Song OF THE Shiver Barrens

BY GLENDA LARKE

The Mirage Makers
Heart of the Mirage
The Shadow of Tyr
Song of the Shiver Barrens

GLENDA LARKE

Song OF THE Shiver Barrens

BOOK TWO
THE MIRAGE
MAKERS

www.orbitbooks.net

ORBIT

First published in Australia in 2007 by Voyager,
HarperCollins*Publishers* Pty Limited
First published in Great Britain in 2008 by Orbit

Map by Perdita Phillips

Excerpt from *Empress*
Copyright © Karen Miller 2007

A CIP catalogue record for this book
is available from the British Library.

ISBN 978-1-84149-607-8

Typeset in Minion by Palimpsest Book Production Ltd
Grangemouth, Stirlingshire

Printed and bound in the UK by
CPI Mackays, Chatham ME5 8TD

Orbit
An imprint of
Little, Brown Book Group
100 Victoria Embankment
London EC4Y 0DY

An Hachette Livre UK Company
www.hachettelivre.co.uk

www.orbitbooks.net

In fond memory of my father
Harold Larke

Acknowledgements

No book arrives at its finished, published stage without the help of a great many people. There are editors, copyeditors, proofreaders, designers, marketing people and blurb writers, cover artists, beta readers and agents and mapmakers . . . and this book seemed to need more hard work than most.

So for all of you, a heartfelt thank you. I couldn't have done it without you, and a very special thanks to my editors Stephanie Smith in Australia and Darren Nash in the UK, all of the UK Orbit team; the cover artist Larry Rostant; the mapmaker Perdy Phillips; my talented fellow authors who know how much I owe them – Karen Miller and Russell Kirkpatrick; other friends who risked being honest and gave of their time – Alena Sanusi, bookseller Mark Timmony, Donna Hanson, Sharyn Lilley, my sister Margaret Larke; and my agent Dorothy Lumley who put me brilliantly on the right track when I derailed.

And to you, my readers – I hope you have enjoyed the ride to get this far, the last book of the trilogy – and thank you all. Please feel free to email me or to visit my blog at www.glendalarke.blogspot.com

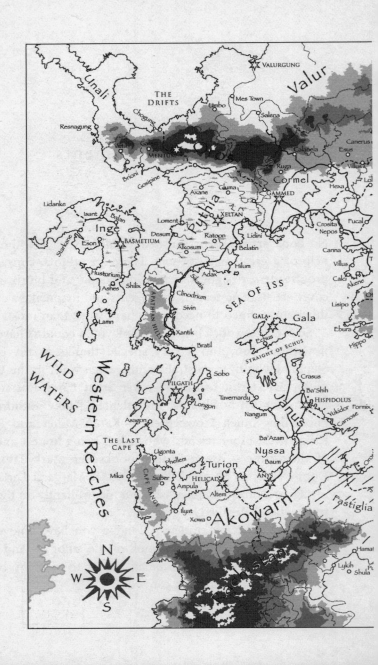

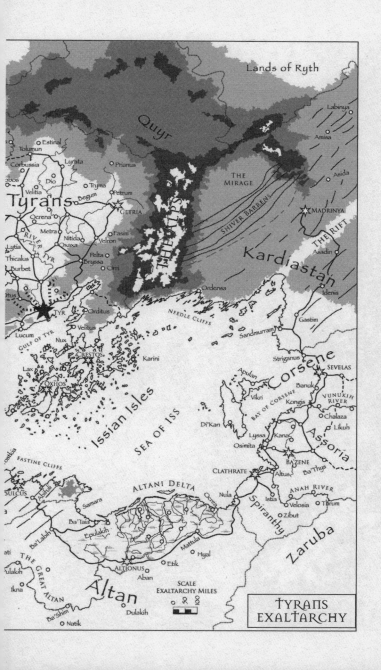

Lands of Ryth

Quyr

Labinya

Amisa

THE MIRAGE

Asida

Estinal
Tolumun
Corbussia
Lyrata
Prianus
Dio
Velitia
Begum
Trjma
Petrum
MADRINYA
GETRIA
SHIVER BARRENS
THE RIFT
Tyrans
Ocrena
Tasimi
Metra
Nitida
Velron
Kardiastan
Oxaxa
RIVER TYR
Lytia
Pelta
Asadin
Thicalus
Bryssa
Burbet
Cirri
Idenis
Ordensa
TYR
Orditus
NEEDLE CLIFFS
Lucum
Velitus
Gastim
Nux
GULF OF TYR
Sandmurram
Striganus
Corsene
SEVELAS
CRESTOS
Karini
Lax
OXHOS
Apulan
Banuk
VUNUKIH RIVER
Vikri
Kongs
Chalaza
Issian Isles
SEA OF ISS
Di'Kan
Likuh
Lyssa
Kanac
Osimita
BAZENE
Assoria
CLATHRATE
Altus
Ba'Thus
FASTINE CLIFFS
Nula
ANAH RIVER
SULCUS
Alshi
ALTANI DELTA
Istia
Velosia
Tarum
Samara
Ocrena
Zibut
Ba'Taia
Spiranthy
Ba'Labih
Epulakih
Zaruba
Mattula
Hyal
THE GREAT ALTAN
ALTIONUS
Etik
ati
Aban
Ikna
Altan
SCALE
EXALTARCHY MILES
Ba'Shim
Dulakih
Natik

TYRANS
EXALTARCHY

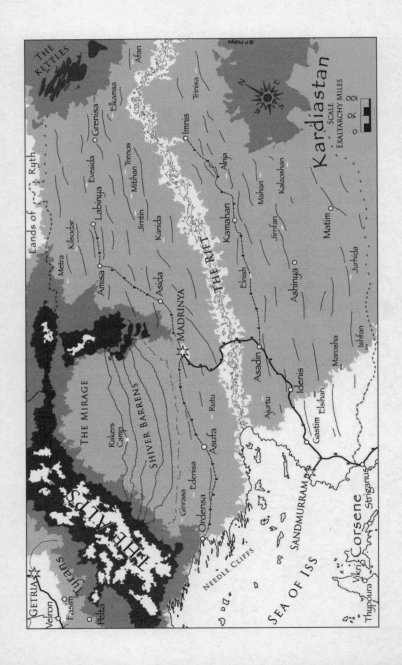

THE KETTLES

Lands of Ryth

THE MIRAGE

Rakers Camp

SHIVER BARRENS

THE HEALIPS

GETRIA

Meiron

Fasim

Lurrans

Pelta

Ginrassa

Ordensa

Edensa

Rutu

Asufa

MADRUNYA

NEEDLE CLIFFS

SANDMURRAM

SEA OF ISS

Corsene

Vikri

Striganus

Thypoura

Gastim

Elsihan

Idenis

Ajurtu

Asadin

Marosha

Ishfan

Jurhida

Ashinya

Matim

Jirnfan

Kalzoshan

Mahan

Elnish

Kamahan

Alnja

Immnis

Tirnisa

Afan

Elkamsa

Grenisa

Evesida

Tirenos

Mitihan

Jirntin

Kanida

Labinja

Kilsodar

Metra

Amisa

Asida

THE RIFT

Kardiastan

SCALE
EXALTARCHY MILES
0   50   100

© D Phelps

PART ONE

FATHERS, SONS AND DAUGHTERS

CHAPTER ONE

Wind gusted and obliterated the whisper, but not before it was overheard. Ligea Gayed may not have seen the man standing behind her rolling his eyes, but she felt his exasperation. 'It's true,' she repeated without turning around. 'I *was* the worst mother in the world.'

From where she stood on one of the two towers that guarded the river, she could see upstream to the walls and domes and columns of Tyr, aglow in the morning sun. The most beautiful city in the world, many said. There, along the riverbanks to her right, were the tiered seats of the Desert-Season Theatre, and the villa on Senators' Row where she had been raised by a Tyranian general. You could no longer find a statue or a plaque or a tomb that commemorated his life anywhere in the whole of Tyrans. Petty revenge perhaps, but she'd do it again.

The wind tugged the flaps of her skirting into streamers, whipping them over her head. Impatiently she thrust them away from her face, regretting that she'd thought it fitting that morning to wear the anoudain of the Kardi people, with its soft slit overskirt and loose trousers. She'd chosen it because this was the day she farewelled the heir to the Mirager of Kardiastan, on his way to take up his place at his father's side.

Arrant, her son.

Behind her, General Gevenan could hold in his acerbity no longer. 'Are you flipping pickled? You raise a lad as fine as Arrant Temellin, and you think you did a shleth-brained job? He's proof of his upbringing, you moondaft woman.'

She was silent. No point in enumerating all the ways she had failed Arrant, starting from the damage she had done to his Magor potential by overusing her power while he was still in her womb. Water through the aqueduct. You couldn't bring it back again.

But Gevenan wasn't finished. He came to stand beside her, saying, 'And I'll be cursed if I see why we are shivering here in a blasted cold seawind without our cloaks, just to wave goodbye, when you already said farewell to the lad this morning.'

'A little breeze upsets the joints these days, does it?' she asked sweetly. 'I want to see his ship sail out.'

'Sentimental mush! And this from a woman who once led an army and slit the throat of her predecessor?'

She shrugged. 'I've earned the right to a little sentimentality. Ah, there they are, see?' Four biremes stroked their way down the centre of the river on the outgoing tide. She was sending her son to his father with an escort from the Tyranian navy, in style and comfort. Not the way she had first gone to Kardiastan, aboard a coastal ship laden with marble.

So long ago. And she'd known so little. 'He's only thirteen,' she murmured.

'Mature for his age. One of the most talented riders I've ever seen, bar none. Good with a sword: he's been well taught, after all,' he added smugly. He'd had a lot to do with that. 'True, he's just suffered a hard lesson about being too trusting, but he'll be better able to judge a man as a result. He's a tad, um, *learned* for my taste perhaps, but he'll get over that. He took responsibility for Brand's death and faced his mistake like a man. It's a fine lad you have there, on that ship.'

'I know. But his command over his power is unpredictable, and that is what is going to count in Kardiastan. He can be dangerous, Gev. People won't like that. And we both know what his Magor magic is capable of when it's out of control.'

'Am I likely to forget?' He repressed a shudder at the memory of the carnage outside the North Gate the day Arrant's power had killed both Tyranian and rebel soldiers. 'But, Ligea, what does it matter now? Kardiastan is at peace; no one needs Magor power to rule. His cabochon can remain a pretty yellow rock in his palm, unused.'

She shook her head. 'I wish you were right. But in Magor society, there's more involved.'

He raised a querying eyebrow, his interest pungent to her senses as it drifted about him.

'It's a Magor secret, Gev. Let's just say that it's the Mirager's power that ensures a new generation of Magor. How can Arrant follow in his father's footsteps if he can't control his power enough to do that? And if Kardiastan doesn't have the Magor, they will be at the mercy of every invader and barbarian who eyes their land.'

'Ah. Well, does he have to be Mirager then? Let someone else be Temellin's heir. Being a ruler is a rotten job for a man of sense.' He ran a hand over his greying hair. 'Although I'll admit I'd feel happier if he took the Mirager's seat at some future point. I don't want Tyrans to fall to some magic-making neighbour intent on conquest.'

'It is the Magor who make the policy in Kardiastan, and the Magor don't behave that way.' Largely due to the restrictions the Mirage Makers placed on their behaviour, but she wasn't about to explain that.

He snorted. 'Power corrodes eventually, Ligea. Not everybody perhaps, but someone, sometime. Anyway, right now we need to catch the whispers about what's happening here in

Tyr. With Rathrox Ligatan and Favonius dead, we have to make sure no one else steps into the vacancy. Because believe me, that's what happens when greedy men seek power. They look for holes they can exploit.'

'Watch the Lucii then,' she said. 'I don't trust Devros. He has always had the ambition to place his well-padded posterior on the Exaltarch's seat.' As she spoke, her gaze did not leave the approaching ships. The banner fluttering from the mast of the second ship told her it was the vessel that bore Arrant. She could make out figures on deck, but they were too small to recognise, so she raised her left hand and bathed her eyes in the glow of her cabochon magic. With her sight enhanced, she saw Arrant was in the bow, leaning against the railing, while Garis, who had come to Tyr to accompany him to Kardiastan, was aft, talking to the helmsman.

'Devros? I never take my eyes off the arrogant bastard,' Gevenan said. 'He makes me want to puke.'

She frowned unhappily. 'I want to leave Tyrans, Gev. I want to go home.' Ah, the irony of that. She had spent less than half a year of her adult life in Kardiastan; half the Magor thought her more Tyranian than Kardi and therefore not to be trusted; and most of the rest would never forgive her because they blamed her for the death of Temellin's wife. Bemused by the oddity of her own sentiment, she thought, 'Yet I still feel it is where I belong. Where I want to be.' Aloud she said, 'I want the Senate and the Advisory Council ruling this land wisely so I can walk away.'

'Go,' Gevenan said. 'Leave the Senate and Legate Valorian and me to manage as best we can. I won't be around forever, but Valorian is young and he's a good soldier. Make a fine general one day, even if he does insist on curling his hair and bedding every pretty athlete in the city. You could even call in those ships down there, right now, and take passage to Sandmurram with them.'

'Don't tempt me, you Ingean devil. If I were to do that, and a man like Devros became Exaltarch, fear of the Magor would drive him to find ways to bring Kardiastan down. He and his supporters already talk of controlling all trade across the Sea of Iss using a Tyranian navy, and it's the ruination of Kardiastan they have in mind. Besides, they would reinstate slavery here in Tyrans.' And to allow that to happen would be a betrayal of Brand . . .

But she wanted to go home so badly. Temellin was there; that was reason enough, and soon there would be another: Arrant. She focused on his face. Serious, too serious for one of his age. Burdened by the deaths he had caused. Burdened already by the responsibilities soon to be his. He was looking directly over the prow of the ship as it approached the booms, unaware of her presence on the tower. He didn't look her way, yet he should have; he should have sensed her. In the stern, Garis had raised his head to gaze in her direction and lifted a hand in greeting and farewell, but nothing in Arrant's demeanour hinted that he knew she watched. She fidgeted, unsettled.

He was going to a home he had never known, to a father he barely knew, to become heir to a position he might never be able to fill. His control over his power was incomplete, and on occasion that power had revealed itself to be as destructive as a winter sea gale. And there would be so many who would not welcome his coming because he was the son of Sarana Solad, Miragerin of Kardiastan, who had become Ligea, Exaltarch of Tyr.

'Gods,' she wondered, 'what kind of legacy have we left for your future, Arrant?'

Arrant fixed his gaze on the sea ahead of them as they rowed through the booms. The River Tyr broadened beyond into the estuary and hence to the Sea of Iss. He didn't glance at the towers on either side, and he refused to look back.

That life was gone, done with. He had to put it behind him, all of it. Even the good things. Like studying in the public library. The luxury of the palace baths. The classes with the Academy scholars. Geometry lessons with old Lepidus. He regretted that; he loved the certainty of mathematics and the shapes it suggested to him. When he looked at buildings now, he saw language in the angles of their structure . . . Did they have mathematicians in Madrinya? He had never asked.

'Don't think about that, you fool,' he told himself. Don't look back at Tyr, at the elegance of the temple columns and the beauty of the caryatids, at the Desert-Season Theatre, at the villas on the hillsides, at the domes of the palace where his mother was right then. 'It's gone, that life is past. You are going to Kardiastan to be Mirager-heir.

'And don't think about the bad things either. Brand dying because you were a jealous fool. All those soldiers dying because you couldn't control your power. From now on, you look forward, not back. Ever.'

He kept his gaze fixed on the open sea, the churning in his stomach a mixture of excitement and anxiety. He was going to his father. Magori-temellin, the Mirager of Kardiastan, liberator, hero, whose other son was one of the Mirage Makers. He'd met his father only once, and his memories of the month they had spent together in Ordensa when he was five were mixed. Childish things, much of them – building sand forts on the beach, playing with the cat, learning to swim. And memories of a man, a tall, brown laughing man with strong arms, carrying him on his shoulders.

And then that awful night when the Ravage had come, choking his dreams with their threat and their gleeful promise of horrible death. He had wanted his father to save him. He had run to find him. Instead he had heard Temellin say to Ligea, 'I don't want him.' Even now he could hear the sound of that voice, the chill of those words.

Temellin hadn't wanted him. It still hurt, all these years later. Perhaps Ligea had told Temellin about his son's inability to manage his power, and that was why Temellin uttered the rejection – a Mirager uninterested in a son who wasn't a proper Magori, for all that his cabochon was gold.

Sweet Elysium, how could he make his father proud of him if he couldn't call on his power when he needed it, if he couldn't control it when it did come? How could he ever be Mirager after Temellin? 'Who,' he asked himself, 'would want a Mirager like me?'

He heaved in a calming breath. He had to stop feeling sorry for himself. He had to learn the knack of cabochon control. He would practise until he was exhausted, if that was what it took. He would study hard. And he would be careful. He would never try to use his power when he was by himself, just in case he hurt someone. He would never lose his temper or give in to his fear, because those were things that might make him lose control. And he would show Temellin that he could be a true Magori, a proper Mirager-heir. 'I have to make him proud of me,' he thought. 'I'll do it, I swear I will.'

Besides, he had to be strong to help Tarran. Tarran depended on him, spending as much time as he could within the sanctuary of Arrant's mind to keep himself sane. *Oh, brother*, he said, not knowing if Tarran would hear, *I'd do anything to make it easier for you. It could so easily have been Ligea who died in place of your mother, and me who became the Mirage Maker.*

'Deep thoughts?'

He jumped, and then cursed inwardly. He ought to have felt Garis's approach; instead he had been startled. 'Yes. I – I have a lot to think about. Magori, can I ask you something about the Mirage and the Mirage Makers?'

'Of course. But don't call me Magori. It makes me feel far too old.'

'But you are. Oh, er, I mean, well – older than me, anyway.'

Garis gave an audible sigh. 'Why is it the young always think of any adult as being in their dotage? My daughter thinks I'm ancient enough to have been birthed before the standing stones were erected. I am ten years younger than your mother, in fact. So, drop the Magori and call me Garis.' He grinned amiably and Arrant smiled back. 'Now, what exactly do you want to know? How much did Sarana tell you?'

'Well, she said the Mirage Makers have become weaker over the centuries. She told me they created the Mirage, but then saw it eroded away by the Ravage sores. And that they hoped – believed – that the advent of a new Mirage Maker, a human embryo, would make them strong enough to resist. But it hasn't worked. Every year, a little more of the Mirage disappears as the sores grow larger.'

Garis gave a quick frown. 'Well, we haven't been to the Mirage lately, you know. We left once Kardiastan was free of Tyrans. That was, what, six years ago? So we don't really know what has happened since. We assume that things have got better – or will get better as Pinar's son grows up.'

Arrant shook his head. 'It hasn't got better.' The Mirage Makers had suffered more as Tarran grew older, not less, but they didn't know why. Maybe they had just made a wild guess at what would help, and had been mistaken. What was it Tarran had said? *I need you. We may not have much longer. Come home. Maybe, if you came, you could think of some way to help us.*

Garis was staring at him, puzzled. 'How would you know it hasn't got better?'

Arrant reddened. 'Er, well, it's more likely it hasn't.' He wasn't going to talk to Garis about Tarran. The Mirager, not Garis, should be the first to learn about the connection between his two sons.

'We have no reason to think anything is amiss,' Garis said.

'But you don't know that.'

'No. Not for sure.'

Tarran was suffering, and no one even knew about it? 'Don't you think someone should go and find out?' he asked acidly.

His vehemence startled Garis. 'Arrant, we have all sworn to uphold the Covenant between the Magor and the Mirage Makers. You will soon, too, at a special ceremony. And that Covenant states that the Magor leave the area beyond the Shiver Barrens to the Mirage Makers. In return they give us our Magor swords, including the Mirager's sword which makes our cabochons. But you know all this, surely. Didn't your mother tell you?'

'Of course she did. But the Mirage Makers made an exception when the Magor were in trouble. They allowed you to live in the Mirage to keep you safe from the Tyranian legions. Don't you think it would be a good idea to check if *they* are in trouble now, and need *our* help?'

'We don't break the Covenant lightly. Besides, if they needed our help, I'm sure they would have asked for it. They speak to each young Magoroth who comes to them to collect his sword, after all. But perhaps you had better talk to your father about all this.'

'I will.'

Garis gave a sudden laugh, but sounded more approving than amused. 'Let's hope it's not too long before your mother follows us to Kardiastan,' he said, and turned to take one last look at Tyr.

Arrant glanced behind to where the two towers guarding the river were now hard to see beyond the shimmering glare from the water. 'I wonder if I'll ever come back,' he said, and hoped he never would.

On the same day that Arrant left for Kardiastan, in a vale a thousand miles from Tyr, a farmer looked up from his fields and worried. A long low bank of maroon cloud hemmed the sky beyond the rake that bordered his valley.

He watched it uneasily throughout the morning as he tilled his melon patch. Any cloud was a rare sight in a land where it never rained, where water came from under the ground, not wastefully falling from above, but he knew enough to understand this was not a rain cloud. Rain would never colour the sky this shade of bruised purple-red. Even as he watched, the blue began to disappear, devoured by the advancing billows. Soft warm breezes blowing from beyond the rake intensified to become vicious hot winds that scorched his skin as the day passed.

When he stowed his tools in his shed in the dying light of dusk, his wife came out to join him, winding her hands nervously into the skirting of her anoudain. 'I've never seen a sky like this before,' she said. 'And there's a smell in the air that I mislike. What is happening, Rugar?'

He put his arm about her and shepherded her back towards the house. 'That's the stink of the Ravage,' he said with certainty, though he had never smelled it before.

'Then ought not someone ride to tell the Magor?'

'It's only a smell and a dust cloud. We'll tell the administrator, next time he comes through. It's not our worry and I have better things to do than borrow a shleth and spend days on the road just to tell a Magor something they probably know about already. Now, what's for supper, lass? That's all I'm dwelling on at the moment!' He patted her rump as they entered the kitchen, and she laughed.

The wind whined around the house all night long, but the morning dawned silent and still under a blue sky, although the smell lingered on until midday. Everything was covered in fine reddish dust. Rugar trickled a fistful through his fingers, and wondered. He'd seen sixty desert-seasons come and go in his lifetime, and he'd never seen a dust storm like this one before.

'Nothing good will come of this,' he thought and, although he wasn't a fanciful man, the hair stood up on the backs of his arms.

CHAPTER TWO

The blast of the afternoon sun outside the unshuttered windows of the Mirager's Pavilion was intense, bleaching the light-drenched adobe, yet deepening the vividness of shaded walls. The heart's-bruise flowers in the garden were a splash of bright blood in the shade and a flock of noisy keyet parrots flickered their vibrant wings and breast flashes at one another as they quarrelled under the vine leaves.

Protected by outer walls of mud-brick an arm's length thick, the Mirager's private quarters were cooler and quieter than the gardens. Sounds from the other five pavilions scarcely penetrated the shimmers of heat and the thickness of the walls; shouts and laughter from students in the practice yard of the nearby Magoroth Academy seemed distant.

'Is it my imagination,' Magori-temellin asked his guest, 'or is the weather hotter these days than it used to be?' He handed a mug of orange juice to Magori-korden, and then poured another for himself. 'Or is it just that I feel the heat more in my old age?'

The older man laughed. Temellin was only forty-two, hardly old by anyone's standards, particularly not that of a Magoroth. Magor power ensured good health well into their longevity. 'Everyone is complaining,' Korden said. 'It is the wind from the northwest. It seems relentless these days, like a blast from the Assorians' Hades.'

'From the Mirage?' Temellin knew his look was as bleak as the reply.

'Well, from that direction, yes. Coincidence, surely.'

'It feels wrong. Evil. I think I've sensed the Ravage in it these past few years.'

Korden was dismissive. 'Are you becoming fanciful in your decrepitude? Even if there is a whiff of Ravage decay, it means nothing. The Ravage sores cannot leave the Mirage, and the Ravage beasts cannot leave the Ravage sores. Let the Mirage Makers deal with it. They never wanted us there anyway, and now they have it to themselves, sores and all. Besides, is not that why your only legitimate child was gifted by Ligea to the Mirage Makers? To make them strong enough to resist the sores that eat away at their Mirage? Or so you said. If that was true, then let that child achieve his destiny.'

Temellin frowned. Korden had once termed Pinar's death murder, and called Sarana a Tyranian traitor for having a hand in her death. Even all these years later, Temellin felt the thread of dislike that wound through Korden's words, made even more obvious by his petty refusal to call her by her rightful name. Korden had not forgiven Sarana, and never would. Even his mention of legitimacy was aimed at reminding Temellin that Arrant would never have been Mirager-heir if his other child, Pinar's son, had been born.

'Or is it you who doubts now?' Korden persisted. 'Perhaps you have had second thoughts as to whether Pinar's murder was justified.'

Temellin curbed his anger only with difficulty. 'Sarana acted in self-defence, and Pinar's actions caused her own death, as was explained to you at the time. Sarana saved my son the only way she knew how.' All true, but Temellin hated the doubt he felt, not about how his wife and son had died, but about whether that son he had never known could do anything to help the Mirage Makers. How could an unborn human child help vanquish the Ravage? 'I wish I could believe in that,' he thought. 'I wish my son could know that his life as a Mirage Maker means something.'

Yet now, now he could smell – no, not smell. He could *sense* the stench of rot on the wind. It touched his fears with the cold of bleak memories. Ravage pools corroding the bright beauty of the Mirage . . .

Korden sipped his drink without looking at him. 'But that is not the reason I came to see you. I wished to inform you of some news I have just received from Tyr.'

Temellin's face went blank as he curled his feelings deep inside, protecting them from scrutiny like a bud closing to avoid the trespass of frost. 'Tyr?' Korden had been in communication with someone from Tyr? 'There's not bad news, is there?'

'Well, you will not deem any of it pleasant. However, it is disturbing, rather than catastrophic. Arrant is unharmed; do not fret. In fact, my correspondent tells me that Garis was readying for his departure with the lad. They will be on their way by now, I dare say.'

Temellin, maintaining a bland expression only with effort, thought irritably, 'Damn the man. He's playing some sort of game here. I wish he would just say something outright for once, in plain language.' Knowing Korden wasn't about to change, he attempted to curb his impatience and said with a calm he did not feel, 'So the disturbing part is—?'

'Doubtless you know that Brand is – or was – the Altani plenipotentiary to Tyr? Well, it appears that he has been sharing Ligea's quarters in the palace, and presumably her bed, for some time. They even travelled to the interior together. Quite the imperial scandal of Tyrans, I understand.'

Temellin sat rigidly still, his face a blank mask. 'Yes, I knew he was there. Sarana told me. And as far as I am aware,' he added quietly, 'such liaisons do not worry Tyranians overmuch. I am not sure why it should worry you, either.'

'Oh, it doesn't. It seems to have been of considerable concern to your son, though. Perhaps not to be wondered at? Unfortunately, he did not display any great maturity in the matter. He became jealous and betrayed Brand to Favonius Kyranon. You will doubtless recall the name – the leader of the Stalwart invasion of Kardiastan? Another lover of Ligea's once, so I understand.'

'Her name is Sarana. *Miragerin*-sarana. Never use that tone of voice when you speak of her. Even if nothing else is of consequence to you, she is your cousin.'

The ice of Temellin's tone did not faze Korden. 'All right. Sarana. Of course. Anyway, here is what I was told. Favonius used Arrant's information to seize Brand, who then became the bait to trap Ligea. Er, sorry, Sarana. In the rescue attempt, Brand was killed. So was the ex-Magister and head of the Brotherhood, Sarana's former puppetmaster, Rathrox Ligatan. He was behind the whole plot, it seems. Sarana was badly injured, although my informant said she would recover. Arrant did not conduct himself with even minimal distinction throughout the affair.'

Temellin's thoughts churned. 'Mirageless soul, Sarana . . . are you safe? And sands blast you, Garis, why have you sent no word of this to me?' He placed his mug down on a table with a steady hand, but his voice, when he trusted himself to speak, was as harsh as a knife on a grinding stone. 'And you just happened by all this information how?'

'Let's say I regard it as my duty to be informed about the lad who is destined to be our Mirager-heir.'

'He already *is* the Mirager-heir, Korden. As well you know.'

'Of course. I meant destined to be Mirager-heir as confirmed by Magoroth Council, rather than just Mirager-heir by birth and his father's wish.'

'An overly fine distinction at this point in time. Arrant is only thirteen.' Tradition decreed Council confirmation took place when the heir was sixteen. 'It seems you've been spying on my son.'

'Nonsense. I have friends in Tyr, merely.'

'There are several gaps in that story that don't seem to make much sense.' Temellin cocked his head to one side, meeting Korden's gaze with a hard stare. 'I am beginning to wonder whether I know you any more, Korden. I always thought you were loyal. A man of honour. You have been invaluable as an adviser to me over the years, for which I am deeply grateful. But I am the Mirager, and my position demands respect and a measure of loyalty.'

'I *am* loyal. But my honour will not allow me to see an incompetent Magori – *any* incompetent Magori – be officially named Mirager-heir by Council. Surely that is understandable. I have heard the lad is without control of his Magor skills, that during the war he slaughtered men on his own side by accident. How can he possibly give our newborn Magor their cabochons if he cannot control his power? This nation cannot afford another disastrous Mirager such as Arrant's grandfather, Mirager-solad.'

Every muscle in Temellin's face went tight. 'You would compare him with a traitor like Solad?' He allowed Korden to feel his fury. 'A harsh judgement of someone you have not even *met*.'

'Perhaps. But by all accounts he has displayed considerable power which he cannot manage with even a modicum of skill. He could be a danger to any of us, especially if he still does not possess the, um, acumen a lad of his age should have. Skies above, the boy trusted the man who was once Legate of the

Jackal Legion! Nonetheless, I am willing to delay any kind of public pronouncement until I do make his acquaintance.'

'Generous of you.' Temellin paused and considered. If he failed to control his temper now, he would be the loser. With all the cold calm he could muster, he said, 'However, you have been misinformed. Yes, Arrant is a more powerful Magoroth than any one of us, even without his sword. He blasted a hole through the walls of Tyr when he was nine. I certainly could not have done that at such an age, especially without the aid of a Magor sword. Just as certainly, it will take a degree of maturity and experience for him to harness such Magor strength. We do know that on occasion he can already wield his power properly, because Sarana has tested him.'

'I'm glad to hear it.'

Temellin thought, 'Not quite a lie, but close,' and continued aloud, 'We Magor fought long and hard to rule this land. I will not relinquish it on my death to an heir who cannot keep it safe, even if he is my own son. You insult me even to suggest that I would be so irresponsible.'

Korden was taken aback. 'I – er, it was not my intention to insult you.'

'Good. I'm glad to hear it. As you can imagine, it's my fervent hope that there is no great hurry for any decision in this matter. I have no intention of dying yet a while, and we have two and a half years after Arrant arrives to train him before his confirmation at sixteen.'

'He shall have that respite, of course.'

Temellin caught the truth of that and breathed a little easier, blessing the Magor ability to hear a lie. He inclined his head in acknowledgement of Korden's promise.

'We both want only the best for Kardiastan, yet you can also be a sentimental fool at times, Temel. We have reason to know that.'

Temellin knew that was a snide comment on his love for Sarana, but Korden, downing the last of his orange juice, gave him no chance to retort. He stood, saying, 'I must take my leave of you. I promised Lesgath I would watch his training session. That youngest son of mine is progressing admirably.'

The smile Temellin gave as Korden left was forced. Alone again, he flopped back into his chair, with a sigh that was almost a growl in the back of his throat.

From the doorway on the other side of the room, another voice interrupted his descent into open irritation and desperate worry. 'The bastard. He's about as subtle as a Sandmurram serpent.'

Temellin turned, suppressing another sigh. 'Hellesia, you shouldn't listen at doors, you know. Korden must have known you were there. I certainly did.'

The woman who entered the room carrying a tray with another jug of juice shrugged carelessly, saying, 'Course he knew. Chided me about it last time he was here. I blamed it on my slave mentality. Was a time when we had to listen because we could be killed if we didn't anticipate our master's wishes, every damn one of them. Everyone knows ex-slaves find it hard to change their habits, particularly one as ingrained in us as that.'

Temellin shook his head in rueful appreciation. 'Slave mentality? Is that what you call your devious nature?'

Once named the most beautiful girl in Madrinya, Hellesia had carried the same serene loveliness that graced her youth into her maturity. Now in her mid-thirties, she did not regard her looks as a blessing, however, but a curse. Much of the horror in her past life had been precipitated by the beauty of her face and the curves of her figure. As a consequence, she drew her hair back into a severe knot at her nape, used no powder, eschewed perfumes, and did her best to appear unattractive. She was not entirely successful.

She laid the tray down on the table. 'I was bringing in some more juice, but once I heard what he was saying, I decided my presence would not be appropriate. Dangerous man as well as an arrogant one, Tem: a friend who thinks he knows what is good for you. Why don't you plant your sandalled foot in his superior backside and tell him not to come back?'

He wondered how to explain it to her; she was not Magor and her history was not his. 'Try to imagine what it was like, Hellesia. Ten Magoroth children, destined to be rulers, but whisked away from home to live in the Mirage with all its strangeness. I was five when we were told that we were the only Magoroth left alive in the world – that our families had been slaughtered.

'Korden was the oldest, the one with the best memory of the life and the families we had lost. I was the Mirager, true – but what does that mean when your country is ruled by invaders? And yes, we did have Illusos and Theuros teachers, but Korden was the one who took on the responsibility of our Magoroth legacy, who became a mentor to the rest of us.

'Picture it, if you can. Orphaned children struggling to be strong when their whole world was gone. A five-year-old Mirager looking up to his ten-year-old cousin. Then ten years old, to Korden's fifteen. Fifteen to his twenty. He was my guide, my teacher, my rock. How can I turn on him now because he questions the suitability of my son to rule after me? In the end, he might be right. And I don't believe he wants to be Mirager-heir, even though he is next in line after Arrant. Even though I know he has always been jealous of me. How could he not be? He knew more than I did, he was the oldest, yet an accident of birth decreed that I was Mirager. Worse still for him when he found out that Sarana was alive and she had more right to be Mirager than either of us.'

'And you don't think a jealous man can also be treacherous?'

'In Korden's case? Never! He struggles with his jealousy all the time, but his sense of honour won't let him give in to it. Besides, he can't lie to me, you know. When he says he doesn't want to be Mirager-heir, I can feel his honesty; to me, it's as real as the smell of the blossom in the garden.'

'A handy skill, that. The one I most envy in you Magor, I think.' She came to stand behind him, placing her hands on his shoulders. Gently she started to massage away the tension in his neck and back. 'Perhaps Korden is as loyal as he can be, as you say. Places the best interests of his own brats over the offspring of any of his friends, though; you ought not forget that. And his love for his family blinds him to their faults. Lesgath? Korden's youngest son is no flashing blade in the practice yard! And that eldest hunk of his? Korden wants to see *Firgan* supplant your Arrant? Not a good man. Not a good human being.'

Temellin closed his eyes, leaning back to enjoy the skill of her fingers as she teased away the knots. 'Firgan? He fought brilliantly during the war, and with great courage. We owe the Rift victories to his leadership.'

'Fine soldier does not always mean fine man, you know that well enough. Fact is, he's a nasty piece of handsome sculpture. Admit it.'

He shrugged, refusing to commit himself even though he knew what she said was true.

'People with mean souls treat a paid servant like me the same way the Tyranians treated their slaves. Beneath notice. And his soul is beyond mean, Tem. Beware.' She paused, then continued. 'Charismatic, though, I'll give him that. Has a following both among the Magor and the non-Magor who served in the army. A fighting-man's man. Dangerous. Bold. Treacherous.'

Temellin leaned back in his chair, impressed. Hellesia was

unsettlingly astute. Firgan had hinted often enough that it was time Kardiastan expanded beyond its borders, and that in order to ensure future prosperity, they should step into the gaps left by the disintegration of the Exaltarchy. The man enjoyed war and the only thing that had held him back so far was that his following was small. Most Magor had tired of fighting.

'And Korden's other children?' he asked.

'I hear the next one, can't remember her name now, has considerable Magoroth skills and a sweeter nature. Unfortunately, totally without ambition, uninterested in anything beyond her growing family. I think she has five children, last count.'

'Her lack of ambition is a disappointment to Korden,' he agreed.

'Can't be much more than twenty-six years old, silly girl. There's a bunch of others after her who I don't know. All wed, living in other towns. Then there's the twins, Ryval and Myssa. Loathe one another, so the servants say, yet don't seem to be able to live apart. Lovers since they were thirteen or so in spite of their antipathy. I know you Magor favour sibling relationships, but that particular one seems a bit twisted to me. After them comes Elvena – she must be about seventeen now. Totally preoccupied with her beautiful self. Her mother encourages her self-obsession. Then Lesgath. Youngest of the lot is another girl, Serenelle. She promises well, I think. Bright. The servants like her anyway.

'But what am I doing going on about such things when you must be hurting? After what he told you about Sarana and Brand and Arrant!'

'You heard that too?' He ran a hand through his hair in a gesture of worry. 'It will devastate Sarana. She and Brand have been friends since she was ten or so.'

'And lovers since, if Korden is right.'

'Oh, he was right.'

'Ah. I'm sorry, Tem. Did you like Brand? Was he a friend?'

'A friend? No. I liked him well enough, but he didn't like me.'

'But you were jealous. I know you.'

'So? I am what I am. He didn't think I was good enough for her.'

'And now he has died for her,' she said, switching her attention to massaging his temples. 'Or perhaps for her son. He won a battle there. She will remember him with fondness for the rest of her life no matter whether she returns to your side or not.'

'She would have done that without the sacrifice. I can't begrudge her that. She owed Brand much, her life included.'

'Oh? Problem will be what his death has done to your son then.'

'Korden said he was not injured.'

'Don't be moondaft, Tem. Sounds as if Sarana's lover died because Arrant was jealous and allowed himself to be manipulated. The boy – if he has any sensitivity at all – will have been devastated because it was all his fault. Have a job on your hands when he arrives.'

He looked faintly surprised. 'Do you think so?'

'Men!' she said in disgust. 'Why d'you never see the obvious? Rule nations with immense foresight, yet can't manage your own families!'

'I've not had a family since the day of the Shimmer Festival massacres.' The day he'd been orphaned and his baby sister had died, slaughtered by Tyranian legionnaires . . .

She ceased her ministrations and went to pick up the tray and the dirty drinking vessels. 'Well, you're going to have to start learning soon. In the meantime, remember what I said about Arrant and Korden. And Firgan, too. 'Specially Firgan. Sometimes much can be told about a man by the way he treats those who hold no rank. Korden may be cold and prejudiced, but at least he has some class. And, yes, honour. He does not treat people such as me with disdain and he loves Kardiastan more than he loves himself. Firgan's just plain rude and arrogant and uncaring. Bet if you look at his campaigns, you'll see he bought non-Magor popularity with money and goods he stole from the defeated, but on the battleground he didn't care a single sand grain for the non-Magor spear fodder.'

When Hellesia had gone, Temellin walked to the unshuttered window to look out at the garden. The keyets flew up from the vines in a panic, shedding stray feathers. Ordinary Kardi birds in an ordinary Kardi garden with all the flowers and plants doing exactly what plants and flowers were supposed to do. 'Damn it, I miss the Mirage,' he thought. 'I miss the wild unexpectedness of it. The bizarre insanity.' He smiled, remembering when he'd been about eight years old and Mirage City had been infested with tiny talking rainbows that recited children's poetry and moved about like loop caterpillars. Singing flowers, creeks that flowed uphill, perfumed birds, kitchen fires with green flames and patterned smoke – he'd seen them all.

He leaned his forehead against the windowframe and thought of Sarana. How was it possible to have shared so little time with her, and yet to go on loving, feeling the ache, for year after lonely year? Arrant had been five when he'd last seen her.

There had been other women come and go on his pallet. Even Hellesia briefly, before he'd realised her history had left too many memories for her ever to be truly at ease in a man's bed, no matter what her initial inclinations had been or how willing she'd seemed. He had an idea she now slept with his cook, an obese ex-slave woman from Corsene, left behind by the Tyranians when they'd fled the city.

Others could fill his arms and some had even caught his

affections – but none of them had been Sarana. And none of them ever would be.

'Skies, woman, come home,' he thought. 'Soon, please.'

Firgan, the twenty-eight-year old son of Korden and Gretha, halted on the threshold of the main hall of the Korden villa and drawled, 'So, Papa, what is this about? A family conclave? All very mysterious.' He ignored the rest of his family and went to lounge on one of the Tyranian divans that littered the room. Once the residence of the Exaltarch's provincial governor, the spacious villa retained much of its Tyranian heritage.

Korden acknowledged Firgan's comment with a nod and glanced around the room with quiet satisfaction. He'd come to love the villa. Built mostly of imported marble and over-looking the lake, to many Kardis it remained a Tyranian eyesore better torn down, but Korden, nagged by Gretha in the after-math of the war and the consequent housing shortage, had moved his family in. He'd not regretted the decision. The elegance of the marble – the clean coolness of it; the grace of the statues and furnishings, still much the way the Tyranians had left them: he loved it all. Gretha even insisted everyone leave their sandals at the door and walk barefoot inside. He now had no intention of ever moving out or, in fact, of disguising the villa's Tyranian nature.

'A small but important matter,' he said in reply to Firgan. 'The Mirager's son will be here within ten days or so and I wish to talk about his presence at the Academy.' He smiled. It felt good to have six of his eleven children gathered in the one room again, no easy task now they were grown.

Firgan, the oldest, was not yet wed and still lived at home, although in his own apartments. The twins Myssa and Ryval were nineteen and undergoing training at the Magoroth Academy in the pavilions, as were the three younger children:

seventeen-year-old Elvena, fifteen-year-old Lesgath, and the youngest, Serenelle, who was just a few months older than Arrant.

Elvena, the beauty of the family, settled herself carefully and arranged her anoudain so that the overskirt would not be creased. 'I am sure you can rely on us to welcome him properly, Papa. We know our manners, and he will one day be our Mirager.'

Ryval guffawed. 'Huh! You think you're going to marry him, do you, Elvie? Fat chance! He's closer to Serenelle in age. You'd have to spend years waiting for him to grow up and by then you'd have lost your looks.'

'I shall never lose my looks,' she said complacently.

Myssa snorted. 'Pity. If you did, you might just be bearable. Thank goodness he's not going to be thinking of *me* in terms of marriage.' Myssa was the least feminine member of the family. She was more likely to be found on the weapons training ground than anywhere else, in a vain striving for equality with Ryval.

'Well, marrying him would be better than marrying Ryval,' Elvena said.

Exasperated, Korden intervened. 'This is not about marriage. Or only as a last resort. Are you so guileless that only marriage matters to you? Arrant is not a proper Magoroth, and my intention is to make this clear to everyone, including his father, so that someone else will become Mirager-heir. We have two and a half years to achieve this goal.'

'But I thought he already *was* Mirager-heir,' Elvena said.

'His father named him so after his birth, yes,' Korden said, reining in his impatience. 'But such an heir, brought up in Tyrans and apparently with poor control of his cabochon, is easily challenged by the Magoroth Council, or even supplanted, if he proves incompetent or otherwise unsuitable. I have agreed to do nothing until the boy is sixteen and of an age for Council confirmation. He will have more than sufficient chances to prove himself. And perhaps he will.'

'As Temellin's cousin, you're next in line after Arrant,' Ryval said. He was picking grass burrs out of his trousers and flicking them at Myssa. 'Would you be nominated heir if this Arrant moonling proves unsuitable?'

'Possibly, if I desired the job. But I do not. I would lose Temellin's confidence were he to regard me as a rival, and I like the power I have right now as his friend and adviser. Besides, by the time Temellin dies, I would likely be deceased myself. No, should Arrant be unsuitable, we need to have Firgan made Mirager-heir, not me.'

Elvena's eyes widened. '*Firgan*? Mirager one day?' She looked at her brother dubiously.

'In which case, you will marry him,' Gretha told her. 'It would be unthinkable that we had a Mirager in the family who then diluted the line of power by marrying outside it. And we all know Firgan appreciates beauty in a woman, so you are the logical choice.'

'I'd like to think I had some say in the matter, Mother,' Firgan said, but he was looking at Elvena with a predatory smile that brought a bright pink flush to her cheeks.

'He's not very *nice*,' she said, and pouted. 'I think I would rather Arrant was Mirager and I was his wife. He's young, and he'd be, um, marblable.'

Myssa laughed. 'I think you mean malleable, sweetie.'

Gretha looked up from her sewing. 'True, Elvena dear, but Firgan would have more power as Mirager than you would as Arrant's Miragerin. However, it may be advantageous for one of you to marry the lad eventually. Serenelle would be a better match. She is only a few months older than he is. Be nice to him, dear,' she told her youngest daughter.

'I did not convene this family meeting to talk about whom

Arrant is going to wed,' Korden said, now thoroughly out of patience. 'I just want all of you to be aware of the situation. We have a Mirager's son who by all reports is not a competent Magor, and I want proof of his unsuitability for the post, if that is indeed the case. You – all of you – are in a better position than I to gather such information. You will be at school with him. You, Serenelle, will share all his classes. Lesgath, you will certainly share combat classes. Firgan, I want you to begin teaching some of those combat classes.'

'At the *Academy*? Father, I am a warrior! My time is better spent refining the skills of real soldiers, not children who haven't yet blooded their swords.'

Korden ignored his son's indignation. 'I want you all to watch Arrant every minute. Every time he makes a mistake, I wish to hear about it. Every time he fails in his Magor studies, I wish to be informed. Every time he loses his temper, or his cabochon fails him, anything at all, *I desire to know*. Is that understood?'

'It sounds horrid,' Elvena said with a shudder, 'spying on someone. Do I *have* to?'

'If your father says so,' Gretha said, not raising her eyes from her embroidery. She was stitching a spray of flowers onto the bodice of a new anoudain for Elvena and her pride and pleasure in her task were obvious.

'I think it sounds like fun,' Lesgath said. 'Is it all right if we encourage him to fall flat on his Tyranian nose along the way?'

'Certainly not.' Korden frowned. 'Your task, every single one of you, is to watch him until he is sixteen and Temellin has to make a decision to put his name before the Council for confirmation as Mirager-heir. If the Council approves his appointment to that position, it will be very, very difficult to oust him. *If* the lad is not suitable, and Temellin really is unwise enough to put him forward, I want a hundred examples

I can bring before the Council to show that he is unfit.' He took a deep breath. 'That will be all for now. You may all go back to whatever you were doing.'

They were quick to comply. Myssa and Ryval left the room arguing, as did Lesgath and Serenelle; Gretha grabbed Elvena to try on the new overskirt before she could disappear.

Firgan, however, did not move. When the others had gone, he said, 'Lesgath had an interesting point, Papa. Do we trip the little Tyranian bastard up every now and then?'

'From all I have heard, that will not be necessary. It is certainly not honourable. You don't seem to comprehend the point, Firgan: I would not be asking any of you to do this if I believed the lad would become a Mirager of calibre in the end. All you have to do is collect evidence of what I believe to be true. Arrant Temellin is probably incompetent, and a danger to us all. I have the best interests of Kardiastan at heart, no more than that.'

'Of course.'

Something in his son's bland agreement made Korden add, 'Firgan, none of us – particularly you – can be seen to be deliberately undermining the Mirager's son. Is that clear enough? Temellin is my friend and comes to me for advice. I want it to stay that way. The lad will trip himself up, without any aid from any of us.'

'As you wish. I see your point.'

Firgan levered himself up from the divan and sauntered out. In the atrium, he asked one of the servants where he could find his youngest brother. Following the woman's directions, he headed outside and intercepted Lesgath as he walked down the marble steps that led towards the stables. 'Hey, wait up, Les,' he said.

'What is it?'

'It's about that suggestion of yours. With regard to making sure the Tyranian bastard falls flat on his nose.'

'Yes?'

'Father is right. It wouldn't be a good idea. We have to be above suspicion.'

Lesgath grinned. 'Ah. But you have a plan anyway?'

'Boys will be boys. Always indulging in practical jokes, teasing, the odd scuffle. Normal behaviour for lads of your age, right? I mean, making fun of him – there's nothing wrong with that. Aim to make the lad look foolish in other people's eyes, because the sillier he looks, the less he will seem to possess leadership qualities. Aim to make him miserable, because the unhappier he is at the Academy, the harder he will find it to excel. But you have to be extraordinarily subtle in this, brother. If the teachers see you making his life a misery, they will intervene. If you are too obvious, then the sympathy will be for Arrant. There is a fine line between bullying and foolery and you must not be seen to cross it. Think you can do that?'

Lesgath smiled, his eyes glinting with the pleasure of anticipation, and Firgan smiled back. 'I think we understand each other. You'll find me grateful. Here, take this and off you go.' He fished in his money pouch and gave his brother a coin.

Lesgath grinned and took the money.

Firgan watched him go, whistling under his breath. It was handy to have a sneaking, conniving, gullible little brother. If he manipulated the game skilfully, Lesgath would do all the dirty work while he, Firgan, came out of this as shiny as polished bronze. Things were going well; very well indeed.

CHAPTER THREE

'So that's the Rift.'

Arrant tried to sound matter-of-fact, but in truth he was awed. It was so – so *vast*. A long steep-sided valley, snaking its way across the landscape like a trail left by a python of mythical proportions.

The impact was all the greater because travellers came upon it so abruptly. One moment they'd been riding on a flat, featureless tray of land; the next moment the tray ended in a rimless edge and a drop of several thousand paces to the Rift floor. He leaned forward on his mount to peer straight down, his gaze following the jagged turns of the path they would follow. 'Hells,' he thought, 'one careless step, and you'd fall all the way to the bottom.'

He fingered the obsidian necklet he wore, taking comfort from the promise of its giver: 'Put it round his neck, and he'll have the blood of a Quyriot horseman.' Well, he was riding a shleth now, not a horse, but he reckoned something special would be useful on a path like that. He glanced at the far side of the Rift where the North Wall rose in a series of perpendicular folds, then back down to the valley floor where a meandering river of blood-orange mud linked a series of red lakes. He knew the winds that whipped along that Rift were famous for their ferocity.

'Down there is the closest thing you'll find to rain in Kardiastan,' Garis said at his elbow as if he had read his thoughts. 'We'll stay here the night' – he pointed at the nearby wayhouse perched uncomfortably close to the rim – 'and then tomorrow we ride down the zigzag to the wayhouse at the cliff base. A day to cross, another wayhouse, then a final day climbing up. You don't need to worry, lad. You have the best seat on a shleth I think I've ever seen. Sometimes I believe you and your mount speak the same language.'

'Oh!' He basked in the unexpected compliment. 'I guess I spent a great deal of my childhood in the saddle. Horses, shleths – it's all the same to me. And maybe the necklet helps. Did Ligea ever tell you about it?'

'The one you wear? Not that I recall. And now that you are in Kardiastan, you really should call her by her Kardi name, you know. Sarana.'

'Oh. Yes. I'll try to remember.' He touched the necklet again. It was warm beneath his fingers. Funny that, how the beads warmed up whenever he was mounted. 'This is made of fire-gravel – black obsidian – and each bead has ancient writing carved into it. One of the Quyriot smugglers gave it to me when I was born. He told my mother there was stone magic in the runes. Luckily the magic of it seems to work with shleths as well as horses.'

'You think it has some power?'

'Well, the smuggler said I'd always understand my mounts if I wore it. And it's true. It makes me feel as though the mount and I are, um, sort of one entity. I can always tell if a horse wants to buck or rear or brush me off against a tree trunk. I can feel its intention.'

'So that's how you've been thwarting that beast you are riding! I've been watching you, and it hasn't managed to pinch you once with its feeding arms.'

Arrant flashed a grin. Garis's mount delighted in pinching his rider's sandalled toes. He gazed for a while longer at the Rift, impressed by the sheer difficulty of crossing such a barrier. 'There's a paveway from Madrinya to Ordensa, isn't there?' he asked. 'Why do most travellers from other lands come this way, through Sandmurram, when it means making such an unpleasant journey across the Rift?'

'Ordensa is a small port for fishing vessels, along a stormy coast. Sandmurram has a large natural harbour sheltered from the worst seas by islands. Doesn't even need a sea wall. It's closer to our main trading partners, which are to the south, not the west. It's the main reason Tyrans was interested in conquering us in the first place, because it lies on their trading route east. Whoever controls Sandmurram, controls that route. Most of our major towns – Gastim, Idenis, Asadin – are along the tradeway between Sandmurram and Madrinya. The paveway between Madrinya and Ordensa, on the other hand, passes through no major towns at all.' He grinned at Arrant. 'Although my daughter might disagree. Our home is in Asufa, which is about halfway between the capital and Ordensa. She attends the Magor Academy of Healing there.' He smiled. 'It was a good question, Arrant.'

'I had the best teachers.' But having the best hadn't made him wise. *Blast*. Why did everything bring back memories best forgotten? 'So you won't see your daughter in Madrinya?'

'No. I am anxious to get home to Asufa.'

'Oh.' His mouth went dry.

Garis didn't seem to notice his consternation. 'Let's take a room in the wayhouse and see what they have to eat. The next two nights will be unpleasant, let me warn you, so you had better enjoy the comfort here. Even though the wayhouse-keeper is as crazy as a fish in a cloud. Mashet. Poor fellow; they say he went mad down there, crossing the Rift. He keeps hearing voices in his head, telling him to do daft things, and no one can convince him they aren't orders from real people. I guess they *are* real to him. He once wrestled your father to the floor because he thought a perfectly innocent trader was a Tyranian assassin.'

Garis was right, Arrant decided a little later. Mashet was indeed daft. When Garis introduced them, the man gripped Arrant's hand tightly. 'Magori,' he whispered. 'You must be careful. There are people who will harm you. They chase you through the night. Be careful! Be watchful! Be mindful!'

Later that night, at dinner, Mashet's glance never ceased to rove the room, as if searching for the unseen attacker. 'I shall stand guard,' he told Arrant as he and Garis went up to bed. 'I shall keep you safe while you sleep. I shall die in your stead, defending the Magor.'

When Arrant and Garis rose in the morning, they found their room barricaded from the outside with a pile of furniture as high as the door transom. They had to shout for other travellers to come and let them out. Mashet didn't seem to remember what he had done, and served them breakfast with a sunny smile, remarking – as if it were an everyday occurrence – that the voices in his head had warned him crocodiles were flying down the Rift, dropping rocks on unwary travellers.

Arrant was glad to leave the wayhouse, but the two nights in the wayhouses of the Rift were even more uncomfortable. The places were unstaffed, damp and muddy. The wind howled all night long like numina whining for their brethren, and the ride across the floor of the Rift was one of the worst days Arrant had ever spent on the back of an animal. They travelled with a caravan of howdah shleths piled high with goods, and they positioned their mounts next to one of the burdened beasts to lessen the impact of that continuous gale, but even so, at the end of the day the fine silt in the water picked up from the lakes had been driven so deeply into their cloaks and clothing that everything was red and sodden. As far as Arrant was concerned, the only good thing about the Rift was that the memory of it made the rest of the ride to Madrinya seem easy.

What wasn't so pleasant for him was the thought of having to explain what he had done to the father he barely knew. Every time he woke up in the morning, he remembered the reason he felt that pain in the centre of his chest, that twist in his gut, that tightness across his temples.

Brand was dead, and he could never bring him back.

They rode into Madrinya late one afternoon, the shleths padding on silent feet over the hard brown earth of the streets.

'Don't they ever pave streets in Kardiastan?' Arrant asked. He had expected the capital city to be grander than the other towns they had passed through. It didn't seem right that the roads were just earth.

'No, they don't. Why bother? The earth is packed so hard it's like rock anyway, and stays that way because it never rains. Shleths are soft-footed and we use them more than wagons, which would break up the street surfaces, so there's no need for paving.'

'I suppose not.' He wasn't convinced though. Dirt underfoot in the land's greatest city seemed, well, uncivilised. Although he was glad to see that the streets weren't covered in shleth droppings. Horse dung, he remembered, had been one of Tyr's problems once Ligea had banned slavery. No one had wanted to pay to keep the streets swept clean.

'The Tyranians did pave some of the more important thoroughfares,' Garis said, 'and those we have left like that, even though some of the City Council wanted to rip up the

stones simply because they were perceived as being Tyranian.'
He shook his head in amusement. 'Temellin managed to
convince them that the paving was good native Kardi rock.
People who think with their hearts instead of their heads can
be a trial to a ruler sometimes – as you will find out one day.'

He blinked, startled. The words gave an unwelcome imme-
diacy to something that had always been distant and vague. He,
Arrant, one day governing a land of which he had no experience, ruling a people who were strangers to him? The notion
was suddenly preposterous.

Around him there was so much that was still strange to his
eyes. Instead of fountains, there were wells, and each one had
people lining up with ewers, awaiting their turn. Instead of
water channels and pipes, there were water sellers, with
amphorae of water transported up from the lake in howdahs
on the backs of the pack shleths. He overheard one woman
berating the seller for trying to sell her smelly water.

The streets were lined with adobe walls, punctuated every
now and then by closed wooden gates. When someone opened
a gate as they passed, sounds and smells spilled into the street
– a child's laughter, an odd snatch of music played on a strange
instrument, the scent of nectar-laden flowers mixed with a
tantalising whiff of cooking food. He glimpsed a garden within
the walls, a blaze of red flowers, fruit vines climbing the brown
adobe walls of a house. So many new sights and sounds and
scents. It didn't seem like home, and he wondered if it ever
would. Yet the emotions that stirred inside him were sympathetic; even with the earthen roadways, part of him liked what
he saw. The language of the streets was his, the tongue he associated with being a child at Narjemah's knee, or sharing
childish secrets with Ligea. The people looked like him. For
once, it was good to look into another's eyes and see the same
shade of brown gazing back at him. For once, he knew for

sure that his appearance didn't label him as unusual, as not quite belonging.

'What are those boys doing over there?' he asked, reining in to point with his shleth prod to where a youth of about his own age appeared to be attempting to pull another from the saddle of his shleth.

'Ah, that's a game of dubblup. Doubling-up – two people on one shleth. The aim is to get yourself from the ground into the saddle behind the rider, all done at a gallop.' They watched as the runner tried to put his foot into the palm of the shleth's feeding arm, while the youth in the saddle hauled him up. Garis winced as the rider tumbled off instead, and said, 'You'll be doing it yourself soon, I suppose, and end up being better than everyone else too, I'll wager. There's not a lad who hasn't tried to perfect the technique, and not a mother who hasn't scolded a son for trying and a father who hasn't secretly been proud when he succeeded.'

The words, meant to comfort and encourage, served only to remind Arrant that he was an outsider, about to meet his father again after a gap of eight years. Gods, he knew Garis better than he knew Temellin. It was hard to love a father he could hardly remember, except for his moment of rejection. Garis, on the other hand – Garis had been there in the first days after Brand's death, stilling his panic, gentling the terror he'd felt at the idea of living with what he'd done, encouraging him when he'd wondered if he wanted to live another day. Garis had been there to remind him that the only way he could make sense of Brand's death was to make something of his own life.

On the month-long journey he had done more: he'd prepared Arrant as far as he was able for all that lay ahead. He'd spent hours describing the workings of the Magoroth Council. 'Your father is the overall ruler of Kardiastan, make no mistake about that,' he'd said, 'but a Mirager has to have the consensus of his peers on policy matters. So every major decision has to go to the Magoroth Council for debate.'

'And ordinary Kardis?' he'd asked.

'Oh, they have their own realm of authority. They govern the day-to-day life of the cities and towns and villages largely without interference, although each area has its own Magor administrative adviser reporting back to Temellin.'

Best of all, Garis had talked about the people Arrant would meet: who they were, how they interacted, who would be likely to make trouble for him, and who would be friends. 'As for the list of potential troublemakers,' Garis had said, 'Korden's at the top, although Temellin probably wouldn't agree with that assessment. Korden's intentions are always noble, and he's been a good friend to Temellin.'

'But?'

'He didn't like Sarana and he hates all Tyranians with a deep loathing. That is going to prejudice him against you.'

'That's silly. I'm not a Tyranian, for a start.'

'You were raised there, by a woman who was raised there. That's the way he sees it. Don't forget, almost everyone he knew as a child, his parents, his older sisters – they were killed by Tyranians when he was ten years old. He will regard your loyalties as suspect because you were brought up in Tyr. He will question your abilities because there have been rumours you can't control your power. People say he would like his eldest son to be Mirager-heir, a man called Firgan.'

'But you don't like Firgan.'

'For someone who doesn't have a working cabochon, you are uncannily acute, Arrant Temellin.' Garis hesitated. 'He's not my kind of man. He likes war and killing too much. He has a vision of expansion for Kardiastan and he is constantly bringing these ideas before the Council. He makes young men restless with stories of conquest and power. I find his father cold and impersonal and Firgan seems to have inherited tenfold that aspect of Korden. I don't see his heart. A good soldier, a brave man, a leader – those attributes don't necessarily mean an ... an *upright* man. I have never felt empathy from Firgan. But then, I've never felt ill will either.' He shrugged. 'Best you make up your own mind, rather than listen to me. Anyway, you will have Temellin to guide you and he knows far more than me. I was forever roaming the Exaltarchy, not living in Madrinya.'

Roaming the Exaltarchy. With Brand.

'Gods help me,' Arrant thought, 'why must I keep remembering?'

He repressed a shiver. As a five-year-old, he'd loved his father. But now Temellin was someone he knew only by reading his words on an occasional letter-scroll, or by hearing others speak of his exploits. Hero, warrior, liberator ... tales gave Temellin a stature that made Arrant proud to be his son, but didn't make it easier for him to contemplate the meeting ahead.

'Scared?' Garis asked.

He nodded. 'Do you know why my father didn't want me to come back until now?'

'Well, it made sense at first – believe me, when the Ravage takes a dislike to you, it's better to be somewhere it is not. And to hide a child with a cabochon outside of the Mirage in a country occupied by legionnaires on the lookout for anyone with a gemstone in their palm would not have been easy. So it made more sense for you to stay hidden in the mountains of Tyrans. But once we ousted the legions from Kardiastan? Well, we all thought you should have come back. Only Temel said you should stay where you were. None of us could understand it. I guess you'll have to ask him. I can tell you this: it would not have been a decision made on a whim.'

He pointed. 'You can see the pavilions from here. Traditionally there have always been eight, but the old Magoroth Council Hall was burned to the ground during the Shimmer Festival massacres and the others were deliberately razed by the legions later. We haven't rebuilt them all yet. The tallest one there in the centre is the new hall, those to the right are the three Academies. Right now we'll go straight to the Mirager's Pavilion, the one closest to us.'

'Will my father be there?'

'Probably. That's not just where he lives, but where he works, too. It's the heart of our administration. You will stay with him in the Mirager's private apartment, at the back.' He glanced across at Arrant. 'There's nothing to be afraid of.'

But Arrant was anxious, nonetheless. Perhaps Temellin had already heard what his son had done. The couriers who carried letter-scrolls from Tyr to Madrinya and back were known for the speed of their journey, and they took the Ordensa route, while Garis and Arrant had travelled at a more leisurely pace. How would Temellin react, knowing Ligea had been injured?

'Cabochon help me,' he thought. 'How can I ever explain without saying why I was jealous of Brand?' Yet his jealousy was the only explanation he had, poor as it was, for the behaviour that had ultimately betrayed Ligea to her enemies.

'It's got to come from you, you know,' Garis said gently. 'I'm not going to tell Temellin a thing.'

Arrant swallowed and nodded.

Garis continued, 'He'll certainly hear the details one day, from someone, somewhere – and probably garbled. It will be better if it comes from you.'

'He might have already heard.'

'It's possible.'

Arrant subsided in misery.

'You can't run from this, Arrant. Remember that once confronted, problems often seem to diminish in size.'

His voice was gentle rather than admonitory, but Arrant didn't believe the words. 'I don't know him. It's hard to talk to someone you don't know.'

'No one said this is going to be easy. But he is a fine man who has been looking forward to this day ever since you were born. And it won't be as difficult as you think.'

Yes, it will. His brother, popping into his head, unheralded as usual.

Arrant jumped, startling his mount in turn, and had to spend a moment calming the animal.

Thanks, he replied sourly. *That's just what I wanted to hear. What are you doing here now anyway? Come to see our papa nail one of his sons to the city gate for terminal idiocy?*

Don't be ridiculous! As if he'd do any such thing.

He doesn't have to, Arrant thought morosely. Just facing his father and having to tell him what had happened was punishment enough, but he kept that thought tucked away in the private part of his mind.

I can give you moral support if you need it, Tarran said. *And I want to see Madrinya. I've never been here, you know. Besides, Temellin's my father too, and I haven't seen him for years. Not since he left the Mirage along with everyone else when you and I were, what, seven or so? Arrant, I want you to tell him about me. I want him to know me. I want to talk to him, through you. I – I want to have a father. Sort of, anyway.*

That would be wonderful! But – um, later, huh?

Yes, of course. Today, you need to get to know him, and he needs to know you, too.

Why do you think it'll be difficult for me to talk to him, apart from the obvious point that I have to tell him I behaved like a brat, got Brand killed and Ligea hurt?

Mirage Maker memories tell me he has a temper. He was very jealous of Brand, you know. And he once tried to kill Ligea.

Arrant was appalled. His jaw dropped. *He what?*

'What's the matter?' Garis asked.

He closed his mouth. 'Oh, um, nothing.' *He tried to kill her? He threw his sword at her from a few feet away. She would have died, except that she had fitted her cabochon into the hilt. Do you know what it means if you do that? Neither the sword nor its magic can ever hurt you. And you had better stop looking as if you've been clobbered with a wet fish, or Garis will think you're moondaft.*

Arrant attempted to look unflustered.

'Just tell him the truth,' Garis said.

'I've just heard – um, I mean, I heard that he has a temper.'

'You're his son, Arrant. He's not going to be mad at you.'

'Oh, gods,' Arrant thought. 'Yes he is.'

He was not looking forward to this.

Shortly after Arrant left Tyr, Ligea announced to Gevenan that she wanted to visit Getria, Tyr's sister city at the foot of the Alps. 'Rumours have spread about how I was badly injured by Rathrox Ligatan, so I need to show the Getrians I am not only alive, but quite capable of ruling Tyrans,' she told him by way of explanation.

He just snorted and made a remark under his breath about mother hens – feeling bereft when their chickens fled the coop – having to fuss about something or another. She glared at him, irritated. Damn the man, she couldn't keep anything hidden from his probing shrewdness. She did indeed need to do something, and a ride to Getria promised diversion.

She took Gevenan with her and stayed half a month. She met with city leaders, made appearances at a number of city banquets and plays, lit votive lamps at several of the city's temples, and donated generously to the Temple of the Unknown God in support of indigent ex-slaves. She even made a call on Paulius Vevian, head of the Getrian branch of the Lucii, and his wife.

'Horrible man,' she said to Gevenan after they had returned to the Exaltarch's Getrian villa. Paulius had grumbled the whole evening about how he couldn't be a proper host because his servants didn't work as hard as slaves and if he threatened to whip them, they had the audacity to leave. 'He could hardly contain his distaste for having me in his house, and his wife took me aside to beg me to reinstate slavery – just to placate him so she has a husband who is halfway bearable!'

He raised an eyebrow. 'You look as if you've drunk a goblet of vinegar. Did he upset you that much?'

'No, not him. It was something one of their servants told me when I went to the latrine. An ex-slave, of course. Apparently Paulius left Tyrans recently and spent a few months in Gaya. When he returned, the servant overheard enough of a conversation between him and his brother to suggest the Lucii are planning a rebellion against the Senate and me, with Gayan help. A rebellion that would reinstate slavery if successful.'

'Ah. Funny how people always underestimate ex-slaves.'

'Moneymaster Arcadim told me sometime ago that the Gayan ruling house is short of money.'

Gevenan nodded. 'I did hear they have some fine ex-legionnaires they can't afford to pay. Bad policy that – not to pay men who have swords and spears and fighting experience. Good way to commit suicide, in fact. But if they sold the services of their army to the Lucii, they'd have gold in their coffers, more than enough to pay their soldiers to fight a war here. Definitely good tactics.'

'Look into it, Gev. See what you can find out.'

'Right. Ligea, you need to tap into this pool of ex-slaves

more. They worship the very air you exhale, and they are a fine source of information.'

She frowned. One of the senators had been nagging her about the very same thing. 'You want me to set up another Brotherhood? To spy on our own citizens? Led, perhaps, by another Rathrox Ligatan?'

'Sarcasm, sarcasm. Don't be so sour. It doesn't have to be a Brotherhood exactly. Although, quite frankly, I can't see any reason this side of Hades why traitors shouldn't be spied upon.'

In her heart, she knew he was right. She nodded, loathing the idea even as she agreed with its necessity. She had to set up some formal structure to gather information, otherwise she might not know what was happening until they were on the verge of a civil war. But anything that resembled a Brotherhood would turn her stomach. 'All I want,' she thought, 'is enough stability in Tyrans to enable me to leave and know that all I have achieved here will remain, that Kardiastan is safe from another Tyranian invasion in the foreseeable future. Is that too much to expect?'

'Knew you'd see reason,' he said amiably. 'Pragmatism before sentiment, that's the Ligea I know best.'

She swore at him.

He grinned. 'You hate it when I'm right, don't you?'

CHAPTER FOUR

They rode into the entrance courtyard of the Mirager's Pavilion just as the Mirager strode out of the main door, closely followed by two other Magoroth. A servant stood holding the Mirager's shleth ready; Theuri attendants milled around with their mounts, their bright boleros and sashes a contrast to the brown shagginess of the shleths and the dry earth underfoot.

Too many people. Too many witnesses to a meeting Arrant had desperately wanted to be private.

He recognised his father at once. He was exactly as he'd pictured him: a head taller than Garis, lean and tough and slim, with eyes that laughed in a face Arrant knew well, even though he hadn't seen him for eight years. The Mirage Maker's gift to Sarana, a lump of Mirage clay, had shown him his father's changing appearance, day after day, year after year.

By contrast, Temellin's glance slid over Arrant without recognition. Instead, his eyes sought the person his senses told him was there: Garis. He took the steps down from the pavilion door two at a time, broadcasting his pleasure. And then his gaze flew back to Arrant, realising who he must be.

You're hiding yourself, as usual, Tarran remarked. *He can't sense you. Stop being so tight-arsed, Arrant.*

But Arrant had no intention of releasing the hold he had

on his inner core of being, even if he could work out how to do it with ease. He had too much hidden there . . .

They stared at one another, neither knowing what to say. Temellin's expression was one of shock. It was one thing to know that your child must now be a young man; quite another to have him in front of you, all the childish curves melted into the form of a youth, and with an adult's emotional suffering showing in his eyes. And just then, Arrant's wretched cabochon decided to work, so he felt the blast of his father's emotion like sand against his skin. Anger – no, *rage*. Hurt, grief, sorrow. None of the joy that there should have been; not in that first reaction. He heard Garis's sharp intake of breath and knew he had felt it all too.

Garis dismounted and Arrant followed, sick to the stomach. 'He knows,' Arrant thought. 'He has heard. Someone has written. Not Ligea; someone else.'

He saw it all there, on his father's face; he felt it in that single blast of rage and mangled emotions, quickly hidden. Someone came forward to take the reins of their mounts. Then Temellin was there, placing his hands on Arrant's shoulders and scanning his face, trying, perhaps, to see in the youth the child he had so briefly known. His father pulled him into a tight embrace, all emotion masked, his smile welcoming, giving the hug owed to a son he hadn't seen in so long.

And Arrant thought, 'This is his public face. His heart isn't in it.' His own heart wobbled, stricken.

'Is she all right?' Temellin asked, the words no more than a whisper directly into his ear as they embraced. 'Tell me. I've heard no details. I've been worried sick.'

'She's fine. Really.' Then an amendment, striving for honesty. 'Physically fine.'

He felt a skitter of relief from his father before it was suppressed. After that, things happened in a blur. He was introduced to so many people, one after the other, it was hard to remember them all. Korden and his son Firgan, however, etched themselves immediately into memory. Korden first; tall, urbane, handsome, greying into a distinguished middle age. His eyes unfriendly, even as his voice welcomed with words so formal they meant nothing.

'Mirager-heir Arrant,' he said, 'this is a much-delayed pleasure. We have been pressing the Mirager to bring you here under our care for several years now, and I, for one, am delighted you have finally arrived.' He held out his left hand and Arrant placed his own so that they were cabochon to cabochon. The man's welcome tingled up his arm, sharp suspicion mixed in with a genuine gladness.

I don't think he meant you to feel that. The suspicion, I mean, Tarran said as Korden's clasp lingered beyond what was normal. *Quick, let him feel respect in return.*

Arrant did his best, but from the look on Korden's face he had an idea he must have let loose less appealing feelings as well.

Korden continued, 'May I present my eldest son, Magori-firgan? Some of my other numerous progeny you will meet later. I have a son, Lesgath, a few years older than you are, and a daughter, Serenelle, almost the same age, both at the Academy. I hope you will forge friendships. It must have been lonely for you in Tyr, being the only Magoroth.'

'Hardly the only one,' Temellin interrupted.

'The only Magoroth child,' Korden said in smoothly delivered amendment.

Arrant extended his hand to Firgan, who ground their cabochons together in a crippling handclasp. And as their gems met, a stab of personal spite passed from Firgan's into his own, a molten streak of malice that took his breath away. Something inside him wanted to cringe before it, but he allowed none of that to show on his face. Firgan's eyes were unpleasantly knowing.

Emotions passed that way aren't visible to others, Tarran said. *That was for you alone.*

Then the man just made a mistake, Arrant said, hoping he was right. *He told me he was an enemy, and it's always good to know who your enemies are.* Ligea's wisdom.

Temellin turned his gaze from Arrant to address the two men. 'Korden, Firgan, as you can imagine, I want to spend time privately with my son. Why don't the rest of you go ahead with the hospice visit?'

Arrant exhaled, relieved. *Vortexdamn, Tarran, this is difficult. I can feel their emotions everywhere, dashing all over the place. It's like they are all shouting at one another.*

That's what the Magor do, Arrant. You should join in. You should be exuding your happiness to be here, your gratitude at the welcome. You are puzzling them by your emotional silence.

Ravage hells. Will I ever learn all this?

Fortunately, he didn't have to plunge straight into an intimate conversation with his father. At Temellin's suggestion, Garis whisked him away first to have a bath and change into clean clothes. 'He's giving you time to calm down,' Garis said as he showed Arrant where to bathe. 'You look as if you swallowed a raw fish and the fins got caught in your gullet. Relax, lad.'

Relax? He had never felt less like relaxing in his life.

'Oh, and remember water is precious here. We use as little as possible for washing. One jug. If you stand over the grid, the water runs out to the garden cistern where it can be used for watering the plants afterwards.'

He thought of the public baths and fountains and aqueducts of Tyr, of the way no one ever worried about how much water they used. He was going to miss that splendid profligacy. Why had the Kardis never thought of building aqueducts to bring spring water to the cities of Kardiastan, the way they did in Tyrans?

By the time he arrived in Temellin's private quarters, he had managed – he thought – to erect a façade of calm.

That's the wrong thing to do, Tarran growled at him, catching his satisfaction. *You are supposed to be leaking your calm, not putting up a barricade that imitates it.*

He sighed. Would he ever learn how to be a proper Magor, let alone a Magoroth?

Do you want me here? Tarran asked.

I – no, I guess not. I have to do this on my own. Do you mind?

No. I'll go back to the Mirage, then. I just couldn't resist coming here for a while. To see him, especially.

The ache Arrant heard in his tone made his breath catch. 'Sweet Elysium,' he thought privately, 'what must it be like never to be able to speak to another human being but me?'

I ought to go back anyway, Tarran added. *The Ravage is widening in the north and the Mirage needs the strength of every single one of us, just to withstand the spread.* He paused, and his next words were telling. *We don't try to repair the damage any more.*

Not knowing what to say, Arrant let his concern spill out instead.

I'll be all right, I promise, Tarran said. *I'll come back in a day or two when you have settled in. Good luck.* With that, he was gone.

Temellin looked up from where he sat as Garis and Arrant entered the room. He raised an eyebrow at Garis, querying his presence.

Garis sucked in his cheeks. 'Looks as if you are on your own, Arrant.'

'Samia is in Madrinya, staying with her aunt,' Temellin said.

'I sent for her as soon as I realised you were here. She's probably already waiting for you down in my reception room. She
should keep you nicely occupied.'

Garis brightened and left, trailing anticipation. Arrant
caught that much, and then his cabochon faded.

'Sit down, Arrant,' Temellin said, running a hand through
his hair in a worried fashion. 'It is good to have you here. I've
– I've looked forward to this day for as long as I can remember.'
He hesitated, then added, 'Unfortunately, it's been marred by
the news I had that your mother was hurt. I also heard Brand
died and that it was all your fault. What happened?'

Arrant heard the unspoken words hang in the air: *Please
tell me this is a lie.* He felt his father's longing to be told a
different story. And it was the one thing he couldn't say.

'It's all true,' he said, his voice husky as he acknowledged
yet again that Brand was dead. That he was culpable. His hands
started shaking, so he sat on them. 'But Mater is fine now.'

'Mater?' The word sliced the air, sharp with distaste.

He'd made a mistake, he realised. Used a Tyranian word.
'Mother,' he amended and hurried on. 'Her arm was slashed.
Favonius did it, but I was able to start her healing immediately and then Garis came, and he did some of the final work.
There doesn't appear to be any permanent damage. She, um,
she has sent you this letter.' He dug in his pouch, pulled out
a scroll tube and handed it over. 'There's a whole lot of papers
as well, about trade and stuff. They are still in my saddlebags.'
Only when he stopped did he realise how cold and unfeeling
his rush of words had sounded.

Temellin put the tube down without opening it. Arrant
could not sense his emotions, but he didn't need to – his father
was furious and having trouble not showing it on his face.
'They can wait,' Temellin said. 'I want to hear what happened.
From you. Please.'

Arrant looked down at his feet. He still had his sandals on, which felt all wrong. He couldn't meet his father's eyes, not while he was telling this horrible tale. He began to stumble and stutter his way through the skeleton of the story, omitting reasons, dealing only with the fleshless ribs of the facts.

'I was angry with M – Mama because she never had time for me. It was stupid and childish, I know. I found a way I could leave the palace without her knowing and that was when I met Favonius, who used to be the Jackal Legion Legate. I didn't know that. I thought he was being kind. Interested in me for myself, not just because I was the Exaltarch's son. All the time he was working with Rathrox Ligatan. They used me as bait in a trap for Mother and the Altani Plenipotentiary, Brand. When they sprang the trap, there wasn't anything I could do about it because I couldn't find my power. In the end, Favonius and Rathrox and Brand were all killed, and Mama was wounded.'

'You left the palace without anyone knowing? More than once?'

'Yes.'

'And trusted a man you did not know?'

'Yes.'

'Why? Surely your mother must have told you of the dangers!'

'Yes. But I was angry with her. I – I don't have any other excuse.'

'That last is a lie. Arrant, you can't lie to me. Don't *ever* lie to me.' His rage was growing, but still carefully corralled. 'Now, what was the real reason? What went wrong between you and your mother that this thing could have possibly happened? Why did you not *talk* to her?'

Arrant felt sick. He *couldn't* tell him the true reason. How could he say that his jealousy of Brand had scarred his relationship with Ligea? How could he say that he was furious with her because she was sleeping with the Altani? 'I – I didn't see that much of Ligea. There were always so many other things taking her time. I was angry with her from the moment I found out about my Mirage Maker brother and how she killed his mother. I blamed her.'

'What in the name of the Mirage are you talking about? If your mother hadn't killed Pinar, Pinar would have murdered her and *you* would be the Mirage Maker, not your brother. She must have told you how it happened, surely. You should be grateful! Sands, Arrant – Sarana almost died because of *that*?'

'I was very young when I found out,' he stammered, but the words sounded juvenile, the proffering of a pathetic excuse. As indeed it was. And it hadn't been his mother who had spoken of it. Tarran had told him, not Ligea.

'Perhaps so, but you are thirteen now!' Temellin snapped. 'Of an age to wear a Magor sword. And to be truthful. You are hiding something; do you think I cannot tell?'

In deepening dismay, Arrant sat silent. This was going from awful to worse.

Temellin took a calming breath. 'Skies above, here we are, father and son who haven't seen one another in years, and we are verging on argument. Let's start again, shall we? Let me explain. I love your mother, Arrant. I always have and I always will. It is a constant grief that she is not here, sharing my life. And I worry about her, living as she does in a land where she has so many enemies. To hear of her being harmed, and yet to be unable to go to her, or to help her – it hurts more than I can say. And a fine man who cared for her welfare, whom I thought would help to keep her safe, whom I admired, died before his time. He protected her. He was her closest friend. And now he's gone and she is alone. To know that it was your foolishness that started this sequence of events – it's – it's upsetting.'

Arrant swallowed. The understatement of the last word was worse than anger would have been.

Temellin continued, 'All I ask is a reason that makes sense. I want to understand how it could happen. You are my son. *Our* son. So let us discuss this with honesty and openness, and then you and I can put it behind us and build a new relationship. No secrets between us, not on this matter. What do you say?'

Arrant sat rigidly still. Here was a chance to make it all right. All he had to do was explain how he'd felt about Ligea's relationship with Brand. His father would understand; in fact it would make him angry, too. He'd be furious. Sweet Elysium, he'd tried to kill her once simply because she'd lied to him . . . The truth would surely hammer a wedge between his parents, might destroy a relationship already made tenuous by distance. His own anger burgeoned. Why had Ligea slept with Brand when she professed to love his father? Damn her for putting him in this position!

'I – I don't really have anything else to say,' he muttered, knowing he sounded both ungracious and dishonest.

His father's expression hardened in anger and hurt at the rebuff. 'I see.'

Arrant said woodenly, 'It started when I found out about Tarran, as I said, and it just got worse as time went by. I was stupid and my stupidity killed Brand.'

'Your mother wrote once that you had an imaginary playmate you pretended was your brother. You called him Tarran. You surely don't *still* indulge in such silliness, do you? I mean, that was when you were eight or nine.' The words, honed with anger, were scathing. 'What may pass for acceptable in Tyr for a lad of your age is not necessarily what is expected of a Magor here, let alone of the Mirager-heir. The Magoroth will be judging you. If they don't accept you as heir, it will be very difficult for me to insist. If you are not prepared to carry yourself like a man from the start, you would do better to return to Tyr because there won't be a place for you here.'

Return to Tyr? The words wounded, no, *crushed* him. For a moment he was back in Ordensa, aged five, hearing a similar rejection. His anger grew alongside his pain. 'That is unfair! I did not say that I believe in an *imaginary* brother. I do have a brother. I just call him Tarran, that's all. Ligea made him into what he is and he'll never be human, not ever. I was young when I found that out, so I didn't understand properly and I thought it was all her fault. He has to live with the pain of the Ravage, and I blamed her for it.' He was achingly close to choking, so held himself rigid, determined not to appear weak.

'I'm sorry,' Temellin said. 'I misunderstood. I thought you might be thinking of this Tarran as being real in the sense you did when you were younger. That is, someone who came and played with you. The dream of a lonely, imaginative boy, and understandable at the time, perhaps. I just wish, well – that you would be honest with me now. I can feel that you are still hiding something from me, something important. Arrant, I am your father. Up until now, not much of a father, I know, and I don't seem to be handling this at all well, but I want to do better. Your trust would mean a lot to me.'

Another chance, yet Arrant felt himself drowning in dismay. If he told the truth about Tarran, the odds were that Temellin would think he was as mad as the Rift wayhousekeeper and unworthy of being his heir. If he told the truth about why he had been angry with his mother, then he risked wrecking his parents' relationship. He chose his words carefully. 'What made you so certain that the Tarran I believed in at eight or nine wasn't real? A Mirage Maker communicating with his brother. Why shouldn't it have been possible?'

'To be quite honest with you, I did consider the possibility of your playmate really being my other son. After all, Sarana did communicate with the Mirage Makers when she was in trouble inside a Ravage sore. Did she ever tell you that? But then they used images and concepts, not words, and the conversation was laboured and difficult, until they found a better way and used the Ravage beasts. They manipulated their jaws and tongues to make them speak to her. She wasn't in Tyrans either, halfway across the known world. She was there, in the Mirage. And we do know Mirage Makers can't leave the Mirage or the Shiver Barrens. Usually they communicate only in the Shiver Barrens. Even there they are unable to speak as we do. They twist the song of the sands, as you will discover. The idea that a Mirage Maker could detach himself from the Mirage, travel somehow to Tyrans, locate you, and then speak in a way that is beyond their capabilities – it was simply too outlandish for me to believe.'

'But Tarran is not just a Mirage Maker. He's all human too. And we have a connection – the same father.'

Temellin paused before he answered in words that held no warmth. 'Do you still think the Tarran of your imagination back then was *real*?'

'I believed him to be real at the time.'

'To invent a playmate is common enough in small children. I remember my own sister, Shirin. She made up another brother for herself and used to bring him out whenever I was mean to her. She insisted he had a chair at the table at meal-time, and was served a plate of food. I ridiculed it, but he was real to her.' For a moment he looked stricken. 'She died on the night of the Shimmer Feast massacres.'

There was a long silence before he added, 'You were a lonely boy, that's obvious, and so you took what you knew to exist and made it – him – into something that gave you comfort. Look, soon we will take you to the Shiver Barrens to receive your Magor sword and you will meet the real Mirage Makers. Then you will understand. Your brother will probably be there, inside the entity. Perhaps he might even be able to speak to you, after a fashion. But that's *all*, Arrant. That's all there will ever be. He was human once, but then he became a Mirage Maker. He's not like you, and never could be.'

Arrant didn't reply.

'You don't *still* believe in that childhood playmate do you?' Temellin's dismay bordered on repugnance, so strong even Arrant could feel it.

Desperate to have his father's respect, he said, 'I don't have an imaginary playmate, Father. As you pointed out, I am thirteen now, not a child seeking companionship. And I am not mad, either, hearing imaginary voices in my head like that crazy keeper at the Rift wayhouse.'

Temellin frowned. 'So why ask how I knew your playmate was not real? Arrant, I need your assurance that you have put all this childishness behind you. Tell me now that you don't believe that your Mirage Maker brother and your playmate were one and the same. Tell me you don't believe you have ever spoken to your brother.' He was begging, desperate to find in Arrant a son he could admire and love in spite of what had happened.

Arrant paled. His dilemma seemed unsolvable. If he told the truth, then Temellin would think he was daft. He would condemn him for believing something he thought to be childish silliness. If he lied, then Temellin would know it and still think exactly the same thing – that he believed in an imaginary playmate. The silence dragged. He confined his emotions deep inside him. He obliterated all feeling, stopped his fear dead, blanked emotion from his mind. He looked Temellin in the eye and said coldly, 'I think you will just have to believe in me. I am your son, after all. Do you think I am silly enough to have imaginary conversations with someone I falsely imagine to be my brother?'

Temellin stared at him, uncertain. Finally he asked, 'Are you going to tell me the truth about what took you out on the streets of Tyr without your mother's knowledge?'

'I – I can't.' Arrant watched the last warmth in Temellin's expression fade, and felt his own spirit diminish. Something that had been within his grasp was slipping away, and he didn't know how to bring it back. Where had it all gone so wrong? That hard, cold lump of his boyhood was back, huge and unyielding inside him.

Temellin drew in a deep breath. 'With regard to Brand's death and your mother's injury, we all make mistakes and sometimes they have unpleasant consequences. There's not a person in this world who has lived a life utterly free of folly. You have been unluckier than most, that's all, in that the consequences were so tragic. They are better not dwelled upon. I want you to put it all behind you, forgotten.' Cold words said in chilled tones. Words too formal to be comforting, tone too flat to be free of resentment.

Arrant's thoughts were bleak. 'He doesn't want me. I am nothing to him. He wanted a different kind of son and he's disappointed with what he's got.' Forget what happened? No, there was no forgetting. And never could be, not by either of them. Let alone by Ligea. Brand was *dead*, by all that was holy! And Temellin didn't explain how it was possible to forget the shrivelling horror of the scenes imprinted within him . . . Brand dying, Ligea bleeding – *Vortex, so much blood* – the light dying in Favonius's eyes.

Temellin made an obvious effort. 'Your problem is your lack of control over your power. If you'd had the control of a normal Magoroth boy of your age, this would never have happened. So, what we have to do now is concentrate on developing your control. Here in Madrinya we have general academies for the Theuros and Illusos and Magoroth. You will start in the Magoroth Academy. When you have settled in a bit, we will leave for the Shiver Barrens, so you can get your sword.' It was the Mirager speaking to one of the Magoroth, not a father to a son. Any chance of rapport had vanished.

Arrant nodded. His emotions strangled him, all of them so entangled he couldn't even decide what predominated.

'Don't look so worried, Arrant. You will soon catch up with the others of your age. Now go and get those papers from Sarana. Oh, and that's another thing: please don't call her Ligea. Her real name is Sarana. It always was. Do you think you can find your way back to your room, or shall I send someone with you?'

Arrant turned in a full circle to look around his bedroom. He had not expected anything as luxurious as the palace in Tyr, but he had thought the Mirager's Pavilion would be better than this. The floor was tiled with terracotta, not marble, and strewn with shleth pelts. The bed was just a pallet on a platform, the bedding woven of undyed shleth wool. There was no statuary, no wall niches for ornaments. Furniture was made from cane and reeds, not wood. A starkly plain room, sunny and bright, but bare.

He bit his lip. This wasn't Tyr and he had to stop comparing the two.

He undid the straps of his pack to extract the gifts and documents Ligea had sent to Temellin, and tried not to think about his father's anger. Tried not to think about the way he had dodged speaking of the brother he knew. Tried not to think about the implications. Tried to make excuses for himself, for his father. 'I wanted him to like me. I wanted him to be proud of me . . . I couldn't tell the truth. And I shouldn't blame him for being angry; Ligea almost died because of what I did. Just as bad, she almost lost everything she had fought for. He loves her. Who wouldn't be angry?'

Dragging his feet, striving not to think about what had just happened, he went downstairs to where his father was waiting.

As he raised his hand to knock at his father's door, an unwanted thought popped into his head: 'What about Tarran?' Tarran wanted to use him to get to know his father. More than that too. What was it Tarran had said just before they'd left Tyr? *Maybe, if you came, you could think of some way to help us.* And, he, Arrant, was the only clear line of communication between the Mirage Makers and the Magor.

'Acheron's mists,' he thought in deep misery, 'what have I done? I've as good as told my father Tarran doesn't exist, when I should be convincing him he does – because it's important.'

CHAPTER FIVE

From the city of Getria, Ligea and Gevenan followed the paveway to the town of Begum in order to visit the legionnaire camp there. 'Morale boost needed,' Gevenan had said when he'd proposed the addition to their trip. 'They need to see their Exaltarch alive and well.'

Ligea enjoyed being out on the road again, away from the protocol and hypocrisy of the highborn life in a city. Of course, she was now accompanied everywhere by a contingent of her Imperial Guards, not to mention an astonishing number of attendants all apparently necessary for her comfort. 'Whoever authorised all these people to come along?' she'd asked the very first time she had travelled away from Tyr as the Exaltarch.

'No one,' Gevenan had replied. 'It's just the way it has always been done. Don't change a thing, or you will upset everyone from the flunkies of your own palace kitchen to the lowest potboy in every wayhouse you stay in.' So she had sighed and acquiesced and dreamed of being Sarana Solad in Kardiastan.

Just after the Petrum River bridge, one of the legionnaires came riding up to her from the front of the column. He saluted, saying, 'Exalted, there's a Quyriot horseman up ahead, says he wants to talk to you. Old fellow, dirty, with a pony covered in tatty bear-skins. Both of them stink, man and beast. Says he knew you before you were Exaltarch.'

She brought her senses into play and exclaimed to Gevenan, 'It's Berg Firegravel!' She had not seen the horse-trading smuggler since she had granted the Quyr their independence from Tyrans.

Gevenan snorted. 'That old reprobate? Watch your belongings, legionnaire. He'll steal the saddle from under your backside without you knowing it was gone.'

Berg hadn't changed. As usual, he was adorned from hair to boots with jewellery, most of it made of obsidian, the rest glass beads in a variety of colours. His pony, untied, grazed nearby. Ligea slid down from her mount and they bowed to one another in mutual respect. 'Hoy, lady,' he said in greeting.

'What can I do for an old friend of the mountains?' she asked, waving her guards away to a discreet distance. 'Is my friend in need?'

'The mountains call me.'

She knew the phrase; it meant he was anxious to conclude his business and go back to where he belonged on the plateau beyond the Alps. 'How did you know I would pass this way?' she asked, curious.

He tapped the beads of the necklet he wore. 'The runes tell me. They tell me many things. They say yus get has left y'side and gone to a strange land.'

'My what—? Oh, you mean Arrant. Yes, he has gone to his father in Kardiastan. One day I shall follow.'

'Ah.'

'What worries you, my friend?'

'The runes he wears. They ached at m'throat once, beggin' me to gift them to him. So I did. I had another, after all. Now I wonder if I did yus all an ill turn. They are old, those runes, made by strange folk clawed like animals, coming from a land that vanished long ago, or so the legends say. Under the sea, some say. Eaten by the sands, say others. The clawed folk vanished too, along with their land and their mines.'

Ligea frowned, looking for the relevance in what he said. 'You think the beads might *harm* my son?'

He shrugged. 'They've no interest in your lad, not one way, nor t'other. Runed beads are ever tied to creatures, not men. 'Tis why we wear them – to understand our beasts. But m'beads yearn towards his'n. I feel the tug of his'n through m'own. There be some strangeness in the air where he goes, and my runes feel the unsettling of it. The carvings twist and squirm. I know not what meaning there be in that, and there be no point in asking, because there's none alive to tell us.' He looked down at his necklet. 'These rest not easy as they listen. Tell him not to wear his necklet. Would be safer that-wise.'

She nodded. 'I will.'

'Then I'll be gone.' He gazed around at the plain they travelled and shuddered. 'Flat lands attack a man's soul. Yus are too far from the sky here.' He took up the reins of his plateau pony and went to mount.

'It wasn't your runes that told me I'd come this way, was it?' she asked with a smile.

He grinned at her sheepishly. 'No. Heard yus was in Getria. Then the tollkeeper told me yus'd come this way, so I waited.' He pulled himself into the saddle and rode away, without looking back.

'Bad news?' Gevenan asked as Ligea remounted.

'Just some superstitious nonsense.'

'Right.'

'Um, have a scribe and a courier attend me as soon as we reach the wayhouse.'

He sucked in his cheeks. 'Right. Always wise to record the ravings of prophets and shamans.'

'Shut up, Gev, or I'll stuff a piece of Berg's bearskin down your throat.'

He laughed and rode on.

'Superstitious nonsense,' she thought. 'That's all it is. A stone necklet can't hurt anyone . . . can it?'

Ungar was a Magoria in her thirties who loved teaching the beginners' class. None of her pupils was over six years old, and that was the way she liked it. She loved the way they had such fun with the weak power of their gems; she loved the way they grew in pride as they first learned to manipulate that power to do simple things, such as find someone in a game of hide-and-seek, or see objects placed at a distance, or hear words whispered on the other side of the grounds. There were so many games you could play with small children, and they never tired of them.

Arrant was different. For a start, he was over thirteen and, although polite enough, he was also aloof. He didn't want to play games; he wanted to learn. He desperately wanted to learn. She could sense that much.

Temellin had called her in to assess the lad so that they would have an idea of where to place him – which was wise of the Mirager, as trying to assess Arrant himself would have been a disaster – but she wished he hadn't then stayed in the room, watching. The boy was nervous enough without the father he scarcely knew sitting there observing. But he was the Mirager, and much older than she was as well, so she didn't have the gall to tell him to leave. She wished she was like Garis, who, although the same age as she was, would have sent the Mirager packing without a qualm.

Poor Arrant. He seemed so unhappy, and he must have been tired. He'd only arrived the evening before, and here he was, first thing in the morning, being put through his paces like a thoroughbred mount that had been bought sight unseen from a shleth trader. He looked as if he hadn't had a good night's sleep, too.

She chatted to him for a while, trying to put him at ease, telling him about how classes were selected according to talent, not age, and how it was perfectly possible to be advanced in one aspect of Magoroth studies and elementary in another.

'So we need to find out just where to slot you in for all the different aspects of cabochon usage,' she said brightly, trying not to be depressed by his solemn intensity. If only he would smile, he'd be an attractive lad. He had his father's good looks . . . 'Warding, far-sensing, battle, positioning, emotion-reading, cloaking and so on. So I am just going to ask you to do a few things to see how you go.'

He nodded, but everything about him suggested tension. He was carefully *not* looking at his father, for a start. The expression on his face was so wooden she suspected that it hid deep-felt misery, but she could not gain the slightest hint of his feelings.

'Well, to begin with, I think we shall be placing you in the advanced class for cloaking,' she said with a laugh.

He looked startled. 'Cloaking? What's that?'

'Hiding your emotions from others. You're the only boy I know of your age who could have sat there and not leaked a thing while I was talking. You can even hide your presence; did you know that? I'd have trouble knowing you were in the room if I just passed by without looking in.'

'My mother did tell me that.'

'It's usually a sign of particularly strong Magor power, you know.'

He looked surprised. 'No, I didn't know.'

'So, let's try something else. Call some colour up into your cabochon first.'

He sat perfectly still, then said, 'I can't.'

'Try.'

'I just did.' He opened his hand to show the cabochon lying there in the palm. It was a pale yellow and glowed not at all.

The simplest of all Magor abilities, available to even the youngest Theuros, and he couldn't do it. She was appalled, and shot an alarmed look at Temellin. The Mirager did not move.

'Sometimes I can,' Arrant said. 'Mostly, though, it just happens when it feels like it, not when I want it to.'

'But I don't understand. You are still cloaking yourself. How can you do that with a dulled cabochon?'

He shrugged. 'I don't know. It just happens. Like a habit.' He struggled to explain. 'I need power to *un*cloak myself, not to hide in the first place.'

She tried not to show her consternation, and asked him to try some far-sensing instead.

Only once in the next hour did he have any success. His cabochon suddenly flared into colour when she asked him if he knew how to build a killing beam of power. 'Oh yes,' he said, his tone as bitter as a frost-burn, 'I'm very good at that.' He looked down at the glow in his hand, and then pointed it at the empty fireplace. Destructive power blossomed against the brickwork and then died as suddenly as it had occurred. One of the mud-bricks was now just glowing powdered dust on the hearth. A wisp of smoke trailed upwards from its centre.

She was shaken. 'I'll be sun-fried!' She gaped at the hole gouged in the brickwork, then back at his cabochon, almost colourless once more.

When she looked back at Arrant, he pulled a wryly amused face and shrugged, palms outwards. 'Only thing is, I can't necessarily do that when I need it.'

'That was impressive,' she told him. 'It takes a lot of power to do what you just did. And you showed excellent control to contain it all to that one brick. Quite frankly, Arrant, I don't think there are many students your age who could be quite so precise. Or so, um, *thorough*.'

Temellin interrupted at that point, rising to his feet. 'I think it's time for your morning class, Ungar. Thank you for doing this.' Politely, he opened the door for her, and followed her out as she stepped through. 'Wait here a moment, please, Arrant,' he said before pulling the door shut behind him. 'Well?' he asked. 'Have you any ideas on how to help him?'

She shook her head, still trying to hide her dismay.

'Have you ever had a pupil with similar difficulties?'

She shook her head again.

'The truth please, Magoria.'

There was a weight in her chest and she exhaled, as if she could lighten the load of it. 'I'm confused. If you'd asked me that earlier, I would have said that I've never seen anyone with so little control and so little power – well, except for his remarkable cloaking abilities. But what he did just then? Mirageless soul, the power he had. I *felt* it as it left his cabochon. The resonance of its passage hit me in the diaphragm.' Deeply embarrassed, she rushed on. 'Someone who has access to that much power could be dangerous if they can't control it. But I don't know where to begin. I'm sorry, Magori.'

'Build his confidence, perhaps? I don't know, either, Ungar. I can tell you this much: he has – with his cabochon alone – done some things that none of us could do with our swords in our hands. Do you think you can help him?'

She fidgeted uncomfortably. 'Temel,' she said, addressing him as a friend, rather than as Mirager, but with an awkwardness she found hard to hide, 'do you remember that day, on the rake – when we were returning to the Mirage hoping we could stop the invasion across the Alps by the Tyranians? Sarana came to us as an essensa.'

He nodded, tensing.

Silly question. As if he could forget. They had all been in a panic after Garis had arrived with news for Temellin. Ungar hadn't really understood it all then, but it was apparent that Arrant's mother had cut open Temellin's pregnant wife and given the baby to the Mirage Makers. Even worse, the Mirage was under attack from a Tyranian legion and a man called Favonius.

Ungar shivered at the memory. They'd all been afraid the Mirage would fall to Tyr . . . 'There were two essensas that day,' she continued. 'Zerise said the other was Sarana's baby. Would that have been Arrant?'

'Yes.'

The word was a whip crack, but she plunged on. 'That was a lot to ask of an unborn child. We could be looking at damage that was done a long time ago, before he was even born. It may – may not be fixable.'

'I know that.'

She castigated herself silently. 'You fool, Ungar. Of course he would have thought of that.'

'Will you try?' Temellin asked. 'For his sake, as well as mine?'

'I'll do my best. For all our sakes.' But no plan came to mind and the weight in her chest grew heavier.

'If you would. Please don't mention his problems to anyone just yet.'

'There – there have already been rumours—'

'I know. But let's not give them substance. Give Arrant a chance. I think it would be best if you taught him personally for a while. Best that we don't put him into a class with other students. He needs to build confidence. Anyway, we'll talk about it again later.' He opened the door and went back into the room.

She took a deep breath and started out for the Academy.

The bell on the roof, rung by one of the senior students using a power-created wind, sounded for first class, so she took the shortest route: the back stairs that led to the alley running between the walled gardens, and thence to the Academy practice ground.

In the alley, she bumped into Firgan.

Something told her he had been waiting for her, and her heart started to thump painfully. Everything about him unsettled her, and always had, ever since the days when they had been children together in the Mirage. Later, they'd been lovers for a time, but something about him had worried her and she had stepped back from the relationship. She'd suspected since that he had not forgiven her for that. In Firgan's world, *he* was the one who decided to leave.

'What's the hurry, sweetheart?' he asked. His smile was, as always, warm and teasing.

Her heart thumped faster. 'Sweet damn,' she thought, 'he still has the power to attract me. Even after all this time. And I *know* he's a bastard.'

'I'm late for class,' she said aloud, and went to move around him.

'You've been giving a private lesson to the Mirager's son, haven't you?' he asked, anchoring her by a grasp on the arm. 'Is he any good?'

'None of your business, Firgan. Let go of me. I'm late.'

'Of course it's my business. It's everyone's, including yours. The lad is in line to be our Mirager.' He released her, but his next words were enough to make her hesitate. 'Come on, Ungar, lovely one – you can tell me. Do we all have reason to worry about our future?' He smiled ruefully. 'If you can look me in the eye and say the boy is truly talented and a worthy successor to Temellin, I shall be on my way.'

Too late, she reeled in her emotions, but not before he'd

sensed her anxiety – no, her *shock* that the Mirager-heir had no control over the potent power he evidently possessed.

She couldn't meet his gaze and dodged around him to continue on. He didn't follow, but she knew that if she turned there would be a dimpled smile on his face, and his attractive eyes would be twinkling.

'Charm,' she acknowledged to herself. 'But it covers an inner darkness.' The combination produced a titillating sense of danger.

She hurried on.

Arrant felt sick. In truth he'd felt ill ever since his conversation with Temellin the evening before. He had to redeem himself, yet didn't know how. Now, of course, he had something else to feel sick about: facing his father again after his failure to manage his cabochon. If only he could have done all the things he did the day his mother had last tested him. He'd managed everything perfectly then, and he still had no idea why.

He fingered the edges of his bolero. It felt strange to be dressed as a Kardi. He wasn't used to the full sleeves of the shirt. They ballooned out before being caught in at the wrist, and he'd dipped one into the sauce served with his breakfast. The servant assigned to him, Eris, had been obliged to show him how to wrap the cloth belt around his waist and how to tuck the trouser legs into the leather lacing of his sandals. Which was another thing he found hard to get used to – wearing sandals indoors.

As Temellin stepped back into the room, Arrant said quietly, 'I did tell you it could be like that. I never know what will happen when I reach for my power. I can misjudge and harm innocent people. Or I can try the simplest of things – and nothing happens at all.'

Temellin didn't answer immediately. He sat down opposite Arrant. After a long silence, he said, 'You don't like using it, do you? Could that be your problem? Your reluctance?'

'No, I don't like using it,' he said, his tone measured. 'I shredded people to bits with it when I was nine. It rained blood, did you know that? There's a place just outside the walls of Tyr that they call the Bleeding Fields. They say if you walk there barefoot, you still pick up splinters of bone in your soles. They say that when it rains heavily in the wet season, the blood leaches out of the soil and runs crimson into the River Tyr.

'No one knows how many people I killed there. There were no whole bodies to count, you see. Just blood and bits of bone. And teeth. Mustn't forget the teeth. There were teeth everywhere, like seeds in a melon. They don't even know which *side* of the battle the dead were on. No one could tell from what was left.' He took a deep breath. 'Foran died there. Nobody could find him afterwards; there was nothing left to find. Nobody goes there after dark now. No one plants anything. It is a barren waste.'

Temellin's hand reached to cover his son's as he said gently, 'I'm sorry, Arrant. No one should have to go through that, least of all a child. But it wasn't your fault and you mustn't blame yourself. Right now, we have to look to the present. We have to find a way to give you control. For the time being, I want Ungar to give you private lessons.'

He met his father's gaze and held it. 'All I can promise is that I will strive to learn. If you think there's no hope that I'll improve, then perhaps it would be better if I did go back to Tyr.' He wanted to hear Temellin deny that would ever be necessary. He wanted to hear him say he couldn't bear it if his son left him, but the words remained unsaid.

Instead, his father nodded. 'I know you'll try your best. You can start ordinary combat and academic classes at the

Academy tomorrow. I think you need to get your Magor sword soon, so that we can see if that makes a difference. Perhaps with its hilt in your hand expanding your cabochon power . . . we'll see. We'll give you a couple of weeks to settle in, and then go to the rake. Once there, you will have a chance to meet your brother, and you can ask the Mirage Makers about this difficulty of yours. Who knows, they may be able to help you. Ask them.'

He wanted to shout, 'I have. I've asked Tarran a thousand times . . .' And Tarran had asked the other Mirage Makers, but they had said his problem was unique. They had no idea what had caused it, and therefore no idea how to mend it. The gall in his chest tightened as he remembered. Finally, he asked, managing to sound unruffled, 'Will you be there too?'

'Of course! I was the one who first showed your mother the Shiver Barrens, and I'll show you in turn. Right now, you must excuse me, though.' He rose to his feet. 'I'm due to meet with the City Councillors over the quality of our water.'

Arrant looked up quickly, interested. 'There's a problem?'

'It's a sewerage problem really; waste from some quarters of the city is contaminating wells and the lake. The old network of drains is just too ancient to be viable any more – the Tyranian building programme put too much pressure on it. A new system has to be designed and we Magoroth will have to use sword power to excavate some new channels under the city. But first we have to locate the old ones. So now you know the truth, Arrant: the Magor are no more than ditch diggers.'

'How do you locate the drains?' Arrant asked.

'Vale-ferrets. The city engineers send tame vale-ferrets down and then we Magor use our positioning powers to follow the animals through the sewers. Unfortunately, the City Councillors are quibbling about payment for all this.' He pulled a face. 'They always do. Some of them even seem to think we

Magor should work for nothing, although just how they expect us to earn a living if we don't charge, I have no idea.'

Arrant looked blank.

'Didn't Garis get around to explaining all this to you? We don't tax people the same way Tyr does. Each town or vale has its own local government. They pay levies to us for particular services and we pay the individual Magor who does the job. It's a perennial problem, because our Covenant with the Mirage Makers states that we are not supposed to use our powers for personal gain. The Covenant Tablets also say we have to use our enhanced abilities to better the life of the non-Magor. We all swear to that – you will too, once you have your sword. So some non-Magor say we should do it all for free.'

'Garis did explain some of this. It sounded horribly complicated.'

'It is. We get around the moral restrictions that the Covenant demands by never accepting money directly from non-Magor for the services we render. A Magor healer, for example, is paid out of the Magor Treasury for every patient he treats. The patients themselves pay the local civil authorities where they live, and they pass the payment on to the Treasury. Doubtless it's hypocritical. Certainly it's cumbersome, and we are always fighting corruption in the system. Magor healer ethics, for example, decree that no sick person should ever be turned away – but it often happens because the civil authorities insist on payment first. And I suspect much of what is due to us gets skimmed off somewhere along the way.' He gave a rueful smile. 'It is indeed complicated. In the end it works because it is in the interest of the non-Magor that we Magor don't have to spend our time working at other more mundane jobs. After all, what would be the point in having a healer living down the street, if they were always busy being a bricklayer in order to make ends meet? I know it must seem idiotic, because we have to negotiate every new deal, like this drainage one, without ever mentioning something as crass as coinage, but we manage.'

'Can I look at the plans for the new drainage system?'

His question bewildered Temellin. 'What do you mean, plans?'

'Hasn't anyone drawn up plans on parchment?'

'I don't know. I think it's all in the head of old Barret. He's the Madrinyan buildermaster.'

Arrant, tutored by the best academicians of Tyr, was shocked. 'And what would happen if he died? Everything should be recorded!'

'This is not our concern. We just supply the Magor skills and power when they are needed. The city authorities worry about the building and the design.'

'Can I come with you to the meeting?'

'Well, yes, I suppose so, if you want to. But it will be mostly about money, not the drainage problems. Still, it would be an opportunity to meet the Councillors, and you could ask about the plans.' He looked doubtful. 'Are you sure you won't be bored?'

Arrant shook his head. In truth he was much more interested in drainage and how to fund a new system than he was in starting combat class or cabochon exercises, but he didn't think he'd better say that.

The next morning, Arrant woke just as the dawn light crept into the room. He had left the shutters open so that he could see the night sky as he fell asleep. There had been a madman's moon that night, when a black circle moved across the yellow disc until the moon looked like a broad bright wheel with a hole in the centre. Folk said if you looked at the dark circle too long, you'd go moondaft because the hole sucked away your sense.

The Tyr Academy scholars had told him it was just the shadow of the moon's child, and he preferred their explanation.

Now, in the first dawnlight, he watched the stars disappear and thought of the day to come. Temellin was going to take him to the Magoroth Academy for his first combat lessons. He was nervous, but determined. He would try to make his father proud. He had to redeem himself. That first meeting had been so disastrous he didn't even want to *think* about it. How could he have made such a *mess* of things?

He had enjoyed listening in on the discussion with the City Councillors, though, but his understanding of city financing (drummed into him by the chief scribe of the Asenius Counting House) and city drainage problems (part of his lessons from the architectus scholar of the Tyr Academy of Learning) were not going to impress his father. Temellin needed him to have Magor skills.

And he had made everything so much more difficult for himself. How was he ever going to introduce his brother to his father now that he had practically denied Tarran's existence? And so much might depend on it. What if the solution to the problems of the Mirage Makers depended on future cooperation with the Magor?

He grimaced, missing Tarran and knowing that he was suffering somewhere, fighting a battle that never seemed to result in a victory for the Mirage Makers. Every thought he had of his brother was tinged with a poignancy that almost broke his heart. Tarran didn't deserve his fate.

When the knock came at his door – Eris with a ewer of warmed water for his morning wash – he was relieved. It was better to be doing something than lying there, thinking.

The first thing Ligea did each morning when she left her bed was to pick up the lump of clay the Mirage Makers had sent her. She would hold it in her palm until it altered shape and re-formed to become a bust of Temellin's head. Each time she did so, she saw a representation of his reality. It was her way of reassuring herself that he was alive and well. Her way of remembering. She would study it for a moment, thinking of him, thinking of her son.

And then she would put it down, and get on with her life.

That morning as she cupped the head in her hands, Temellin seemed severe, unsmiling, preoccupied.

'Perhaps Arrant hasn't arrived yet,' she thought. 'He wouldn't look like that if his son were with him, would he?'

Of course not. He'd be overjoyed. But Arrant would arrive soon, and they'd be together. Father and son. 'Not long now,' she whispered. 'Love him. Tem. Do a better job than I did.'

CHAPTER SIX

'There are two kinds of combat class,' Temellin told him as they walked to the Magoroth Academy after breakfast. 'The normal kind given to all warriors, no different to the training you will have had in Tyrans, and the Magor sword training that you will begin once you have received your sword. Firgan teaches some of the classes, mostly the more advanced ones, and a Theuros called Yetemith does most of the intermediate ones. Bit of a sour fellow, but he's a fine teacher.'

Arrant nodded, hoping Firgan wouldn't be around that day. He hadn't forgotten the nastiness of the man's welcome, cabochon to cabochon. He had meant it to be unsettling, and he had succeeded. 'Damn him,' Arrant muttered under his breath. 'He's made me fear him, right from the beginning.'

When they arrived at the practice yard of the Magoroth Academy, Garis and Yetemith were sparring in the centre while students watched from adobe benches along the sides. High walls surrounded the yard, and the students had clustered where one wall cast shade on the seats. Heads swung Arrant's way, there was a muttered whisper or two and a flutter of excitement before the students resumed their interest in the fight.

Arrant used their preoccupation as a chance to scan them unnoticed. Seated nearest to him was one of the most beautiful young women he'd ever seen. She would have been even more attractive if she hadn't been wrinkling up her nose in disgust at the sweat the two men were flinging into the air with the rigour of their battle.

'Elvena Korden,' Temellin whispered. 'Seventeen. I doubt if she'll ever graduate from this particular class.'

Arrant nodded. Further down the line he thought he could pick out another two of Korden's children: they had the same lean, aristocratic faces as their father. 'Rather like thorough-bred horses,' he thought. 'Handsome, but haughty.' The boy must be Lesgath, the girl Serenelle. Garis had said something about them both on the last day's ride into Madrinya. What was it again? 'Serenelle is the same age as you are, and the best of the bunch, not that saying *that* means much.' About Lesgath he had been even less enthusiastic. 'The lad strikes me as shifty. Not sure why. Watch yourself around him, Arrant.'

He turned his attention to the fighting. The two men were enjoying themselves, using wooden practice swords and buck-lers, but no Magor power. They were evenly matched. Every time one of them appeared to have the upper hand, the other would reassert himself and seize the advantage. Clearly, the winner would end up being the one who had the most stamina, probably Garis, seeing as he was at least ten years younger than his opponent.

Arrant had been taught his swordplay by the best, the same teachers who had hammered technique into Ligea's legions. Even General Gevenan himself had tutored him. Arrant had started young but as the years had gone by, his passion for fighting had waned. His lessons, however, had continued sporadically, and he'd practised with grown men who had known life-and-death struggles on the battlefield. He could recognise a skilled veteran when he saw one, and to his enor-mous surprise, he wasn't seeing one in either of these two men.

They were competent, but no more than that. Several times he saw opportunities missed and strokes fumbled. Gevenan would have skinned them alive, had they been his soldiers.

'What do you think?' Temellin asked.

'I expected better. They're not very good,' he blurted, then blushed. He looked around, but no one was looking his way.

'What makes you say that?'

He was uncomfortable, but gave an honest reply. 'If they fought against experienced legionnaires as Ligea's army did in Tyrans, and made the kind of mistakes they are making now, they'd both be dead.' *Damn*. Sarana. He should have called her Sarana. He was relieved when Temellin laughed.

'You are probably right. You see, Arrant, they are both Magor. And that means they carry other skills with them wherever they go. Unfortunately, it also means that they have less incentive to perfect battle techniques that don't involve the cabochon.' He watched them for a moment longer. 'They are both experienced. They have killed more battle-scarred veterans than they would ever care to count. They just did it with a combination of physical skills and Magor power.'

The fight ended just then, with Yetemith calling a halt, pleading fatigue. Garis went off to clean up and Temellin introduced Arrant to the armsman.

'We are glad to have you here,' Yetemith said, giving a neutral cabochon clasp. Up close he had the appearance of a battle veteran: his face was scarred, and part of an ear was missing. 'Do you want to watch him put through his paces, Mirager?'

'Not now,' Temellin replied, much to Arrant's relief. 'I'll leave him in your hands.' He smiled at Arrant, and left the yard.

Yetemith looked Arrant up and down. 'You are much the same size as Lesgath. You can have a practice bout with him in a moment and we'll take a look at you. But in the meantime,' he cast a look around the watching group, 'you lot, you just watched two experienced soldiers fight in practice; what did you learn, if anything? Grantel, what about you?'

A large pimpled boy of about sixteen, who had obviously been daydreaming, jumped. 'Um, oh – the way the Magori ducked under that thrust by dropping into a roll, then coming up behind you – that was solid.'

'Solid?' Arrant wondered. 'What in all the seven layers of hell does that mean?'

'Dangerous though,' Lesgath remarked. 'What if you'd been a bit quicker to spin around, Theuri? You would have caught him still on the ground.'

Several of them argued the point, until Yetemith directed a question to Elvena. 'You are very quiet, Magoria. Have you nothing to offer about the fight?'

'All that sweat is horrid.'

Several students guffawed; others muffled their amusement. Yetemith glared. 'You are just wasting your time in this class, girl, and you are too much of a distraction to the others. I am going to recommend your removal.'

Elvena perked up, not bothering to hide a smile, but the armsmaster was already fixing his attention on Arrant. 'And what did you think, lad?'

'Er, nothing, Theuri.'

'Nothing? Have you not been trained, then?'

'Yes, um – of course.'

'He said neither of you are very good,' Serenelle piped up. 'And that you both would have been dead in a real war.'

Arrant flushed, furious. He knew she had not been close enough to have heard that with normal hearing; she had eavesdropped. He'd been careless. He'd forgotten that everyone here could enhance their hearing. It was a mark of bad manners, of course, but doubtless that wouldn't stop it happening altogether.

Yetemith raised an eyebrow at him in a sharp arch. 'Is that so? Perhaps the expert warrior would like to explain why?'

Arrant winced. He knew he should keep his mouth shut, but spoke up anyway. This was the future fighting force of the country he now called his own, the land his father ruled. He had to tell the truth. 'You both took too many risks for too small a return. You fought as if it didn't matter if you made a mistake. Perhaps it doesn't on a practice field. Perhaps it doesn't when you have Magor power at your disposal in a real battle, but it's dangerous to assume you always will. That was how Magor died during the war – when they had exhausted their cabochon power.'

'Perhaps you'd like to demonstrate your superior skills?' Dislike, barely disguised.

Arrant flinched. *Fool.*

Yetemith beckoned to Lesgath. 'Step into the ring. Grantel, get Arrant a practice sword and a buckler.' He turned back to Arrant. 'The rules are simple, young man. If you take what would be a maiming or killing blow with a real sword, you lose. If you are disarmed or rendered ineffective, you lose. If you step outside the circle, then the other steps back to allow you to re-enter. No magic allowed except emotion-sensing and cloaking.'

Arrant was wary, knowing he was going to be under intense scrutiny.

Lesgath nodded to him as Grantel handed over a practice sword, and said, 'This should be interesting. You will have different techniques. You are Tyranian-trained, aren't you? Your teachers were legionnaires?' He said the words pleasantly enough, but there was something in his smile that made Arrant wonder if he was not deliberately pointing out Arrant's foreignness, and his ties to Tyr.

He smiled back and tried to broadcast a general air of

approachability. 'Not entirely. My first armsmaster was an Ingean. The second was a rebel from Pythia. Miragerin-sarana tried to use the best of all methods in her training programmes.'

'Oh. A sort of mongrel army.' Still pleasantly said, but Arrant had no doubt he was being needled. He shrugged carelessly. 'Yes, I suppose so. Best of all breeds. Shall we get to it?'

He raised his sword in salute and the fight began. The first strokes and parries from them both were tentative, testing the other's reactions and level of skill. Lesgath was no fool, rushing in when he hadn't had time to size up his opponent. His cabochon glowed gently, doubtless searching for any stray emotion that might help his attack.

Arrant had been carefully taught; he knew how to assess a fighter. Watch the way muscles tightened and relaxed; take note of eye movement, even the way your opponent blinked; be alert to the subtleties of his stance and be aware of the instant his weight shifted. He soon knew himself the better fighter: more skilled, better trained, more experienced. He toyed with the idea of ending it quickly, of humiliating Lesgath with the magnitude and speed of his defeat, but then thought better of it. For a start it wouldn't be kind; moreover, he didn't want to alienate the watching students by being perceived as boastful.

He allowed the fight to continue, blessing those hours of training and Gevenan's years of nagging that had kept him practising long past the threshold of boredom. He blocked and dodged, pretended a vulnerability he didn't feel, and feigned a few fumbles. Lesgath's eyes widened as he began to wonder if he was being played with; Yetemith probably guessed as well, but Arrant doubted the others who watched had the experience to tell.

As Lesgath tired, his frustration grew. His cabochon must have deepened in colour because the glow around his sword hand was brighter. Arrant could see the fury in his eyes. 'Soon you will do something stupid,' he thought, and decided to bring the bout to a close. He didn't want to risk being hurt by a blast of Magor power because he was unable to raise a ward.

He made a clumsy lunge, pretended to lose his balance, and went down on one knee, with his right hand to the ground, a manoeuvre that he and one of his teachers had perfected after long practice. Like all Magoroth, he and Lesgath fought with the sword in the left hand, and Arrant's right side was wide open, his sword arm low and towards his front. Lesgath failed to note Arrant's poise and swung his wooden blade. He intended to slam the flat of it across the right side of Arrant's neck from above.

Arrant, though, was perfectly balanced for what he wanted to do. Instead of raising his right arm with its buckler to protect himself, as might have been expected, he swept his buckler from right to left, throwing his weight behind the move. The edge of the shield slammed into the side of Lesgath's knee. He toppled with a gasp, his blow sailing over Arrant's ducked head.

Arrant rolled as he followed through, and was back on his feet before Lesgath. He pressed a foot gently but firmly to Lesgath's sword arm, pinning it to the ground as he placed his sword point at his throat. Then, without waiting for any sign of capitulation, he stepped back, saluting him with the swordblade.

There was silence in the yard while everyone stared, gaping.

'That,' Yetemith said finally, 'was quite the ugliest piece of action it has ever been my misfortune to observe. You blocked your own line of sight and deserved to have had Lesgath's sword remove part of your face.' He shook his head, as if he couldn't believe in Arrant's foolishness. 'Still, you did win. Just remember that victory is pointless if you are badly injured in the process.'

Arrant said nothing. Lesgath stood up, glaring, and limped

to take his place among the watchers against the wall. Several of the boys clapped his back, including Grantel, commending him on his fight.

The lesson continued. There were exercises to practise, as repetitive and dull as always. Towards the end of the morning, the pairs of students were matched up to put what they just been taught into practice, while Yetemith walked around, his eyebrows drawn together in an unpleasant glower, commenting. There were an uneven number of students, so Arrant was left without a partner. He would have been content for it to stay that way, but one of the boys then twisted his foot and his sparring partner sought Arrant out. He was a fair-skinned youth with serious eyes and straight brown hair that seemed to grow in all directions, like a clump of spiny grass. His smile was tentative, yet admiring. His name, he said, was Perradin Jahan. 'That was trim, what you did to Lesgath. It wasn't an accident, was it? Do you reckon you could teach me how to do that—?'

'Less chatter, you two,' Yetemith growled. 'Practise, please.'

Perradin shrugged and lifted his sword. 'Some other time,' Arrant promised as they crossed blades.

When the bell rang to signal noon and the students prepared to leave the practice ground, Yetemith singled out Arrant and Lesgath. 'Go collect all the practice swords and bucklers,' he ordered, 'and return them to the racks in the armoury store. The rest of you go to lunch.'

Arrant and Lesgath eyed each other cautiously. 'Yetemith did that deliberately,' Arrant thought. 'He must know Lesgath is furious with me.' He pondered that, wondering if the arms-master was a petty man who wanted to provoke ill will between him and Lesgath, or if he wanted to throw them together hoping they'd learn to like each other. He had a horrible suspicion it was the former.

As he collected the swords, he took note of those who made a point of bringing their weapon to him, and those who deliberately dropped them wherever they happened to be. It seemed a good way to decide who might be a friend in the future, and who not. Perradin was one of those who handed his sword over personally. So, unexpectedly, was Serenelle Korden.

'Where's the armoury store?' he asked Lesgath after the two of them had collected the swords.

Lesgath nodded to a building at the end of the yard. 'There.' He led the way wordlessly and together they stored the weapons in the racks, still in silence. By the time they had finished, the yard was empty of students and they were alone.

'They say your cabochon is useless,' Lesgath said as he pulled the door shut behind them. 'Is that true?'

'No, it's not true.'

'I also heard people died because you couldn't control your power.'

Arrant shrugged. 'Then my cabochon can't be useless, can it? And just maybe you shouldn't make me mad,' he added, 'for fear of what I'll do. By accident, of course.'

Lesgath grinned. 'You dare not. The moment you make a muck of using your power, there's no way you'd ever be confirmed as Mirager-heir, with the Council's approval and all.' He took a step closer. 'I reckon I can do whatever I like.'

'I wouldn't if I were you. After all, what happens if I tell a teacher? Or my father?'

'You wouldn't do that. You know why? Because if you do, students will scorn you as a tattle-tale. And adults will scorn you as a weakling who couldn't even raise a warding to save his own pride. You need the Magor to see you as a leader, not as a reed too weak to stand straight. Sure, I'd get into trouble, but it would be worth it.'

'Why?'

He wasn't answered. Without warning, Lesgath hit him in the stomach with a beam of gold power. Razor-sharp jags raced outwards, ploughing furrows of agony from a central well of pain so deep Arrant doubled up and collapsed to the ground. He rocked to and fro, unable to speak, dominated by the appalling torture radiating from his midriff. 'Pain,' he thought. 'This is Magor pain-giving, nothing more. It's not doing any damage.'

But knowing that didn't help.

He glanced up and saw Lesgath looking down on him, laughing. He closed his eyes. He could not have spoken to save his life.

Time passed. The pain went away enough for him to move, only to find himself enclosed in a prison of power. 'A ward,' he thought. 'The bastard built a ward around me.' He strained against it,' but it didn't move. And where he lay, in the shadow of the armoury, he wasn't visible from any overlooking window.

He lay helpless on the ground, unable to do anything at all.

CHAPTER SEVEN

Someone was looking down at him. A girl. She had freckles across her nose, uncommon in a Kardi. She was not one of the class; too young, he decided. Still young enough to be as skinny as a stick, without any budding breasts or the beginnings of shapely hips. He found he noticed things like that more nowadays, even, apparently, at inappropriate times.

'Lesgath doesn't like you,' she said.

'Yeah, I know.' He tried to rise, but he was still trapped. At least the pain was gone.

'He wants you to look like a fool.'

'I know that, too.'

'You ought to get out of there.'

He gritted his teeth. 'Tell me something I *don't* know. Like, how did you know Lesgath made the ward?'

'Wards always carry signatures of the maker. Didn't you know that? I know him, so I recognised his mark.'

'Ah.'

'So why don't you get out?'

'I don't know how.'

She thought about that. 'He didn't use his Magor sword. That means it's a weak warding. It'll only last a couple of hours.'

'I don't want to stay here that long. Can you break it for me?'

She shook her head. 'I'm only an Illusa. It's going to take another Magoroth, one who's already got a sword. And even then it might be difficult.'

'Then go and get one of the teachers.'

'I don't think I ought to do that.'

He repressed a swear word. 'Why not?'

'Don't you know *anything*? Cos the other sprouts don't like a tattle-tale. Lesgath will get into *real* trouble if you tell on him. If you do, *nobody's* going to like you.'

'All right, I won't tell on him. Just get a teacher to get me out of this.'

'Then you'll get into trouble for not telling who did it.'

She was really annoying him. He tried to relax his clenched jaw. 'Better than lying here being laughed at. I lose either way, and he wins. Just do it, girl.'

She considered. 'He probably intends to come back before the next class to release you himself. After all, he doesn't want to get into trouble. Easy for him to lift his own ward. If I were you, I'd wait.'

'I'd rather not be around for the humiliation of that.'

She tilted her head to one side, thinking. 'Well, I could get you out of there without breaking the ward, I think.'

'Then *do* it!' he shouted.

'Don't yell at me. *I* didn't do this to you.'

He took a deep breath. 'Sorry. If you can get me out of here, please do. I'd be grateful.'

'Like this.' She pointed her cabochon at the ground alongside the edge of the ward and scoured it with a beam of red light. Dust – coloured red by her cabochon's glow – billowed up in a cloud that obscured everything.

'Gods,' he shouted, 'are you mad? You'll cut me in two!'

'No, I won't,' she said calmly. 'My power won't penetrate the ward.'

'So what in the seven layers of Acheron are you *doing*?'

'Digging you out,' she said. 'I'm digging a trench along the side of the ward. The ward is anchored, but it doesn't go down into the ground. I should be able to make a hole big enough for you to wriggle through. Don't move and you won't get hurt. Least I don't *think* you will.'

Fortunately the ward kept most of the dust from choking him, but he couldn't *see* anything. She was like a hare digging a scrape, sending dirt flying furiously. After a while he felt the earth beneath him lose its stability. He squawked a protest.

She ignored him.

He squished himself over to one side of the ward, away from the area of her excavations, and watched mesmerised as the earth trickled out under the ward. It seemed an age before she stopped and the dust started to settle.

'There you are,' she said, allowing the red glow to subside. 'You should be able to squeeze through there.'

It was a tight fit, but he did it, edging flat to the ground under the length of the ward. He stood and brushed himself off. 'Thanks,' he said trying to be gracious. 'That was a, er, trim solution.' He kept his next thought to himself: 'Hades, rescued by a girl of what, ten? Eleven? Great, Arrant. You'll go far.'

She grinned. 'Let's put the earth back. No point in them knowing how you got out.' She started pushing the soil into the trench, and he helped to stamp it down, until the ground looked more or less flat again.

He liked the idea of them seeing an empty ward, sitting there like a dusty food cover. That would make them wonder.

'What's your name?' he asked.

'Sam,' she said. 'And I got to go.'

She turned and walked away in the direction of the outer gate. He watched her, wondering who she was.

*   *   *

There was still plenty of food on the long trestle tables when he entered the dining hall. He looked around, saw Perradin and sat down next to him.

'I was wondering what happened to you,' Perradin said. 'Lesgath came in ages back. I was going to go and get you if you didn't come in soon. I suppose that sand-weasel left you all the work cos you're younger than he is. He's about as mean as they get, Lesgath is.' He shoved a plate of roast venison in Arrant's direction. 'Here, have some. The meat tastes good, but it's as tough as dried hide strips.'

The lad next to him grinned. 'There was some sauce to go with it, until Perry here dumped the lot in his lap.'

'The bowl was slippery,' Perradin said in his defence. 'You'd been pawing it with your greasy hands. Arrant, this is Bevran, who thinks he's funny. Never believe a word he says.'

Arrant found himself looking at someone of about his own age, who had a mouth far too wide for his face. The overall effect was odd enough to make Arrant want to laugh. Bevran grinned as if he knew his looks were innately amusing and rejoiced in it.

Arrant nodded awkwardly, and wished he'd had more to do with boys his own age before now. He found he rarely knew quite what to say. 'Do either of you know a girl called Sam? An Illusa? Bit younger than us?'

'Sam? Nah, I don't think so.'

'No,' Bevran said. 'Don't know any Sam. But then, I don't know all the crimmies, or the weeds.'

'All the *what*?'

'Crimsons and greens – Illusos and Theuros.'

'Oh.' It was going to take him time to learn all the student slang. 'And what's a sprout?'

Perradin answered that one. 'Hey, there's lots of stuff you don't know, isn't there? That's what the girls call us boys. And we call them buds. Because of—' He made a gesture in the chest area and Bevran rolled his eyes appreciatively.

Just then Arrant caught sight of Lesgath making his way out of the hall, using the door that would take him back to the practice ground. He was alone, and he failed to notice Arrant. It seemed Sam had been right; Lesgath had intended to release him. When he turned away, Serenelle Korden caught his eye. She had her head cocked to one side and was watching him, her gaze thoughtful. Or was it calculating? She had made him look a fool on the practice ground.

He turned his attention back to Perradin and Bevran. 'What do we do after lunch?' he asked.

'Classroom stuff.' Perradin counted the subjects off on grubby fingers. 'History and geography, mathematics and geometry, the theory of Magor magic and healing, battle theory and logistics and ethics. It's all right, I s'pose. Some of it's interesting stuff, and Lesgath and Grantel and their barbarian hordes aren't in our class, thank the Mirage. Serenelle is though. I never know what the sands she's thinking. Are you any good at geometry?'

'Not bad. It was one of my favourite subjects.'

'Solid! You can help me.'

Arrant's first days at the Academy were not as bad as he had feared. Much of the normal class work he had already covered with his Tyranian tutors. He enjoyed the classroom atmosphere, even though he sometimes found the other students childish, a stray thought he was wise enough to hide. They had not lived the kind of life he had. Their early childhood had been spent in the Mirage, cradled by the charm of Mirage Maker eccentricities.

Lesgath ignored him most of the time. If the combat class necessitated some kind of interaction, he was polite, if distant.

Arrant, knowing Lesgath's private face did not match his public one, was equally polite but cautious. Serenelle always seemed to be watching him, assessing. He guessed she continued to eavesdrop, and he was circumspect in what he said to Perradin and the others, but as far as he could tell, she did nothing to harm him. Firgan came to watch his combat classes several times. He did not speak, and as usual Arrant felt nothing of his emotions, but the critical assessment of his gaze was unfriendly.

Unfortunately, within a day of his arrival, everyone seemed to know that the Mirager's son had no reliable control over his cabochon and had to be specially tutored by Ungar, who usually taught the elementary classes. Worse still, he was soon the victim of a series of petty indignities as well as anonymous and malicious innuendo. When he left his writing tablet on his desk one lunchtime, someone scratched a message into the wax: *They won't wean you till you learn how to pee standing up.* Perradin told him that some of the senior students were openly wondering if he should really be Mirager-heir, given his disability. One of his fellow students, a girl called Vevi, asked him, in front of many of their classmates, if he could really melt them all by accident, as the rumours said.

'Don't take any notice,' Perradin said.

'But could you really?' Vevi persisted.

Because she sounded more interested than nasty, he answered honestly. 'Probably, but I'd have to be trying to hurt you first. Don't worry, I shan't mince you or splinter the Academy by accident.' And yet, even as he spoke the words, there was a cold, hard lump in his stomach. 'At least, I don't think so . . .' he added to himself.

Vevi looked disappointed, but Perradin nodded equably. Nothing seem to faze him, not even his constant mishaps due to his clumsiness. Perradin never did seem to *see* things. At first his lack of passion irritated Arrant, more used to Tarran's bright exuberance, but after a day or two of Perradin's calm, he began to appreciate his new friend. He was reliable. Kind.

But he wasn't Tarran.

He kept waiting for Tarran to return, but the days went by without any touch of his mind. He remembered his brother's last words: *The Ravage is widening in the north and the Mirage needs the strength of every single one of us, just to withstand the spread.* Arrant wanted desperately to talk to his father about it, but without Tarran, he had no way of proving he could communicate with his brother. He quelled the urge.

All the other students stayed in the Academy, eating in the refectory and sleeping in dormitories, but Arrant remained in his own bedroom, taking his supper every night with his father.

They were awkward meals, with both of them feeling their way, trying to find some common ground, searching for a mutual trust, but never truly finding it. Temellin never again alluded to the events that had led up to Arrant's leaving Tyr. Arrant knew his father was trying hard to be kind, to be fair, to be loving, but he never forgot that first unguarded moment, when Temellin's feelings were written on his face for him to read. He never forgot his father's disbelief at a time when he'd needed his trust, or that Temellin had once rejected him. He remembered, but he still strove to please and be the kind of son Temellin would have wanted.

It hurt to see the worry in Temellin's eyes as Arrant continued to fail to control his cabochon power reliably. Temellin doubted his son's competence.

'Did you know,' he asked Temellin one evening, as they sat beside the fire in the Mirager's apartments after dinner, 'that many of the students in the Academy believe that my position as Mirager-heir will never be confirmed by the Magoroth?

That the Council will try to declare Firgan Mirager-heir in my stead?'

'Student gossip. It doesn't mean that it will happen. Arrant, there has to be consensus – and that includes *my* consent as well. We have yet to see what happens to your power once you get your Magor sword.'

'What if – um, I mean, won't it be better that Kardiastan has a skilled Mirager, rather than one like me?' He shivered and moved closer to the fire. 'But not Firgan,' he thought. 'Please, not Firgan.'

Temellin shoved another bundle of tightly bound reed fuel onto the coals before answering. That was another thing Arrant had found out; wood was scarce in Kardiastan, far too scarce to be burned. 'If there were a suitable candidate in the line of succession, I might consider it,' his father admitted, his honesty painful. 'But *Firgan*? Believe me, you would be a much better Mirager than Firgan. True, he is popular with many who fought alongside him. If I could be sure he was also a wise and compassionate man, I would say to you – let him be the heir.'

He ran a hand through his hair in a troubled gesture. When his fingers snagged in the leather tie, he pulled it off in exasperation. 'Being the Mirager of Kardiastan is a thankless task. I thought once that I loved the power, but then I had to give up the woman who has meant more to me than any other; I had to marry a woman I did not much like; I had to separate myself from my son and see him come back to me as a stranger. I had to lead a nation into war and watch as good people died.'

'It's not a fate I'd inflict on my son if it weren't necessary.'

'But you think it is? Necessary?'

'If you aren't the heir, then it will be either Korden or Firgan. Korden doesn't want it. He thinks he has more influence being my adviser, and that I would trust him less if he was my heir. Not necessarily true, but he believes it is. As for Firgan? I don't like him. During the war he had a reputation for being need-lessly ruthless. He's charming when he puts his mind to it, generous with money, and Korden won't hear a word said against him – but I dread the idea that he might rule this land. There's nothing tangible I can use to discredit him; he's too clever for that.'

Even though all the shutters were closed, the chill of a frosty desert night had entered the room and he warmed his hands at the flames. 'Gretha – Korden's wife – is a singularly silly woman who has alternately spoiled her children or played them off against one another. She has never instilled any ethical values into any of them. She's just taught them to present a respectable face to the world.'

'You think *I'd* be a better ruler?' Arrant couldn't help the surprise that slid into his voice.

'Yes.'

The brevity and certainty of Temellin's answer took Arrant aback. 'But you don't know me.'

'I know Sarana. I know Garis. I know what *they* say about you. And I am getting to know you. I like what I see. I am hoping that one day you will trust me with the truths that you hide, whatever they are.'

Arrant sidestepped that subject. 'But what about my power? I've killed people when I didn't mean to and I've been unable to call on my power when it was necessary.'

'We'll find a way to train you in its use. Arrant, this land needs a future Mirager of better calibre than anyone in Korden's family. The world is changing with the break-up of the Exaltarchy. The Magor are generally too inward-looking, so we need someone like you, who knows more of the world. I'd like you to come to terms with your destiny.'

He wanted to reject the idea outright, but heard instead the echo of a voice in his head: *I have to be able to live with myself.*

Or rather, I have to die knowing how I have lived. Brand's words to him, spoken with the knowledge that he was soon to die, asking Arrant to remember, asking him to have courage. Gods, how could he have forgotten that? Brand, showing in his last moments that you had to accept duty, responsibility and sacrifice as being part of any life lived well. Arrant choked on the denial he had been about to voice.

Temellin noticed his turmoil but did not remark on it. He went across to the table and poured himself some wine. 'Would you like some?' he asked. 'I can add some water.'

'Yes, please.'

As he came back to the fire and handed over the goblet, he said, 'There's something else I need to tell you. I have no tangible basis for saying this – it's just a gut reaction that I have, born perhaps of many years of war and other horrors. Be very careful around Firgan.'

Arrant remembered the shaft of malice from the man when they had met, and stirred uneasily. 'You mean he might try to harm me?'

Temellin paused, as if embarrassed. 'I'm probably overreacting.'

Arrant stared at him, trying unsuccessfully to sense something of his emotions. He fell back instead on his own instincts, thoughts flying, and asked, 'Gods of Elysium – *that's* why you delayed my return to Kardiastan? You thought I might be in danger from Korden's family? That Firgan might want to *kill* me?'

'Well, that wasn't the reason in the beginning. At first it was because of the Ravage and the danger posed by the legions. But once we were free again, and back in Madrinya? Yes. By then Firgan was older and without a war to occupy him, and I feared what he might do to a young boy.' He shrugged. 'I had no proof, nothing – just something in my gut. No one can close themselves to Magor scrutiny all the time, you know – not even you! Some whisper of my sensing power when Firgan is near urges me to caution. It's why I want you to continue sleeping in this pavilion and not with the other students. I'm being careful. Just think of the trouble I would get into from Sarana if I let something happen to you.'

They looked at each other, imagining – and exchanged grins.

'Would it be all right if I go out into the city?' Arrant asked. 'Buildermaster Barret has sent me an invitation to look at the drainage on the next Academy rest day. I suppose the City Councillors must have told him I was interested.'

Temellin looked puzzled. 'Well, it seems an odd thing to want to do, but go ahead. Tell Eris when you want to go, and he will find a guard to accompany you. I'd rather you didn't go alone. If you want to go out with the other students any time, that's fine too. They often go down to the lakeside to practise dubblup and I am sure you will want to try that. Just make sure you are never alone.'

Arrant nodded, pleased that Temellin trusted him not to disobey. 'Why would Firgan ever do anything violent, though? I mean, what about our Covenant with the Mirage Makers? Misuse of power would mean no more Mirager swords and therefore no more cabochons and therefore no more Magor power. No Magor would risk that happening, surely.'

'What if he didn't *care* what happened after him?' Temellin shook his head as if he, too, didn't quite believe it could happen. 'I'm not convinced Firgan does care. Arrant, please, I do ask this of you: do your very best to be confirmed as the Mirager-heir.'

Later that night, lying on his pallet with his hands behind his head gazing through the open shutter out at the bright studs in the night sky, Arrant considered that. And terror rippled through him because he knew something Temellin did not.

Something Tarran had told him. *We may not have much longer,* Tarran had said back in Tyr. *Come back home.*

If Firgan realised that, then what would stop him from breaking the Covenant and behaving as reprehensibly as he liked if he became Mirager one day? After all, the outcome would be no different to what would probably occur anyway as a result of the death of the Mirage Makers. Arrant remembered the deliberately painful cabochon clasp the man had given him. He remembered the malice. With his powers and the help of a few like-minded Magor, Firgan could destroy the hard-won peace of the nation and turn Kardiastan into his personal arena of cruelty and arbitrary despotism.

A light wind rucked the surface of the vale lake, but that wasn't what startled the young lad fishing at the lakeside. It was the smell that travelled across the water on the breeze, an odour of putrefaction as if a whole herd of animals had died out there somewhere, and been left to rot. The boy gasped at the stench, at its intensity. It burned the insides of his nostrils and the surface of his throat, scorched his skin like flame. He looked up and saw a cloud of dust bearing down on him. It curled over the jagged edges of the crest of the First Rake and poured down into the vale like thick soup.

'Mirageless soul,' he thought, 'what is going on?'

He pulled in his line and threw everything into his fishing bag in a mixed-up jumble, including a couple of uncleaned trout. He headed for home along the shoreline, fumbling at the ties of his bag as he ran.

The cloud overtook him as he raced through Kallard's vegetable farm. A wall, a moving wall, so thick it seemed solid ... At the last moment he stopped running, knowing he was going to be engulfed. He turned instead to face the wind, as if to defy it, and saw something glaring at him from the cloud.

A face. The kind of thing you saw in your worst nightmares, only this was alive. Real. He heard the rage of it above the wind. He saw its hungry eyes, its fangs with serrated edges dripping saliva. It howled. It clawed at the air.

He swore, panicking. And then the dust billowed over him, around him. He coughed, choked and dived into Farmer Kallard's mustard greens, burying his face in the plants and pulling off his bolero so he could use it to cover his nose. The noise of his panting was obliterated by the whining of a wind that sounded the way he felt: lost, despairing, alone. The sound of a thousand abandoned children, calling out their terror. Something fell nearby, shaking the earth on impact.

And then it all began to fade. The wind passed on, the whining died to a far-off skirl and then into nothing. An uncanny stillness settled over the farms and the lake. Stillness, but not quite silence. He heard snuffling, snorting grunts nearby. He stirred and dust trickled from his clothes in rivers of red. He shook his head, showering his shoulders with dust, surprised to find himself still alive. He hauled himself up into a sitting position to look around. He blinked. He didn't recognise his world. Everything was silted with red dust. The stalks of the mustard greens were broken, the leaves wilted and brown. The surface of the lake beyond was filmed thick with a scum of dust. When he stood, whorls of powdery red eddied in the air once more, reluctant to settle.

Stumbling, coughing, he again started out for home. Some fifty paces further on, in Farmer Malthorn's yam patch, he found the source of the snuffling. A creature sprawled across the way, its tail lashing in the irrigation ditch on one side, its face leering at him from the centre of the path. There was intelligence in its calculating gaze. Its body had split open when it landed and greenish liquid oozed from a gaping tear in its side. The grass under its body shrivelled and smoked and died.

The lad's gaze locked into the stare of slitted black pupils and golden irises. No matter how he tried, he couldn't drag himself away from the attraction of those calculating eyes. Strange thoughts filled his head; memories, each one unpleasant, of when he'd been in some kind of trouble or another. His little sister, whom he loathed and tormented and loved in equal parts, figured in most of these recollections, usually crying. They weren't memories he wanted to recall because they invariably featured an act of his own meanness, but he couldn't stop them filling his head.

He took a step towards the beast, and then stopped, puzzled by his own behaviour. And yet then he took another step, as though it was drawing him on, slave on an invisible thread. He knew he should flee. That was the awful part; he knew it would kill him, yet he couldn't stop. He even knew what it was, though he'd never seen one before: a Ravage beast. They weren't supposed to be able to leave the Mirage, yet here it was, in the vale, about to kill him.

He couldn't run. Couldn't even scream. He took a step closer. Cold skimmed down his back. He took another step, and another. Closer. The beast smiled and lashed its tail.

And then it gave a shudder and more liquid spilled out of its wound in a sudden flood, to pool in the irrigation ditch like stagnant bog water. The creature groaned, and died.

When his father came looking for him sometime later, he found his son shaking on the path, unable, in his terror, to speak. The monster was already rotting.

CHAPTER EIGHT

Half a month passed before Tarran appeared in Arrant's mind again, an interval marked by a confusing mix of loneliness and awakening friendships, or of despair at his humiliating failures and pleasure in his occasional successes.

He'd spent a wonderful day exploring Madrinyan drainage with the buildermaster and discussing the plans for a new system. In Tyrans they built with stone and marble; in Madrinya they used sun-baked bricks strengthened with reed strips, so they'd had a long conversation about how that influenced building techniques. On his way back through the city, his guard trailing behind, he'd seen the streets with a more appreciative eye. He was beginning to love the simplicity of the buildings now that he noticed the way the austerity was always coupled with the intricate beauty of a smaller feature, perhaps the flamboyant fecundity of a garden, or the patterns of an agate path, or the inlays of decorative stones on a balustrade or the carvings on window shutters.

He'd also enjoyed his first attempt at dubblup. His necklet had been so warm it had almost burned his neck, and he suspected the magic of its runes had played a significant role in the shleth's cooperation, especially in its willingness to extend its feeding arm at the crucial moment during mounting. He felt himself more in tune with shleths than he had ever been with horses, and as timing was so important when you wanted to mount a moving animal, that connection proved invaluable.

Afterwards, as he led the shleth he had borrowed from the Mirager's stables back towards the pavilions, Serenelle dropped into step beside him, her gaze fixed on his face. He raised a questioning eyebrow.

'I've never known anyone to succeed on their first try, let alone do it twice,' she said. 'Are you just lucky, Arrant Temellin, or have you been practising?'

He shrugged. 'I understand my mount. No more than that.'

She frowned. 'There's more to you than meets the eye, isn't there? That stupid brother of mine might have picked up more than he can lift.' And she turned and walked away before he could ask what she meant. Or which brother. Was she warning him out of kindness, or in order to make him fearful? He had no idea. She was an enigma.

Balancing out his dubblup successes were his failures in his classes with Ungar, and his humiliation in several of his general classes when he couldn't call any colour into his cabochon as had been required. Worse, he'd found several unsigned notes among his things, written in different hands, deploring his presumption in thinking he should be Mirager-heir, and whispers continued to circulate about how he could be a danger to other students.

His first combat classes taught by Firgan, however, had gone relatively well, although Firgan had several times subtly pointed out to the rest of the class how foreign his fighting style was. It was cleverly done, seemingly without malice – but Arrant knew it had been a deliberate move to make him appear less Kardi and therefore less suitable as a future Mirager.

'You just have to ride it out,' Temellin said one evening over dinner. 'Ignore the rumours and innuendo and act in a manner which shows that you are a true Kardi with our interests at heart.' He didn't say how it was possible to show himself to be a true Magoroth, however. They both knew his success with his cabochon was crucial to his acceptance, and it wasn't happening.

'I shall arrange for our trip to the Shiver Barrens,' Temellin added. 'It's time for you to get your sword.'

As he left the Mirager's rooms a little later, Arrant tried to convince himself that his father was happier with him. He didn't succeed. Temellin could not quite hide his unease or his disappointment and Arrant was unable to blame him. They had not discussed it that night, but it lay there like a canker eating away at his soul: Arrant would never be confirmed as heir, indeed even Temellin would not countenance it, if he could not learn the secret behind power control.

As he lay in bed that night, Arrant fingered his cabochon, depressed. Instinct told him that there would be no miracles for him – no sudden awakening of a latent talent. The unpredictability of his control over his power had been determined before he was even born, and nothing would ever change that.

When he woke in the morning, his brother was there, in his mind. And something was terribly wrong. He thought it must have had something to do with what had happened in the Mirage and he started to ask, but Tarran interrupted.

How could you do that?

'Do what?'

Deny my existence to my father!

'What are you talking about? I didn't!'

You know what I mean. It's all there in your head—

'You've been rooting around in my memories while I was asleep? How could you do that!'

How could you deny my existence?

'I didn't!'

Yes, you did! As good as. You implied it. You implied that to believe in me would be silly, and you weren't so stupid. You don't want me to know my father. You want to keep him all to yourself—

'Of course I don't! Don't be ridiculous. Anyway, you had no right to go rummaging in my memories when I was asleep.'

But Tarran would not be diverted. *No, you had no right to deny me to my father. I wanted to know him. I was dependent on you, and you failed me! Without you, how can my father know me? I needed you to tell him about me. Instead, you denied me. After all we have been to each other – how could you do such a thing? Why did you do such a thing?*

Tarran's sense of betrayal filled his mind with devastated bitterness. Arrant tried to justify himself, but stuttered in his explanation, knowing some things can never be excused. 'It was just – I was going to tell him – I was waiting for you to come back. How could I explain you if you weren't there? We can go and see him now—'

But Tarran had gone. Arrant tried calling after him, but the silence was the soundless emptiness of something that had vanished more thoroughly than a pricked soap bubble. He was gone, and he wasn't coming back.

Aghast, Arrant thought, 'Acheron's mists, *what have I just done?*'

That evening, as usual, Arrant made his way to the Mirager's quarters for dinner. When he entered the dining room, it was to find that he and Temellin were not alone. Garis was there. And the skinny girl who had helped him escape Lesgath's ward. He stared at her, mind racing. A fragment of remembered conversation from the last time he had seen Garis in this room surfaced: his father saying, 'Samia is in Madrinya, Garis, staying with her aunt.' Samia. Sam. Garis's daughter. Of course.

Garis grinned at him. 'How have you been surviving your first half month, Arrant?'

He smiled back and tried not to lie. 'I'm, um, all right.'

'You haven't met my daughter, have you? This is Samia the Savage. She persuaded her nurse in Asufa that she really, really needed to see her aunt in Madrinya.' He looked at her fondly.

Samia pouted. 'I came cos I *knew* you wouldn't come home through Ordensa, and I was sick of waiting to see you again.'

'And you were fed up with school. Admit it.'

'Not with school. I like school. Well, most of the time. But I *was* sick of being looked after by Theura-viska. I'm too old for a nurse. Besides, motherless girls of my age need to see their aunts. For women's talk.'

Temellin sucked in his cheeks, and Garis waggled a finger at his daughter. 'I was not born yesterday, young lady.' He looked over her head to grin at Temellin. 'Now say hello to the Mirager-heir.'

'Hello, Magori,' she said politely.

'Hello, Illusa.' He held out his left hand and they clasped cabochons, neither of them betraying by as much as a blink that they had ever seen each other before.

'Arrant, sit down. The food's getting cold. And I have news for you.' Temellin passed the platter of unleavened bread around. 'We have decided to take you to the Shiver Barrens tomorrow. At first light.'

Arrant's heart did something in his chest that resembled a somersault. At last – to enter the sands and receive his sword, the symbol of Magoroth manhood. To walk beneath the sands, to meet a Mirage Maker face to face, to see his brother for the first time. His heart thumped. 'Oh! Good,' he said inadequately and turned to Garis. 'You're coming too?'

'We are. Samia and me, both. She has been nagging to see

the Barrens since she was old enough to ride a shleth, so this seems like a good chance. To get home to Asufa we have to take the same paveway part of the way anyway – as far as the Three Wells Wayhouse. That's where the turn-off into the Barrens starts. Going to the First Rake will add a few days to the journey, but as she's missed so much school anyway . . .'

'I promise to make it up when we get home,' she said.

'Don't talk with your mouth full.'

The pang Arrant felt as he listened to their banter delved deep into his mind, turning over his memories, pushing regret to the surface. He exchanged a look with Temellin and he knew they were both thinking the same thing: 'This is what we missed, not being together. This is what we missed, not being a family.'

He woke just before dawn with the impression that someone had entered his room. He sat bolt upright, all the hair rising on the back of his neck. In the dim of pre-dawn light filtering in through the windows he never shuttered, he thought he saw his brother standing in his open doorway.

Tarran! he cried, and the overwhelming joy and relief he felt was as intense a pleasure as he'd ever known. And then he woke properly, and realised there was no one there, and never had been. The door – improperly latched the night before – had swung open in the breeze from the window. It swung gently to and fro on its hinges in the silence of the night.

And it came home to him, yet again, just how much he had thrown away.

Oh, Tarran, please come back.

He lay awake until Eris came. After he had washed, he dubiously eyed the clothes that had been laid out for him on the bed. 'Aren't these a little, well, um, fancy?' He had been about to say 'flamboyant', but changed his mind, not wanting to offend the man. Eris was an elderly non-Magor with cataracts, and he was unfailingly helpful in his attempts to make a proper Mirager-heir out of Arrant. 'I mean, we are going on a journey, not to a banquet or something.'

'It's what your father had especially made for this trip, Magori.'

'Oh! Oh, well then, of course.' He resigned himself to wearing a bolero of bright scarlet with a matching cloth belt; an ivory-white shirt that tied with a bow at the throat, and a broad-brimmed hat of shleth leather to match his riding sandals. At least the trousers were plain enough, as was the cloak of warm shleth wool, although it had an ornate brass clasp.

'It's because you're getting your sword,' Eris explained. 'It's a very special event in a young man's life. A time for celebration. 'Specially for you, being the heir and all. City folk will be lining the streets to cheer you this morning.'

He was horrified. 'The non-Magor? They will? But it's so early in the morning—'

'Never you mind that. They'll want to get a look at the lad who'll be Mirager one day, all dressed up, fancy-like, looking as handsome as can be. I've packed your ordinary gear as well, but today you wear this. And the day you walk into the sands, too. You've got to show respect to the Mirage Makers.'

Half an hour later, as he rode through the streets with his father at his side and Garis and Samia behind, he wondered if this was how slaves had felt being paraded before customers in a market. Every eye seemed to be on him, assessing. Girls threw flowers and blew kisses, until he was sure his face was the colour of his bolero.

'Oo-er, handsome!' a young woman shouted.

'Smile and wave,' Temellin hissed out of the corner of his mouth.

He obliged, although his smile was sickly, especially when he heard Samia chortling behind him once she had somehow divined his discomfort. '*Girls,*' he thought in disgust, although the truth was he'd had little to do with any until now.

Only once they had left Madrinya well behind did Arrant understand how tense he had been ever since arriving in the capital. With the city and the Academy disappearing into the distance, though, he began to relax and enjoy the ride, even revel in the way his Quyr necklet warmed on his neck until he felt at one with his mount.

'I'll see Tarran in the Shiver Barrens,' he told himself. 'We'll make it up. I'll promise to talk to Temellin, and maybe everything will be all right again.' He had to make it right, because Tarran needed him, needed the shelter of his mind. How could his brother stay sane otherwise? 'He has to come back. He has to.'

He tried to stop thinking about it. 'Do we really need guards?' he asked his father. There were several Theuros guards and non-Magor servants riding with them, in front and behind, all discreetly out of conventional earshot. Several of the large transport shleths, their howdahs fully laden with supplies rather than people, accompanied them on leads.

'Probably not. But it's traditional since the rebellion, so I go along with it. There was a time when I didn't bother too much with servants, either, but now it seems expected of me.' He grinned at Arrant. 'I'll guarantee you and Sarana know all about that.'

He gave his father a heartfelt look. 'Gods, yes. It was so hard to be alone, sometimes. Or to have a conversation that wasn't heard by half a dozen people. Ex-slaves were the worst. They were so used to having always to be in earshot to answer their master's every whim.'

His father grimaced. 'Oh, I know. But I think everyone here

knows to keep their distance in order to give us some privacy, if they want to keep me happy.'

'Can I do that to Theura-viska when I get home?' Samia asked her father.

'No, you cannot. She is *supposed* to keep an eye on you.'

Samia gave an exaggerated sigh and screwed up her nose at Arrant. He laughed and the two of them dropped behind a little to have their own conversation. 'How come you don't have any control over your cabochon power?' she asked.

'How come you don't have a gold cabochon like your father?' he countered.

'You answer my question, and I'll answer yours.'

'All right. I don't know.'

'That's not fair! "Don't know" is *not* a proper answer. That's such a sprout thing to say.'

'Well, I don't. It might be because my mother was in a lot of danger when she was pregnant with me and kept using up all her power to save us.'

'Oh.'

'Your turn. Why isn't your cabochon gold?'

'Well, Papa's parents were Illusos, not Magoroth. So he's the odd one, not me. Mama was Magoroth, though, so I guess everyone hoped I would be too. It doesn't matter much, cos I want to be a healer, and Illusos are good at that.'

'A healer?' he asked, amused. He could not imagine her being gentle and nurturing. She was rarely tactful, never still, always inquisitive. He couldn't make up his mind if she was a pest, or a fun person to have around, but he had a good idea that things would never be dull in her vicinity. At least she was more amusing than the bloodthirsty and bossy Vevi, and less calculating than Serenelle Korden. He decided he would have liked to have a sister like Samia Garis.

*   *   *

They rode straight down the paveway towards the fishing port of Ordensa, stopping at the Tyranian-built wayhouses every night. Constructed to ensure Tyranian legions could deploy rapidly, the road followed an old shleth route serving the small vales to the southwest of the capital, before reaching the town of Asufa and then heading for the coast. It was not as heavily travelled as the major paveway that joined Sandmurram and Madrinya, and once they were more than half a day away from the city, they passed few long-distance travellers.

The Three Wells Wayhouse sat at a fork where an unpaved shleth trail, heading northwest to the First Rake, parted company from the paveway that curved more directly southwards. The architecture of the wayhouse was pure Tyranian: rooms, arranged around tiled and fountained atriums, looked narcissistically inwards. Floors were patterned with mosaics, and a terracotta tiled roof topped the one-storey structure.

'Where do they get the water from?' Arrant asked Garis as they rode through the archway into the entrance yard and servants came to take the mounts. He could hear water running somewhere within the building.

'An underground channel,' he answered. 'Comes from a source under that hill over there. Enjoy a bath tonight, because there's no wayhouse at the end of the track. We Magoroth are the only people who ever go there, after all, and only when we have a youngster in need of a sword. There's a soak that supplies enough water for us and the animals, plus a few storage huts beside the First Rake, where we keep grain and feed, but that's all.'

'Why did we need to come this far south?' Arrant asked as he slipped down from the saddle. 'Isn't a part of the First Rake closer to Madrinya than this?'

Temellin nodded. 'The distance between the rakes is broad near Madrinya; too far to cross to the next rake in one night.

Anyone attempting it would die. Further north still, where it does get narrower, the rakes are high and rocky, rugged enough to be impassable. So we always crossed to the Mirage around here, and it became the traditional place for a young Magoroth to receive their sword. Your mother actually got hers on the Third or Fourth Rake.' He fell silent then, and Arrant knew he was thinking of Sarana, regretting her absence.

A pang of longing gripped his heart. He missed her too, even though his anger at her infidelity sometimes returned to haunt him. Her relationship with Brand had sparked so much grief . . .

Just two days after the Mirager and his party had left for the Shiver Barrens, a courier arrived with a letter for Arrant from the Exaltarch. Temellin's scribe gave it to Eris who placed it, still unopened, on the small table in Arrant's room, to await his return.

It was a long ride from the Three Wells Wayhouse to the First Rake, with only one brief stop at a vale too small to have a proper lake. A few villagers lived alongside a soak where they grew what food they needed for themselves, and maintained a livery stable for mounts which they rented to the Magoroth who passed that way.

Several hours after leaving the village, Garis was finally able to point ahead and say, 'Look, Sam – that red line along the horizon? That's it. That's the First Rake.'

For several hours more, the red line was still only an edging to the sky where it met the flat plate of the land. In the late afternoon the line sharpened into a jagged contortion of peaks and indentations like clay pummelled with the thumbprints of a divine sculptor and then baked in the sun. Alternately shadowed and sun-blasted, the red rock of the rake vanished off to left and right as far as the eye could see. Arrant's breath quickened. All his life he had been heading towards this moment, towards this place, where he was to leave his childhood behind and slip his hand into the hilt of a sword that would amplify his powers. 'Please, let it happen,' he thought. 'Let this solve all my problems.'

Yet, used to the grand peaks of the snow-capped Alps, he found the height of the rake puny as they approached, its slopes more impressive for their artistry than their majesty.

Garis laughed, reading his lack of wonder. 'Believe me, when you are riding the Barrens, with the frost breaking up under the paws of your mount and the sands escaping the crust to begin their deadly song – any rake looks very desirable indeed.'

Arrant nodded, and felt regret; crossing the Barrens would never be something he knew. The Mirage on the other side was banned to them now. The agreement giving them access – made by his grandfather, Mirager-solad, and the Mirage Makers – had ended. Besides, the Mirage was now far too dangerous. The Mirage Makers had been unable to prevent the Ravage killing people there, even before the decision had been made to leave. *Tarran. Gods, Tarran, I'm sorry* . . .

'Come,' said Garis, 'I'll race you to the top!' He urged his mount forward onto the red rock, and Sam raced after him. She was at the crest first, and Arrant had an idea that Garis had not let her win, either. As Arrant joined them, her father was protesting, 'You have an unfair advantage – less weight for the beast to carry uphill . . .'

But Samia wasn't listening. She was groping for words to describe what she thought of the Shiver Barrens. 'Creeping cats! That's – that's—'

'Creepy?' her father suggested.

She pulled a face at his silliness. 'No! It's wondrous.'

Arrant had to agree. The landscape below fascinated, drawing him. Another red line just visible on the horizon, and between him and that far-off barrier . . . purple sand, swirling through the air in thick whirls and eddies like windborne spume whipped up from restless surf. The grains sang as they flew.

He slid from his mount and began to walk down the slope towards the edge of the rock, where the sands lapped at the rake like waves slipping up and down a seashore. Gods, it was beautiful. And *scary*. He shivered, fear prickling in his throat. These sands could kill without thought.

'Can you hear it?' Temellin asked, coming to stand beside him on that strange shoreline.

'Yes.' Oh, yes. The whispered song was tuneful, yet somehow just beyond the range of his understanding. He strained to hear properly, thinking he ought to be able to make out the words – but the harder he tried, the more indistinct the meaning became. 'Like sounds carried on the wind in snatches,' he said. 'It never quite makes sense.' He turned to Temellin. 'Why don't the grains blow away in the wind?'

'They have an attraction one to the other. You can't separate any one grain too far from the rest. If you were to take one and bring it up here in your closed hand, the moment you opened your fingers it would fly back down again to join the others. My feeling is that the sands are all one entity. Semi-sentient, if you like. A being like none other, but alive nonetheless. Not everyone agrees with me. Korden thinks I am moondaft, but it would explain why the sands never blow away in the wind.'

'When can I walk into it?'

'Not today. It is already too late. The Mirage Makers won't be there now, not when the sands begin to stop dancing towards dusk. Tomorrow, in the heat of the day, they will call you. You must not enter unless you hear that call, otherwise you'd be doomed. It is not a pleasant death.'

The wariness in his voice widened Arrant's eyes. 'He's afraid,' he thought, surprised that even a man like his father, who must have crossed the Barrens countless times, could still regard them with such respect.

'Memory stirs old griefs,' Temellin said softly. 'I have lost friends in there. But it does not hate us. It just doesn't care.'

Ligea – no, Sarana – had told him that, too. The grains of sand killed without remorse. They frayed clothes into no more than a heap of thread. Then they abraded you to death, rubbing the skin away in slow excoriation, rasping the flesh with their tiny shivering particles. Flesh oozed, then bled. Sand bounced into the ears, driving the victim mad as the eardrums perforated and grains penetrated deeper. Eyelids shredded under the onslaught. Eyes were scored to blindness. No bodily orifice was safe from the squirming, scouring, rasping erosion. If you were lucky, you choked on sand. If you weren't so lucky, you died when your flesh finally bled too much for you to live.

Temellin withdrew his sword from its scabbard. 'Out there, on the Shiver Barrens, there is only one magic that works. Look.' He swung the weapon in an arc towards the sands. The translucent blade flared briefly once at the top of the curve. 'The flare tells us the direction of the closest part of the next rake. It was how we found our way.'

'More accurate than following stars,' Garis added.

'Why doesn't other Magor power work here?' Arrant asked.

Temellin answered. 'Who knows? Some say the Shiver Barrens feed on it, draining our cabochons and our swords. The odd thing is that the Mirage Makers' powers are undiminished. I've often wondered why. What is it that makes their power different from ours, when ours has its origins in theirs?' He shrugged. 'I don't suppose it matters really. It's just a minor mystery that niggles my intellectual curiosity.'

Samia's eyes shone as she bent to touch the grains of sand dancing at the edge of the red rock. They curled away, and she laughed.

'Try your left hand,' Garis said and Samia did so. Grains of sand nestled in the heart of her palm, gathering around her cabochon.

'They are all different colours!' she exclaimed. Arrant leaned over to look. It was true: the grains were all the colours of the rainbow when seen individually. She giggled. 'They tickle.'

'Listen, they're humming,' he said. It was true. When he bent to listen he could hear their song, but the words were still out of reach.

'Do you remember?' Temellin said softly to Garis. 'It seems like only yesterday . . .'

'I remember.'

'Remember what?' Samia asked.

'When Arrant's mother saw the Shiver Barrens for the first time.'

'You were here then too?' Arrant asked Garis.

It was Temellin who replied. 'Yes. And Brand, as well. The four of us.'

They were all silent. Arrant was embarrassed. Speaking to his father of Sarana and Brand in the same breath made him want to sink into the ground with shame – his shame, and hers. Samia, oblivious, asked, 'Who is Brand?'

It was Garis who replied. 'An Altani rebel, the same man who helped us when we were attacked just before your mother died. One of the finest men who ever lived. He was killed in Tyr saving Mirager-sarana's life.'

'Oh. That's sad.'

'It is,' Temellin said. 'And that's why we honour him with our memories, and those he died for go on living as he would have wanted.' He laid a hand on Arrant's shoulder. 'Tomorrow you become a true Magoroth. Garis, get the others down here to set up the camp, will you?'

He waited until Garis and Samia had gone, then he said quietly to Arrant, 'I've been a fool. I saw your face just then, when we were speaking of Brand. I felt your emotions. I should have realised earlier. You were jealous. *That's* why you stopped talking to Sarana. You knew they were lovers.'

'*You* knew that too?'

'Yes, of course.'

'She *told* you?' Arrant flushed, his face and neck warming with embarrassment.

'She did say Brand had returned to Tyr and was staying in the palace.' He shrugged. 'She really didn't have to tell me any more. Cabochon, Arrant, of course I knew. They'd had a relationship before. He was her closest friend and he loved her. What did it matter? I wasn't there, could never be there. If I had been, it wouldn't have happened.' He sighed. 'Why is it that children refuse to see their parents as human beings with adult needs? Listen, up until then, your mother and I had so little time together as lovers. A little over a month if you include that time in Ordensa when you were five. That's *all*. We loved each other so much – but in fact, that's all we've *ever* had. Would you have had us be celibate for the rest of our lives?'

Arrant's flush deepened. He felt uncomfortably hot, and he couldn't think of anything to say. He felt a fool.

Temellin was relentless. 'I've had other women in my bed. There have even been women I had a deep fondness for. But they weren't Sarana. And as much as she loved Brand, he wasn't me. I'll admit I was jealous at first, but once I was sure of her love, it didn't matter. I *liked* him. Probably a lot more than he liked me. I was glad she had a true friend in the midden heap that was Tyr. It never made the faintest difference to the way we felt about each other and it was just too bad that you were not mature enough then to understand. A lot of people paid for that mistake.

'And you made another mistake when you arrived here: you should have told me what was bothering you. We have some damage to repair, you and I, and you have to forgive your mother. You understand me?'

Arrant looked down at his feet, shame sweeping through him. He nodded.

Temellin turned him to look at the Shiver Barrens. 'Tomorrow you become a man out there, in more ways than you can imagine. That sword you'll claim brings responsibility. Like all Magoroth, you become a guardian of this land. Unlike others, you could one day rule it. You can't be a child any more.'

'I understand.' And he did. 'And I do have things to tell you.'

'We'll talk tomorrow, afterwards.' Temellin smiled, gently chiding. 'Right now, you dropped your reins and walked away from your mount. Never a good idea anywhere, least of all here. Go and attend to the beast.'

Arrant scrambled to obey.

CHAPTER NINE

The moment he felt the call, mid-morning of the next day, he knew what it was. It had a familiarity. He had touched the essence of the Mirage Makers before; because of Tarran, he knew the whisper of them through his mind.

He scrambled to his feet and looked across at where his father sat, leaning against a rock in the shade of one of the serrated peaks of the rake. 'They are calling me,' he said.

'Then it is time.' Temellin came across and walked him down to the edge of the sands.

Garis had to grab Samia to stop her from following. 'No,' he said. 'This is a private moment for a man and his son.'

She thought about that, and nodded. 'Do you feel bad that you will never do this for me – bring me here to receive a Magor sword?' she asked.

He smiled at her, and shook his head. 'No. Why should I? I think you will do very well without one.'

'So do I. But Arrant needs his. He needs it badly.'

'Yes, I'm afraid he does,' he said softly. They turned as one, to watch.

Where sands and rock met, Temellin stopped. Arrant held out his left hand and they clasped cabochons. Arrant felt nothing and suspected his father didn't either; no layers of communication, no knowledge of the other's emotions, a lack that honed an edge to the regret each felt.

Temellin said quietly, 'Tell him – tell him I think of him often. Every day of his life, I have thought of him, and wished that things had been . . . somehow different.'

Arrant held himself rigid. Temellin wasn't talking about Tarran; not really. He meant the brother he thought Arrant had never met. Aloud he said, 'He may not be there.'

'He will be. Of course he will. Listen, once you are under the sands, you will see very little. Walk towards the voices you hear. Afterwards, to get back to the rake, well – if your sword is working, you can use the flare from it to tell you the way to go, as I showed you.'

'And if it doesn't work?'

'You'll have to rely on the Mirage Makers. They always wait until the recipient of the sword is back safe on the rake. While they are there, the sands will not hurt you. If your sword doesn't flare the first time you take hold of it, ask them what to do. In days gone by, they used to talk to us mostly with visions, illusions really, but since your brother has been with them, they seem able to use language more.'

He nodded, quelling his nervousness. Of course the Mirage Makers would help. There was no need to be afraid. He held his head high and turned to walk into the Shiver Barrens. The Quyriot necklet was strangely hot at his neck; that had never happened before unless he was mounted. 'The sun must have warmed the beads,' he thought. He tucked his shirt collar under them to keep them from his skin.

Ahead of him the sands parted, just as they must have done for his mother fourteen years earlier. 'This is my second time,' he thought in wonderment; she had been pregnant then, with him.

The ground was hard beneath his feet, and the sands deepened as he walked in: up to his knees, then his thighs, then his waist. Nothing touched him; the grains swirled and twisted, a whirlpool with him at the centre. It was like walking into the ocean and not being touched by the seawater. He went deeper and the singing intensified, became more frenzied. Words caressed him – he could have sworn they were words – yet he could make no sense of them. He thought he felt his necklet move, and laid a hand over the beads. The runes shifted under his fingers, and he snatched his hand away. 'You over-imaginative fool,' he muttered.

He felt a yearning to communicate in the air, an alien entity's desire to speak. The whisper of the sands was there, in his mind, but he could not understand.

'Surely the Barrens *are* alive,' he thought. 'They feel as if they are.' He wondered if the runes were trying to tell him what they said, the way they tried to tell him about his mounts.

Shoulder height. He looked back at the rake. Temellin remained where Arrant had left him, motionless, a hand shading his eyes against the glare as he stared. Behind him and slightly higher up the slope of the rake, Garis stood, hand in hand with Samia. Arrant waved and turned to follow the call he still heard ahead. Not the sands, he knew; the Mirage Makers. But that yearning? That was something else, new to him.

The sands whipped over his head, cocooning him, filtering the harsh light of the sun into a purplish gloom of cool air, swept with the capricious wind the sands themselves created with their movement.

Arrant . . . Arrant . . . this way.

Words whispered, not quite as Tarran spoke to him, nor yet as a person spoke, either. Tarran's words he heard in the same way he heard his own thoughts. These words he seemed to hear whispered close to his ears. 'They are using the song of the Shiver

Barrens somehow,' he speculated. 'Twisting it to shape their words, because they have no true bodies and no true voice.'

He obeyed their call and at last he saw them: shadowed, nebulous, unreal, half hidden by the undulating curtains of sand. Formed to give a semblance of humanity. Yet they weren't really there, not in a tangible human sense. They were just an extension of the Mirage.

'Tarran?' he whispered.

He is not here.

Grief tore through him, shredding uncertainties, defining what was important with new clarity. He said, 'If you are here, then he must be too.' Words that tried to salve a wound that would not heal until he felt Tarran in his head once more.

No. He will know later what happens here. But now, he does not hear us. He has cut you free. He feels you betrayed him.

'I did not mean it as a betrayal,' he protested. 'But I *was* thoughtless and stupid and muddled. I – I have *tried* to call him back. When this is over, I want to talk to my father, but Tarran should be there. Please tell him that. Besides, he *needs* me. How can he survive without the safety of my mind?'

The choice must be his. He grows older. We will shield him as much as we can.

'But it's also important that we communicate! Together we might find a solution . . .'

None of the Mirage Makers will survive what is happening, Arrant. You must realise that. It is just a matter of time. Perhaps that is as it should be: every being comes to an end of his road and looks out into the unimaginable infinity of death beyond. It is soon to be our turn.

He wanted to rail against the Mirage Makers' certainty. Scream at them all to fight, Vortexdamn it, never to give in. As if they didn't battle and never had. They were already fighting, every day of their lives.

Arrant took a deep breath to steady himself. He subdued his frustration and said instead, as if to plead his brother's case, 'Tarran is only just starting out on his life. The rest of you have centuries behind you. And all he has ever known is the pain of the Ravage. There must be a way to stop what is happening. Together we must find it.'

He has known your world. And in it, an absence of pain. You have given him that much.

'I would give him more, if I knew how. He once thought perhaps I could help you. Somehow. *You* thought that, I know you did! So what can I do?'

Yes, we thought he would make a difference. But there is something we missed. His presence here was not enough.

'If I could use my cabochon properly, would that make a difference?'

To us? We don't think so. The gem in your hand, in every Magor's hand, is a concentration of energy continually renewed by pilfering from other sources – the sun, the wind, heat. It enhances your Magorness, the essence you and all Magor possess at birth. We can feel that personal power of yours, as well as that of your cabochon. Both are there, true and strong. You just do not recognise it. Cannot reach for it.

'There is something wrong within me?'

There was a heavy silence. Then, *We believe so.*

Oh, sandhells. It really was his fault. His own sodding, pickle-brained *fault*. 'Then how do I learn? How do I overcome this? Tell me!'

This time they were silent, and he knew they knew of no way.

'I will never give up,' he said, defiant. 'Won't having a Magor sword help?'

Probably not.

A wave of nausea swelled, then retreated. *Sweet Elysium.*

We are sorry, Arrant. We would help if we knew how. If we thought there was a way.

He changed the subject. 'Tarran. I need to talk to him. If I could only explain—'

There was another heavy silence, and then more truths he didn't want to hear. *You think it easy to wipe away the footprint of betrayal? Ask your mother, she will tell you the pain of betrayal lasts a lifetime.*

'Will he never forgive me?'

He thought you were prepared to obliterate him in order to appear in a better light before your father. He wondered if you were jealous, the way you were of Brand – and wanted to keep your father's love to yourself.

'It wasn't like that!' He refused to allow the shuddering in his chest to spill over into the release of tears. He was too old for tears. 'If he would just speak to me—'

Give him time. We will send him back.

'Tell him I'm sorry. I wanted to unsay it the moment I said it—'

He will know. We Mirage Makers are all one, remember? Whatever you say to us, he will know the moment we leave the Barrens. But hurt needs time to subside.

Arrant felt as if he had been cleaved with pain. He couldn't speak.

Then, while he struggled with his shame, they spoke again, more information he had not wanted. *We are losing our hold on the Mirage, Arrant. And we know not where it goes.*

'I don't think I know what you mean.'

The Ravage beasts have learned to use the winds. The gales come down from the mountains, drawn in by the heat, and sweep away the earth where once we thrived. Tell the Magor to beware; your people will become their prey, food to those who now devour us.

Arrant wrenched himself away from his personal pain to

deal with this new threat. 'You mean the Ravage beasts are leaving you to attack us? But we can fight them for you. The Magor are warriors—'

Can Magor warriors defeat monsters streaming out on the wind in the thousands? We fear our death dooms you all. Once we were all that was beautiful and gave you shelter. Now we house within us the end to all you hold dear. Tell the Mirager.

The idea was almost too much for him to grasp. The Magor had feared the death of the Mirage Makers and an end to the magic that made the Magor special. Now it seemed they were looking at the possible annihilation of the Magor – an end to their lives, not just their power.

It is not only that, the Mirage Makers said, as if they understood his thoughts. *All of Kardiastan will fall to the Ravage beasts unless you find a way to do what we could not.*

No words came to him in answer. He had come full of hope to receive his sword, and now all hope was annihilated by the magnitude of the disaster foretold.

While he stood there, stricken and speechless, a sword appeared in the air in front of him. A Magor sword.

Take it. It is yours.

He hesitated, swamped by all that had gone before. More than ever, he needed a sword that worked. The Magoroth would soon be called upon to save the land again. His desire to be a true Magoroth warrior so mingled with his fear of failure that he found it difficult to move. Finally, he reached out and plucked the weapon from the air. His cabochon slotted into the hollow on the hilt. The clasp of his hand felt right, as if it belonged. The balance of the blade was perfect. It was his.

But nothing happened.

No flare of colour. No surge of power.

Instead it was his pain at the failure that flared, the fire of it running through his mind and body in searing streams.

Failure.

He would never be a true Magoroth. His sword was just an interesting artefact, sharper than most. He stood staring at it, hardly hearing what the Mirage Makers were saying.

There is a responsibility that comes with this weapon. This is not a sword that drinks blood for the sake of power; it is an instrument of service to this land and all who live here. Use it for personal gain, pursue corrupt goals, and you break the Covenant made by your forebears. Never turn it on your peers with lethal intent. Are you willing to accept this gift?

He swallowed back his pain. 'I am.'

And then the presence of the Mirage Makers was ripped from him. The sands continued to sing – they were still urgent and fervid as if they strove to make him understand their hidden message – but there was no one else there. He was isolated, surrounded by humming sand grains.

The shock of the abandonment shuddered through him. The Mirage Makers had been sundered from the Shiver Barrens, torn by a power he could not recognise. 'Wait!' he cried, terror swelling. '*I don't know how to go back.*'

He whirled around, staring, searching, but had no idea which way was out.

He fumbled for control over his cabochon. Nothing. No colour. And nothing flowed from his cabochon to his sword. In his hand, a Magor sword was no different to a weapon crafted in the blacksmith's alley of Madrinya. He clamped down on his panic.

This was so *stupid*. No one else had been so abruptly abandoned. No one else had problems returning to the rake after receiving their Magor sword. But when he swung it to and fro, waiting for it to flare and direct him to the rake, it was quiescent.

He licked dry lips. *Tarran?* he asked, the request apologetic. *I am in real trouble. Can you help me? Please?*

There was no reply. Yet he knew Tarran would come if he heard. He *knew* it. Something had happened, something terrible, and the Mirage Makers had been wrenched away. He was on his own.

The sands weren't attacking him. Yet. Fear settled over his shoulders, a cloak of creeping terror. How long did he have before the remnant influence of the Mirage Makers dissipated and the sands turned on him in their mindless dance powered by the heat of the sun? He had no idea. A quarter of an hour-glass? Less?

He was disoriented. Cut off from the sky, from sounds, from smells – from anything that would indicate which way he should go.

He shouted, calling out to Temellin. Tentatively, timidly at first, then bellowing. First one direction. Then another. But even to his own ears, his voice was muffled by the singing sands. How would Garis or Temellin or anyone else hear him?

'Goddess, this is ridiculous,' he thought. 'I can't die out here, within a hundred paces of safety, just because I don't know which way to go. It's absurd!'

Carefully he thought about the direction in which he had just moved. A circle. He'd turned in a circle. Which meant he still had his back to the rake. So if he turned around, he ought to be facing the right way. 'The trick,' he told himself, 'will be not to walk in a circle once I start.'

He set off. After fifty paces, nothing had changed except that the dancing of the sands seemed more frenetic. The day was hotter, perhaps that was why. He had no idea where he was. None. And the first grains had brushed his skin, slid down his neck to rub against him under his shirt. One tiny sliver bounced into his eye, and began to edge itself under his eyelid. Horror made all the hairs on his neck stand up. And the grains of sand caught on them.

He started sweating. *Tarran, Please!*
Silence.

Samia was restless. It was so hot on the rake, a dry, crisping heat. Even seeking out the shade didn't seem to help. The red rock soaked up the sun's rays like a snake in the sun and then radiated the heat back at them. Most of the servants and guards, scattered in the indentations of the rake, were asleep.

'I feel like bread in an oven,' she complained, wilting.

'Take a nap in the cave,' her father said, referring to where the two of them had spent the night. It was more a deep fold than a cave, but it was cooler there and spread with sleeping pelts. The dew run-off had made a pool in a niche nearby, and she would have loved to bathe in it if there hadn't been so many people about.

'I don't want to miss Arrant coming out of the sands. What's taken him so long? All he has to do is get a sword. And it's not even a Mirager's sword.'

Garis glanced over at the Barrens. 'Well, it doesn't take this long normally. But Arrant is not a normal youth. He has a brother among the Mirage Makers, for a start.'

She knew the story. It was so sad . . . What could you say to a brother who was a Mirage Maker?

She looked down at the edge of the sands, where the Mirager waited. He leaned against a tall finger of rock, arms folded, looking out in the direction Arrant had taken. He was stern, his grimness intimidating. 'I'm glad I have a father who's so much fun,' she thought. 'I bet Arrant doesn't have as much fun as I do. He often looks sad.'

'Why don't you go down and ask him about your mother,' Garis suggested. 'It'll take his mind off Arrant and make time seem to go faster.'

She thought about that, but made no move.

'It will help him,' Garis said gently.

She brightened. She liked to be of use; it was why she wanted to be a healer. She scrambled to her feet and walked over to stand in front of Temellin, her hands behind her back, a solemn expression on her face to match his. 'Papa says I should ask you about my mother. Did you know her?'

He smiled, and she thought he looked much nicer. He had the kind of smile that lit up a face. 'Of course! She was funny and sweet and brave and very, very young. I was so sad when I heard she had died.'

'She was only seventeen when I was born. I'm eleven now. Well, almost. But I don't miss her. Is that wrong of me? I don't remember her, you see. I try hard, but I don't remember a thing.'

'No, it's not wrong. But *she* knew *you*. And loved you. She shared your life for two whole years, even though you don't remember them. You would be a different person if she had not loved you and taught you and played with you. Nothing can take those years away, Samia. Part of you is the way it is because she was there, loving and caring for you when you were tiny.'

She thought about that. 'I like that. It means she left part of herself behind in me. How did you know that?'

'Maybe because you remind me of her. Maybe because I, too, lost my mother when I was young. I do remember her, though, a bit. Just not as well as I would like.'

'Arrant lost you when he was young, too,' she said. 'But now he has a chance to know you. He's lucky.'

He gave a rueful smile. 'I hope he thinks so.'

She looked over her shoulder at the sands. 'He's been in there a long while.' She frowned. 'Did you know he's just started to walk away from us again?'

'Again?' He stared at the Shiver Barrens. 'I can't feel hi—

Oh, *shit*!' he said. In one fluid motion he grabbed both his cloak and Arrant's from where they'd been flung over a rock, and raced into the sands. As he dashed past her, he roared over his shoulder, '*Noise*! Make a noise.'

Garis came up at a run. 'What happened?' he asked Samia. 'Did the Mirage Makers call Temellin in too?'

'No. Arrant's going the wrong way.'

He stood stock still. 'I can't sense him at all. The sands are blocking everything.'

'Can't you? I can. And I think the Mirager did too, just then. Arrant started back this way, then he went that way' – she pointed to the right – 'then he gradually turned and started going away from us. He's scared, Papa. The Mirager says to make a noise.'

'*Vortexhells*.' Garis went white, staring at her. Then he turned to shout at the guards, calling them down to the edge of the sands. He slipped an arm around her shoulders, but his gaze had returned to the Shiver Barrens. 'The Mirage Makers must have gone. If the sands are active again, both of them are dead. Can you still feel him, Sam?'

'He's stopped.'

His arm tightened. They were both thinking the same thing. Perhaps, attacked by the Barrens, he'd fallen. Perhaps he was dead.

'What about Temellin?'

'I could at first, but not now. He went too deep. But he did seem to know which way to go, at least at first.'

'Magori?' One of the guards spoke behind them. 'Is there trouble?'

'Yes. There might be. And I want everyone to make as much noise as they can. Yelling, screaming, hitting the rocks with cooking pans – anything at all. I want them to keep it up until the Mirager returns with his son. If they can hear us, they can get back. Understand?'

The man nodded, already turning away to shout the orders.

'Unbuckle your stirrups from your saddle, Sam,' Garis said. 'Bang them against the rocks. Can you sense them?'

'Arrant's moving again. Back towards us.'

'Temellin?'

'I don't know. Why can I feel Arrant and not Temellin?'

'Perhaps it's your healer's empathy. You feel his need, his—'

'Pain,' she finished for him. 'He's hurting.' She shivered. Pain was filling her head with its rawness, and it was hard to shut it out. She wanted to bury her face in her father's chest for comfort. She wanted to feel his arms about her, keeping her safe. Instead, she went to unbuckle the stirrups.

Tarran? Gods, Tarran, please come. I am in real trouble . . .

He sank to the ground, pausing to pull his bolero off and wrap it around his face. He still had no idea which way was out. His panic unfurled his emotions and set them free, spinning out of his control in all directions. Perhaps someone would feel them. But what could they do anyway? The sands were slowly changing from grains obedient to the Mirage Makers' restrictive hold to the free spirits they normally were, free to kill with their heedless dance.

He could feel a few jiggling in his ears. Only it was more like an army marching down his ear canal with copper studs in their sandal soles. He extracted the grain in his eye, but others were already hitting his closed eyelids in relentless attack. Each was a tiny pinprick, almost unnoticeable of itself, but each was also part of a battle line of millions. His face was beginning to sting. The backs of his hands were raw. When he gasped, a phalanx danced into his throat. They crunched when he gritted his teeth, yet refused to be still even in his mouth.

He was going to die by pinprick. One tiny wound at a time. Maybe the Mirage Makers would come back. They had come from the Mirage to give him his sword, so they must have been aware of his arrival on the rake. Just as they were of all the young Magoroth who came to receive their weapon. So why wouldn't they be aware of him now?

'Because,' the voice of reason told him, 'you are under the Shiver Barrens now, blocked by the sand, and the sands eat Magor power. And because something tore them away – which might be the same thing that would stop them returning . . .'

Tarran would come if he heard. And in the past he had always known; right across the Alps, he had known. But perhaps his brother had blocked him out of his part of the collective mind that was the Mirage Makers. Perhaps he didn't *want* to hear from Arrant.

'Oh, mirageless soul,' he thought wretchedly, 'once Tarran realises how I died, he'll blame himself.' He unwound his cloth belt and flapped it at the surge of sand erupting in his face. And saw a formless lump of a shape crossing in front of him from right to left, almost swallowed up by the swells of sand. He screamed, 'Wait! Wait!' And choked on grit.

The shape stopped, turned and came stumbling towards him. His first thought had been that it was the nebulous form of a Mirage Maker, but now he realised this was a person, wrapped in a cloak and clutching a Magor sword. Suffering, just as he was. The golden glow from the weapon spluttered ineffectually like a guttering lamp flame.

His father pulled him into a hug and wrapped him in a second cloak just as the sword's light dimmed and vanished.

CHAPTER TEN

'There's got to be something else we can do,' Garis thought wildly. 'We can't lose them. What about a whirlwind? Maybe I can push a path through the sands. If I stand on the rake, then my power will work . . .' No sooner had the thought come, than he used the power of his sword to start a whirl of air. He built it up high and fast. He whirled it stronger and tighter. Around him people yelled and banged and clapped. The guards slapped the flat of their swords against their bucklers. The servants battered metal kitchen pots together. He turned the whirlwind into the Shiver Barrens, trying to bludgeon a way through. To plough a path through to Arrant and Temellin. If he could find them.

It didn't work. The sands ate the whirlwind. They drew it downwards and sucked it of power, sucked it dry just as children suck juice from an orange, until all that was left was an aimless breeze that stirred the grains not one whit.

'What about water?' Samia shouted at him. 'Fill the wind with water, keep it well above the sands so that they can't suck away the power, and then drop the water. Would it, um, flatten the grains, do you think?'

He thought of the Rift, of the winds that carried water in them, drenching all who rode that way. 'Worth a try.'

He built another whirlwind of power and used it to sweep

up all the water he could find in the crannies and hollows of the rocks, and from the soak behind the rake. But when he dropped it from above, the grains parted to let the shower fall to the ground, then closed up behind it. Their frenetic dance did not slow. Garis swore.

He changed his tactics. He drew lines with water, thin trickles dropped by the whirlwind, falling in patterns like the spokes of a gigantic fan-shaped spider's web, with himself at the apex. Pathways to safety – if there was anyone alive to see one of them.

Temellin swung his sword in an arc. The faintest flare of colour came into the blade and disappeared before Arrant could be sure he had seen it. Grains flew into his eyes and he was forced to close them.

Temellin put his mouth against Arrant's ear. 'Keep your eyes closed. Grab me around the waist. Keep your head buried in my back.'

Arrant did as he was told, and stumbled in his father's wake as they moved off. His thoughts were jostling horror. How could Temellin see unless he kept his eyes open? He needed to see the flare from the sword to keep a straight line to the rake. Arrant thought of the single grain of sand jiggling under his eyelid. He thought of enduring the rasping of countless grains against the eyeball. And in his despair, he thought his heart would stop. *Temellin would go blind*. He shuddered. Not once, but in endless spasms.

Temellin ran at a shambling gait, doubled over, one eye closed, the other looking directly down at the ground. He had wound his cloth belt around his head, to swathe his nose and mouth and his closed eye in its folds. He held his sword with the point in his line of vision. The top of his head faced into the swirls of sand.

'Sweet hells,' Arrant thought, 'how can he survive?'

The pain continued. Pinpricks on top of pinpricks. Sand grains ricocheting off the walls inside his ear. Slivers burrowing under his fingernails, leaving trails of fiery pain like red-hot sparks. Grains coming up from under the cloak in their blind dance, to find and irritate the crevices of his body. Grains pushing at his eyelids. Grains joggling into his nose. He knew he was bleeding, and disregarded it. It must be worse for his father. Much worse.

It seemed to last forever. Pain, stumbling, more pain, skin rubbed raw, desperation. Then Temellin stopped. Arrant cracked his eyelids apart and saw him swing his sword through an arc, only to have it remain quiescent.

'No more power,' Temellin told him, and coughed, an unpleasant rasping sound. His uncovered eye was streaming blood. 'We'll have to guess from here on in. Hope my sensing abilities return. Listen for a noise, Arrant. It might be our only chance.' He rewound the cloth about his head, uncovering his protected eye.

Arrant choked, knowing what that must mean. He bent his head in despair, fumbling to cover his own face – and saw a mark on the ground. His eyes teared, a desperate attempt to rid the eyeballs of the grains that scratched at them. He tugged at Temellin's arm and pointed. There was water on the rock beneath their feet. A thin trail of water, leading away to the right and the left.

'Garis,' Temellin whispered. More blood wept from his nose and mouth and ears. 'Ingenious.'

'Which direction?' Arrant asked. There was no way to tell whether to turn left or right. No way to know in which direction to follow the trail.

'Listen.' Temellin tried to enhance his hearing, and failed. Arrant, who had never been able to do so with any reliability, used his normal hearing instead. And heard nothing either. His necklet writhed unpleasantly at his neck. He touched it and felt the carved runes move under his fingertips once more. This time he kept his hand there long enough to be positive he wasn't imagining it. The grooves in the obsidian writhed. He was overwhelmed by smell. And feelings. Such odd emotions. Boredom. The pleasant sleepy boredom of someone – of lots of someones – who enjoyed doing nothing. Sandhells, was he going mad? He strained, trying to pin down the location. Looked at his cabochon. No colour. Closed his eyes, wanting to scream with the irritation under his lids. Not his cabochon. His *necklet*. Warm at his throat. Not people, animals. *Shleths*. Sleepy, bored, smelly shleths. He pointed to his right. 'That way,' he said with certainty.

And Temellin accepted his certainty. He pushed Arrant down under the cloak again, and they moved off. Arrant kept his eyes closed. And thought of his father, who could not. Who had to watch that thin dribble of water that was going to lead them to safety.

Some time later, Arrant had no idea how long, Temellin staggered and fell. Arrant knelt beside him, rewrapped his head to protect his injured bleeding eyes, and then tried to lift him. He wasn't strong enough.

'I can't go on,' Temellin whispered. 'Follow the water, Arrant. Your chance. You must live.'

Arrant hesitated. *Leave* him?

'That's an order from your Mirager.'

But Arrant caught the echo of Brand's voice in his head. He thought now he really understood what Brand had meant. When you die, you do so knowing how you lived. And if you haven't lived well, then your death is hard and bitter. He said, 'Papa, I couldn't live with myself if I did that. Put your arm around my shoulders. I know where the camp is. It's not far, and I don't need to use my eyes to find it now.'

He hauled his father up and thought of the shleths, heard them, smelled them. The fire of the necklet runes branded his skin with pain. And the two of them staggered on.

There were hands grabbing him, voices crying out. The cloak was flung off. He opened his eyes. His sword – so dearly bought – clattered to the rock, and lay ignored at his feet. His gaze sought his father. Temellin had dropped to his knees, his hands covering his face. Garis and Samia were kneeling beside him. Garis was peeling off his clothing. Samia grabbed the Mirager's hand, cabochon to cabochon.

Someone took Arrant's left hand and his pain halved in intensity. Someone else was stripping his clothes off, too. He wanted to protest, he desperately wanted to go to his father's side, but one of the Theuros guards, Farrenmith, kept a firm hold on his arm. 'We've got to get your clothes off,' he explained, 'so any remaining grains of sand can find their way back to the Shiver Barrens. And then we want to start the healing process.'

'Father?' he asked, coughing. His throat felt dry and raw. Blood trickled from his nose and from the corner of his lips. Something still jiggled in his ears. A thunderous noise, deafening him. 'I want to know—'

'Garis and Samia are the best healers we have here,' Farrenmith said, patting his shoulder. 'Samia says your father is worse off than you are, so they are attending to him. Lie back, Arrant. Hey, someone get water here!'

His thoughts were muddled. Samia – she had said she was training in healing, but she was only a child. What could she know? He strove to hear what Garis and Samia were saying, but someone pushed him down onto some soft pelts in the shade. Too weak to struggle, he was forced to acquiesce.

'We will wash the blood away and start the healing process,' Farrenmith told him. 'I am going to pour oil into your ears. Lie still.'

Absurdly he began to feel drowsy. He didn't want that, and tried to push sleep away. 'Will he be all right?' he asked. He was naked and someone was washing his face. Liquid trickled into one of his ears, then the other, mercifully stilling that horrible battering against his eardrum.

'He's fine,' Farrenmith said, his tone soothing. 'His skin's seeping, just like yours, but that we can fix. It's only his eyes they are worried about.'

Only his eyes. Only. Vortex*damn* it! He tried to struggle up, but slipped further towards sleep. 'Blast them,' he thought. 'They are doing that.' The Theuros. In their efforts to aid his body's healing, they were pushing him into rest. 'Rot them all . . .'

When he woke, it was night. The sky was ablaze. Stars. The luminous glow of towering nebula clouds. He'd thought he'd never see them again. He felt sore, all over. His eyes stung and teared. His ears hurt, bruised inside and out. His skin felt raw everywhere. It was bitingly cold; his nose, peeping out of the pelts heaped on him, was freezing. He turned his face to the left and saw the pristine white of a peaceful Shiver Barrens, frozen into stillness by the sparkle of frost. He saw the guards, who'd built a fire using dried pats of shleth dung, warming their hands to flames that smelled of burning grass.

He turned his head the other way and saw the wrapped bundle that was his father. Oil lamps placed on the rocks burned steadily in the still night air, but he could see little. Garis sat cross-legged beside Temellin, holding his hand. There was no one else close by.

'Garis? How – how is he?' he asked, and dreaded the answer.

Dreaded it with a burrowing fear that lodged deep in his gut, that dug into his bones and ached there.

Garis relinquished his hold and stood to come across to him. He knelt, sitting back on his heels, and said, 'He's not in any danger, don't worry. He has eaten, and he is sleeping.'

'His – his eyes?'

There was a pause that told him everything he did not want to hear. Then, 'They appear to be badly scarred. We have tried to set healing in motion, but I don't think the prognosis is good. The damage is, um, severe.'

'What in the seven layers of hell does that mean?'

'Right now he can't see, Arrant. He can't see at all. I'm sorry.'

'He's – he's *totally* blind?'

Garis nodded. 'It looks that way. It's hard to say at this time. Maybe it won't be as bad as it looks.'

'No. Oh, no.' Hoarse words stuck in his throat. Garis levered him up and gave him a sip of water. He drank, spluttered, then clutched at the Magori's hand. 'It *can't* be,' he whispered. 'I mean, how did things go so *wrong*? It wasn't supposed to be like this. I didn't – oh, gods, Garis, why didn't I think more about how I was going to get back? I didn't realise what it was going to be like in there. So – so difficult to see anything. I couldn't find my way. I would have asked, but the Mirage Makers just – just *vanished*. And then the sands started to change.'

'It was our fault,' Garis said. 'Mine and Temellin's. We should have given it more thought. We knew you had problems with your powers. We should have sent you in holding a cord, or something. Ravage hells, Arrant, I'm sorry.' He closed his eyes and dropped his head, struggling with his emotions. 'It wasn't your fault. How could you know the Mirage Makers would disappear before you reached the rake? They've never done that before.'

Arrant battled the impulse to cry. He felt like a three-year-old again, not understanding the larger world. A short time ago he had looked forward to receiving his sword. Things had gone wrong so *fast*.

He didn't sleep again after Garis went back to his healing of Temellin. He lay awake looking out on that night sky, the lush black greying with the coming of dawn, the twinkling beads of the stars fading as he watched. The frozen clouds of the horn of the Cornucopia dimmed from fire-red to orange as the sun crept up to the horizon. The Shiver Barrens themselves looked so harmless: glistening blue-white, so untouched, so faultless, so cold, so silent. How could these be the same sands that had taken his father's sight with their horrible dance?

He rose and moved across to Temellin. Garis relinquished his place to him and left them together. Temellin was wrapped tightly in his cloak, apparently still asleep as light stole into the world once more.

Another day. A new dawn. Arrant had his Magor sword, somewhere. And his father was blind. Made blind in exchange for a blade that was useless in his son's grip. Arrant dropped his head into his hands, but he couldn't even cry. He felt he'd never cry again. Some griefs were too bitter – and corroded too deep – for tears. His father had said he must leave behind his childhood. Well, he had. His Magor sword may not work for him, but he was a man now, for all that.

We failed him, you and I, Tarran. And now he is blind. Did you hear me, brother? Did you hear me and not come?

He couldn't believe that. He *wouldn't* believe it. A Ravage attack had prevented him from coming. Or maybe it was because the Shiver Barrens was a world where Magor magic was always dimmed, and Tarran simply hadn't heard him. The

Shiver Barrens, it – they? – had their own magic, he knew. They were different, alien, and they smothered the power given to the Magor by the Mirage Makers. He shuddered. People underestimated the Barrens. They weren't just lethal: they were *alive*. Sentient in some bizarre way. They spoke a language. The trouble was that no one could interpret it. His necklet had brought him to the edge of understanding, but had been unable to take him a step further, to communication. Just as it made him aware of the feelings of his mounts, but nothing more.

He tried not to think about how to tell his mother what had happened. And it was better not to remember that, when Temellin next opened his eyes, it would be to a world of darkness and the knowledge that he would probably never see again.

'Think instead about the Mirage Makers,' he told himself. 'Think about how to help them.' Think about why the Mirage Makers needed to use the Shiver Barrens. Could it be because, to communicate, they needed more than an illusion? They had to have something that was *real*. Like the song of the Shiver Barrens, which they then twisted into the speech they needed. He fingered the necklet runes and wished he understood more than he did.

As the camp started to stir with the dawn, he found there was a limit to how much he could distract himself. When his father groaned in his sleep, and murmured his son's name, Arrant wondered if he was always doomed to cause the people he cared about pain, disfigurement or death. His father, blinded while saving his life. Brand, killed saving Sarana from the consequences of his betrayal. Sarana, injured saving him from his folly. Foran, dead because Arrant had wanted to get closer to the battle. Soldiers, disintegrated because he couldn't control his power. Tarran without his sanctuary because he, Arrant, had betrayed him.

'I should have kept on walking into the Barrens . . .'

He hadn't spoken out aloud, but a hand gripped his in a strong, solid clasp. His father's hand, finding his unerringly, his powers still strong. Closing over his fingers in comfort. His voice was hoarse as he said, 'Thank you. You saved my life back there.'

'I put you in danger.' Arrant faltered with his apology. 'I – I am so *sorry*.'

'Not your fault. It was theirs, the Mirage Makers. They vanished, didn't they? Long before they should have. We should have considered the possibility, even if it hadn't happened before. I'm paying a heavy price, but so be it. Had you died, the price would have been *unbearable*. Beyond any hell of any religion's devising. Believe that, Arrant. Because it is a truth I can't even *begin* to explain to you.'

He sat up and pulled Arrant's head down to his chest, and stroked his hair as if his son were a small boy again. And for the briefest of moments, Arrant's cabochon worked and he felt a surge of love swell through him, then ebb like an ocean wave passing on its way. He sighed as the colour in his cabochon faded.

His father may not have seen the colour vanish, but he must have felt the power seep away because he said, 'You have a purpose even though you may not yet know what it is. Never doubt it. Being blind is not so very bad for one of the Magoroth, you know. For instance, I can tell you where every person in this camp is at this precise moment. I know who they are. I can tell you how they feel as they go about their business. I don't need to see their faces. I even know where every shleth is tethered.'

His father's courage made Arrant choke with pride. Temellin

the Mirager was already considering his strengths, not his weakness.

'Now, tell me, was your brother there?'

Arrant sat up, burying his own weakness deep. 'No.' He hesitated. This wasn't the time to speak of the reality of Tarran. He drew in a deep breath and wadded his emotions tight. 'No, he wasn't there. I need to talk to you about him, but it can wait. More urgently, the Mirage Makers had a message for you. They are all dying, my brother included. They spoke as if they are close to the end.'

'Ah.' Temellin moved uncomfortably, whether in pain or grief or worry, Arrant couldn't tell. 'That is not good news. Although "close to the end" may be a while yet, when time is counted by a being that has lived hundreds of years. Still, I did wonder if the only thing that would account for their disappearance before they saw you safely to the rake would be a disaster in the Mirage.'

'There's more. And it's not good, either.' Arrant swallowed and told his father all the Mirage Makers had said about the Ravage and the wind.

There was a long silence before Temellin spoke again. The sadness in his voice then said it all. 'When the legions were defeated, I thought our fighting days were over. It seems I was wrong.'

'What can we do?'

'I need to take this to the Council. We thought to obey the Covenant and stay away from the Mirage, but it has not helped the Mirage Makers nor, it seems, our own future. Perhaps we need to break the Covenant yet again and return to the Mirage. Perhaps we need to fight again, a different kind of battle this time, and one I have little stomach for. Too many of us will die. Yet not to fight – that cannot even be an option, for if this battle is lost, it seems Kardiastan dies.' His fingers fiddled restlessly with the cloak covering him. 'I haven't received any reports of Ravage beasts appearing in Kardiastan yet, but they could have. The areas closest to the Shiver Barrens are sparsely settled.'

Arrant was silent. He recalled his dreams and tried to imagine those creatures let loose on the waking world. In a city street perhaps. Slavering jaws. Gleaming eyes. Insatiable hunger to rend and tear and consume . . .

'The Mirage Makers – were they able to help you concerning your powers?' Temellin asked.

'They said my power is there, I just don't know how to use it. They didn't seem to know why, except to say they doubted I would ever learn. They didn't think I'd ever be able to use my sword.'

Another long silence.

'Papa, is it my fault?'

'Is it someone's fault if they are born with overly large feet or a withered arm?'

'No.'

'Then you have your answer.' His clasp on Arrant's hand tightened. 'You must write to Sarana and tell her what happened here today, before she hears some other way.'

Arrant nodded, and then remembered his father couldn't see. 'Yes, of course.'

'You're not still angry with her, are you, over Brand?'

He thought about that, surprised to realise how hard it was to remember the extent of his resentment and jealousy. 'It seems so stupid now,' he admitted. He had the sudden thought that if he'd been foolish about his mother's relationship with the men in her life, then maybe he'd been foolish about other things too. He said, 'I remember you talking to her when we were in Ordensa. I heard you say you didn't want me and even then I knew you couldn't lie. I remember being upset.'

'Did I say that? I'm sorry you heard it. It was only true in one sense. Of course I wanted you to stay. Both of you. But I was worried more for your safety in the Mirage, because of the Ravage, than in Tyrans, where all we had to worry about were legionnaires. Besides, I didn't want to deprive Sarana of you, or you of your mother. Arrant, she was so alone. She was surrounded by enemies, running for her life, trying to build something worthwhile out of a corrupt and rotting empire. Perhaps it was revenge she needed, but she also did it for us. For Kardiastan. So that we could be free. That would never have happened, had she not brought the Exaltarchy to its knees. You were all she really had then. She *loved* you. It tore her in two to bring you to Ordensa with the intention of giving you up. Her pain sliced so deep she couldn't hide it from me. How could I tell her I wanted you? So I told her instead that a child's place was with his mother. Sending you away was one of the most difficult things I've ever had to do. When you have children of your own perhaps you'll understand just *how* difficult.'

He fell silent, thinking. Remembering, perhaps. When he did speak again, it was to change the subject. It was time to go on with living, as though nothing had happened. 'Arrant, hand me my clothes, will you? We need to get moving if we are to start back to Madrinya. And Garis and Samia have a long way to go to get to Asufa.'

His courage stopped Arrant's breath in his throat.

'Oh,' Temellin added, 'one other thing. Remember back there in the Shiver Barrens when I told you to leave me behind?'

'Uh, yes.'

'Next time you disobey a direct order from your Mirager, I am going to have you shovelling manure in the pavilion stables for the next year and a half. Is that clear?'

Arrant grinned. 'Perfectly, Mirager-temellin.'

'Good. I am proud of you.'

*   *   *

Garis stared as Temellin moved among the men. The kerchief he'd had around his neck when they'd left Madrinya, he now wore as a bandage over his eyes, and he no longer strode as he once would have. Someone had tied two shleth prods together for him to use as a walking stick. His steps were tentative on the uneven rock, yet he smiled and chatted as if there was nothing different from the day before, as if nothing had changed, as if he didn't need time to adjust to the horror that had overtaken him so swiftly.

'Dry hells, now there goes a man,' he murmured.

'I can't sense his emotions,' Samia said, standing at her father's shoulder. 'He hides everything in a way I've never felt him do before.'

'A man often does when he feels too much grief.'

She shivered. 'I want to go home.'

'We'll leave this morning. We will ride with the others as far as the paveway.' He looked down at her. 'I thought you might be sorry to go back. You seemed to get on well with Arrant.'

She shook her head as if exasperated at his lack of perspicacity. 'Well, he's only a *sprout*. But it's not that. It's just that – well, he hurts too much. All the time. I don't like it.'

He stared at her, surprised. 'You mean you can sense his emotions? No one else seems to have much success.'

'Um, no, I can't feel the ordinary surface emotions that keep changing, either. It's what's underneath. There's so much sorrow, and it – it looms so large. It's like a big dark animal inside him. I don't like being around him. It's too *sad*.'

Garis didn't say a word, but the dismay he felt was overwhelming.

'There's something else too. Something odd. He has wounds like burns around his neck. They haven't responded very well to healing, and they weren't made by the sands either. They feel—' She struggled to find the right words. 'Foreign. The other healers are puzzled too.'

'His necklet?' he ventured.

She shrugged.

'Shiverdamn, where are we all going with this?' he wondered, riddled with anxiety. 'Ah, Sarana, I wish you were here.'

That morning, when Ligea cradled the clay in her palm and studied Temellin's expression, she knew something was wrong. His eyes were lifeless. Her hand trembled as she stared. *No.* She would *not* believe it. She would *never* believe it. He couldn't be dead. He *couldn't.*

She put the head back in its niche, watched it turn to a formless lump. She waited an endless, torturing moment, and then picked it up once more. This time he was smiling, a sad smile, but still – his expression *had* changed. He couldn't, then, be dead. She started breathing again.

Yet there was something wrong. His eyes . . .

Dear sweet gods of Elysium. His eyes. This was the gaze of a sightless man.

She sank down onto the nearby divan, her head bowed over the sculpture she cradled in her hands, as if she could protect it from harm. As if she could protect *him* from harm. Knowing as she wept that it was already too late.

CHAPTER ELEVEN

Arrant waited before he sought another private moment with his father. Temellin was still fatigued by the battering he had suffered under the Shiver Barrens and by the healing necessary afterwards, not to mention the emotional shock he suffered from knowing he was blind and likely to remain so for the rest of his life. Arrant didn't want to put him under more stress, so he waited. They persuaded Temellin to rest another night on the rake, and then headed back to the Three Wells Wayhouse. That evening in the wayhouse, he penned a difficult letter to his mother, explaining what had happened. There was no easy way to do it, and when he'd finished, he felt emotionally empty, a hollow shell of what was possible. In the morning he would give the scroll to Garis, who would be heading south with Samia. They would take it as far as Asufa and then send it on by paid courier to Tyr.

He turned in for the night, but before he could fall asleep, Tarran came to him.

Relief shuddered through Arrant's body at the familiar touch in his mind. 'Are you all right?' he asked, sitting bolt upright on his pallet. 'Please don't leave again. Please! I'm sorry about everything.'

There was a short silence, as if Tarran didn't know what to say. Then, *I'm sorry too.*

'I'd like to talk about it.'

Me too. We should have talked it out.

'It wasn't as bad as it seemed, really. I just didn't know how to tell him about you when you weren't there.'

I shouldn't have ransacked your memories without your permission. And I was wrong not to turn up in the Shiver Barrens. It was your first chance to meet a physical manifestation of me – and I denied it to you. I guess I wanted to punish you. It was not nice of me. And the other Mirage Makers have scolded me nonstop about it ever since.

'We were both such – such *sprouts*. I am sorry, truly. Tarran – what went wrong? Why did the Mirage Makers leave so quickly?'

Another Ravage attack. The worst ever. Every Ravage beast in every sore rebelled against us. We had no choice; we have to be whole at times like that. There were deaths, Arrant. We are fewer than we used to be.

'Oh!' He was shocked. He had not known that individual Mirage Makers could die while the Mirage itself went on living. 'That's – that's awful.'

We have to get used to losing part of ourselves. Things will only get worse.

'You don't know what happened to us, do you?'

To whom? When?

'To me. To Temellin. In the Shiver Barrens. I couldn't find my way back, and Temellin came to help. The sands blinded him, Tarran.' He opened up his memories of all that had occurred and allowed his brother to see.

Tarran's shock flamed through his head. *Oh no. No, no, no. Oh Ravage hells, this is my fault! Why wasn't I there? I should have been there. If I had, it wouldn't have happened!*

Arrant winced. His head ached as though it were clamped in a blacksmith's vice. He said, 'If you had been there, you would have disappeared with the other Mirage Makers. It was no one's fault. It just happened.'

There was a short silence. Then, *I suppose so. It just seems . . .*

'So bloody stupid. I know.'

I suppose you called me. If you did, I didn't hear you, because of the Barrens. I am so, so sorry.

They were both silent again.

Then Arrant said slowly, 'A strange coincidence, wasn't it. Just when I needed help to leave the Barrens, everyone was pulled back to the Mirage by what the Ravage was doing.'

What are you trying to say?

'Could they – the Ravage beasts – could they have known where I was?'

He felt Tarran's assent. *They know most things about us, and we know about you. But why would they single you out?*

'Why did they send me Ravage dreams when I was a mere child in Tyrans? It must have been them, because I knew what they looked like before I saw your memories of them. Did they want to scare me away? To make sure I never came here to Kardiastan? Perhaps they thought I was special.' He shrugged unhappily. 'The son of Ligea and Temellin should have been special, a Magor warrior of unusual strength and skill.'

Tarran thought about that, then added, *Maybe it's because they realised you and I would be able to link, and they don't want the Mirage Makers chatting to the Magor on an everyday basis.* He paused, then added, *It's a pity we aren't as clever at reading their twisted minds as they seem to be about reading ours.*

Arrant shivered. The idea that the Ravage would go to those lengths to kill him was terrifying.

Fear crawled around the edge of his thoughts, and it was an effort to keep it from Tarran. 'We have to talk to Temellin about this. If the Ravage doesn't want us talking to each other, then we'd better start talking. If they really did want me dead, then we have to find out *why* they fear me, because I'll be damned if I can think of anything.'

Oh, I don't know. I think your mind is a very scary place . . .

Arrant smiled. The old Tarran was back, and he was glad.

With Tarran still in his head, he went to knock on his father's door at dawn, and found him awake. He was sitting by the window with the shutters open. Beyond was the atrium, still shadowed, where fish swam in lazy circles around the base of the fountain, and water trickled from stone fish mouths.

'It's strange,' Temellin said, without turning around. 'I find I like to see the dawn. The night is too dark – if awake, I see nothing . . . Then the sun rises, and I see the light. My world takes on form. There's an atrium out there, isn't there? I can hear the water and sense the fish. And your cabochon is working this morning. I can feel the power. What brings you here so early?'

'I need to talk. It's time to tell you about Tarran.'

'Ah. You said he wasn't in the Shiver Barrens.'

'No, he wasn't. But that first day that we met, I didn't tell you the truth. I didn't exactly lie, but the truth wasn't there either. That was wrong of me.'

'I'm not sure that I understand. What didn't you tell me?' Temellin turned to face him and indicated a nearby chair.

'Everything.'

'Go on.'

Arrant came forward and sat down. 'When we were in Ordensa, and I was five, I had a Ravage dream. No one had ever told me about the Ravage, yet I dreamed they threatened me. That was the night Tarran first came to me. He has been coming to me ever since. He is inside my head right now.'

Temellin stood up abruptly. 'I don't think I want to hear this.'

Arrant took no notice. 'I spoke to the Mirage Makers when I was under the Shiver Barrens. One of the things we spoke of was Tarran and all that we had been to each other over the years. If he had been imaginary, they wouldn't know about that, would they?'

Temellin, fumbling for his chair, sat down again. He sat so still he could have been made of marble. Arrant waited.

It'll be all right, Tarran said. *You'll see.* He couldn't keep the excitement out of his tone.

Sweet Hades, do you know how hard this is? Arrant asked. *He's wondering if I've been staring at the madman's moon.*

When Temellin spoke again, his tone was so neutral it did nothing to allay Arrant's anxiety. 'Start at the beginning and tell me everything.'

Arrant began again, groping for words that didn't seem to want to come. He told him everything he knew, not just about Tarran, but also about his Ravage dreams. He couldn't feel his father's doubt, but he was sure it was there. His hurt at Temellin's earlier disbelief, at Ligea's dismissal of his imaginary playmate, dragged itself out, and he felt it again, fresh and humiliating. Doggedly, he continued.

At the end of his tortured recital, he added, 'You can sense that I'm telling the truth.'

'I can sense a deliberately told lie, not the absolute truth, or otherwise, of a statement. There is a difference. All I can tell is that you *believe* what you say is true. The issue is whether you are deceived.'

'Like the madman at the Rift Wayhouse? Hearing voices in my head?'

'Yes.'

Blind eyes stared at him, and Arrant stared back. They both kept their pain encapsulated and unreadable. 'So what will you believe?' Arrant asked. 'That I've lost my reason?'

Tarran interrupted. *You really can be a shleth's arsehole, Arrant. You wouldn't want an idiot father who'd believe any kind of weird story without thinking about it would you? He's a ruler, for Mirage sake! He has to be sceptical.*

Arrant flushed at the fraternal disgust and said hurriedly, 'We can prove it.'

'We?'

'Tarran and me.'

'How?'

'Ask Tarran – through me – something about your life in the Mirage. Something that only a Mirage Maker would know, that I couldn't possibly have learned from anyone else. Tarran is part of the Mirage Makers and has their memory.'

Temellin was silent for a moment and then said, 'When I was about eight I had a secret hiding place—'

He used to hide his hop-square tors under a loose stone on his windowsill, because Korden wanted to pinch them.

'You hid your hop-square tors under a loose stone on your windowsill.'

This time Temellin's shock had a physical dimension. Arrant felt the blow of it, striking somewhere under his heart. 'You hid them from Korden,' he added.

Temellin, white-faced, bent his head. When he spoke again, his voice was husky with emotion. 'Once before I made a terrible mistake . . . I didn't believe your mother when she spoke the truth, and we all suffered for it. We could have lost the Mirage to the Tyranians as a consequence and she almost died.' He turned an anguished face to Arrant. 'Now it seems I have repeated that mistake with you. I'm sorry. Of course it's the truth, and I don't know why I couldn't see it.'

Arrant felt a rush of affection.

'Forgive me. Is he all right? Tell me about him. Is he with you now?'

Tell him Tarran has a matchless intelligence, a peerless wit, an exemplary character, a modesty supreme—

For once, Arrant couldn't muster up a brotherly insult. Aloud he said, 'Yes, he is. Tarran? He's, um, well, he's kind and bright and funny. And so very brave. You – you would like him. A lot. But he's not like us. He's a Mirage Maker first, and – and my brother second.'

For once Tarran didn't have anything to say.

'Father, there are things we have to tell you. He's going to die. He can't save the Mirage. He's not strong enough and the Mirage Makers don't know how to save themselves. They have no answers and know of no way we can help them.'

'Is he – is he listening? Can he hear us?'

'Yes, of course.'

'What can I say? My *son*!' His feelings ranged free, as if he no longer had the strength to contain them, but there was far too much there to read. When he did manage to speak, it was with a depth of open emotion that Arrant had neither heard nor sensed from him before.

'Have him ... Tarran ... could you tell all the Mirage Makers that we will do anything – anything at all to help them, even if it means we lose what we are, the Magor, in the process. We have that because of them. We have been special, and blessed, because of them. Kardiastan is free because of the powers they gave us. Now we would gladly die if it would save them. Save *you*, Tarran.'

Arrant relayed Tarran's reply. 'He says to tell you that the Mirage Makers don't know of anything that will make any difference.'

The pain on Temellin's face was stark. 'No,' he said. 'We aren't going to give up. Not just like that. How can we? This is just where the fight begins!' He stood up, as if to emphasise his point. 'Tarran, we need the Mirage Makers' permission to break the Covenant. We have to return to the Mirage.'

Ligea's letter-scroll was the first thing Arrant saw when he entered his room on his return to Madrinya. He unbuckled his Magor sword and his belt pouch and laid them down on his pallet before opening the scroll case.

She would not have received his letter about Temellin, of course, but he was astonished to find most of the contents concerned his necklet. He sat down on his bed, frowning. He read the last part twice: *Berg Firegravel seemed to think your necklet might become dangerous, possibly because it is returning to the region near where it was made – and its makers were perhaps as much animal as human. Don't wear it, Arrant. Just in case.*

He turned to his belt pouch and emptied it out. The necklet was there, along with his coins, his whetstone and his flint firemaker. He ran a finger over the beads. The runes were cold under his fingers, but he carried scars at his neck where they had burned him. Unlike the scars caused by the Shiver Barrens sands, healed by Samia, these had not vanished. They were rough and raised to his touch. He had removed the necklet to give them time to heal.

He ran the string of beads through his fingers. Dangerous? Perhaps. But he and Temellin were still alive because of them. Deliberately, with steady hands, he reclasped them around his neck. There was power of some sort there, and he needed all the help he could get. He would ask Tarran what he knew, next time he came. In the meantime, he was prepared to take the risk.

He had an idea it would be better not to tell his mother that.

'Temellin.' Korden stood for a moment in the doorway, emotions spilling out.

Temellin raised the bottom edge of the black bandage over his eyes and saw the blur of a shape against the light behind. If he hadn't been able to feel Korden's presence, the amorphous shadow could have been anyone. Or anything. 'How I hate this,' he thought with sudden savagery. And then, despairing, 'This is the rest of my life. Get used to it.' Aloud he said, and his voice rang with good humour, all of it false, 'Korden. Come on in.'

Korden's dismay was palpable as he came across the room to where the Mirager sat at the window, a glass of wine in his hand. 'Damn this, Temellin. I came as soon as I heard. I am so sorry. I don't know what to say.'

Temellin considered Korden's emotions. 'It's more than dismay,' he thought. 'He's horrified. And his grief is genuine. Why then does he always make me feel so uncertain of his loyalty?' The answer was there, the same one as always: because Korden was jealous and always had been, for as long as Temellin could remember. Korden had wanted to be Mirager and, being the eldest of the Ten who had escaped the Massacre of the Shimmer Festival, he thought he had a better right to the Mirager's sword than Temellin. He had the most memories of the world they had lost, of the Magoroth who had died, of the richness of the life they had once lived. And now Temellin was blind and, as much as Korden might grieve over that, it gave him another reason to believe he would make a better Mirager.

Temellin smiled and waved at the chair next to him. 'I'll survive. It's not so bad. Have a seat. Would you like some wine?'

'Thanks, I will. You shouldn't drink alone. No, don't get up;

I'll help myself. When can you take the bandage off? What do the healers say?'

'The bandage comes off tomorrow, but the damage is permanent. I am totally blind in the left eye.'

'And the right one?' Korden asked as he poured himself a drink and sat down.

Temellin hedged to avoid a lie, keeping his voice even, his tone upbeat – and his emotions carefully concealed. 'I have some vision, enough to get by. I won't be doing much sword-play though.'

'I'll talk to the healers.'

'They'll tell you exactly the same thing.' They'd better, after the trouble he had taken to conceal the extent of his blindness. It was marvellous, he reflected, how much you could deceive without telling a single lie, as long as people assumed you had no motive for deception.

'I just want to make sure that everything is being done that can be done,' Korden said.

'Oh, skies above, as if the healers aren't falling all over themselves to do their best for me. And the truth is, I had one of the best immediately after it happened. Samia Garis.' He winced as Korden tapped his fingernail against his cabochon, apparently without noticing the irritating sound it generated.

'Sweet waters, she can't be more than ten years old, and an Illusa at that.'

'Eleven, I believe. And there's plenty of evidence to suggest that Illusos make the best healers. She did a good job. I was lucky she was there or I could be worse off.'

'It is a shame that it occurred at all. Temellin, I heard you entered the Barrens deliberately, to save Arrant. And you had to do that because his sword did not have power. We almost lost our Mirager because of your son's Magor incompetence.'

Temellin gritted his teeth. It was too much to ask, of course, that the whole story wouldn't have spread through Madrinya as fast as a sandstorm before the wind. Too many people had seen what happened. He said, evenly, 'It seems the Mirage Makers vanished abruptly after giving Arrant his sword. The sands then returned to their active state. He didn't have much chance.'

'If he'd been able to control his sword, then he would have known which way to go. I heard he headed off in the wrong direction. Temel, he is a danger to himself, and possibly to others.'

'How so? It was the first time he held a Magor sword in his hand. Give the lad a chance.'

'Temellin, he has problems. If you cannot see that, then consider the pressures you are exerting on him. Arrant has power but no control over it. Yet he is being pressed to perform to the level of his peers, or better, in order to match his position as Mirager-heir. Are you being fair to him? Are you perhaps being both a poor father as well as an irresponsible Mirager?'

Temellin stilled. 'The bastard,' he thought. 'He knows how to hit me at my most vulnerable spot.' Aloud he said, his tone as cold as he could make it, 'Let me be the judge of that.'

'I would, if it concerned only your son. But it does not. It is a matter of Magor concern. Of Kardi concern.'

'You promised me two and a half years, Korden, until Arrant is sixteen. He's been here under a month, and you're already making up your mind?'

'I did not know he was going to place his father's life in jeopardy. I did not know you were going to end up purblind. Sweet hells, Temel — it is his incompetence that has left you this way. And now you need a competent heir to aid you.'

'I will hold you to our agreement.' His expression bland, he pondered inwardly, 'And that is an interesting choice of word, my friend: purblind. Do you mean dim-sighted or dim-witted?'

Korden did not notice his abstraction. 'Confound it, I didn't come here to argue with you!' He sipped his wine, then continued in a lower tone, 'I just wanted to say how deeply I regret what has happened. And ask if there is any way I can assist you. Temellin, you've laboured so hard these past few years. Perhaps you might consider resting a little.'

Temellin gave a faint smile. 'I am not sure I would know how. What do you suggest I do, Korden? Doze in the sun by the seaside? A little fishnet weaving to occupy my time, perhaps? My friend, there is work to be done.' Briefly he related all that the Mirage Makers had told Arrant of their present situation.

Korden was horrified. 'Mirageless soul! You cannot be serious.'

'Am I likely to joke about such a thing? Anyway, there has been confirmation. When we came back from the Barrens, there was a report waiting from a vale up near where the Alps meet the rakes. They found a Ravage beast, apparently deposited by a wind. Fortunately, it died, but not before it had almost lured a young boy to his death. I'm calling a Council meeting about all this. We have to consider a return to the Mirage, to fight for them. No, to fight for ourselves. For our own future.'

'We can't do that. What about the Covenant? Anyway, all those years we lived there, we never managed to get rid of a single patch of the slime.'

'We never really tried,' Temellin pointed out. 'At first we were too young and too few, and then we concentrated on the Tyranians. We have an added advantage now: Arrant has a direct line of communication with his brother. He can speak to him, even while he is here in Madrinya and his brother is in the Mirage.'

Korden stared at him with a shocked expression. 'That's impossible.'

'Apparently not. It seems Arrant is not as useless as you assumed after all. And I have already received permission from the Mirage Makers to move our warriors back to the Mirage.'

'I – I see. I'll organise a small group of volunteers to cross the Shiver Barrens and take a look—'

'That's a good idea. Do it. Get started on it today. I shall want them reporting back as soon as possible to a full meeting of the Magoroth Council, in twenty days' time. In fact, I want a Magor meeting as well, immediately following. Send the word out to every corner of Kardiastan. I'd like a representative from every Magor family. Oh, and do bear in mind, Korden, that the last time I looked, I was still the Mirager. I rule this land and I make the decisions. My eyesight is poor now, but there is nothing wrong with my brains. I am quite capable of organising another war, albeit a different kind of one.'

'Damn it, Temellin. No one is suggesting you are not the Mirager. But you are injured and half blind. Let others take on this burden. Why don't you go down to Ordensa again? Rest. Arrange to meet Ligea Gayed there. I'm sure she would jump at the chance.'

Temellin rose abruptly to his feet, spilling his wine. 'You already have my answer. I think I said it plainly enough? There is a war to be fought. Now will you excuse me?'

Aware he had overstepped the mark, Korden put down his drink and muttered an apology. He started for the door, but before he reached it, he turned back. 'Temel—'

'I know, I know. You have my best interests at heart. You always have. And believe me, I have never been less than grateful. You have always been the older brother I never had.' His thoughts were a less charitable, 'Yet I grow to dislike you more with each passing day.'

'I – yes. Skies, I'm so, so sorry.'

Temellin remained standing until he was sure Korden had gone. Then he groped around, cursing, to find and clean up the wine he had spilt, using his neckerchief. Sands, but this was so damnably *frustrating*.

He lowered himself back into his chair. Was it true; was he being unfair to Arrant? Or was he merely preparing him for what was his birthright? It was just as easy to argue that, if he accepted Arrant's disability as incurable, then he was denying him his place as Mirager, or even his future as one of the Magor.

'And admit it,' he thought, 'you cannot bear the idea that one of Korden's children might step into your shoes. Korden himself wouldn't be so bad because he at least cares for Kardiastan. But Firgan? He cares for nothing but Firgan.'

So, was he prepared to push Arrant into something he might be incapable of doing, simply to keep Firgan from sitting in the Mirager's seat one day?

And the answer was clear: yes, he was. Arrant would be a fine man one day, worth a hundred Firgans. In peaceful times, his lack of control over his Magor power wouldn't really matter – but Temellin couldn't fool himself about that, either. No Magoroth Council would ever accept a Mirager who couldn't call up Magor power into his sword at will, because how would such a Mirager ever bestow cabochons?

And that led him to another, more immediate problem. Would the Magoroth Council accept a blind Mirager when there was another war to be fought? As he stared sightlessly out the window, he didn't think it would come to that. He was popular; much more so than either Korden or Firgan. He had proved himself a wise ruler, or he thought he had. His strategies had won Kardiastan its freedom from Tyranian rule.

Besides, it would be a terrible thing to ask a ruling Mirager to step down. He would either have to die, or leave the country and go far enough away for the Mirage Makers to consider he was dead, as had happened to Sarana as a child. If the Magor did ask him to abdicate his position, maybe he could threaten them with the idea of Sarana being the next Mirager. He grinned inwardly. No, no one was going to ask it of him.

But still, he didn't want the Council to know just how damaged his eyesight was. He pondered for a while and then called for Hellesia. She came immediately, as he knew she would. Ever since he had arrived back, she had hovered within call, even sleeping on a pallet in the room off his bedroom, although he had assured her it wasn't necessary.

'Yes, Magori?'

'Is there a bird sitting on the branch out there?'

She looked through the unshuttered window. 'Yes, one of those pesky mellowbirds. They have been wreaking havoc on the figs, confound them. Oh! You can *see* it?'

'No, no. But I am aware it is there. Which gives me an idea. You told me earlier that Jahan and Jessah were waiting to see me?'

'Along with half the Magoroth Council, the townmaster of Madrinya and half *his* city councillors, your son, the head of the—'

'All right, all right. I get the picture. Go and fetch Jahan and Jessah now. And Arrant too. Tell the rest to come back this afternoon.' Her disappointment was obvious; she had thought for a moment that his eyesight had improved, only to have him dash that hope. He wanted to weep.

When she returned with the three of them, he asked her to stay. As Jahan and Jessah said all the things one could possibly say to someone who had so suddenly lost their sight, he tried to remember their faces, the way they smiled, Jessah's mannerism of tilting her head to one side as she listened, the habit Jahan had of rubbing his thumb against the side of his nose before he spoke. Temellin had to remember, because he'd never see them again. They were brother and sister as well as husband and wife, a tall honey-skinned couple, alike not just in looks but in personality. Quietly thoughtful rather than brilliant; stubborn and dogged rather than brave. Temellin valued them most for their good counsel and their steadfast loyalty. Jessah's worst character flaw was that she nagged; Jahan's that he lacked initiative. Apart from Garis, they were his closest friends and, of all the Magoroth Council, they were the two he trusted above all others.

'I'll never see them grow old,' he thought, 'none of them. Not even Arrant. I'll never know what he looks like as a man. How strange!'

How sad.

'Jahan, Jessah, I owe you both an apology for keeping you waiting,' he began, burying his distress too deep for them to find. 'In truth, I didn't know what to say, because the truth is about as bad as it can get. Let me start with the personal. I am blind. I am, however, trying to give the impression to everyone, by implication, that I have considerable vision remaining in my right eye. It's not true. I can see the difference between light and shade. And I can make out movement, at least of people and anything larger, but that's about it.'

Jahan's and Jessah's shock was sharp in the air. Arrant he could not sense at all. He continued, 'Why am I pretending it's better than that? Because Kardiastan needs a leader they have confidence in. So do the Magor. I don't want people to think I can't do my job. And in this, um, manipulation of the truth, I need your help.'

No one said anything, but he felt their cautious expressions of support, so he continued. 'I want people around me who will keep the secret and who are clever enough to cover any mistakes I make. Or better still, prevent me from making them in the first place. I need a personal guard and a new scribe. I shall retire Scribe Hasneth on the grounds that there will be more to do now that I can no longer read and write, and he is too old. One of the first things I will do is visit all the major towns to show that I am not some old hulk of a cripple.'

Jahan gave a low laugh. 'A sly scrub-fox in his prime more like it. You know full well that Jessah is a damn good scribe and there is nothing I'd like more than to be responsible for your safety. Of course we'll do it. Now that Perradin, our youngest, is grown, we've no problem with gadding about, have we, Jess?'

'We can move into the pavilion tonight, if you want.'

He let them feel his relief. 'Thank you. You may as well know this too – we are going to the aid of the Mirage Makers. We are going to fight the Ravage.'

He felt the warmth of their attention focus on him. Even Arrant's leaping approval was obvious, overriding his barriers.

'Us?' Jahan asked, broadcasting his surprise.

'Not just us, personally. The Magor as a whole. But I need Council approval first. Jahan, help Korden there. I've already spoken to him. I want as many Magor in Madrinya as possible in twenty days or so.'

'What about Arrant?' Jessah asked. 'He should be making his Covenant vows now that he has his sword. Perhaps we could arrange to have it at the same time as the Council meeting – it would be a good way to introduce him to Magoroth from all over the land.'

'No. I want to postpone that as long as possible. We'll use my blindness as an excuse. Subtly suggest that I am hoping my eyesight will improve enough to appreciate seeing my son's swearing-in ceremony. After that I'll have another excuse. I'll be preoccupied with the preparations for war against the Ravage.'

He felt Arrant's bafflement. He explained: 'Everyone will be watching you as you come out of the Hall of the Covenant after the swearing-in. They will expect to see your sword filled with colour. If it is not, they will question your fitness to be Mirager-heir. I want you to have as much time as possible to train with your weapon before that day arrives.'

Arrant was usually so good at hiding his emotions that his open display of pain disconcerted Temellin, who quickly added, 'At the same time, I intend everyone to know of your connection to Tarran. I want them to think of you as special, as someone who might bring us victory because of your connection to the Mirage Makers. If people look up to you for that, they will be more inclined to overlook your control problem. Jahan, Jessah, I hope that in your spare time, you can work with Arrant on managing his power.' He turned to Hellesia. 'I am going to need your help too. I need more light about the pavilion, even in the daytime. I can see the glow of lamps. I want all passages and rooms lit, all day, so I can get around without walking into walls. You can say I need more light because of my sight. No need to let anyone know that's *all* I can see. When I travel to other cities and towns, I'd appreciate it if you always came along, to see to that kind of thing. To all the things that help conceal the extent of my blindness.'

He turned back to Arrant. 'Son, I want you to become an animal lover overnight. Especially fish, I think.'

Arrant stared, bemused. '*Fish*?'

'Fish in bowls. Mellowbirds in cages. Frogs in jars. Lizards in boxes hidden behind statues. Whatever. I may not be able to sense the emotional life of a salamander, but I can sense their presence. If there is a fish swimming in the bowl on the table, I know where the table is and how high it is. If there's a bird in the cage near the door, I know where the door is. If we have lights and fish all over the place, I think I could walk all over the pavilion without a stumble. It will be your job to look after them. I would like people to think it is all your doing.'

He didn't see Arrant's sudden grin, but he caught his rush of gladness.

'And I'll make sure the furniture is never moved,' Hellesia added. 'And no low stools where you might trip over them.'

'We can do this,' Temellin said, but he added to himself, 'We must. Because I will *not* be some broken-down old man huddling in his rooms. I am the Mirager of this land and I intend to rule it well.'

Aloud, he said, 'And now Arrant is going to tell you exactly what the Mirage Makers told him about what is happening to them. I want you to spread this to all the Magor, before the Council meeting, so they have time to think about what we should be doing—'

Arrant's admiration for his father deepened with every word he heard. As the Mirager made the plans for war, for marshalling the forces of the land, both Magor and non-Magor, he made little reference to his blindness. He intended to lead, just as he had done before.

When the discussion was over, Arrant – in answer to a gesture from Temellin – stayed on after the other three had left. 'About your classes,' Temellin said. 'I am going to place you in the class for beginning ordinary Magoroth sword magic with Magoria-markess. Once you pass the beginners' tests, you can start the intermediate sword-powered combat classes. In the meantime, you will continue the normal swordfighting classes with Yetemith. But for cabochon usage, well, Ungar doesn't feel you are progressing with her, so you can drop those sessions. Jahan, Jessah and I will try to help you instead.'

Arrant felt sharp disappointment. He liked Ungar, and he

had hoped to please her; now it seemed she was giving up. 'I'll do my best,' he said unhappily.

'I know you will. You will continue to take all the normal classes, of course. From what I've heard, you've been more than holding your own in all subjects, except perhaps Kardi language. Illuser-stanus was telling me he thinks you ought to be teaching geometry, not studying in it.'

Arrant brightened. 'He did? He's exaggerating. He's brilliant. I love his classes. He was Tyranian-trained, of course. He worked under the legion's buildermaster here in Madrinya during the occupation: Xanus Cristan. Even I'd heard of *him*. And I can work extra-hard with the language until I catch up. I don't care about Kardi poetry though; it has too many rules. I prefer Tyranian, but I don't plan on telling anyone else that.'

Temellin laughed. 'It's an acquired taste. To tell the truth, I never did like poetry much myself. And now I have a suggestion. I want you to write down every single instance when your power has done *exactly* what you wanted of it. And then I want you to put down precisely what the circumstances were. Including what you had for breakfast, if you happen to have remembered.'

Arrant was incredulous. 'You think what I *eat* might have some relevance?'

'Who knows? But I think we should look for a common factor. Either something that was there – or something that was missing. Every little thing that you can think of. Ask Tarran about it next time he comes. Have you spoken to him in the last day or two?'

Arrant shook his head. 'No. I wish I had. I worry about him.'

'So do I,' said Temellin. 'So do I. Oh, and one more thing. Give some thought to whom you want to take into the Hall of the Tablets to witness your reading of the Covenant.'

'I thought that would be you!'

'Well, I'd be honoured, but nonetheless you may want to think about it a little more. You need allies, Arrant. Traditionally, the person a Mirager-heir takes will be their closest supporter. The person who stands at their shoulder when they are in trouble.'

'Who did you ask for yours?'

'Korden,' he said. 'I asked Korden. And Sarana,' he added softly, with the ghost of a smile as he remembered, 'asked Garis.'

Ligea rubbed at the cabochon in her palm. An old habit that, and something she did whenever she was worried. She looked across at Gevenan where he sat, his bare feet on one of the low marble tables. His soles had the gnarled appearance of the bark of an ancient olive tree.

'All right,' she said. 'I'll give you authorisation to draw money to pay informants. I want every member of the Lucii family watched here in Tyrans, and I want every bit of information from Gala that you can glean. We must know if they are assembling an army and the ships to transport them. We must know where and when they land on Tyranian soil. Information is the key – our army will be useless if it waits for them at the wrong place. Devros must be followed everywhere he goes, because he will have to lead any invading army if he is to be credible.'

'Why don't I just kill him?' Gevenan asked. 'Easier.'

'Because that's what Rathrox would have done.' She refrained from adding that she could well have been the one to do it, too, back in those days. 'Don't tempt me. Anyway, it would have a down side. The highborn have a marked objection to being assassinated. They close ranks, and I might find myself faced with more, not less opposition.'

'True.' He removed his feet from the table and stood. 'I'll

get on to it. What about you – have you heard from Kardiastan?'

'Yes. The courier came in today with a letter from Arrant. I was right. Temellin has been blinded.'

'Ocrastes' balls!' He stared at her in shock. 'Are you going to Madrinya?'

She shook her head. 'I can't,' she whispered. 'How can I, when Tyrans teeters on the edge of another war?'

He let out the breath he had been holding.

She wondered if he had any idea of what that decision had cost her.

CHAPTER TWELVE

Arrant woke to the sound of his brother shouting in his mind. 'What—?'

Wake up, you sleeping log of a lazy sluggard!

Arrant opened an eye, looked towards the shutters, and groaned. 'Dry hells, Tarran, the sun's not even up yet.'

Why do you human beings spend so much of your lives asleep? It's a waste! And who knows how much time I will have? At the moment nothing much is happening here, so I think I can sneak away for a while.

Arrant opened the other eye. 'I have classes. I need my sleep. Is Father all right?' Temellin, having received Council approval for his plans to fight the Ravage, had already left for the Mirage with the first contingent of Magor and non-Magor warriors. Arrant worried every time he thought of his father fighting things he could not see.

He's fine. Any luck with your sword skills?

'No.'

Ah. I assume from the terseness of that reply, that you have been making a fool of yourself.

'Pretty much, yes. I burned a hole into the armoury wall yesterday. Firgan said I should be banned from using the sword within half a mile of the city. Four months, Tarran, and I haven't progressed one iota.'

Arrant's head swung around to scan the room. *What's all these scrolls?*

'Stop that! I'll manage my own neck, thank you.'

They had discovered back in Tyr that Tarran could move Arrant's body in a limited fashion, but that was not something he usually made a habit of doing.

Sorry. He didn't sound particularly contrite. *So what are the scrolls?*

'Temellin asked me to write down all my cabochon successes and try to work out what the common factor was.'

Hey, that's a good idea. What did you come up with?

'I'm not sure. At first I couldn't find any common factor. Nothing. Not the time of the day, or what I ate for breakfast, or where I was, or whether you were with me. I even checked the phases of the moon and the tide timetables! I went through every variable I could think of. I used Tyranian mathematics. And then maybe I found something.'

Which was—?

'I have a near-perfect rate of success when you are inside my head. Only trouble is, there haven't been all that many times that I have deliberately used my magic while you've been with me. There may not be enough data to be statistically significant.'

Um, I'm not sure I understand what you mean by that last.

'Never mind. Let's just say it looks as if I manage my cabochon perfectly when you are around, with one obvious exception.' Arrant felt his brow wrinkle. 'Stop it! Will you be serious?'

I like the feel of it. Ah – I don't remember any failure.

'At the North Gate! The day I blew up the wall and a gorclak legion and a whole lot of injured rebels. You were there.'

Not when it actually happened, I wasn't. Shiverdamn, Arrant

– I would never have left you, not for anything, if I had been there when you did that.

This time it was Arrant who frowned, trying to remember. 'You came, you told me I'd better kill that legionnaire who hit Foran's ward, because the ward was breaking and he would kill me.'

That's right. And then I left. You had control of your cabochon, so I thought you'd be fine.

'Oh! To tell you the truth, my memory becomes a bit vague after that. It was too – awful. I always thought you were still there.' He spent a moment pondering the significance. 'I wonder if that's what went wrong? I had all my power, because you'd come. I could control it, because you were there. Then it went spinning out of control, because you left.' He swallowed. He still couldn't think about it without wanting to lose his last meal. 'I should have thought of all this earlier. But I was confused by the fact that sometimes I have perfect control when you are *not* around. At those times, it just seems perfectly random.'

Let's try your sword right now.

Arrant went to where he'd hung his scabbard on the wall and drew out the blade. 'I'll be sun-fried,' he said, feeling the power leap from cabochon to the sword. It blazed gold. He practised some of the things he'd been trying to learn in class: drawing a ward, extending power beyond the end of the blade, lighting the wick of a lamp. Unfortunately, he burned a hole through the lamp and spilled oil on to the floor, but otherwise he felt he'd done quite well. 'Is it you who's controlling my power then?' he asked.

I don't control your cabochon.

'Are you sure? Because you *can* control my body. You can make me move. You even breathed for me once . . .'

Magor power is yours. I'm a Mirage Maker. I deal only with illusions.

'But Mirage Makers can make illusions real. Making me

breathe when I was unconscious and choking – that was no illusion. You kept me alive.'

Arrant, I have never tried to touch the power that comes to you through your cabochon. That was power you were born with, because you were born Magoroth. The Magor swords are illusions made, and then materialised, by our powers. A Mirager's sword made your cabochon, that's true, but all your cabochon really does is collect power from other places to fuel the, the – he hunted for a word – *the enhancement of Magor magic. Your sword should enhance it even more. Whatever power you have is yours, and yours alone.*

'Then why do I seem better able to manage it when you are within me?'

Maybe because when I'm here, your mind works better. The connections, um, connect *better? It's not something I consciously do, really it's not.*

'I hope you can come when I swear to uphold the Covenant. Temellin says it's important people see that I can use my sword.' He stirred uncomfortably as he spoke, wondering if what he was suggesting was ethical.

I'll try, I swear. And why shouldn't it be ethical? he added, indicating that he had caught Arrant's stray thought. *It doesn't matter what you use to control your sword as long as you can. But relying on me could be a problem. It's becoming more and more difficult for me to leave the Mirage, and I am rarely sure exactly when I can be spared. And who knows how much longer any of us Mirage Makers will be around?*

'The Magor might make a difference. You shouldn't give up.'

We aren't. But we're not thinking about the far-distant future either. Are you going to tell Papa that it's the presence of his second talented son that makes the difference to your control?

'Of course. As soon as he returns. Tarran, there's something else I want to ask you.' He picked up the Quyriot necklet from the table beside his bed. 'Do you know anything about this? About what it is, or who made it?'

I know you've always worn it when you ride. And sometimes at other times too. Bring the lamp over here so I can see better. I don't think I've ever really had a good look at it.

Arrant didn't bother with the lamp. Instead he illuminated the necklet with his sword, showing front and back, and the intricate intertwining of the clasp.

There's something in my memory about similar runes, Tarran said at last. *There was writing like this carved into the rocks when we first left Kardiastan proper and went north of the Shiver Barrens. We couldn't read it. There were pictures, too, of animals. Or maybe they were men. They walked upright and they carried weapons and tools and baskets. But they had pointed teeth like cats, and claws on their hands and feet. And pelts instead of skin.* He shrugged Arrant's shoulders. *We didn't know who they had been, or if there were any of them left. We never learned to read the runes, and in the end it was covered up by the Mirage. Why do you want to know?*

Arrant told all he knew about the necklet and ended by saying, 'I was just worried it might hurt me.'

Tarran was unperturbed. *None of the runes hurt us,* he said. *Arrant, it's getting light. Show me what's outside.*

Arrant stepped through the shutters onto the narrow balcony outside his room. He leaned against the balustrade, and circled his head around slowly so that Tarran could see it all: a city beginning to stir under a dawn sky. The flat-roofed adobe buildings, the scents of the many blossoms that opened only at night, the call of the furred roof-scurriers that had glided in to feed in the rooftop gardens; Arrant was still seeing it with a newcomer's eyes as well. Strange, but alluring.

It's beautiful. Why is our sky so much brighter than that of Tyrans?

'Foran used to tell me it was because there is less moisture in the air here.'

In silence, they watched the sky lighten, changing colour through pinks and reds into an early-morning azure.

It's so serene, Tarran said as the sun came up.

'Can you stay with me today?'

No. I should go back now. One other thing first. Something else I wanted to say: I found a speck of wisdom in your chaotic thoughts. About Firgan. Beware of that man. I didn't like the way he felt when he received his own sword as a youth.

'You weren't alive then, surely.'

No, but it's in my memory now, like the runes. Nothing we can identify – just the feeling that he covets power for what it can bring him, rather than for the good it can do.

'Wouldn't the Mirage Makers refuse him a Mirager's sword then?'

No. It is part of the Covenant that we don't interfere in the affairs of the Magor, remember? We supply the swords. What you do with them is up to you. If we changed the rules, we would damage the magic, and I am not sure that we would know how to fix it. Magor magic was made so long ago that we have indistinct memories of how it was done. We did not keep the knowledge alive by thinking about it – there seemed no reason to do so. Of course, if a Mirager broke the Covenant, then there would be no more swords. But then, that's going to happen anyway, isn't it? No more swords, I mean. Soon, too.

A lump formed in Arrant's throat. He wanted to say all sorts of things: *Fight it. Don't die. Stay with me. I can't bear the thought of you gone. I'm frightened* – but he curbed the desire. Tarran needed his strength, not his fear. Instead he asked, 'Are you scared?'

I – I don't want to be nothing.

'You will become one with the land, as we all do when we

die. To nurture those who follow us. To be part of them. We'll
be together one day.'

I'd rather be the way I am.

'I – I know. I'd rather you were too. But it's better than
nothing.' *Maybe.* He wanted to say something comforting,
but did not have the words. His gaze followed the drift of a
flight of roof-scurriers. Standing there in his nightgown,
Arrant felt the chill of the morning air and thought of death.
Of Tarran dying.

'How soon is soon?' he asked, his voice husky.

But his brother had already gone.

'That's not good news,' Firgan said. He was speaking to his
father, but his eyes were on Serenelle where she sat sewing. It
was a humid day and her anoudain was sticking to her breasts.
His eyes feasted. She glared.

He smiled at her and continued, 'The other day you told
us Temellin still won't give up any of his power in spite of his
blindness, and now you say he is postponing his brat's
swearing-in again? I was hoping it would be soon.'

'He's still in the Mirage and he wants to be present, which
is hardly surprising,' Korden replied.

'The boy is going to fall flat on his unresponsive sword and
people will remember when the time arrives to vote on his suitability as Mirager-heir. Temellin is postponing the ceremony,
hoping Arrant will improve with time.'

'Is his sword unresponsive?'

'I haven't taught him yet. Ask Serenelle. She attends some
of the same classes.'

'It's unpredictable,' she said. 'Same as his cabochon.
Nothing's changed.'

'What do the other students think of him?' Firgan asked her.
She shrugged. 'How would I know? I don't ask them.'

'Then guess,' he snapped.

She winced and answered. 'He has a certain amount of respect. He never gives up when he fails, which is all the time as far as his Magor power is concerned. If he failed at everything, maybe the students would mock him. But he doesn't. He's at the top in every class except Magor studies. He can ride better than anyone I've ever seen – remarkable seeing he'd never ridden a shleth at all until he came to Kardiastan. And the students respect the fact that he can beat them with one hand tied behind his back when it comes to normal swordfighting. He's good, Firgan. And then there's his ability to talk to his Mirage Maker brother. That gives him a certain, um, status.' She picked up her sewing and left the room before he could comment.

'Perhaps we'll make a Mirager of him yet,' Korden said.

'He might be lying about being able to speak to his brother.'

'In which case, we would know, would we not?' Korden asked drily.

'We can't sense anything about him most of the time,' Firgan pointed out. 'Maybe he *can* lie to us. Anyway, the fact remains – I will never allow this land to have an official heir who can't manage his cabochon!'

'Neither will I. But he still has a couple of years to prove himself. His determination to learn control might lead to success eventually.'

'Father, this country needs vision in its leaders, and we haven't got it. In any sense. I am not interested in following either Temellin or Arrant into oblivion.'

'Oblivion?'

'Read the signs! The continuity of Magor power is doomed. We will lose this war against the Ravage because we don't know how to fight beasts you can't easily kill. Skies, Father, you know: cut a Ravage beast in two and they don't die – you just have two beasts instead of one!'

'They can be sword-burned.'

'Use power like that and a warrior soon has an empty sword. It's not our kind of battle. What if the Mirage Makers do disappear, and we have no new Magor? What if Kardiastan ends up being decimated by Ravage beasts? We need new horizons. New wealth. With proper planning and strong leadership we could conquer and control Tyrans and Corsene. We could abandon Kardiastan to the ordinary Kardi – if they wanted it – and leave to rule elsewhere.'

'Protection of Kardiastan is our sacred duty—'

'Rubbish. The Covenant is broken, or will be the moment our children fail to receive their cabochons. Our duty is to find a safe home for us, and for all who care to follow us. Every Kardi alive, if they want.'

Korden stared at him, uncomfortable. Firgan smiled. It wasn't the first time he had broached such ideas, but it was the first time that they had seemed to resonate with his father. 'Dripping water wears hollows in even the hardest of rocks,' he thought.

'No.' Barret, buildermaster of Madrinya, shook his head as he pored myopically over the parchment on the table. 'There wouldn't be sufficient lateral force, Magori. You've factored in the weight of the water channel, but you've forgotten about the weight of the water. Your aqueduct wouldn't hold up if the channel was full.'

'Oh. So it would need buttressing?'

'Yes. Here and here, to pass the thrust. But looking at the land contour and your flow map, I think a siphon might be a better solution for that valley anyway—'

Outside, a bell started tolling and Arrant jumped. 'Skies, I've got to get back. I have a meeting with the Mirager.'

There was no doubting the pleasure in his voice, but Barret felt a pang of sorrow. How long was it now since the lad had arrived in Kardiastan – five months maybe? Yet he had hardly seen his father for more than a couple of weeks at a time. Others may envy the Magor, but Barret knew the price they paid for their power. 'Come again any time,' he said.

'Thank you, buildermaster. I'd like to.'

Barret accompanied him to the door and watched him ride away through the streets of the city, trailed by two mounted guards. The Magor might mutter about a lad who couldn't control his sword – he'd heard the rumours – but Buildermaster Barret was well pleased with the idea of a Mirager-heir who spent his spare time designing aqueducts and bridges over imaginary landscapes.

Out on the street, there were so many people thronging the city that Arrant found it hard to urge his mount at more than a walk. For the past few months, Madrinya had been chaotic. First there'd been the full Council meeting followed by the wider Magor gathering, and after that there had been a steady build-up of armed men, most of them Magor, and auxiliaries, all non-Magor, not to mention their mounts and the howdah shleths that would be transporting men and goods. Early reconnaissance troops had left first, then the major contingent, led by the Mirager. They had been followed by a second contingent, after which Temellin had returned. Arrant did not expect him to stay long. He was planning to visit Asida and Amisa to the north.

'Hey, Arrant!'

He turned in his saddle to see Perradin calling to him. He was with Bevran, Vevi and Serenelle, and they were all leading shleths. 'We're off to have a game of dubblup by the lake – want to come?'

'Can't!' he replied. 'The Mirager wants to see me.'

'Too bad,' Serenelle said, and smiled. He never knew how to take her smiles. Bevran, who swore he was in love, was always asking her to join them, even though she never evinced the slightest interest in him. It was Arrant who was the target of her considering gaze and the sweetness of her smile, but he was never sure why. Was she angling for a husband who might be Mirager one day? Or was she just spying for her family?

'Damn it all,' he thought as he rode on, 'I might have more of an idea if I could control my sensing abilities better.' He wasn't sure he liked the way she made his breathing quicken. The last girl he wanted to dream about would be any member of the Korden family.

When Arrant entered the room, Temellin was alone. He had become used to seeing his father giving orders and making plans, always surrounded by people. Feeling his son's surprise, Temellin flashed a smile. 'I wanted to see you alone,' he explained. 'This may be my last chance before I ride out tomorrow, and I won't be back for a while. After Asida and Amisa, I will head for the Mirage.'

'Oh, Father, again?'

'Why not? I have my senses. I don't need to see.'

'I should be with you, in case the Mirage Makers need to communicate.'

'Until you can reliably control your power, you are not going near the Ravage.'

'But with Tarran in my head—'

'Arrant, you told me yourself that Tarran said he cannot be sure if he can always answer your calls in an emergency. You will stay in Madrinya for the time being, and that's final. What I wanted to tell you was that we will hold your dedication ceremony on your fourteenth anniversary day. There's no need to delay any further, not if you can plan ahead so that Tarran can be with you to help you with your control. I will return for that. In the meantime, I intend to keep Firgan away from

Madrinya as much as I can. I'll try to arrange it so that when he's here, I will be too. It may not always be possible, but that's my aim. When I'm not here, either Jessah or Jahan will be, so you'll always have someone you can rely on. And although everyone knows about your ability to communicate with Tarran, I would continue to keep quiet about the fact that having Tarran in your head gives you control over your power.'

'Why?'

'It gives you a last line of defence.'

Against Firgan, he meant. 'All right. I haven't told anyone yet. Not even Perry.'

Temellin came forward holding out his left hand. 'Take care, son,' he said as their cabochons met. 'Write to your mother often. She will worry, you know.'

'Father, I don't think the Mirage Makers feel you can win.'

'The Mirage Makers aren't warriors. They deal in illusions and the bizarre. Their lives have been centred around the joy they take from their creation of the Mirage. What do they know of combat? But we Magor know. We fought the might of Tyr's legions. And we can afford to lose this war even less than we could have the last one. We have strong motivation, Arrant, and I have the strongest of all. I will hand on to my successor a land that is whole and free, one that contains a Mirage. I swear it.'

But Arrant knew neither of them had any way of knowing the future.

Almost a month later, when Temellin stood on the last rake at the edge of the Mirage, the certainty of future victory appeared more remote. He could smell the rot. He could sense the Ravage, and it was everywhere. In front of him, several of the Magor were extracting Ravage beasts, one at a time, out of a sore with a grappling hook and a chain hauled by a shleth.

It was hot, nasty work. Once a hook was embedded the men found it difficult to remove without being ripped to pieces themselves. The beasts had to be kept apart from one another until they died, because if they were heaped together, they managed to exude enough liquid to start another sore – the Magor had learned that the hard way.

He turned to Garis, who was standing beside him, and said, 'Let's walk back to camp. I want to know what you found out there.' Garis, after a month of risking his life deep inside the Mirage, never knowing when he lay down to sleep at night whether he would still be alive in the morning, now knew more than anyone about the state of the Mirage.

'It's flatter than it used to be,' came the reply. He strained to keep his voice neutral, but nonetheless Temellin heard the reflection of his troubled thoughts. 'All the valleys where the lakes once were, they are now filled with Ravage sores. What's left of the Mirage is bare. Flat grassland, mostly. No buildings, no roads. Oh, there are some absurdities, just as there used to be, but they are fewer, and further apart. Sands take it, Temel – the bloody grass is *green*! Plain, ordinary green.'

Temellin didn't know whether to laugh or weep. 'Our water supply?' he asked at last as they approached the huddle of reed roofing and makeshift shelters, known as Raker's Camp, on the Fifth Rake. He had long since realised water could be a problem. There never had been any large rivers in the Mirage. The snow-melt from the Alps to the north soaked into the porous soils of the foothills and disappeared, only to emerge as lakes in the low-lying areas throughout Kardiastan, but if most of the lakes in the Mirage had become Ravage sores . . .

Garis replied, 'The Mirage Makers did as Tarran promised they would. There are ponds out there, and enough grazing for the shleths. How's the fighting been going while I was gone?'

'Well, pulling the creatures out of the sores is tough, as you can see. We did try nets, but they get torn by claws and teeth. I've sent word to Madrinya and Asufa to make more hooks. In the meantime, we forge what we can using sword power and whatever metal we have to hand. I have the mastersmiths working on it. I want to start with eradicating some of the smaller Ravage sores and their beasts, tackling them a few at a time. We need more victories; our forces need to feel we can make a difference.' As they walked, he glanced over his shoulder at the Mirage as if he could see it. There was pain there, a continuous blur of it like a background buzz of bees. 'Sandhells,' he thought. 'My son endures that, day after day?' He flinched at the image in his mind. 'Do you have any ideas, Garis?'

'I was wondering about salt. It kills things. What would happen if we dumped blocks of salt into a Ravage sore?'

He considered that. 'It might work, but I doubt we could bring in enough to make a difference to the bigger sores. Salt is scarce and expensive. We buy most of ours from Assoria and we could never get enough for that job. Though the Mirage made salt once . . . I'll have to send a message back to Arrant to tell him to ask Tarran if they can do it again.' He shook his head in exasperation. Arrant was right about one thing; it would have been easier if he'd been here. He added, 'I want you to come back to Madrinya with me at the end of next month, by the way, for Arrant's dedication ceremony. I shall be taking Korden and Firgan too.'

'Arrant won't thank you for that.'

'They need a break from the Mirage, just like everyone else – and I prefer to be there in Madrinya when Firgan is, if I can.'

'You don't trust him?'

'Would you?'

Garis laughed. 'About as much as I'd trust a Ravage beast.'

CHAPTER THIRTEEN

The passageways beneath Madrinya had begun their existence prosaically enough as cellars that made the most of a natural network of caverns. At the time of the Covenant between Kardis and Mirage Makers, part of them had been set aside to house the Tablets of the Covenant. When the Tyranian legions invaded, the passageways became escapeways and the Tablets were spirited away to the Mirage, to be returned only after the Kardi victory.

The day he was to read them and take his oath of loyalty to the Covenant should have been one of the happiest in Arrant's life. Tarran was with him, so he didn't have to worry about his sword not reacting to his touch. His father was back, unharmed; so was Garis. The Mirage Makers were cautiously optimistic because the Ravage sores were no longer spreading. Sowing the smaller ones with salt had been successful. True, emptying the larger ones of Ravage beasts would be a huge task and no one yet had any idea whether it could be done, even in a generation, but at least the battle had begun. He should have been happy; instead, as he waited in one of the underground chambers to be called for the ceremony, he was consumed by a nebulous feeling of dread.

Whatever is the matter with you? Tarran asked. *Your mind is like an ant trying to climb the sloping sand in an ant-lion trap, scrabbling all over the place yet never getting anywhere.*

'I don't know. I've been feeling strange ever since we came down here.'

You're not one of those people who can't stand being under-ground, are you?

'No, that doesn't worry me.'

Let me probe a bit deeper.

'No thanks. I'll manage my own mind, if you don't mind.'

Your stomach feels weird too. Can't you manage it better? It makes me feel terribly odd.

'I'll tell my stomach to behave. I'll threaten to eat a bowl of those fried anchovies you like so much if it doesn't.'

Are you being funny?

'Trying. Never mind. I'm sure this is nothing.'

It's Firgan. He's targeting you with his hate.

'Are you serious?'

Am I ever anything else?

'All the time. Did you just probe my mind?'

Tarran avoided answering. *I've seen this done before, or rather the older parts of me have. He's focusing his hate on you. Deliberately, I suspect. To unsettle you. Which it does.*

'Can he do that without other Magor noticing?'

Well, most are far too sloppy with their emotion sending to do it themselves, so I suppose they don't recognise it when it happens. But it is possible. It's even recorded in some of the texts we gave your mother. It needs lots of practice.

'You're sure it's him?'

Positive. No one else has such a nasty streak. It's like a, um, a signature seal. I grew up with him living alongside me in the Mirage, remember.

Arrant was about to describe what he would like to do to

Firgan, when Tarran said, *Here comes Jessah. You'd better stop talking to yourself.*

The Magoria had already helped him dress that morning, in a new suit of clothes. The bolero was a lush deep maroon to match a cloth belt. The shirt was of Corseni silk. Temellin had sent along a shleth-leather scabbard, set with rubies, and a silver clasp for the bolero. The scabbard was empty; his sword had been taken away from him the day before and would be returned during the ceremony. Advised by Ligea before he'd left Tyr, where anything except a short haircut was considered a barbarian custom worthy only of the uncultured, he had been growing his hair, and it was long enough now for Jessah to tie back with a leather thong, Kardi-style. When she'd made a mirror by sandwiching water between two wards, giving a better reflection than the polished metal ones he was used to, he was pleasantly surprised by what he saw. She'd laughed at his bemusement. 'You *are* handsome,' she had assured him.

Now she came bustling in again, saying, 'It's time to go. Everyone's waiting.'

'Magoria, will you do something for me when we go out there? I had asked Perry if he would be my witness—'

'Yes, I know. He is proud as proud can be.'

'Well, that's just it. I don't think I can ask him any more. I need to ask someone else.'

Her initial warmth faded and it was a moment before she could reply. 'Well, of course, it's your choice.'

'Could you just warn him?'

'Yes, I think I had better. He won't be happy, Arrant.'

'I know. Tell him to trust me, if he can. I will explain afterwards, and it is important.'

She pinched up her lips but nodded anyway. 'In that case you'd better let me go out first to give me time to drop a word in his ear. Count to twenty slowly and then follow me. I hope you've thought this through, Magori.' She turned on her heel and left the room.

So do I, Tarran said. *You've made her angry. You're not going to do something silly, are you?*

'Probably. I gave it a lot of thought before I opted for Perradin. He's my closest friend here. But now . . . I think this is a better idea. I need to know where I stand.'

What idea?

'You'll see.' The ache within Arrant gripped his insides like claws as he stepped outside the waiting room into the long passageway beyond.

He stopped dead. He had not expected what awaited him. A line of Magoroth on either side of the passage raised their swords in salute, each blade shining gold. Many of the Magoroth, wearied by their Ravage battles and in need of respite, had returned to Madrinya with their Mirager, and now they had come to honour his son. Garis and Jahan were there, and Korden. Then there were others who had not yet gone to the battle: his teachers, his fellow students. Perradin, Bevran, Vevi, Serenelle. Even an unsmiling Lesgath.

Arrant was overwhelmed. A rush of emotion wafted his way: encouragement, congratulations, goodwill, friendliness. And one vicious stab of loathing. Firgan. He stood at the end of the line, close to Temellin and Korden.

Arrant's heart raced. His cabochon gleamed in his palm in response to the wash of welcome as he stepped between the archway of swords. Temellin's smile for his son expressed his pride, and Arrant felt his strong affection. But his blind gaze remained an indictment, even though it was not meant to be so.

When Arrant reached Perradin halfway along, he returned his puzzled look with a shaft of appreciation. *I hope he will understand*, he said to Tarran, *because I don't know what I would do without his friendship.* When he reached Temellin, who stood in front of a pair of huge wooden doors, he halted.

'Beyond these doors are the Tablets of the Covenant,' Temellin said. The warmth of his words had a physical dimension as he added, 'You are to read them all. Whom would you like to accompany you to testify that you have read all the Tablets and understood their meaning?'

'Magori-firgan,' he replied with a ringing clarity that did not echo the anxiety he felt. Firgan's hatred sawed at him, focused and cutting.

There was an audible intake of breath down the passageway. The astonishment on his father's face was as obvious as the stillness of Firgan's. Korden was blank with surprise.

She did that too, you know. His brother, laughing in his mind. *Did what? Who?*

Firgan stepped forward, radiating suspicion for an instant before he thought to cloak it. 'I am honoured to be chosen,' he said formally. The smile he gave as he inclined his head to Arrant was smooth. His eyes twinkled. But his smile couldn't mask his wariness, or the solidity of his hate, not to Arrant, not with Tarran inside his head.

Your mother, Tarran said. *You and she are swords made to fit the same scabbard. Temellin expected her to ask him, but she asked Garis, to be annoying, and now you've annoyed him again by asking this horrible fellow. Why? He has a heart like the Ravage.*

With a gesture of his hand and a flare of cabochon light, Temellin opened the doors.

'Enter,' he said.

Arrant stepped forward, Firgan at his shoulder. *I didn't do it to annoy Temellin. And I don't think he's annoyed. Just surprised. He's wondering what I'm up to.*

Temellin's your father. Of course he's annoyed. This should be a special moment, and you ask a man like Firgan, you worm-brained brat?

The doors closed behind them with a soft click and Arrant looked around in wonderment. The light from the half-dozen lamps petered out in the darkness that hid the soaring cavern roof. In the centre of a dry sandy floor stood five stone tablets, as large and as imposing as the stele that marked Tyranian graves. The words of the Covenant were engraved on them.

We made them glow like starlight for her. Tarran sounded wistful, as if he would have liked to have done the same for his brother.

She did tell me that, Arrant replied. *I think they look grand the way they are.*

'So,' Firgan drawled, 'why does a little runt of a Tyranian bastard like you ask me to accompany him? Need me to read the Kardi words for you, do you? I did hear your mama couldn't read them, the Tyranian bitch that she was.'

Arrant stiffened. *Gods, I'd like to kill him here and now.* After all Ligea had done to save Kardiastan, someone could still speak of her this way?

You asked for it when you named him, Tarran said.

Yeah, guess I did at that. He smothered his feeling of outrage. 'I read Kardi very well,' he said, as mildly as he could. 'In fact, I also read, write and speak Tyranian, Assorian and Altani. Can you?'

Firgan snorted. 'So you're a stuffed-head scroll-lover. Might have known it. So then, why me? Scared of the dark and want a *real* warrior to protect you? I hear you can't manage your cabochon enough to even warm your left hand on a cold night. This ceremony is a mockery and should never have taken place. Your sword should have been taken from you the moment it became clear you can't use it properly. Let me tell you something, Arrant Temellin: I will do everything and anything to prevent you from becoming the officially endorsed Mirager-heir.' He stabbed his hate at Arrant, driving it deep between his eyes. 'Do you feel that? Do you?'

'It's not exactly subtle.'

'Why did you bring me in here? To mock me? To change my mind?'

'Why? To know you, that's all. And now I do.' *Tarran, you can't make them beautiful again now, can you? Just to show this bastard a thing or two?*

No, I'm afraid not. Arrant, we're too weak. And too far away. My other selves cannot even see this far any more.

Arrant took a step towards the Tablets so that he could read them, but Firgan was there before him. He shot a beam of gold from his hand and with a few muttered words, made a cabochon ward to prevent Arrant from approaching close enough to read the Tablets.

Arrant looked at him in astonishment. 'You want to play silly games?' he asked. 'If you were Lesgath, I might expect that, but you're twice my age and a man who thinks he'd make a better Mirager-heir. Grow up, Firgan.'

Tarran danced agitatedly in his mind. *'Ware, Arrant. He's more dangerous than you think.*

He'll hardly try anything here, Arrant scoffed. But the way Firgan glared started a feathering of fear along his backbone nonetheless. He met the angry gaze with a stare of his own, and hid his anxiety.

Firgan quirked an eyebrow and smiled. 'If you want to read the Tablets, then break my cabochon ward with the power of your own gem. I made it weak enough for any true Magoroth to be able to do that. Otherwise, I am not going to allow you near them and you'll have to march out there and admit you couldn't read the Tablets because Firgan stopped you with an elementary cabochon ward.'

'You wouldn't look so great either, spoiling my ceremony with your childish spite.'

Arrant, we can break that ward, Tarran said.

'Many people will say I was right to expose your weakness,' Firgan said. 'You little maggot, I'll take you apart piece by piece in the eyes of everyone out there. I am going to make damn certain you never pick up the Mirager's sword, and I don't care how I do it.'

Tarran, let's do the unexpected instead. You know what's on the Tablets, don't you? Exact words?'

Of course. We wrote them, after all.

Then stay with me, please. He put his head on one side, regarding Firgan with open contempt. 'You know what? I think I'd make a better Mirager-heir than you ever would.' He turned abruptly on his heel and opened the hall doors with a push of gold power from his cabochon. Firgan, caught by surprise, was left flat-footed and had to hurry to catch up as Arrant left the chamber bathed in a golden glow and came to a halt in front of his father.

Temellin looked past him to Firgan. 'Has the Magori read and understood the Tablets of the Covenant?' he asked in formal ritual.

'Er, well, no, Mirager-temellin,' Firgan said. He rubbed his forehead in an embarrassed way. 'He didn't seem able to read them.'

Arrant turned to look at him, surprised. 'Whatever gave you that idea?' he asked, striving to sound both innocent and puzzled. Then he turned back to Temellin. 'Firgan seems to have forgotten that there is such a thing as Magor far-sight. I'll recite the Tablets word for word, if you like.'

Temellin's cheeks hollowed, as if he had sucked them in. 'Go ahead,' he said, his tone expressionless.

Korden, apparently guessing that no matter what happened

next, his son was going to look a fool, intervened. 'That won't be necessary—'

But Arrant had already begun, following Tarran's recital in his head. '"Herein lies the history of the agreement between the Mirage Makers and the Magor of Kardiastan, the Covenant that has been agreed upon by all those who come here to read these words. And you who read this—"'

Firgan was forced to stand beside him, looking pleasant and blurring his emotions into an unreadable mixture. His hands were clenched tight. Several people tittered.

When Arrant finished, Temellin said, 'Then do you solemnly swear not to indulge in mirage-making, and not to use your powers for personal gain or in pursuit of selfish motives? Do you solemnly swear to use your enhanced abilities to protect the land of Kardiastan and to better the life of the people you serve? Do you solemnly swear you will do everything in your power to protect the Mirage from violation? Do you swear to uphold the decisions of your Mirager, as sanctioned by the majority of his peers?

'If you are prepared to swear these things, place your left hand on the hilt of your sword and say: "I do so swear."'

He extended Arrant's sword to him and smiled. Arrant took a deep breath, and uttered a silent plea that the sword would flare this time. His hand closed on the hilt.

Colour leaped from the translucent blade. A brilliant gold light blossomed outwards, radiating higher and higher, illuminating the roof far above, blasting its brightness into every corner and cranny. Most of those watching raised their hands to block out the glare. Arrant, both elated and shocked, gaped – until Jessah elbowed him in the back. 'I do so swear,' he said, and a grin split his face.

The Magor hail in answer was unusually ragged as the gathered Magoroth recovered from their surprise. 'Fah-Ke-Cabochon-rez! Hail the power of the cabochon!'

Someone muttered, 'I thought he was supposed to be incompetent. That just about curled my eyelashes.'

Well, that was very satisfactory, Tarran said, sounding smug.

People gathered around, wanting to give Arrant a cabochon clasp in congratulations, the senior Magoroth first, followed by the students. When it was Perradin's turn he took Arrant's hand without hesitation. 'I can see why you did that. And I'm glad you did. You made Firgan look a real shleth brain.'

Arrant blinked. That had not been his motivation, but he decided that if his friends thought it was, he would let them. 'I wish it could have been you, nonetheless,' he replied, and sent his gratitude and thanks through the direct touch of his cabochon.

'Wonderful!' Vevi crowed as she took his hand. 'I never did like Firgan Korden.'

To his surprise, Serenelle was the next person to seek him out. She didn't offer her hand – in fact, she clasped both hands behind her back – but she looked at him from under her lashes and said, 'Congratulations. And happy anniversary day.'

'Thank you,' he said politely, desperately searching for some indication of her emotions, in vain.

'My brother hates to look a fool. You just made a huge error,' she said.

'I don't think I made any difference to what Firgan already thought.'

She considered that. 'Maybe not. And I doubt whether you did it to make him look a fool, either. But I don't suppose you are going to tell me the real reason.'

He smiled and said nothing.

'You really are infuriating,' she said, and walked away.

Some time later, Temellin came and slipped an arm about his shoulders. 'Get me back to my quarters, Arrant,' he said in a whisper. 'If I have to listen to one more person tell me how well I cope despite being blind, my cabochon will melt under the sheer heat of my irritation.'

Arrant nodded, and they set off down the passage, away from the chatter and the crowd. Temellin, still draping his arm around Arrant, was able to stride out confidently as if he had perfect vision. 'So, suppose you tell me what all that was about? With Firgan?'

'I sensed that he was really angry. Angry enough to make a mistake. I wanted to be alone with him for a moment, and yet be safe, at the same time as catching him off guard. Gev – General Gevenan – used to say that is the best way to know your enemy: attack when he doesn't expect it and see what he does.'

There was an edge of amusement in Temellin's voice as he asked, 'And what did he do?'

'He tried to stop me reading the Tablets by building a ward. In other words, he can be foolish when he doesn't have time to plan. He also threatened me. I think you are right, Papa. He'd kill me if he could get away with it.'

'Indeed. And that is what you wanted to know for sure, one way or the other, I suppose. Clever of you, but I don't know that it was wise. Now that you have made him look a fool in everyone's eyes, he'll be more determined than ever to get rid of you. Korden was furious with him too, so he'll have his father scolding him as well. You are a very unusual fourteen-year-old, do you know that?'

'Yeah, well, I haven't had much of a chance to be ordinary. We always had to be so careful because Sarana had lots of enemies, and I didn't have a working cabochon that could warn me when there was trouble. Besides, everyone was wary of me, after what I did at the city gates. It was – it was hard to find a friend of my own age.' His bitterness seeped through into the words as they climbed the stairs to the Mirager's quarters. He knew he left traces of it behind him like a scent trail. 'I spent most of my time with my tutors. And with soldiers, men we knew from the Stronghold who became part of the Imperial Guard. Or with people like Gev and Narjemah.'

And Tarran, his brother said.

'And Tarran, of course.'

The guard opened the door to the Mirager's Pavilion, and they continued down another passage to the Mirager's quarters.

'I'm sorry,' Temellin said. 'But they were not times to be ordinary in. Not for any of us. Your power just then – it was impressive. Even I could see it, and I don't see too much these days. And you had perfect control. That I could feel too. Is Tarran still with you?'

'Yes.'

'Well met, son.'

Well met, Father.

'Thank you for helping Arrant. People saw a true Mirager-heir just then. Someone they could look up to.'

'Is that, um, all right?' Arrant asked.

'What do you mean?'

'Well, it's not *my* power control. In a way, it seems like a deception.'

Stop fussing, said Tarran.

'I use my cabochon and my sword,' Temellin replied. 'You use Tarran as well. The method doesn't matter as long as you achieve the result. The trouble is that Tarran cannot be with you all the time, or even every time you call on him. And that could be a problem. We aren't deceiving anyone about that. They all know your power comes and goes.' He opened the door to his private apartments and gestured Arrant inside. 'Has Hellesia left some drinks for us?'

'Yes,' Arrant replied and went to pour them both some wine.

As Temellin took the goblet, he said, 'I want to ask you something. A serious question. Do you *want* to be the Mirager-heir? Or, more to the point, do you want to be Mirager once I'm dead?'

Ah, wine. That's good. Drink it up, Arrant.

Shut up, you tosspot.

He sat opposite Temellin, aware he was being offered a way out, a way of avoiding the problems that would only increase in the days to come, if he continued as the heir. A way in which he could live an ordinary life, and not have to worry himself sick about his powers being unpredictable, even deadly. Gods, how he wanted that. An uncomplicated life where he could make friends who liked him for himself, where he could one day marry whom he chose, live where he liked and how he wanted.

He opened his mouth to say, 'Can I? Can I really?' but the words that he whispered instead said something entirely different. 'What do *you* want me to do?'

'Right now I want to know how you feel about this. It's your decision. Your life. The life you have to live once I am not here to guide you. I worry about whether I am being fair to you, if you don't have cabochon and sword control.'

Once again Arrant started to say what he wanted, only to stop as the first words formed. 'No. No, it's not about me,' he said. 'It's about what is best for Kardiastan, isn't it?'

Temellin nodded. 'Yes, I'm afraid you're right,' he agreed sadly. 'It is.'

'So, um, what is best? Will it be good for Kardiastan to have a weak Mirager who can't manage his gem, nor therefore his sword, in any reliable way?'

'Do you think that Firgan will ever ask the question that you just did: "So what is best for this land?"'

Slowly, Arrant shook his head. 'No.'

'Perhaps your power will always be unpredictable,' Temellin said. 'Whereas he will be a powerful Mirager, we both know that. Magor-strong. And he will have a following. A *military*-based following too. On the other hand, people are suspicious of you, because of who your mother was, because of your history. You would not have an easy job. You would have to build a power base that was not founded on Magor strength, but on other things: decency and learning and wisdom. Not always easy. Ask your mother about that one. So, do you want to be Mirager when I am gone?'

Arrant still wanted to say no. He wanted permission to be a nobody, and it seemed he was being offered it. Perhaps, then, he would be able to forget the other things. The rain of blood and the splinters of bone shooting like darts into the ground around where he stood, all that remained of men; the kindness of Brand's smile as he died; knowing, as Temellin guided him out of the Shiver Barrens, that his father would never see again.

Yet Brand's words came back to him once more: *I have to die knowing how I have lived.* And so he heard himself say, 'If it means keeping that bastard from putting his hand to the hilt of the Mirager's sword? Yes. Gods above, *yes.*'

'Well, he really made you look a fool yesterday, didn't he?' Lesgath grinned at his eldest brother. 'You looked a real hollowhead. And I could hear Papa grinding you down to grape juice about it afterwards, too.'

Firgan wondered for a moment what the penalty would be for decapitating his brother. One of these days . . . 'The little Tyranian bastard did not use his farsense to read those Tablets. He can't control his senses well enough to see a pimple on his own backside. He'd learned the Covenant by heart, obviously. Temellin must have coached him. I'll get my own back. I've made myself a promise: he won't be so smug once he fails to be confirmed as Mirager-heir, and he certainly will never be Mirager. You just do your part, brother.'

'I'll have to, won't I? Cos you'll be off fighting battles with green slime in the Mirage.' He grinned at his brother.

'Oh, no I won't. Not all the time. It's one thing to fight Tyranian legionnaires, it's quite another when the enemy is a pile of clawed beasts in a pit of pus. I intend to stay right here in Madrinya as much as I can. I am taking charge of the training of non-Magor soldiers as well as all the senior Academy arms classes. My skills in combat need to be passed on; that is where I am of most value to Kardiastan. Father organised enough backing of Councillors to force Temellin to agree. From now on, I'm on a rotation of three months here, one in the Mirage. Most of the others have three months fighting and one month off.'

Lesgath stared at him. 'That's clever. Fighting the Ravage is probably a wasted battle anyway. One our family shouldn't be associated with. And I don't believe that the beasts are really going to come flying out on the wind like grit in a sandstorm. Do you?'

'I doubt it. Anyway, what I want you and Serenelle to do is keep needling Arrant. I want his life to be a misery. One day he will lash out, and then we'll have him.'

'How so? You mean, goad him into using his Magor power against one of us?'

'That's right.'

Lesgath frowned. 'You want to get me fried?'

'Don't be silly; we're talking about *Arrant* here. He couldn't fry a quail's egg in the sun at midday.'

'I'm not stupid, Firgan. I was at the dedication ceremony! Anyway, I heard that he lost control and sliced up a whole legion before he was old enough to wear trousers. His Magor tutor among them.'

'Exaggeration. He says his tutor died from a legionnaire spear, for a start. Lesgath, *think*. The moment he uses – or tries to use – his power against another one of the Magor, he has doomed himself. He hides his emotions pretty well, but there is one feeling I read from him all the time: frustration. He burns with it. We have to play on that. You know what they used to do to Magor who sent killing power against another one of the Magor?'

'Yeah. They cracked their cabochon so all their power leaked out. Not enough to kill them, just enough to stop them being Magor. But that hasn't happened, oh, for at least a hundred years. Not with one Magor doing it to another.'

'Exactly. Now doesn't that sound like a pleasant ending for that Tyranian lowlife? All you have to do is enrage him and make sure you have your warding ready. He won't have enough power to do any real harm. We just have to catch him trying.'

'He's not that stupid. And I'm not stupid enough to provoke him to that point.'

'All right, I'll fix it so you won't get hurt. And he will indeed be that stupid by the time we've finished with him. And we have two years, brother. We can do *a lot* in two years.'

Ligea read the scroll three or four times.

Vortexdamn it, Tyranian letters were so blasted formal, and Arrant's tutors had all been Tyranians. She had to scan it again and again to pick up the subtle nuances between the florid nature of the greetings, the coldness of the information, and the formality of the farewells.

Temellin was blind, that was a fact. But Arrant and Temellin seemed to have laid the groundwork for a good relationship, if she read the nuances correctly. Arrant hadn't learned to manage his power reliably yet. However, he had given a spectacular show at his dedication ceremony, which had bought him some respite from Magoroth criticism. He would explain all about that when he saw her next. (Damn the boy for hinting at things. She'd have to ask Temellin what he meant.) The Ravage had stopped expanding, but the battle seemed stalled, with neither side gaining the upper hand. They believed the Ravage was going to leave the Mirage and prey on Kardiastan, given the chance.

She frowned. If that was true – gods, they were in trouble. She read on. He didn't see much of Garis. All the Magor who weren't too young or too old were taking tours of duty in the Mirage. Temellin was fine.

She grunted in exasperation. Now, what the Hades did *that* mean?

'News from Madrinya?'

She'd been so engrossed in the letter, she hadn't heard Narjemah enter the room. 'Now how did you know that? It could have been some dry document on the state of Tyr's road system.'

'You always get this dreamy look when either the Mirager or Arrant writes.'

'Rubbish. The Exaltarch of Tyrans is *never* dreamy.'

Narjemah snorted. 'How is the Mirager's eyesight?'

Ligea capitulated. 'It's from Arrant.' She gave an outline of the news contained in the scroll. Narjemah crossed to her side, sombre now. She had been a Theura once, before the legions had cracked her cabochon. She knew the significance of the news.

Ligea handed her the parchment to read. And as the light breeze from the loggia stirred the curls of her hair, she remembered things she would rather have forgotten. Being submerged in a suffocating emotion so thick she could barely breathe. Being hit by hammer blows of an outpouring of malicious loathing. Being enveloped by a gaze of gleeful, cruel hunger.

She had always felt there was something horribly *human* about the Ravage. As if it were all the bad things humans could be.

She thought about those beasts moving into Madrinya. Beasts out of one's worst nightmares feeding on children in the streets . . . 'I've got to go back to Kardiastan,' she said.

Narjemah looked up from the scroll, nodding. 'When?'

'Soon,' she said and added silently, 'as soon as I can be sure Tyrans won't fall apart the moment my back is turned.' Kardiastan would need every sword they could get.

Before the next desert-season, Gevenan brought the news she had been dreading.

She was eating her evening meal with Narjemah when he plunged into the room, roaring at the guard to get out of his way. She waved away the Imperial Guardsman clutching at his arm, remarking mildly to Gevenan that he'd trained them to protect her, so it was hardly fair that he condemn them for doing just that. But the general wasn't in the mood to be amused.

'A mercenary army just invaded from Gala,' he told her. 'Fortunately I was right – they landed at Lisipo. Devros met them there. I had two legions waiting for them.'

'So why do you look as if you've eaten a crab without shelling it first?'

'They had help. That bloody idiot, the King of Janus, has sent his forces to land a second army at Ebura. Ligea, I'm sorry. But we have a proper war on our hands. This is serious. Janus has more resources than Gala. We need you.'

She stifled an impractical desire to wring Devros's neck. For a long while she didn't answer, but sifted through the implications, and with every heartbeat, she felt a further chill at the thought of another conflict. She said at last, 'Everything will depend on how much support they can garner here. The

Acanicii family that Devros married into is from Lucum. Expect trouble there. And Devros's sons have commercial interests in Burbet. They control the port and trade in much of that region. Watch for an uprising there. And they all follow the Cult of Melete. I wouldn't mind betting Antonia has raided the Cult treasuries for gold to pay the troops. She still hankers after reinstatement to the Temple on the Forum Publicum and she'd sell her soul to anyone who would promise to give it to her. Watch the paveways for priestesses on the move and search their wagons.'

'It's the slavery issue,' Gevenan said, and ran a hand over the close-crop of his grizzled hair. 'There are just too many highborn in Tyrans who won't accept your refusal to reinstate slavery. Especially those with interests in grain growing. Bloody ploughmen.'

'I won't ever go back to selling people like cattle, Gev.'

'No, I know. And I'm glad. Leave the pretty boy here in Tyr to keep things quiet' – he meant Legate Valorian – 'and come with me to Ebura. We need that bloody gem in your palm. We need you.'

She thought, despairing, 'So does Tem. And Kardiastan.'

He said, as if he'd read her mind, 'Without your power this could drag on for years. You know that. The Mirager of Kardiastan has tens of warriors with stones in their palms. We have only one. Tyrans is not ready to do without you.'

Grief swelled inside her, for she knew he was right. Peace came with a price, and you had to be prepared to pay it.

PART TWO

BROTHERS
AND
ENEMIES

CHAPTER FOURTEEN

Arrant dreamed.

There was no air. Nothing to breathe. He was struggling in thick liquid that ran into his eyes and ears and throat; a burning, stinking sludge that contaminated with its touch. He choked. Tears streamed. Skin shrivelled. He couldn't hear, but he could see: deformed shapes striking out at him with curving claws and yellowed fangs, slimy ropes of living foulness insinuating themselves through the fluid to wind around his legs, to squeeze, pressuring, then tighter, crushing. He sweated, vomited fear, struggled . . .

He reached for his father, to implore, to beg his help, his arms opening out in supplication. Temellin was there, but his eyes were unheeding and indifferent. Blind eyes. Arrant called to him: *You came once, why not now?*

The rope-beast pulled its coils still tighter.

You blinded me, his father said. *You made me useless. How can a blind man help anyone?*

Guilt. It was all his fault.

He thrashed, arms flailing, legs kicking – and woke.

He was alone on his pallet. No nightmarish creatures. No Ravage corrosion. The fine-woven sheets were twisted about his legs, the pillow was wet with sweat.

He let out the breath he had been holding and began to ease tightened muscles, one by one. The same dream, always the same dream. Only the creatures differed each time. Different beasts, but the same pain, same fear, same horror. Some foetal memory stirred to the surface by sleep? Or was it just a fertile imagination playing with stories of the past; stories of his own beginnings? He couldn't tell. All he knew was that he'd had that dream – or a variation of it – long before he could recall his mother, or Tarran for that matter, telling him of the Ravage and of how he'd suffered its horrors prior to his birth.

He unwound the sheets, stood and padded across the bare tiled floor to the open balcony shutters. It was the hour just before dawn, when light and dark vied for supremacy. Beyond the garden, the silhouette of the Madrinya skyline was sharp-edged against a pale sky, mostly adobe buildings now. In the six months since his dedication ceremony, several of the Tyranian monstrosities arrogantly blocking out the sky had been pulled down. They'd used the marble to pave the main market. Other buildings, less offensive, had survived because they'd been planted over with creepers to hide the stone walls and blend them in better with the Kardi adobe of the homes between. The Tyranian buildings around the lake edge, with the sole exception of Korden's villa, had disappeared even before he'd set eyes on the city. There, the traditional parkland and coppices along the shore had been replanted in an attempt to regain what had been lost. Young trees now added the softness of curves to the skyline silhouette.

Strange, he thought, how when he'd seen Madrinya for the first time, he'd seen it through Tyranian eyes. Now, any evidence of how it had been degraded by the Tyranian occupation tore at his heart. The city had slowly crept into his consciousness and forged the power to move him.

'Cabochon only knows why,' he thought. 'I can hardly say I've been happy here.'

Temellin was away in the Mirage most of the time, and Arrant worried about him. Ligea wrote to say Tyrans had been invaded and several parts of the land had risen in rebellion against her and the Senate. Not only did that mean she could not come to Kardiastan, but she herself was leading her legions into battle, all of which added to his burden of anxiety. He was beginning to wonder if he remembered what she looked like any more. Would she recognise him? He had grown taller, but not much broader. He was going to be like his father: slim and athletic, rather than muscular and solid. Quick and lithe, not large and strong.

But of what use was an athletic physique if his control over his powers did not improve? Even when Jahan, Jessah or Temellin were around, they rarely had the time to help him. Markess, who taught sword power classes, was sarcastic and unsympathetic.

At the Academy, the childish campaign to subject him to an endless series of minor irritations continued. His belongings would go mysteriously missing, only to be found torn, broken or dirty. A library scroll was found defaced, and he was the last person to have used it. The hilt of his practice sword was rubbed with itching powder, ink was spilled on his work scrolls, a model he was making in the geometry class apparently fell from the bench and smashed.

He thought he knew who was to blame, especially when he found out from Perradin that Lesgath now had a single room instead of sleeping in the student dormitory, supposedly because his snoring disturbed the other students, which meant he could sneak out into the classrooms at night without being detected. In public, however, Lesgath maintained a distant but polite façade, and when Arrant wanted to tackle him about the breakage of his model, Perradin warned him against doing so.

'You don't *ever* ask a Magor a direct accusatory question unless you have some tangible proof of the accusation,' he said. 'It is considered a terrible breach of good manners and an invasion of privacy. Only the Council can do that, in criminal cases, and get away with it. People would condemn you as a crass Tyranian if you did it just to have a suspicion confirmed. Nor would it get you anywhere; Lesgath would just refuse to answer and he would be in his rights to do so. It wouldn't mean anything.'

So Arrant had continued to endure the pricks and pretend he didn't mind, even when he felt like pounding Lesgath into the ground. No, he hadn't had an entirely happy time at the Academy.

He shrugged and turned towards his pallet with the intention of getting more sleep before Eris came to wake him.

You've been dreaming about the Ravage again. The comment slipped into his thoughts, unbidden. Tarran.

'Yes. How did you know?'

You get morbid. And tense. Your mind gets sort of hunched up and rigid – a bit like a constipated fisherbird standing on one leg at the lakeside. Anyway, I'm sorry that sodding bog and its ghastly tenants have been scratching around in your dreams again.

'Ah, it was just a nightmare. And what's a mere dream? Your pain is *real*.'

I survive. Thanks to you. Who knows what would happen to me if I couldn't slip away to you like this? Your mind is my sanctuary. Such as it is.

'Well, if you're going to be critical—'

I can go back to the Mirage? No thanks. Not yet. But honestly, Arrant, you should hear yourself think sometimes. So . . .

muddled. It must be because you use words so much. They are very confining, you know. Try thinking with concepts, blocks of knowledge—

'Not now, Tarran. It's far too early for intellectual discussions. I've just got up.'

Sleeping alone again?

'Of course I am! Sandhells, Tarran, I'm not even fifteen years old yet!' He turned around in a full circle, showing his brother the room.

How dull. One day I shall come when you have a girl with you on your pallet. I want to know what happens.

Arrant reddened because, although he spent a lot of time thinking about girls, there had been a distinct lack of any practical endeavours to ensure anything tangible ever happened. It didn't bother him that Tarran knew of his preoccupation, but he hated anyone knowing how slow he was to do anything about it. After all, most of his peers – of both sexes – had long since started to find themselves a steady companion of some sort, even though most may not yet have progressed to the sharing of a pallet. Even Perradin, usually half a step behind anyone else, had a girlfriend from the Theuros Academy.

That's a curious emotion! Tarran exclaimed. *What are you doing?*

'You've embarrassed me.'

It feels like that bad case of sunburn you had once. Embarrassment? That's never been an emotion I really understood.

'No, I know. Just as you don't understand privacy either, you insensitive wraith.'

How can I? he asked sensibly. *You know that I'm joined to my fellows, irrevocably. Every nuance of what I think or feel is known to them, just as I know their every thought, their every pain. Right back into the past. The closest I have ever come to*

*being alone is when I am inside your head. At least things are
very simple here.*

Arrant sighed. 'Tarran, you have a wonderfully tactful way
of putting things.'

I do my best.

'Oh, Vortexdamn, has it been very bad? Has anyone been
killed? Hurt? Father?'

There was a moment's blankness in his head, as if Tarran
had left; then a subdued reply. *Two Theuros died the day before
yesterday. A Ravage sore crumbled at the edge when they were
pulling out some beasts for slaughter. Father's fine. It's frustrating.
We don't seem to progress. The Magor kill the beasts, and more
of them spring up out of nothing.*

'As long as it doesn't get worse.'

*No, it's no worse, but no better either. Which means we don't
get any stronger and the pain is pretty bad at times.*

Old angers bubbled up. 'Damn her – she should never have
done this to you.'

*Who are you talking about now? Sarana? Ah, let's not start
that again. You know she had no choice. You should be grateful
that my mother lost the fight and yours won. Otherwise you'd
be the one battling those vile beasts and the fester they live in,
instead of me.*

'Maybe that's the way it should have been. After all, it was
my grandfather who made the bargain. It would have been a
more ... honourable solution if I'd been the one to fulfil it.'

Tarran laughed. *So what? He was my mother's uncle, and my
father's uncle, too. Anyway, I'm none too sure I understand what
this 'honour' thing is. Every time you've tried to explain it, it has
sounded rather ridiculous. Am I glad I wasn't born to a human
body! People are so – so – illogical. Why, I suppose you think I
should feel guilty too. After all, I was supposed to be the solution
to our troubles with the Ravage, yet every time I wish they'd go*

away and leave us alone, they never seem to take any *notice.* He sounded innocently puzzled.

Arrant laughed reluctantly. Tarran was right of course. The idea of Sarana calmly submitting to Pinar's madness out of a sense of honour was absurd, just as it was absurd to blame either Tarran or himself because they were not quite what they should have been.

How about going for breakfast, eh? I'm hungry.

'You don't have a stomach.'

All right, you're hungry. Anyway, isn't it time you were getting dressed? You asked me to come today because you had a test, remember?

Arrant sighed and reached for his trousers.

Next time, how about a long-legged lovely on your pallet, eh?

'What do you care about long legs?'

Believe me, I enjoy what they do to you. I've seen you look at Elvena Korden.

'Oh, shut up. Er – and thanks for coming. Magoria-markess is always looking for some excuse to fail me, even when my cabochon works and things go well.'

Daft woman. She's been twisted inside out since the legions killed her husband.

'She thinks I'm too Tyranian.'

A knock came at the door, followed by Eris entering with a ewer of warm water, the way each day began.

'Good morning, Magori,' Eris said. 'Sword skills on the agenda today, I believe. I shall lay out your combat clothes. I had those sandals of yours repaired—'

Arrant smiled and allowed the prattle to skim by, leaving only the hint of its meaning behind like a retreating wave discarding flecks of foam on a beach. Eris, and this bedroom just down the hall from Temellin's, and all the perks of being the Mirager's son, were an embarrassment to him. The other students of the Academy slept in dormitories of the school. They ate in the refectory and bathed in the communal wash-rooms. But Temellin remained adamant that Arrant stay in the Mirager's Pavilion.

'Nothing's changed. You must remain under my protection,' he said when Arrant tried to explain the ribbing he received about his preferential treatment. 'And that is the end of the discussion.'

And so another day started with Eris fussing about whether his scabbard was polished to his satisfaction. Arrant pulled a face when Eris wasn't looking and went to wash.

Don't worry, Tarran said cheerfully. *We can do this, no problem. We'll show 'em what Temellin's sons can do, even if they don't know I'm here.*

Arrant looked around the training area. The seniors had come to watch, Lesgath and the Korden twins among them. *I'd like to wipe the smirk off their faces, for a start*, he told Tarran.

The test began with a series of timed exercises. Each student, armed with their Magor sword, took their turn shooting power at an assortment of targets moving past in quick succession at varying distances and heights and speeds. Serenelle went first and had trouble with accuracy. Perradin followed, hitting most of the targets, but – in typical Perradin fashion – rather messily, because he found it difficult to limit the width of his power beam. Lesgath and his friends hooted and shouted insults until Markess glared them into silence. Bevran made a joke of his run and turned it into a performance, which pinched Markess's face into a picture of ire. There was nothing much she could say, however, because his score was excellent. Vevi, next up, was even better, achieving a perfect score just within the maximum time limit.

To Arrant's dismay, by the time his turn arrived, the audi-ence had swelled. Korden and Firgan were there; so were a number of other parents of members of the class, including Jahan. He suspected his own presence may have something to do with the number of people. There was far too much interest in his progress for his comfort, and this test was an important one. It would determine whether he would be allowed to take the class on using the Magoroth sword for combat.

When his turn came, he had no problem calling up his power, but it was clear he'd had too little practice using it. As a consequence he missed the five faster, smaller targets, and struck too deep on another. Markess glared at him, but Arrant knew he hadn't done badly enough to fail.

See? Tarran crowed happily.

'The next test is something you haven't done before,' Markess said when everyone had finished with the targets. 'There's no skill involved. However, we find it a good way to measure the strength of a Magoroth's sword power. You see those stone blocks over there? There's one for each of you. Cut yours in half, without using the edge of your blade, as quickly as you can. Arrant, you first.'

Easy, Tarran told him. *That's no bigger than a doorstep.*

I've never tried to chop a stone in half, Arrant replied, calling colour into his blade again as he approached one of the blocks. He extended the power out an arm's length beyond the blade.

Pretend the extension is the blade itself and slash down. Don't worry, it will cut like a dagger through a guava.

Arrant took his sword in both hands, and instead of trying to cut the block widthways, he slashed down at it lengthwise. *May as well make it worth watching,* he said to Tarran, knowing every eye would be on him. He had braced himself, thinking the cut would jar his wrists and arms. Instead, the beam of power sank into the stone, parting it cleanly. Hiding a pleased smile, he stepped to the side and struck another blow, to separate the stone block widthways into four equal pieces.

Just like a guava, Tarran said.

'Braggart,' Bevran muttered beside him, but he was grinning.

When Arrant looked up, it was to find himself the target of every eye. All the other students had stopped to gape at what he had done. The silence was total. Even Markess seemed speechless as she made a fluttering gesture at the other students to send them back to work at their own stones. Then, with a baffled look in Arrant's direction, she scribbled a note in his personal test ledger, and moved it to the bottom of her pile.

Watching the others as they struggled with the task, Arrant's eyes widened. *I guess that is usually quite difficult*, he said. *I didn't realise.* And Magoria-markess was furious, thinking he didn't try hard enough at other times. He couldn't win.

Indeed, she glared at him as she announced that the last part of the test was to be conducted in the saddling yard of the Academy stables.

'Any idea what this is?' Arrant asked Perradin.

He shook his head. 'She changes the tests every year.'

Once they arrived at the stables, Markess waved a hand at the six unsaddled shleths in the yard. 'You are to ward a shleth – a single animal – out of the group,' she said, 'while you yourself are riding a shleth. A more difficult task than you are used to. This will show how adaptable you are to circumstances, and how much you have really managed to learn about the building of sword wards.' She looked down at her test ledgers. 'Arrant, you're first.'

He went to walk towards the riding shleths tethered to the hitching rail, only to find a stable lad thrusting the reins of a mount into his hand. He took a moment to speak to the animal and pat its nose, but it flung up its head nervously. Warmth flared in the Quyriot necklet, and he became aware of how uncomfortable the shleth was. Something wasn't right. He turned to tell Markess, only to feel her fury with him. She was trying to suppress it, but he caught the tendrils that escaped.

'Get up and do it,' she ordered, scowling.

Harridan, Tarran muttered. *She's worse than sour plums.*

Arrant mounted and the shleth reared, a move he anticipated. *Damn. I don't know what's wrong with this beast, but something is.*

Let's get this finished quickly, then.

Right. Still struggling to keep his animal under control and grounded, Arrant scanned the six shleths. *I'm going for the old grey with the white patch on the neck,* he said. *It's a nice docile fellow.* He wasn't quite sure how he knew that. He managed to edge his mount in the right direction, and caught the eye of the grey. When it signalled which way it was going to move, he built a ward, anchoring it to the ground and the wall of the yard to cut off the animal's line of retreat. The grey sensed something and poked at the ward with a feeding arm, then looked back at Arrant in a puzzled way.

That's my beauty, Arrant thought. *You have to be the sweetest natured beast in the stable.*

Probably just ancient, with creaking joints and a slow mind, Tarran said.

Who cares, as long as it stays still. His mount reached back and tried to pinch him. He knocked the feeding arm away, but the shleth was determined and tried with its other arm. When Arrant blocked that as well, it bent its neck and nipped at him. Arrant felt under siege. The animal was unhappy and determined. He pulled it around in a tight circle, erecting another ward at the same time to stop the other shleths from joining the old grey.

Another tight circle and he managed to erect the last ward needed to keep them separate. To make sure the completed warding was obvious, he coloured it gold before slipping from his mount. He grabbed the bridle at the cheek strap to stop the agitated shleth from pulling away.

Markess nodded without smiling, but the burst of chatter and clapping from the watching crowd told him he had done well.

Brilliant, said Tarran. *Is that all you have to do for the test?*

That's it, I think. Do you have to go?

I'd better. Don't forget, a long-legged lovely. He was gone before Arrant had time to thank him.

Arrant walked his mount towards the stables. The shleth was still edgy, but had calmed a little since he had dismounted. In the stables, the stableboy offered to take over, but Arrant shook his head and unbuckled the saddle girth. He had to dodge yet another nip from the animal as he removed the saddle.

'She's not usually like that,' the stableboy said.

'Here's the reason,' Arrant replied. He'd whisked off the saddlecloth to find a handful of burrs stuck to the underside. 'That's enough to make any shleth cantankerous.'

The stableboy paled. 'Oh! I dunno how that happened. Them burrs grow in the weeds—'

'Who saddled the shleth?' Arrant asked.

'I did, M-Magori,' the boy stammered. 'It's his own saddle-cloth. We always use the same one for a mount. It's kept next to where he's tied up. I – I guess I didn't check the underside.'

'And who asked you to make sure I used this particular mount?' he asked, even as he thought, 'Gods, I'm being daft. This was accidental, surely.'

'N-no one, Magori. This one is always first, and y-you were the first s-student.'

Arrant was bewildered. Markess had chosen him to go first. But she wouldn't involve herself in a nasty prank like this. 'When did Magoria-markess tell you to do the saddling?'

'Why, just now, Magori. She sent one of the senior students across with the message. Magori-lesgath.'

Not so daft after all. 'What's your name?' he asked.

'Avarmith, Magori.'

'All right, Avarmith. You can take the animal now. Look after his back and see that he's not ridden for a few days until the irritation is healed. Pamper him.'

He walked back to the class to watch the others build their wards and observe how Markess selected the order. It was simple; the next person chosen was the one whose name was on the student ledger at the top of the pile. When that student was finished, the ledger went to the bottom. And his had been on top because he had been the first student to cut the stone block in two. Plenty of time for an observant senior student, sent to the stables on an errand, to put burrs on the saddlecloth. If for some reason, Arrant had not ridden that shleth, well, it didn't matter. If anyone found the burrs, they would deem it accidental.

He looked across the yard, and locked his gaze on Lesgath. And Lesgath stared back defiantly. 'As guilty as a hornet at the honey pot,' Arrant thought. 'I'm not going to let you get away with this, Lesgath. Not this time.'

When Lesgath went to his room that night, he found a note, scribbled on a scrap of grubby, used parchment, on his pallet. Grantel, passing by his open door, grinned and asked, 'Hey, got a girl writing you love notes, Les?'

He ignored that and opened up the note. It was badly penned over the top of a shleth feed bill, and the spelling was so poor he could hardly understand the words. When he finally deciphered it, he thought it read: *Big trouble. Had to tell about burrs. Meet me in stable at day's end. Avarmith.*

He licked dry lips. Day's end. That was what some of the

poorly educated folk called midnight, he knew that. Damn. This was from the stableboy, obviously. He swallowed, wondering who knew, fearful of what Firgan would say if he knew Lesgath had been caught. He lay back on his pallet, feeling ill. 'I'll kill that sneaking little bastard if he's told anyone,' he thought.

He felt under his pallet and drew out his dagger. He waited over an hour until he was sure everyone was asleep, then rose to dress and sneak out. He was adept at using the dark to cover his comings and goings. There were guards at the outer walls and the Academy gate, but as he never tried to leave the compound, they did not present a problem. When he reached the stableyards, he realised there were still too many people about. The stablemaster and the shlethmaster were leaning against the hitching rail, chatting. He could hear stableboys still awake in the loft of the feed store, where they slept. He had to wait. He settled down under an orange tree. After a while, he dozed.

When he jerked awake, it was to find everything in darkness, and quiet. He had no idea of the time, but he walked over to the main stable building anyway. The door was barred from the outside, so he lifted the bar and walked in, believing he would find it empty except for the shleths. He paused, waiting for his eyes to adjust to the gloom, irritated because he didn't have his sword. Students were not permitted to keep their weapons in their sleeping quarters.

As he expected, the shleths were sleeping together, cosily heaped up in the middle of the building, their feeding arms flung over one another. Hay was piled into a wooden feeder at one end of the room, and he was standing beside a long watering trough. A door at the far end led into the tackle store. He peered around, looking for the stableboy, trying to sense his presence using his cabochon. Nothing. 'Avarmith?' he whispered.

'Avarmith is not here,' Arrant's voice said from behind him. Lesgath swore. He hadn't sensed a thing.

The outside door swung shut. 'He didn't send that note; I did.' For a moment the darkness was complete, then a Magor sword glowed softly and the figure standing in front of the door was thrown into relief.

'What are you doing here?' Lesgath asked, and his mouth went dry. *Arrant's sword was working.*

'Come to teach you a lesson, you creepy little dunghill. You went too far today, Lesgath. It's one thing to spread rumours, or muck up my scrolls with ink, or melt my wax tablets. It's quite another to interfere with a mount I'm using. Quite apart from the fact that you could have endangered me, I won't stand for animals being hurt by a poisonous serpent like you.'

Lesgath smiled, his heart lifting. *No one knew, except Arrant.* He hadn't told anyone, the stupid moonling. 'So, what are you going to do about it? Use your sword on me? You'd be kicked out of the Academy.'

'Oh, no. That's just to give us some light. But I am going to give you the thrashing you deserve.'

Lesgath laughed. He was two years older and a recent growth spurt meant he was now much taller and heavier than Arrant. There was no way the Tyranian bastard would beat him in a fist fight. He waited until Arrant jammed the point of his sword into the earthen floor so his weapon remained upright, casting light in a circle, then he pounced. To his surprise, Arrant wasn't there. He'd leaped sideways, and as Lesgath floundered off balance, he was seized by the neck of his bolero and the seat of his trousers. He struggled, swinging his arm backwards, trying to hit Arrant's nose. Before he could find his target, he was unbalanced still further, as Arrant pushed his head down towards the water trough and kicked at the back of his knee. Horror dawned as he realised he was in trouble. How had the bastard done all that so *quickly*?

He grabbed at the front side of the trough and tried to lever himself upwards. He might have done it too, only Arrant kneed one of his wrists and his arm collapsed down into the water. A hard shove to the back of his head plunged his face below the surface. He spluttered and struggled and tried not to breathe. The water tasted heavily of shleth. And Arrant held him there. For one wild, despairing moment, he thought the sod was going to drown him.

Then Arrant hauled him out and threw him face down on the ground. While he was still choking, drawing air into his lungs in gasping shudders, a foot was planted on his left wrist to ensure that his cabochon was flat to the ground.

'Not bad for a lad trained by a mongrel army, eh, Lesgath? You see, when people don't have Magor power to rely on, they learn other ways to fight, and I was well taught. Don't *ever* underestimate me, or you'll end up dead.'

No sooner had he stopped speaking than the stable was plunged into darkness. Lesgath was vaguely aware that the door opened and closed, and he was left alone. For the first time in his life, he had been thoroughly humiliated, and he was having a hard time believing it.

Outside, Arrant paused to sheath his sword. He was grinning, and addressed the weapon in a whisper. 'For once, you decided to stop working at just the right moment.' And then he drew in a deep breath and set off back to the Mirager's Pavilion. In his heart, he knew this hadn't been the end of the fight; it was just the beginning.

'Temel, it's cold out here at this time of the evening. Shall I get your cloak?'

Temellin gave a faint smile. 'Mothering me again, Garis? I'm not cold.' He held up his hand, gesturing for silence. 'Listen.

They are singing for me. They know I can't see any of the things about them that are still beautiful, so they sing for me. I come here every evening to hear them.'

Garis looked around. There wasn't much to see. The Mirager was sitting on a gentle grassy slope that led down to a distant Ravage sore. Temellin's shleth grazed nearby, nervously avoiding a clump of long grass that was humming a complex melody and exuding a pleasant smell. 'Your son's way of saying goodnight?'

'Perhaps.'

'I like the smell.'

'A whole year, Garis, and all we seem to be doing is running on the same spot. And we have to battle so hard to do that. We lost another man yesterday, bitten in half by a beast.'

'I heard. Here's something to cheer you, I hope. I came out here to give it to you. It just arrived – a letter-scroll from Sarana.'

Temellin's face lit up. 'Read it to me.'

Garis opened the scroll case and started to read aloud by the light of his cabochon, blessing Sarana's reluctance to write love letters. She could have been writing to her moneymaster.

Temellin, the war here goes no better than yours, I fear. We are bogged down in snow-season rains at the moment, and snow has closed all the passes. My navy blockades Janussian ports in the hope of cutting off supplies to their invading army, and Gevenan swears he will send them packing next summer.

However, I write regarding another matter. The Ravage beasts.

I always thought they were the manifestations of abstract things, like hate and malice and greed. I saw the unpleasant side of myself in them. No, they showed me that unpleasant side. It was a nasty experience, like being brought before the gods for judgement and having to acknowledge that you are not as nice as you had fooled yourself into thinking you were. There is something very evil about them, yet there is something so human, too. And I don't mean that in a noble sense. The snide assessment in their eyes, the avaricious cunning of their smiles, the gleeful mockery of their laughter . . .

I was struck by another thought last night, hence this letter. Although we Magor can feel the presence of animals, we do not feel their emotions. That is something we can only do with humans – and the Ravage. Perhaps we should think on this.

I suggest you send Arrant to the library in Madrinya. Ask him to talk to Illuser-reftim about the books and scrolls that the Mirage Makers gave to me. They were new then, but they are copies of things so ancient they predate our nation's memories. Perhaps the answer is not in the present – but in the past.

My thoughts go with you all, as always,

Sarana

Temellin nodded his thanks, but didn't speak for so long, Garis began to wonder if he was falling asleep. Then he roused himself to say in an amused way, 'She shames me.'

Garis was startled. 'In what way?'

'I never thought to look for a non-violent solution. She's right, of course. We ought to be devoting more of our time to working out what the Ravage is and where it came from. Only when we understand it, will we know its weaknesses and how to defeat it. Send this letter to Arrant, Garis. Tell him it is my wish that he and Tarran follow her suggestion.' He scrambled to his feet and whistled to his shleth. 'Come, ride with me back to Raker's Camp. I am hungry.'

CHAPTER FIFTEEN

'Do you think that Sarana thinks the Ravage beasts were once humans?' Arrant asked Tarran, as they walked to the library.

Tarran was indignant. *And we are some kind of jailors? Trapping them inside us? I think we'd remember that, don't you?*

Arrant thought Tarran sounded unsettled and said, 'You don't much like the idea of investigating the nature of the Ravage, do you?'

Just worried what we'll find out.

'Perhaps Mirage Makers were human once.'

Tarran snorted. *Of course they weren't. Human-like, maybe.*

'You don't really know that. You don't remember back as far as your beginnings. The Magor believe you were once people who started making illusions until the illusions took on solidity and the people lost reality, until they were no more than their own creations. Hundreds of years afterwards, they clashed with Kardis who had a talent for illusion, which is when the Covenant came into being.'

So? People aren't necessarily human. For all you know, we were the clawed folk who made your necklet.

Arrant, who had not even thought of that, was fascinated. 'Is that poss—?'

No, it is not! We can't even read those runes.

'What I really don't understand is why my mother thinks these books could be helpful. After all, aren't the contents of all those texts inside your memories somewhere? If there was something useful in them, you Mirage Makers would already know it, surely.'

Tarran was slow to answer. *Your mother*, he said at last, *has an interesting, analytical mind. And one that has developed since the time we knew her in the Mirage, all those years ago. Perhaps she has fingered something that may be of import.*

'Which is?'

Humans and Mirage Makers can look at the same object, yet see two different things.

The library was a pleasant room, designed to be bright with diffused sunlight deflected inwards from outer walls white-washed with lime. The smell of old parchment, vellum and newly made reed-and-wood shelving all combined to give the place a distinctive and not-unpleasant odour, bringing back childhood memories. An Assorian moneymaster's library, if he remembered correctly, in Getria. That was the place he had first fallen in love with the idea of libraries and reading.

Reftim the librarian was a plump man, with red cheeks and a round puff-ball nose. He should have had a jovial nature to match his looks. Instead, he was a tense, fidgety man, given to long periods of silence and, Arrant suspected, guilt-ridden introspection. *I know the signs*, he said ruefully to Tarran. *Although I hope I don't look as harassed.* What the librarian had to be guilty about, though, he hadn't the faintest idea.

I shall tell you, Tarran volunteered, *afterwards.*

Good. It drives me crazy.

As he explained to Reftim why Sarana had sent him, the man gazed at a point somewhere over his shoulder. Arrant had to restrain a desire to look behind himself to see who was there. By the time he had finished explaining what he wanted, though, the librarian's eyes gleamed with the shine of a man in his element. He scurried across to a book cabinet along the wall, talking over his shoulder. 'The nature of the Ravage? I have just the text. It has always been my contention that no one pays enough attention to our literature; we can learn so much from the past.'

He opened the cabinet and ran a gloved finger along the vellum covers. 'We Kardis lost so much of our written past when the Tyranians came. Most of the valuable texts were kept in the pavilions you see, and they were burned. It was a great blessing that the Mirage Makers gave these to your – to the Miragerin-sarana. They are not at all old, of course. Books didn't exist when these were first written. They were probably recorded originally as wax tablets, then later as scrolls. It was the Assorians who had the idea of binding many scrolls inside vellum covers for their accounts ledgers. And thus the book was born.'

Arrant's eyes rolled up as Reftim chattered on, and he growled at Tarran, *Stop that!*

Well, he is a prosy old bore.

He's going to be an angry old bore if he thinks I'm being rude, Arrant said, regaining control of his eyeballs.

Reftim took a book down from its shelf and laid it reverentially on a nearby table, where he turned over pages, looking for the relevant passage. 'The book itself is the history of a man called Nadim. He was a Kardi living in the days before the Covenant, one of those whose illusive powers upset the real Mirage Makers. One of the first, in fact, to have real intellectual contact with the Mirage. The trouble is that, although the book tells an early story, we don't know who wrote it, or when it was first written down – it's very doubtful that the original writer was contemporary with Nadim himself. I suspect the language is much more modern than that. This actual volume is one of those created out of Mirage memory, given to your mother—' He blushed, mottling red and white as if Arrant had caught him ripping pages out of the library's most precious volume.

Huh? What's all that about? Arrant asked.

Tell you later, Tarran replied.

Reftim, recovering, found the correct page and added, 'We don't know if it is an accurate copy. We don't know if it is legend or history or fiction.'

Do you know this story? Arrant asked Tarran, as he read the first few lines.

Yes, of course. It's an old tale. But you read it without talking to me about it. That should be the whole idea behind this exercise: whether you can see something that we Mirage Makers don't.

Arrant nodded and began to read.

Nadim was riding between Kilsodar and Metra, two vale villages to the west of Labinya, when he came across a Mirage. In length it measured not even half a day's ride; its width was even less than its length. Nadim, in great fear and wonder, entered the place riding on his shleth, Gyrlan. Gyrlan was the most favoured of all his steeds, an animal of speed and great cunning, and friendship between man and beast was as close a brotherhood as swordblade to scabbard.

Great was the beauty of this mirage. Silver waters streaked with verdigris sparkled over stones of red and orange and gold, and the waters were filled with swimming beasts and weirdling creatures. The flowers and plants were strange indeed to Nadim's eyes, for where else would he have found, when he lay to rest beside the waters, such vines as those that caressed him, first arousing his manhood and then satisfying the longing of his arousal? Where else could he have heard maidens singing sweetness from within the flowers as he passed by? Many were the curious episodes Nadim knew then.

But all was not well within this magicked Paradise. In the beauty there lurked a Horror that not even brave Nadim had the courage to face with steadfast heart, nor yet Gyrlan, his mount, could pass with firm tread.

This Horror was a Scourge, a Sore of Evil, that ate at the heart of the Mirage's beauty, with its foulness streaming forth to corrode. And within this putrid liquid swam obscene Greed, and cynical Hypocrisy and cruel Depravity and all those things the makers of this Paradise had tried to leave behind when they remade themselves.

The Evil flowed out to surround Nadim and Gyrlan, and the creatures therein reached out to clutch and rend man and mount. Nadim slashed at them with his sword, but where he made two, both lived, and his enemies were doubled. So, when all his battling achieved naught but further trials, he mounted brave Gyrlan and put the steed with courageous heart at such a leap as will be remembered for all time. Impossible for such a spring to succeed – the Scourge was surely too wide – yet the great Gyrlan hurdled the ravaging sore even as its hideous creatures threw themselves upwards to disembowel him with their talons. They brought death to Gyrlan, but he landed his rider safely on the other side of the Sore. There his blood and entrails spilled from his belly, draining his life from him.

Deep was the grief of Nadim as he bade his steed goodbye; many were the tears he shed, ere he walked forth from that Mirage, swearing never to return to such a place, no matter how enticing its beauty. For Evil is never obliterated. It is ever with us.

Arrant looked up, to catch Reftim's eye across the room. The librarian looked away immediately to a point somewhere over Arrant's head. *Just what did he do, Tarran, that makes him so jumpy around me?*

Oh, he tried to poison Sarana once when she was imprisoned under his care. My mother put him up to it, but Sarana sensed the poison. Which was just as well, because she was pregnant with you at the time.

Arrant felt his eyes widen. *In* prison? *Ravage hells, there's a lot about my mother I don't know, isn't there?*

Heaps. Better you don't know most of it. But that's why Reftim acts so oddly around you. He's as embarrassed as a skinned wood possum – he almost murdered you before you were born.

As he thanked the librarian for his help, Arrant had trouble hiding his bemused shock.

Out in the sunshine again, he delayed returning to the Mirager's Pavilion. He found a deserted corner of the gardens of the Theuros Academy instead and sat down on the stone bench there. 'I need to think,' he told Tarran. A flock of keyet parrots appeared out of nowhere and dived into the pomegranate bushes lining the wall, from where they gazed at him in an interested way as though they expected to be fed. 'I need to pick your brains. The Mirage Makers' memory.'

Go ahead.

'The Ravage beasts eat the Mirage, and multiply. The Ravage sores erode away at you and grow in size. What sustains you, the Mirage Makers?'

Our power. Which comes, ultimately, from the same places yours does. From the sun, from the spinning of the earth, and the pull of the world and the moon.

'*Really*? That sounds, well, *bizarre*. The moon *pulls* us? Pulls us where? And if the world spins, why don't we all go flying off it? Or get dizzy or something?'

No idea. We just feel the power and feed off it; we don't understand how it works. From his tone, Arrant guessed he didn't much care, either, and didn't understand why Arrant asked.

'Ah. Right. I'll accept that. And let's accept, too, that Mirage Makers started out, er, human-like. Their creativity and artistry became the Mirage. Their sense of humour became the Mirage's eccentricities—'

Eccentricities? Tarran was indignant. *We are* not *eccentric! You* are *the ones who are odd.*

'Be quiet and listen. More unpleasant human-like traits had no place in the beauty of the Mirage. So they were encapsulated and ignored. The Mirage Makers strove to build only on the beauty and the good things about themselves.'

Shiver the sands! You are saying we created the Ravage? From ourselves? *We have no memory of doing that.*

'Well, that's what the writer of the Nadim story implied. "All those things the makers of this Paradise had tried to leave behind when they remade themselves." Is it possible?'

Tarran's confusion was a background whisper in Arrant's mind. *Our memories are hazy. Our recollection of once being separate beings is there, but it is so – so* vague. *None of the others can ever remember having a name, for example. In fact, to them, to be a separate individual would be their idea of, well, Hades, I suppose. They don't understand how I can stand being with just one entity – you. The idea appals them. When I first visited you, they were always trying to drag me back to them, thinking I would go moondaft in your head.* He paused. *With some justification.*

Arrant snorted. 'You still have all your human traits, that's for sure. Rudeness and lack of tact included.'

Tarran ignored that. *Go on with your theory.*

'Well, how about this: for years the Mirage Makers managed to keep their own evil encapsulated, restrained. Maybe the fluid of the Ravage is the putrescence exuded by the beasts as a suitable medium to live in. But something went wrong. The Ravage started to spread, to multiply . . . why? Probably because as the Mirage Makers grew older they also grew weaker?'

Tarran snorted. *Even if it's true – how does it help? What good is it to know that we are being killed by the remnants of our own failings? And what about the most obvious hole in your theory?*

'And what's that?'

Why would the remains of our failings want to destroy us? They wouldn't get any benefit from killing us. In fact, they wouldn't have a place to live in.

'That applies to the Ravage beasts no matter what they are,' Arrant pointed out. 'They are killing you, and in the long run that kills them too because they don't seem very good at suriving out of a Ravage sore.' There were several reports now of Ravage beasts being found in vales bordering the Mirage. They had even killed Valemen, but all of the beasts had died in the end. He paused to think, then added, 'Perhaps they are not accidentally swept up by the winds. Maybe they think it's the only way they will survive, one final desperate attempt to escape dying along with you. They are wrong, fortunately.'

So far, Tarran said, the words grim in Arrant's mind. *None of this makes sense, you know.*

He was right. It didn't.

As always, Arrant walked to class along the laneway between the Mirager's Pavilion and the Magoroth Academy, a short, uninteresting walk, boxed in by a solid gate at either end and walls too high to see over in between.

That morning he was deep in thought. He'd just realised, to his bemusement, that he had forgotten his fifteenth anniversary day. It had passed unremarked several days earlier, even though Temellin happened to be back in Madrinya. When people were fighting wars and risking their lives, he thought wryly, when a country was losing its warriors to creatures that ate them when they lost, a fifteenth anniversary meant nothing at all.

The sound of the gate being opened roused him from his

reverie. As he normally had the lane to himself at that hour in the morning, he looked up, startled, to see Lesgath, Serenelle and their twin siblings, Ryval and Myssa, entering the lane from the Academy. He stopped dead and waited for them to walk up to him.

'What are you all doing here?' he asked.

'Come to talk to you,' Ryval said. 'We've been patient, Arrant, but we're running out of patience. Serenelle tells us you still don't have good control over your power.'

'You've been attending the Academy for over a year, and it seems you haven't improved at all,' Lesgath added.

'We don't want to have a Mirager-heir we can't trust,' Myssa said, coming to stand immediately in front of him, with her hands on her hips. 'It's bad enough having a blind Mirager who can't win a war against a pack of animals after even a year of fighting, but to think his successor is going to be even more of a lame lizard . . .' She grabbed Arrant's left hand, to turn the palm upwards. His cabochon was quiescent and colourless in his palm. She shook her head sorrowfully. 'Look at that. We want you to tell the Mirager you don't want to be heir any more.'

'You'll get your chance to say what you think when it comes to a Council vote,' Arrant said. He tried to push his way past Myssa but the alley was narrow and Ryval and Lesgath came and stood on either side. Serenelle hung back. Arrant shot her a contemptuous look. She was always tagging along, never quite participating. Never quite showing approval of her family's point of view – or disapproval either, for that matter. More like a crow waiting to pick up the pieces, after the dogs finished fighting over the carcass. *Hells, why was he thinking about that now?*

There were four of them, three of them bigger and older than he was.

'Going somewhere, Arrogant?' Myssa asked, reaching out to pull the tie from his hair. She tossed it on to Lesgath, who fumbled the catch.

'Oops. Sorry. Dropped it,' Lesgath said, smirking.

Arrant didn't answer. And he certainly wasn't going to pick up the discarded leather thong and put himself in a vulnerable position by bending over. 'I think he might be thinking of going to our combat class,' Lesgath said.

'*Your* combat class?' Ryval asked, feigning incredulity. 'Surely not. Your class is for the Magoroth, not for a bum-licking sonofabitch.'

'Son of a Tyranian bitch at that,' Lesgath chortled as Arrant tried to sidestep around them.

Arrant scowled. Bastards, the Vortexdamned bastards. They weren't trying to hide their emotions and their mockery was as sour as a drunkard's breath.

'We used to kill Tyranians once,' Lesgath said, barring Arrant's way yet again as he tried to pass. The youth's fury loomed, full of hatred. He put his hand flat to Arrant's chest and pushed him back. 'Pity we can't do it with this puny little one. But he hangs around his father's trouser legs.'

'Never mind, his papa isn't going to *see* anything, that's for sure,' Myssa said with a high-pitched giggle.

Arrant felt his anger rise like a swelling wave. Gods, don't let him lose his temper. That's what they wanted . . . He said evenly, 'What's the matter, Lesgath? Upset by your dip in the shleth trough? It was no more than you deserved. Taken you a while to plan your little revenge, though, hasn't it? And I see you had to bring along your big brother and sister too.'

'You listen to me, you runty little maggot,' Lesgath said, coming closer and breathing into Arrant's face. 'How *dare* you come here, swaggering like a legionnaire, when you can't even colour up your cabochon! Go back to your mama's skirts and get her to teach you to pee straight before you dream of being Mirager-heir.'

Arrant raised an eyebrow. 'Did you have your eyes closed the day of the last testing, Lesgath? Didn't you even *notice* that I did better than your own sister in the sword power tests? Your father and Firgan noticed, I'm sure.'

Lesgath's anger mounted. 'We'll see you lick Korden family arse before we'll see Council support you.' He looked across at Ryval. 'How about it, brother? Why don't we get papa's precious darling to show us the respect a Tyranian lowborn should give to a true Magoroth?'

Arrant tried to push past them again, but they moved as one to block his way. Too late he realised this was not just a haphazard piece of name calling; they had planned this. Myssa and Ryval grabbed an arm each. Lesgath spun around, loosening his cloth belt and pulling his trousers down. He looked back over his shoulder as he bent to present the twin moons of his bare buttocks. 'Go on,' he said, 'lick 'em!'

Arrant went berserk. He pulled and kicked and pushed. He landed a punch into the softness of Myssa's stomach, and the girl doubled up. Then Ryval grabbed him from behind and twisted his arm violently up behind his back. Arrant stamped hard on his instep. Ryval yelped but didn't let go. Arrant was forced to bend forward or risk a broken bone. Myssa, still grunting in pain, grabbed Arrant's right leg from under him and pulled it backwards. Helpless, he had to hop on one foot to stop pitching forward.

Merciless, Ryval rammed his head face downwards against Lesgath's buttocks.

'Lick 'em!' he snarled.

Waves of anger roared through Arrant's ears like thundering surf. He called on his power, he scoured his body for it, dredged into the deepest veins of his being for some way to bring it forth. Memory tore through him – *Brand being beaten, his own searching for power to save him, his cabochon nothing but an empty promise* . . .

Ryval ground his face into the smooth skin of Lesgath's backside until he had to open his mouth to breathe. They laughed – laughed so much they couldn't hold him any more. Suddenly released, he fell to the ground. Ryval and Myssa ran down the alley, still doubled up with laughter. Lesgath pulled up his trousers as he followed. Serenelle leaned her back against the adobe of the wall and watched them disappear through the Academy gate before switching her attention back to Arrant. She lowered her chin and gazed at him from under her lashes, her expression scornful. 'You know what? You sprouts really are pathetic. Like scorpions flexing their tails before battle, until one scurries away to hide.'

He took several deep breaths before he spoke. 'Oh, shut up, Serenelle. I've had it with your family.'

'You should be nice to me. I'm your only ally among the Kordens.' She pushed herself away from the wall, picked up the leather thong for his hair and passed it to him. As their hands touched, she ran the tip of her tongue slowly around her parted lips.

He stared at her and took another deep breath to steady himself. 'You're all crazy, d'you know that?'

'I'm not. I'm the only sane one in this family, with the possible exception of Papa, who is just purblind. They are going to get you, you know, Arrant. You haven't a chance. You're the scorpion without a sting who can't find a hole to hide in. The only thing you don't know is when the predator will strike.'

'And you enjoy the watching. That's *sick*.'

She smiled and shrugged. 'So what? And what will you do now? Go home to lick your wounds – or turn up at class?' She didn't wait for an answer, but walked down the lane after the others. He watched, unable to look away. He couldn't help himself even though he knew she revelled in his interest. She was so Vortexdamned sensual.

He dusted down his clothing and walked after her, trying not to remember the feel of Lesgath's buttocks in his face, nor to recall the feeling of utter helplessness. How could he have let them do that?

'How could I have stopped them?' he pondered miserably. Called on Tarran? Brought him all the way from the Mirage to put an end to a stupid bit of bullying? 'I have to stand on my own feet, win my own battles. That's what it means to be Mirager-heir, damn it.'

'Being late is arrogance, boy,' Theuri-yetemith said. 'A way of saying you think yourself superior to those you keep waiting. Remember that.'

'My apologies, Theuri,' Arrant replied politely.

The man looked him up and down in disgust. 'You are a sight, Arrant! You should be ashamed of yourself. You look unwashed, and why isn't your hair tied back? Since when do we come to a combat class with our hair blowing around our faces?'

'I'll fix it,' he said.

The expression of distaste on Yetemith's face deepened. 'Go and stow your sword and get your practice weapon,' he snapped, and turned back to the rest of the class. 'And what are all you lot doing, standing around like a mob of shleths? Get back to it! Left lunge! Quickly now . . .'

''Ware,' Perradin murmured behind Arrant as he turned to obey. 'Firgan's there, in the armoury.'

Arrant nodded and started towards the building. Even when teaching the class, Firgan usually ignored Arrant to the point of rudeness, but nonetheless Arrant would rather not have to come face to face with him.

He frowned as he walked. He didn't like the smell of what was happening. First Lesgath and the twins, and now Firgan. 'And less than a year to stop me being confirmed as Mirager-heir,' he thought. The Kordens were stepping up the pressure.

The door to the single room of the armoury was on the side facing away from the practice yard. Arrant was acutely aware that no one could see inside from the yard, so he did not enter immediately after opening the door. He stood in the doorway, as if waiting for his eyes to adjust to the gloom. Firgan was leaning against one of the weapon racks, a Magor sword held by the hilt in his left hand. He looked up, smiling.

'Well, well, on Yetemith's bad-boy list, are we, Arrant?' Firgan asked. 'Naughty, naughty.'

Using his far-sense to listen, the bastard. Arrant didn't answer. He passed by the Magori to the rack that bore his name, where he took his practice sword from its slot and replaced it with his Magor sword. He turned to leave, but as he passed in front of Firgan once more, his gaze alighted on an empty space in the rack in front of him. Perradin's space. His Magoroth sword should have been there.

Shock rippled through him, sending his thoughts racing. He whirled, to stare at Firgan. To realise the sword in Firgan's hand did not belong to the man; he wore that at his hip still. As if to confirm his suspicion, Firgan leaned across and put the sword he held into Perradin's slot.

Arrant leaped to take up his own sword again. Firgan moved just as fast to block him with his bulk. Arrant ran into him, chest to chest, and had to step back. Shaking, he stared at Firgan. The man was large and solid; all muscle and sinew. A thirty-year-old soldier with combat experience. He could easily have picked Arrant up and flung him across the room, had he wanted. And he stood between Arrant and his Magor sword.

'So, boy,' Firgan said softly, 'what are you going to do about it?'

'Don't you *dare*,' Arrant snarled. He was more than furious; he was frightened. If Firgan placed his cabochon into the hollow on the hilt of Arrant's sword, Arrant could never use it against him. Not only would it not hurt Firgan, but Arrant could end up dead if he tried. 'I shall tell the world,' he added, but the warning sounded hollow to his ears.

Although it was considered the gravest insult possible between two Magoroth, to fit your cabochon into the hilt of someone else's sword was not against the law. Anathema perhaps, but who would blame Firgan if he wanted to protect himself against the unpredictable magic of one of his pupils? Yet as Arrant thought of his sword – with or without its magic – becoming useless as a weapon against Firgan, he went cold all over.

'Sweet goddess,' he thought, 'the bastard probably put his hand to the hilt of every sword in this room.'

'And who will believe you?' Firgan asked reasonably. 'I am a highly respected Magoroth, a seasoned warrior and a hero of the rebellion. You are a poor excuse for a Magor, Tyranian by upbringing for all your claim to good bloodlines, a weak, pathetic boy who just kissed the buttocks of my little brother and therefore hates the whole Korden family and is willing to tell any lie to discredit the man who would be the next Mirager. Everyone knows your accursed Tyranian bitch of a dam had the ability to tell lies and make them believable, and therefore they won't trust what comes from your mouth.'

'That's a filthy lie. You should honour her for all she has done for Kardiastan and the Magor.' Beneath his breath, he swore, thinking, 'This really was planned. All of it. The Hades-bound bastards.' He doubted any member of the Korden family was going to admit openly that they had made the Mirager-heir kiss Lesgath's backside, so the whole episode was probably just to undermine his confidence. They were relying on him being too ashamed to tell anyone what had happened – and they were right.

But this, this was more serious. He had to stop Firgan. Yet how? What could he do? His cabochon was quiescent. And if he called on Tarran, and Tarran was free to come, what then? It was a crime to use power against another Magor. Nor could he use the practice sword he clutched in his hand; the idea of fighting Firgan with a wooden sword was ludicrous.

Shout for help: it was the only thing that came to mind. He opened his mouth to cry out. And Firgan was there before him, anticipating. He hooked his heel behind Arrant's knee and brought him down to the floor, flat on his back. Breath whooshed out. His head rang. Before he could recover, Firgan created a ward that anchored him to the floor, part of it pulled tight across his mouth so he couldn't speak. Couldn't move. Could hardly breathe.

Firgan stepped away, out of Arrant's range of vision. When he returned, he was holding Arrant's sword, his left hand nestling into the hilt, his cabochon slipped into the hollow. 'So much for your Magoroth sword,' he said. 'Not that it was ever likely you'd have been able to hurt me with it, anyway. But with unpredictable power, one never knows, does one? Better for me to be sure.'

He walked away again to replace the sword. From the sounds, Arrant thought he might have picked up several other blades as well, but he couldn't see. When Firgan came back into sight, he casually stepped over Arrant on his way to the door, his smile dimpling a cheek as he passed. The light dimmed as he stepped through and half-closed the door behind him. Arrant heard him calling Yetemith from just outside, asking the teacher if he could speak to him. His bitterness raged as he struggled against the ward. In desperation, he tried to drum his heels, anything to make a noise. But the floor of the armoury was hard-packed earth, and his struggles made little sound.

There was a pause, then Firgan spoke again, the words pitched perfectly for Arrant to hear even without enhancing his hearing. 'Theuri, I apologise for interrupting you, but I have a small problem – a matter of that silly boy Arrant, and Serenelle. He – Oh, never mind. No real harm done. But Arrant being the Mirager's son, I would like to deal with it, in my own way, just confining it to the children, you understand. Anyway, I hope you will forgive me for keeping Arrant for a moment longer. The boy is in need of some advice, I think. And could you send Lesgath to me for a minute as well?'

'Oh course. Take as long as you wish. I am a great believer in pinching off bad behaviour at the root the moment it sprouts.'

Arrant's spirits plunged even lower. Was that what all this about – starting a rumour using innuendo? Planting an idea without ever really saying anything? Discrediting him in a way that could never be challenged, because nothing had ever actually been said. Clever. If people thought the Kordens bullied him, they might be sympathetic towards him, if a little contemptuous. But if he was thought to be making a nuisance of himself with Serenelle, then people would condemn him outright.

Yetemith went back to the class; Arrant felt him go. Which meant his cabochon must be working. Good.

Tarran?

No reply. His power was being obliging on its own for once.

Firgan returned, closing the door behind him. 'See?' he asked. 'And not a single lie uttered. Easy when you know how. Yetemith has just gone away imagining the worst. I shall repeat an even better tale within the hearing of a few non-Magor servants who can't tell the truth from a heap of lies, and you'll be surprised how quickly the story develops.' He heaved a sigh and shook his head with mock sadness. 'Arrant, Arrant, why don't you just give up now, gracefully? I am sure in your heart, you know that you shouldn't be the Mirager-heir anyway. We've given you well over a year to prove yourself, and nothing's happened. If you are wise, you will go to your father and tell him that you wish to relinquish the position of heir. Otherwise you will have to face some remarkably unpleasant consequences.'

Arrant didn't answer. He couldn't, even if he'd wanted to.

The power in his cabochon spluttered ineffectually. The door opened and Lesgath entered. He came and looked down at Arrant. 'Interesting,' he said in approval. He glanced at his brother. 'What are you going to do – stick a sword through his middle?'

'Nothing so crass. No, I just want you protected. Go put your hand into the hilt of his sword over there in the rack, that's all.'

Lesgath laughed. 'Gladly. Now why didn't I think of that?' He slipped out of Arrant's sight, only to return a second or two later waving a Magoroth sword. 'Yours, I believe?' he asked, swishing it under Arrant's nose before returning it to its rack. 'Can I do that with them all?'

'No, of course not. These belong to your Magor sparring partners, you idiot. Someone in the class would soon realise something was the matter if none of their sword magic ever worked when they tried it on Lesgath. With Arrogant here, it doesn't matter; no one expects his magic to work. Oh, and don't tell anyone about this, right? No one. Not even those friends of yours. This is our little secret – yours, mine and Arrogant's here. Now get back to class.'

Lesgath grinned one more time at Arrant and left. Firgan was out of Arrant's line of vision again, and he couldn't be certain what the man was doing, but it wasn't long before he came back to stare down at Arrant once more.

'I am now going to release the warding,' he said. 'Think before you do anything foolish, eh? I am giving you a chance to get out of this with a modicum of pride. Just go to your father and tell him you don't want to be Mirager-heir, because you know you can't walk in his sandals. Do that, and I promise I will never bother you again. I'll even call the rest of the family off. Life would be much more pleasant for you then, wouldn't it? Oh, and by the way, I wouldn't tell anyone about this, either, if I were you. You will only end up looking a fool and no one will believe you.'

The warding vanished. 'No, wait a moment. Perhaps you should tell everyone.' Firgan grinned. 'I think I like the idea of you making a fool of yourself.'

Arrant scrambled to his feet. He took a moment to retie his hair before he bent to pick up his practice sword. 'Perhaps it *would* be better if I never became Mirager,' he said, surprised to find how steady his voice sounded. 'But let *me* tell *you* something, Firgan. I'll see you dead before I let you step into my sandals as Mirager-heir.' He spun on his heel, opened the door and stepped through into the sunlight, without looking back.

As he walked across the practice yard to join the other students, he felt every eye on him. Emotions eddied around and his cabochon obligingly told him what they were. Intense curiosity. Speculation. They guessed Arrant was in trouble and they wanted to know why. Firgan had ploughed the ground, preparing it for the seeds of rumour about to drop, and Arrant doubted there was anything he could do to stop it taking root. Damn his blasted cabochon: why did it work when he didn't want it to?

CHAPTER SIXTEEN

Immediately Yetemith's class was finished, Arrant went to meet his father, glad that the Mirager was in Madrinya. He had no intention of hiding what had happened from Temellin, and he wasn't sure why Firgan thought he might. 'He thinks he knows me,' Arrant muttered under his breath, 'but he doesn't really.' He paused at the doorway to Temellin's rooms, taking comfort from that thought as he braced himself for the conversation ahead.

His father had come to love those rooms, bright with sunlight most of the year, filled with the smell of lemon and orange blossom in the early warmth of the desert-season, or the ripe tang of the fruit as the weather changed. Hellesia, noting this, had arranged for the planting of honeysuckle, climbing jasmine and moonflower vines along the stone walls of the garden.

Fountains were built into the walls of the study, Tyranian-style, and the trickle of running water was now a constant sound. Most Magor who visited him there thought it a foreign affectation, wasteful of water, and condemned the expense. Others, more tolerant, said a man without good eyesight should be allowed an affectation or two; it'd give him something pleasant to hear, at least. Only Arrant, Garis and Temellin knew the real reason; the constant sound of trickling water made it difficult for anyone outside to far-sense conversations within the room. Most of the Magor would not even have recognised that there was a need for such precautions; the taboo against using the senses to eavesdrop was so strong they would never have considered it. His father, however, no longer trusted all of the Magoroth.

To Arrant, everything in the apartment was evocative of things he'd rather forget. The scents reminded him that his father had to be content with senses other than sight; the fountains were a reminder that there were people who worked against the Mirager, some believing his blindness rendered him ineffective, and others who thought his love for his son blinded him to the future needs of Kardiastan. His father's attachment to the rooms was a testament to the way the Mirager's life had shrunk since he had lost his sight. In spite of his forays to the Mirage, a once-vibrant, active man was now far more introspective and sedentary than he had ever been before.

As he entered the room Arrant knew he must have been broadcasting his emotional turmoil because the other two people present, Jahan and Jessah, exchanged startled glances, and Jessah asked, 'Would you like Jahan and me to leave?'

'No, you had all better hear this,' Arrant replied. He took a deep breath and outlined what they needed to know in a rush of words. 'Firgan was in the armoury today. He as good as told me he's going to start a rumour about me upsetting Serenelle with my supposed misbehaviour. Worse, he put his hand to the hilt of my Magor sword. Mine and Perry's. Possibly them all. He then called in Lesgath, who took up my sword, too.'

Their anger was an immediate blast across the room: solid and hot. Jahan's frown was thunderous. 'Perry's too? I'll *kill* the bastard.'

Temellin's hand dropped to the hilt of his own weapon in an instinctive gesture of rage, but other than that he did not move. When he spoke, it was with quiet puzzlement. 'I don't quite understand. Why would Firgan let you *know* he held your sword?'

'A warning?' Jahan suggested. 'A way of saying, "Don't attack us, Arrant, or you'll be the one to die. Your sword power will turn against you, not us."'

'Decent of him, wasn't it,' Temellin remarked, his tone dry. 'And it's also telling Arrant that he is defenceless against Firgan and Lesgath if he relies on his Magor sword. It's telling him that no ward built using his sword will stop those two Korden brothers. It's telling him that Perry won't be able to help.' He shook his head, mystified. 'If Firgan wants Arrant to give up the idea of being Mirager-heir, he has to do better than this. We are missing something.'

'You could ask him if he put his hand to the lads' swords,' Jessah suggested tentatively. 'If he tells the truth, he looks bad. If he lies, everyone will know.'

'He would be under no compulsion to reply,' Temellin said. 'Or he could answer, saying that as a combat teacher, he was merely protecting himself from an unpredictable student. Many wouldn't condemn him for that.'

'He might find it harder to think of an excuse for holding Perry's sword,' Arrant said.

Jahan swore just thinking about it. Temellin considered. 'I could call both Yetemith and Firgan in here, and order them never to pair you or Perradin with Lesgath for Magor combat. I'm not sure that's wise, though.'

'Why not?' Jahan demanded.

'Because it would be a public insult to members of the Korden family. It's like saying they are planning to hurt Arrant. Remember, our aim is to get Arrant confirmed as Mirager-heir. To do that, we need to show him to be a worthy leader. Banning him from training with any of the Kordens, for whatever reason, will rebound to Arrant's discredit. I think we should do what

Firgan least expects. Arrant, tell all your closest friends what happened, in strictest confidence, of course. Ask your children to do the same, Jahan.'

'Oh, for goodness sake, you don't expect they will keep it a secret, surely?' Jessah said.

'Of course not. Everyone will know in a day or two, but it will be hard for Firgan to fight, because no one will openly accuse him. However, if the Korden offspring know everyone is aware of the situation, it will make it hard for any of them to stage an accident without implicating themselves. If anyone other than your close friends asks you directly what happened, Arrant, just say that you'd rather not talk about it as it reflects badly on one of the Magoroth. Refuse to be drawn. That way you will earn respect.'

'You don't think Korden himself had anything to do with this?' Jahan asked.

Temellin hesitated. 'No, I don't think so. He may want his son in Arrant's place, but this doesn't fit with what he would consider honourable.'

Jessah snorted.

'I can't understand why Firgan let you know what he'd done,' Temellin added to Arrant, 'so my advice is this: walk away from confrontation.'

'I've seen him in the library several times lately,' Jessah said. 'And he doesn't strike me as the kind of man who reads for pleasure.'

Temellin looked thoughtful. 'No, but he is a man who under-stands the value of research. He studied the history of Tyranian campaigns in order to learn their battle techniques. He put that knowledge to good effect during the war. Jessah, go to Illuser-reftim and find out from him — tactfully — what Firgan was researching. In the meantime, I want you to act as Arrant's personal guard.'

'Skies, Papa, the other students would never cease teasing me. Forgive me, Magoria, I don't mean to be rude. But, Papa, she's your *scribe*.'

'Your son has to show his own courage,' Jahan agreed, 'otherwise he'll never be able to lead this nation, or the Magor. You can't send him off to the Academy every day with his best friend's mother.'

Temellin struggled with himself. For a brief moment, Arrant felt his frustration, his fierce resentment of his disability and the restrictions it imposed on him.

'They're right,' Arrant said quietly. 'This is a battle I have to fight alone.'

Temellin conquered his feelings and shut down his emotions. 'Very well. But I'm going to get Garis here. I am due to leave for the Mirage again and I want you to have a Magoroth guard I can trust and one which won't be an embarrassment to you. Garis has done too long a stint of duty in the Mirage anyway. He's due to be rested and see a bit of his daughter. She can come with him.'

Arrant nodded, and his spirits brightened. To see Garis again . . . and Samia, of course.

'In the meantime, if anything worries you, bring it to Jessah immediately. And now, I want a private word with you. Jahan, Jessah—?'

He waited until they had gone before continuing. 'We have less than a year in which to decide whether to put your name forward to the Council for your official endorsement as Mirager-heir.'

Arrant murmured his assent.

'You have passed all your exams so far. And you have impressed many of the Magoroth. That day you swore to uphold the Covenant and your power bathed the whole antechamber in light – none of us had ever seen that before. I hear your building of wards for Markess's test was masterful, the cutting of the stone was almost frightening. However, Yetemith and Markess have formed an alliance against you. They are constantly recounting, in public, your failures. Arrant, I will be quite frank with you. It will be difficult for me to endorse your confirmation myself unless we can be sure that you will have enough power to bestow cabochons in the future, without Tarran's presence. Of course, that problem may become redundant if the Mirage Makers all die and my successor never receives a Mirager's sword, but at the moment it still has to be the main criterion.'

Even though he'd known the words were coming, Arrant winced. 'Nothing has changed,' he admitted, the honesty painful. 'Sometimes my cabochon works just as it should, sometimes it doesn't, and I can't predict it. Nor has it improved much since I started at the Academy. I've never lost control again, the way I did when I was nine. That – that was what I used to worry about most, but I think it happened because Tarran left me too suddenly for me to cope with the power I had called up when he was there.' He swallowed. 'If I had a Mirager's sword, and could dictate just *when* to bestow a cabochon to coincide with when I had power, then I think I could do it.' *I can be a Mirager, even without you, Tarran*, he said, even though he knew his brother wasn't there to hear the words. *I can. But, oh, Tarran – I'd rather it was with you.*

The smile that lit up his father's face was one of pride, and yet it made the ache in Arrant's heart all the larger. Because neither of them could be sure there would ever be another Mirager's sword.

He might be a Mirager one day, yet have no way to bestow a cabochon on a newborn child.

Jessah would have liked to spend more of her time in the library. She loved poking about among the scrolls and books, even though the librarian, Illuser-reftim, with his fussy ways inevitably made any user feel like an interloper in his domain. Everyone who entered had to use silk gloves before being allowed to touch anything. He would then hover at the reader's shoulder, ready with advice on how to handle the scrolls or books, or to scold them if they dared to turn a page too roughly.

'They are our legacy from the Mirage Makers,' he was fond of saying. 'They are our history, the records of our past and they point us to our future.' His days were spent cataloguing every single paper and book and scroll – a seemingly endless job, because he'd been at it ever since the library had been re-established in the pavilions, and he still wasn't finished.

This time, though, Jessah was not there to browse. 'Illuser-reftim,' she said cheerfully, 'I wonder if I could have a moment of your time. I have a question to ask.'

Reftim looked up from his labours and laid his stylus down. 'Of course, Magoria. That is what a librarian is for, you know. To seek out the answers to our questions.' He waved a hand at the shelves and scroll racks. 'There lies much of the knowledge of the known world. Did you know that we just received a shipment of copied Assorian histories? Seven scrolls, each as long as this room. The Council approved the purchase after the Mirager's recommendation.' His smile was beatific.

'I'm glad. But wherever did you learn to read Assorian?'

His face fell. 'I can't. I'm wondering if the Council would approve us hiring an Assorian scholar for a year to provide a translation. Do you think—?'

'Well, you could ask, I suppose. Reftim, the Mirager wants to know what Magori-firgan has been doing in the library lately.'

'Oh. Well, reading.'

'Reading what?'

'I don't know whether I should answer that. I mean, it's his business, really . . .'

Jessah arched an eyebrow. 'The Mirager wants to know, Reftim.'

He didn't reply, but said instead, 'They say Firgan wants to be Mirager-heir. Is that true?'

'Yes. Instead of Arrant. You were his mother's guard back in Mirage City, weren't you?'

He flushed a deep red and she had no idea why, but the question prompted him into an answer. 'Magori-firgan was reading some of the books on using Magor swords in combat. There was nothing strange in his request, Magoria. He is training warriors. Wisely, he decided to do some reading on the theory.'

'Do you know which books?'

'Of course. All that I could find on the subject. There were seven or eight of them.'

'Oh. Do you think he found what he was looking for?'

'I was unaware he was looking for anything in particular. He told me he had a general interest. He was careful with the volumes, so I left him on his own.'

Jessah nodded. Reftim oozed honesty. He had seen nothing strange in Firgan's behaviour. She thanked the librarian, and left him to his cataloguing. As she walked back to the Mirager's Pavilion, she knew she ought to have felt reassured, but she didn't.

She was frightened.

Arrant hated saying goodbye to his father. Every time the Mirager rode off, he had a sick feeling in his stomach that he might not come back. When Temellin left for the Mirage at dawn one morning, with the promise that he would send Garis to Madrinya, Arrant went straight to the Academy practice yard early. He felt in need of lashing out at someone, and the straw-stuffed target in the yard seemed to offer the safest alternative.

To his dismay, after he had been practising for a while,

Serenelle arrived. He didn't bother to hide his scowl. He was fed up with the Korden family. She crossed the yard towards him and it was all he could do not to turn away and leave. Or bite her head off.

'You're up early,' he said instead.

'I wanted to see you. I was hoping you'd come early. I've tried to have a word with you for a couple of days, and you always dodge me. That's not very polite.'

'*Polite*? When has your family ever been polite to me? So, what's the plan this time, Serenelle? Another spot of nastiness disguised as Korden humour?'

She snorted. 'Get it out of your head that I involve myself with my brothers and sisters, Arrant.'

'Oh? Yet I seem to remember you watching when the twins pushed my face into Lesgath's rear end.'

'I didn't know they were going to do that. And do you think I *like* having my name bandied about, everyone believing I was somehow molested by you or whatever it is you are supposed to have done? And incapable of protecting myself from *you*? I've heard at least four different versions of what supposedly took place.' She tossed her head. 'Those idiot brothers of mine have less sense than a shleth embryo. They certainly didn't consult me first.'

'Which brothers are we talking about here?'

'Lesgath and Ryval, of course. Who else?'

'Firgan, of course. Who else?'

'Ah.' She put her head on one side, her eyes narrowing. 'Maybe you're not as dumb as you always seem to be.'

He gritted his teeth. 'Is that supposed to be a compliment?' He regarded her dubiously. This had to be another trick.

'Arrant, they mean you harm, you know. All of them. Even Papa, in his own more civilised way. Firgan's behind it, you're right. He will do anything to stop your official confirmation.'

'What are they planning?'

'I don't know. They don't tell me.'

Frustrated, he wondered if she was risking telling him a lie because she guessed he wouldn't recognise it as such. 'Sands,' he thought, 'it must be so easy for other Magor, always able to sense an untruth. How can I be the Mirager if I'll never be able to do that? It makes things so much more difficult.'

'Just watch out. I don't think Firgan will care too much if you end up dead, as long as he isn't blamed.'

He was still suspicious. 'Why are you telling me this?' Maybe the others had just sent her to scare him into deciding he didn't want to be Mirager-heir.

'I don't like being used. Not by anyone.'

He hid a sigh. He couldn't tell if what she said was the truth or not.

'We have to let most of it go, Temel. All the outer edges to the north, east and west. We should concentrate on cleaning out a strip that borders the middle section of the Fifth Rake.' Garis tried not to show his distress. He held out his hands to the fire, to warm his frozen fingers. The burning shleth pats had a pleasant smell like lakeside grass, and supplied a small circle of welcome warmth on the rake in the midst of the chill of the night air. He looked back at the Mirager and then watched a dance of lights along the horizon instead – the Mirage Makers at play, even now – because he couldn't bear to see the pain on Temellin's face. 'I'm sorry.'

'How far did you go in this time?' Temellin asked.

'As far north as we could. I've finished the mapping up that way. We couldn't reach the foothills. The Mirage has vanished there. It's just an ocean of Ravage liquid, suppurating under the sun as far as you can see.'

'How much are we talking about?'

'The portion we can save, you mean? About one tenth of what the Mirage used to be, if we're lucky. We've left boundary markers for the area, and hopefully the Mirage won't mess with them. Not so sure about the Ravage though. There's no large expanse of Mirage anywhere that doesn't have a Ravage sore eating away at its heart.'

'*None?*'

Garis didn't answer.

Temellin sighed. 'It hurts, Garis. After all they gave us, we can do so little for them.' He drew his cloak tighter around himself. 'I want you to go back to Madrinya for a while. Ask Samia to join you. You've been out here too long. You shouldn't press your luck, and I want you to keep an eye on Arrant.'

'Problem?'

'I think so. I'll tell you more in the morning. Go off to your pallet now.'

Garis knew that tone of voice. The Mirager wanted to be alone.

Garis didn't know what woke him. It could have been the screaming of the shleths or the frightened yells of the men. Or perhaps the caterwaul of the wind as it whipped out of the Mirage in skeins of turbulence, each skein a tangle of slavering beasts.

One of the creatures came tumbling down onto the makeshift cover that he'd rigged up. He leaped to his feet, or tried to, but had to struggle out from underneath the fallen cover first. When he emerged, he was in the middle of a battle.

Cabochon light flared around him, red, green, gold: coloured shafts spearing the darkness, searching out the Ravage beasts that had arrived on the wind. He came face to face with the one that had crashed through his hide cover. There was no time to find his sword. The creature was so close that, when he raised his left hand, he jammed the cabochon into its eye.

The head melted into a rain of muck that showered him. He slipped in slime and went down on one knee. While he was there, he managed to find his sword.

He put his back to a perpendicular outcrop of rock, and fought another attacker that seemed to have two heads. When he had killed that, to his satisfaction, he checked to make sure that all its pieces were dead, then stepped away from the outcrop. He didn't even see the thing that leaped out at him from under the fallen hide cover and clamped double rows of serrated teeth around his ankle. He heard the scrunch of cracking bones a split second before he felt the pain. He slashed his sword down and cleaved it in two, then burned each half to ashes – but the lifeless head and jaws were still embedded in his ankle. The smell of blood attracted another; weakness made Garis slow and outstretched claws raked his wounded leg from thigh to ankle. As he killed the attacker, he saw power leaking from him, along with his blood.

'Samia,' he thought as the sword tumbled from his hand. 'Oh, Samia.'

Just as the rumour spread that Lesgath and Firgan had put a hand to Arrant's sword hilt, so did the gossip circulate about how Arrant had pestered Serenelle with unwanted attentions until Ryval, Myssa and Lesgath had retaliated and forced Arrant into licking Lesgath's backside while Serenelle watched.

Arrant wasn't sure which of the stories was the more damaging. He did know it was hard not to think that every snigger he heard was directed at him, hard not to blush when someone gave him a knowing smile. 'It's nothing.' He forced his inner voice to repeat the words over and over. 'Embarrassment is nothing. You weren't the guilty one; why should you feel embarrassed?'

To his further irritation, Elvena Korden was drawn into the

fray, apparently instructed to make life miserable for him. It started when he was in the library, and she built a ward across the floor so that he sprawled at her feet. A simple trick that would not have fooled anyone with a working cabochon. He picked himself up and ignored the tinkle of her laughter.

'Well, well,' she said, dimpling prettily, 'Mirager-heir! Are *you* blind, too?' She could not have thought of a comment better designed to hurt him.

Every time he was alone, she would use her senses to track him down and torment him with similar childish tricks. His inability to sense her approach, or to combat her tricks with a ward of his own, was devastating to his self-esteem. How could he be a Mirager one day if he couldn't even stop the silly antics of someone like Elvena? Which was exactly the way the Kordens wanted him to feel, of course. He thought of taking the matter to one of the teachers, but he knew such a complaint would only make him look a fool.

Myssa and Ryval, when they were not away fighting the Ravage, lent their own brand of torture to his situation, waylaying him as often as they could in the walled lane leading to the Mirager's Pavilion, or somewhere else equally quiet. Ryval's favourite trick was to put a hand to Arrant's back and smile as if they were having a pleasant conversation, only to shaft pain from his cabochon directly into Arrant's body.

'Hurts, does it?' he would inquire. If Arrant strode on, Ryval would keep pace as he chatted. 'What are you going to do about it, lad? Complain? Retaliate with your own power? Of course, most people might remark that a Magoroth who can't raise a ward against a bit of cabochon pain, or even notice a ward raised in front of him, might be a bit of a useless sort of Mirager-heir, wouldn't you think?'

Arrant was often tempted to call Tarran, but resisted. If his brother came in a hurry, believing he was urgently needed, who knew what repercussions it might have to the situation in the Mirage? And so he would endure the pain with as much stoicism as he could muster, fix Ryval with a steady stare and as serene a smile as he could manage and say something like, 'Have you *quite* finished?'

His calm was a small victory, but a victory, nonetheless. He thought it would all end when Garis arrived, only to receive a letter from Temellin telling him Garis had been badly injured, and was now convalescing with Samia in Asufa. It could be months before he would be able to come to Madrinya.

Arrant wrote back to his father, telling him not to worry; he had enlisted the help of Perradin, Bevran and Vevi instead. From then on, the four of them formed an inseparable quartet. If any of the Korden family chose to torment him, there would be witnesses.

In the meantime, when he found his stylus broken or his slate smashed, when he suffered one of the other countless aggravations, he refused to react, and perfected a look of mildly contemptuous indifference. The number and severity of attacks lessened, aided by the need for the twins and Firgan to spend time in the Mirage. When they were away, Elvena faltered in her enthusiasm for Arrant's persecution, and Lesgath confined himself to petty irritations.

'Don't worry,' Arrant told Tarran once when he did come. 'I'm fine. What's my pain and a few indignities compared to yours?' And it was true. When he thought of it that way, he thought he could endure anything.

But he also knew that, as his sixteenth anniversary day approached, he might be in more trouble than he could handle.

A tiny part of his mind whispered a continuous warning: *be careful.*

*   *   *

A beam of gold sliced through the cloth side of the tent and Ligea stepped through the slit. Devros of the Lucii was alone, as she had sensed. He stood with his back to her, washing his face at the bowl on a washstand.

She looked around, assessing where his weapons were, and waited for him to reach for his towel before she spoke. 'You've aged since I saw you last,' she said. 'Balding, I see.'

He started so violently he sent the washbowl flying. For one frozen moment he stared at her. Then recognition came and he dived for his sword where it lay on the table, still in its scabbard. A stab of gold light jabbed him with pain and he doubled up before he reached it. 'Vortex take you, Devros, didn't anyone ever teach you not to annoy someone with a drawn sword standing right in front of you when you aren't armed?'

Gasping and clutching at his stomach, he straightened. 'You son of a bitch!'

She smiled. 'Not really. "Daughter of a bastard" is probably closer to the truth. Now sit down in that chair over there, and listen very carefully to what I am about to say.'

He hesitated, but did as she asked, apparently deciding that if she was going to talk, he wasn't in any immediate danger. 'You won't get out of this camp alive,' he promised.

'Of course I will. I came in without anyone sounding the alarm. Although I must admit, if anyone were to look, they might have trouble finding the guards. By the way, I've placed a ward around this tent. That means no one can come in, so there's no point in yelling for help. But let's get down to why I'm here. Yesterday I stood on a cliff top and watched the last of the foreign armies – what's left of them – sail for home with our navy nipping at their steering oars. You're on your own, Devros. I could kill you now, oh, so easily. Or you could surrender your men, as well as yourself, and live. I'd prefer that, I admit, so I have drawn up a list of my terms for you. Basically it involves a modest existence on a country estate and a chance to see your grandchildren grow up, or death for every adult male Lucii who joined your rebellion and confiscation of all their estates. You choose. Every one of the highborn who followed you into this disaster will receive the same offer.' She withdrew a piece of parchment from her tunic and dropped it on the table. 'Read it and send me word in Tyr.'

She hardened her gaze. 'There won't be another chance. You've seen my power. The only reason it has taken me so long to confront you like this is that I can only be in one place at a time. Now everything I have will be concentrated on you, because your allies are running like rabbits back to their burrows. Think about it. A month, and I want to see you kneeling at my feet in tyr to kiss the hem of my robe in submission, or I will take immense pleasure in hunting you down.'

She touched her sword to his where it lay on the table. The metal of his blade began to droop and then melt around the edges. Devros watched, the fear in his eyes unmistakeable. 'Cold fire,' she said. 'Can you imagine what it would do to your guts? Or would you prefer heat, perhaps?'

She directed the point of her sword out of the tent opening. He had to look over his shoulder to see what she was doing. The ridge of the tent opposite burst into flames. One of his men hurtled out of the tent, yelling. When Devros turned back, Ligea was gone.

Outside the slit at the back of the tent, she said to Gevenan who had been waiting for her, 'I *loved* doing that.' Then added, as she sliced through the guy ropes that held the tent erect, 'Almost as much as I would have loved to wring his neck.'

He handed over her cloak as the tent collapsed. 'Brand did once tell me you had a penchant for extravagant theatre. Let's go home, woman. My knees are aching.'

CHAPTER SEVENTEEN

'Settle down, class!' Firgan's voice boomed out over the yard. 'Gather around. I have an announcement to make.'

Firgan, not Yetemith. Yetemith was there, but quietly leaning against the practice yard wall. The first class was with wooden swords, but Arrant had been hoping that Yetemith would take it, not Firgan. He hated it when Firgan taught. Fear seeped into every moment, contaminating every pleasure he might otherwise have taken in learning, singeing every thought with suspicion.

'Theuri-yetemith and I have been assessing your success with handling your Magoroth swords,' Firgan began. 'We have decided that, apart from the obvious exception among you' – he stared at Arrant – 'you are all doing well.'

Arrant stared back, his face wooden.

'So, we have decided to bring forward this year's two combat tests to this week; that is, both with and without power. Starting tomorrow. With the combat tests out of the way, you will have more time to concentrate on your weaker subjects. Of course, you, Arrant, who are obviously way behind the rest of the class in Magoroth sword combat, may say this is unfair to you. After some discussion, it was pointed out that no matter how much time you have, you never seem to improve, therefore to grant you more time is pointless.'

Serenelle giggled and there was muffled tittering from the direction of Lesgath and his friends.

'Fail the exam,' Firgan continued, 'any of you, and we'll drop you back to join the next class that starts Magoroth sword combat.'

Perradin muttered, 'What in all hells is he up to? Why now, when the Mirager is away?'

Arrant shrugged. 'He wants me to fail. To look bad when I come up to be confirmed as Mirager-heir.' Six months. Only six months more.

'Of course,' Firgan continued, 'it is also perfectly possible that the Mirager-heir will miraculously manage to pass the test. Perhaps he will one day be able to explain why his cabochon works only during examinations.'

More laughter.

'Anyway, expect to be tested as from tomorrow. And as for today's combat classes, they will be a heavy practice. You will be changing opponents often. We'll start with practice swords, then move to the Magoroth sword. We are mixing you in with my seniors to give you a wider variety of fighting styles and levels of skills. Collect your practice swords, please.'

'Sandblast it,' Arrant thought. 'This is *not* going to be fun.'

The students filed over to the armoury shed to rack their Magoroth swords and pick up their wooden swords, then the morning's practice began. Firgan and Yetemith walked around the yard, intervening every now and then to comment on what one combatant or another was doing wrong and how to correct it.

Half an hour into the class, Arrant found himself pitted against Lesgath. Arrant spun Lesgath's practice blade out of his hand in less time than it took to tie on a sandal. Several students noticed and guffawed, which didn't improve Lesgath's temper.

'You are a knucklehead,' Serenelle told him afterwards, when it was her turn to face Arrant. 'What in all the wide blue skies do you think Lesgath will do to you later, when we are all using our *Magoroth* swords?'

Arrant's jaw tightened. Even with practice swords accidents occurred. In his years of training, he'd seen teeth knocked out, wrists broken and ears torn; how much more damage could be inflicted in a Magoroth class when an attacker and a defender were unevenly matched?

He refused to show Serenelle he was worried, but he was. Nothing was predictable any more. He didn't think Firgan would partner him with Lesgath, not when everyone knew his sword was useless against him. But still, the whole Korden family were consolidating their position for concerted action against him in the near future, he knew it. 'Vortexdamn it, how soon?' he wondered. 'While Papa is still away? And exactly what can I expect? Gods, I wish Garis would come.' Garis's recuperation was slow. The injury must have been severe, to incapacitate a Magoroth for so long, and he worried.

In the break between classes, which they spent in the tree-shaded Academy courtyard, he said as much to Perradin and Bevran, and then added, 'They wouldn't dare to hurt me, not with everyone knowing I can't use my sword against Lesgath, even if I could call on the power.'

'Lesgath's awfully mad,' Bevran said. His gaze followed Serenelle as she crossed the courtyard. Perradin rolled his eyes. Bevran's futile hankering after Serenelle had become the worst-kept secret in the Academy. 'I heard him swearing about you to Serenelle a while back. He sounded nasty.' He turned back to Arrant, giving his full attention. 'I eavesdropped, actually. I reckoned if they can, so can I.'

Arrant had to hide a shiver.

'I don't like this,' Perradin said. 'Not with both your father and mine away, and with Lesgath fuming. Too many things happening at once. I'm going to ask my mother to be here to watch the tests.'

Arrant turned away to drink at the fountain to cover the cold sweat of fear along his upper lip. When he stood straight again, he was able to ask calmly, 'Could Firgan be using Lesgath without his knowledge? And Lesgath is so thick he can't see it? It's almost as though Firgan wants his brother to get so mad he'll attack me with his Magor power, knowing I won't be able to defend myself.'

Perradin's eyes widened. 'You mean – he wants Lesgath to *murder* you?'

Arrant shrugged. 'Perhaps.'

'That's – bizarre,' said Perradin, but the tone of his voice told them he didn't think it impossible.

'I could still use my cabochon to defend myself.'

'You're not supposed to use a cabochon, not directly, in a sword class,' Perradin said. 'Still, you might like to consider doing so if you get in a fix. Better to be told off than to be dead.'

'Thanks for pointing that out,' Arrant said. 'Especially when there's nothing to say my cabochon will work.'

'It always seems to work when you're tested. Hells, Arrant, if Lesgath is that stupid, he'll suffer for it afterwards, but that wouldn't bring you back if he's already killed you.'

Bevran frowned. 'Hey, that's right. Your cabochon does tend to work when we have a test. How do you do that, yet can't fix it to work at other times?'

'I just do it that way to annoy Markess and Yetemith,' Arrant said solemnly. Bevran blinked, half-believing.

Arrant laughed and said, 'I will explain one day, I promise. But it comes with a price, and I don't like to do it too often, all right? What worries me, and Father too, is this: if Firgan wants me dead by Lesgath's hand, then why did he have Lesgath put his hand to my sword in front of me? If I *hadn't* known that, and tried to defend myself against an attack by Lesgath, any power I sent his way would rebound back on me, with possibly fatal consequences. Which would make it more my fault than Lesgath's. We both think we're missing something still.'

'Arrant, I think you ought to have a terribly bad stomach-ache,' Perradin said. 'Or a splitting headache. Avoid the test.'

'And who's going to believe that?'

'No one. But you'd be alive.'

'A live coward no one will ever want as a Mirager, or the possibility of ending up a dead hero who's no use to anyone,' Bevran added, brutally frank. 'Not much of a choice.'

Arrant exhaled. 'No, I know. I think I need to get my cabochon working, if I can. You could try warning him, in the meantime.'

'Warn who? *Lesgath*?' Perradin gave him a strange look, and then thought about it. 'I don't think he'd listen to me.'

'He might take notice of Vevi,' Bevran said. 'He used to like her rather a lot.'

Perradin stared at him. 'Bev, how do you always know things like that?'

'I watch and I listen. Unlike some people I know, who never seem to see anything, especially if it is right under their nose.'

'All right, all right. Let's go and have a word with Vevi.' The two of them went off to find her, leaving Arrant alone on the bench.

Tarran, can you hear me?

A long pause made him think Tarran wasn't able to reply, but then he popped into Arrant's head. *What's up?*

Arrant looked around the yard to show Tarran where he was, and what was happening. *I think I might need some help in a moment. And more tomorrow, when we are going to be tested.* He outlined what had happened.

Ah, Tarran said. *You are in a fix. I don't like it, Arrant. You're right, Firgan means to do something.*

How in Hades are you always able to grasp what's been going on so quickly? You glimpse my life in chunks, with great holes bitten out by your absences, yet you're always ready to plunge right in again.

Talent, sheer talent. I'll stay around for a bit and do my best now. Afterwards, I'll talk to the rest of me about staying with you for a day or two. Papa is here, and things are always quieter for us when he is fighting. I wish you could see him, Arrant. He scares the Ravage beasts.

Arrant smiled. *He scares me sometimes, too.*

Instead of being restricted by his blindness, he has honed his other senses and melded them to his Magor abilities to create a warrior who inspires us all. But, Arrant, we worry. He takes such risks for us. One day — one day he will take one step too far.

Arrant swallowed back the rise of emotion into his throat. *That's — that's who he is, Tarran.*

'That's great,' Perradin said, coming back again just in time to note the gold beginning to fill Arrant's sword as he put his left hand to the hilt. 'That'll give Lesgath second thoughts when he sees. And Vevi *is* going to talk to him. She doesn't think it will do much good, but she's going to try.' He nodded at the sword. 'Will you be able to keep it like that?'

'I hope so. The trouble is, I have little experience at using a Magor sword with its power intact. I'm worried about making a mess of things anyway. I have to be extra-careful I don't hurt anyone by accident.'

'And how old were you when you last did that?' Perradin asked. He already knew the answer. Arrant had once told him what had happened, and when.

'Perry, I didn't have a Magor sword then. I have an even greater potential for making a mess of things now.'

Don't think about it, shleth brain.

Perradin looked taken aback. 'That's right. You must have done all that with a cabochon. I never considered that. Skies above, Arrant, you must be the strongest Magori ever born.'

'Yes, sure. Once every ten years when I'm not trying.' To Tarran he added, *Try to give me warning if you have to leave, all right? I don't want to blow everyone to Acheron in little bits this time.*

I'll do my best. Things seem quiet here at the moment. We will get you through this test together. It is important, isn't it? It could be the last in Magor sword combat before your sixteenth anniversary day and your confirmation as Mirager-heir.

'You are very quiet,' Perradin said, staring at him. 'Are you all right?'

'I'm fine. Just thinking. Don't worry.' *If there ever is a confirmation. The Kordens are still trying to make damn sure there won't be.*

'There are times when you seem to be in a vale a thousand seas away.'

'Sorry. It is a way I have when I'm thinking.'

'Yes, I've noticed.'

Perradin's tone was so dry, Tarran remarked, *I think he knows you are talking to me.*

Probably. He's not dumb.

'Arrant,' Perradin continued, 'even as dreamy as you are, and with a cabochon as unpredictable as a desert wind, I sure as the sands are dry hope you stay the Mirager-heir, because I would hate to see Firgan there in your place.'

On the surface it was lightly said, but Perradin let his emotions free, and Arrant could – for once – read them. Admiration, concern, loyalty: it was all there. Even love, of a kind – diffident, embarrassed, but real. He blinked, taken aback. 'Thank you, Perradin,' he said and did his best to show his friend his own appreciation.

He couldn't have been very successful, because Perradin grinned and punched him on the arm. 'Idiot,' he said.

Tarran laughed. *I think you overdid it. If Perradin didn't know you so well, he'd be thinking you made a pass at him.*

Arrant muffled a groan. He just didn't get enough practice at emotional chatter.

For the combined Magor sword combat classes Yetemith and Firgan were stricter about who was paired with whom, taking care not to mix people who were too disparate in ability.

Except, Arrant noted, for himself. When Firgan saw that his sword had filled with gold light, he said, 'We are getting sick of this from you, boy. This sometimes you can, sometimes you can't. It smacks of puerile game-playing. It is time you showed us you are worthy of being Mirager-heir. You can fight someone from the senior class, and I am going to be watching you, every step of the way.' He signalled to one of Lesgath's friends, Grantel, who lumbered over.

'Adjust the power in your swords to its lowest level, please,' Firgan continued, 'and let me see a beam hit the ground in front of you. I want to see no more than a puff of dust.' He gave Arrant a glare. 'Understand me, boy? No funny games out of you just because your sword has colour.'

'No, Magori.'

'And no touching each other with the blade under any circumstances.'

'No, Magori.'

They both demonstrated their control over their power by producing a beam that did no more than nudge softly at the ground.

'Good. Now keep it that way. Begin!'

Arrant knew it would be difficult. Being good with a normal sword didn't mean much in a Magor fight. The cutting edge of a Magor weapon was much sharper and the power of a Magor sword extended beyond the tip of the blade. To use it involved a different fighting technique. In practice fights such as this, the aim was more *not* to touch the other fighter with the blade, for fear of really hurting him, but rather to thrust at him with carefully controlled power subdued to non-lethal levels. A successful combatant kept his opponent offbalance at the same time as he harmlessly diverted any beam of power sent in his direction.

What's wrong? Tarran asked, aware of his brother's ambivalence as he and Grantel circled each other.

Until now a working cabochon and a Magor sword lesson rarely seemed to coincide. I don't have experience at this.

Grantel lunged; Arrant sidestepped neatly and followed up by levering Grantel's weapon sideways with a beam of power. The youth, though, kept his balance. *Gods, it's like trying to fight a tree trunk,* Arrant complained a moment later, as several more of his attacks were brushed aside by the strength of Grantel's arm as an extension of his sword. The youth was almost twice as broad as Arrant.

You could defeat him if you used your power more, um, effectively, Tarran said. *Dig a hole under his back foot.*

With this level of power I don't think I could. Besides, I might hurt him.

Shivering sands, this is a fight, isn't it?

Can you shut up for a moment? I can't concentrate with you chattering like a demented wood-squirrel in my head.

Just then Grantel swung his power beam across to hit Arrant's blade. His power may not have been strong, but the physical strength behind the blow sent Arrant's sword spinning away across the yard. Grantel whooped and laughed.

At least your Magor skills are performing consistently, even if your command of them is, um, amateurish, Tarran said.

Oh, thanks. And stop laughing – you're supposed to be on my side.

Just as well this wasn't the test, Tarran said cheerfully.

'That was pathetic,' Firgan said. 'Arrant, when you are up against an opponent who has greater physical strength, you have to make use of your Magor power, else how can you win? Both of you were doing the same thing – acting as though the power was no more than the physical extension of an ordinary sword. It is *power*, you hollow-brained idiots! Just because it is powered down doesn't mean it can't be used in innovative ways. Go and watch Mikess and Rovanel over there and see how it should be done.' He pointed to where two of the senior students were facing up to one another under Yetemith's watchful eyes. Mikess, half blinded by grit after Rovanel's power had puffed dust in his face, was now using swordlight to blind Rovanel.

Tarran, Arrant said as he trudged to the side of the yard to watch, *we have to think more about why, when you are inside my head, I have power.*

We've been through all this before. You always have power. The difference is that you can find your power when I am here.

All right, put it that way. I just want to know why.

Tarran was silent for a moment, then he said sadly, *I am not sure we will ever know exactly why, any more than – than Samia knows why she has freckles and you don't, or Perry knows why he can't do geometry and you can. It was the way you were born, and I don't believe we'll ever change it. If you keep hunting for reasons or trying to change what is, you will waste your life.* He paused, then added, *Use me while you can. After that – I have no answers.*

The uncharacteristic sadness of his reply so permeated into

Arrant's mind he was incapable of replying. He picked up his cloth from the bench on the sidelines and wiped away his sweat. Perradin and Bevran and Vevi came over to join him, Bevran grinning broadly. 'Hey,' he said, 'I just heard Firgan praising you to Lesgath, and Lesgath is furious.'

'Praising me?' Arrant was astonished. '*Firgan*? Are you sure?'

'He said that you had more power in your sword than the rest of us put together.'

'You eavesdropped again?'

'Of course. Firgan told Lesgath that in battle, you have to expect the unexpected, and he'd be dead if he had a real fight with you. He even told Lesgath he thought you'd beat him every time you fought, because you use your head and Lesgath doesn't.'

Arrant gave a bark of unamused laughter. 'And he just told me I was a hollow-brained idiot. What's he up to?'

'He must have been trying to infuriate Lesgath,' Perradin said. 'You need to be careful if you end up fighting him.'

Arrant didn't comment. Instead, he asked, 'Vevi, did you get a chance to talk to Lesgath?'

'I tried. I suggested he consider if Firgan really has his best interests at heart. I pointed out that if he hurt you, he'd be the one in trouble, not Firgan.'

'What did he say?'

She snorted. 'He lost his temper with me. I'd say he has the brains of a shleth embryo, only I'd probably be maligning the shleth.'

'Quiet,' said Perradin. 'Here comes Theuri-yetemith.'

The class continued for another hour, with Arrant waiting on the sidelines for either Yetemith or Firgan to pair him up with another student again, but they both ignored him. This was nothing new; he normally spent the whole of a Magor sword class idle, but it was galling to have to sit out the opportunity to practice when he had power in his weapon. He spent the time quietly using his Magor power under Tarran's tutelage. He built a series of small wards along the wall. He practised manoeuvring a breeze he created. He made small dust devils. He used his power to rearrange the gravel nearby into patterns. And he envied his friends, sparring in the centre of the yard.

At the end of an hour, Firgan came over to where he stood. 'You can fight Lesgath this time,' he said.

'What are you trying to prove, Firgan?' he asked, rudely dropping the respect due to a teacher. 'You know there's not a blasted thing I can do against Lesgath without risking my own life.'

'Just get out there. If you are worried about backlash, then just use your power defensively – or more creatively in offence. Anyway, no backlash is going to hurt anyone if the sword is kept powered down. Don't be such a baby.' He seized Arrant by the shoulder and pushed him to where Lesgath waited.

There, he addressed them both. 'Maybe with an opponent you don't like, the two of you will show us what you can *really* do. Let me see that your swords are powered down to the minimum.'

You bastard, Arrant thought as he pointed his sword at the ground and allowed it to do no more than stir the dust.

Lesgath grinned at him as he followed suit, but waited until Firgan stepped back before murmuring, 'Winning a swordfight with a wooden sword means nothing, Arrogant. This is where we separate the Magoroth warrior from the Tyranian imitation.'

Right then, Arrant found it hard to remember his father's advice about not losing his temper; his rage simmered to fever heat inside him.

Deep breath, said Tarran.

You don't breathe. What the hell can you know about deep breaths?

Not much, but still, I've heard it helps.

Sometimes you say the weirdest things, Tarran.

Arrant took a deep breath, and kept his voice level, his tone calm. 'And just how am I going to give you the defeat you deserve when you have protected yourself against my sword? You are never going to know your true worth, or lack of it, in combat with me, because you cheated before we even began. Where, then, will be your satisfaction? And if you are so sure of your superiority, why was it necessary in the first place?'

'Because you kill by accident, that's why,' came the sneering answer.

Pleasant fellow, Tarran muttered. *Don't let him rile you, Arrant.*

Oh, I'm riled, Arrant said. *It's a permanent state when any of the Kordens are around.*

'All right, you two, cut the chatter,' Firgan interrupted. 'Salute and begin!'

The two of them gave a token salute which was barely polite. *Gods,* Arrant thought, *if I knew what Firgan really wants me to do, I'd do the opposite. But I don't know.*

They started with some tentative sparring, standing well apart using the extension of power beyond the sword tip, just as he had earlier with Grantel, but that soon palled because neither of them seemed to be getting anywhere.

Careful, said Tarran. *I can sense a slight increase in power levels. His, that is; not yours.*

Arrant thought about that as he deflected another lunge from Lesgath. The beam of power slid over his head as he caught it on his blade and pushed it upwards. He didn't try to take the offensive. There was no point – any magic sent against Lesgath would rebound. Lesgath attacked again and again; each time Arrant blocked and fell back.

Firgan stood with folded arms, a smirk on his face as he watched.

Lesgath was exasperated. 'Who's the coward now?' he asked. 'Fight, you foreign bastard!'

But Arrant continued to be cautious.

You are making him mad, Tarran crowed.

That is not good, Arrant said, irritated.

Firgan watched the two of them with an almost avaricious anxiety. 'Don't drop your wrist like that, Arrant,' he said. 'You lower the tip of your sword and give Lesgath an opening. Which he was too slow to take advantage of, lucky for you. Lesgath, keep your wits about you.'

Take him by surprise, Tarran suggested after another couple of fruitless attacks from Lesgath.

How?

Why not swap your sword to your right hand, and use your cabochon. After all, he's only protected against your sword, right?

Arrant parried another attack. *This is supposed to be a class in Magor sword usage, that's why.*

Who cares?

I do! Firgan would chew me up like a mouthful of nuts over it.

So? You'd be alive. And don't worry, you have perfect control at the moment. You can please yourself just how much power you use.

Lesgath feinted, then twisted his power, imbued now with pain-giving magic. Arrant was slow to block the second thrust and power brushed his bare arm. Pain leaped from the gold light into him, searing his bones, biting deep as it travelled up his arm. This time, though, he had his own magic. He summoned his power and blocked the spread of the agony, then diminished its racking torment until he finally banished it altogether.

Lesgath laughed. 'Hurt you, didn't I? You weren't quick

enough, you son of a traitorous bitch. Why don't you try that on me?' Mockingly, he thrust his bared arm at Arrant and lowered his guard. 'Go on, I dare you!'

He couldn't, of course. The pain would rebound on him.

'Bastard son of a Tyranian Brotherhood bitch,' Lesgath hissed. 'Fight me!'

Arrant threw his sword to his other hand and shot a controlled beam of gold from his cabochon. He aimed it straight at Lesgath's chest. Just enough power there to send Lesgath flying backwards, so he would land ignominiously on his back, but not enough to harm him . . . With his guard so foolishly lowered, the youth would not have time to block the beam. Out of the corner of his eye, Arrant was aware that someone was moving towards him. Firgan, he thought, but all his focus was on Lesgath.

As the power left Arrant's cabochon, Firgan's emotion leaked into the air, splendidly triumphant. More than enough to tell Arrant he had made a terrible mistake. A splinter of time when everything went wrong, and no time to take anything back. No time to stop anything. No time even to understand.

Firgan bellowed in his ear, '*Don't!* For Mirage sake, *no!*' and grasped Arrant hard, on the shoulder. His fingernails dug into the flesh. Under his hand, Arrant's clothing scorched as power burned into his skin.

Gold light billowed from Arrant in a spreading arc, out of his control. The wedge of it mowed down everything in its path, gouging furrows into the hard earth of the yard. Lesgath flew through the air, his clothing and hair on fire. He still held his sword in his hand. Pain exploded in Arrant's head, behind his eyes, in his chest, through his gut. He lost control of his bodily functions. His muscles began to fail, to become too soft and weak to hold him upright.

Tarran screamed, a terrible sound that wouldn't stop,

splitting Arrant's head like an axe blade, fracturing his thoughts into uncomprehending shards.

Beyond the flying fireball that was Lesgath, Perradin stood, frozen as the billow of gold engulfed him. Behind him, Serenelle had her sword thrust out, as though she could stop the burning magic as it rolled towards her. People screamed, but Arrant could no longer hear them. As he fell, gold in the air in front of his face blistered into molten bubbles, then curled and crisped around the edges like burning papyrus, until it turned as black as a starless sky, and he saw and felt nothing more. Knew nothing more, except that he had killed again.

That shard of knowledge he took with him into oblivion.

CHAPTER EIGHTEEN

When he woke, his immediate awareness told him time had passed. He wasn't in the practice yard; he was in his own room. And it was night-time. A single lamp, turned low, burned on the windowsill. His awareness expanded, telling him he wasn't alone; someone was sitting by his bed, outlined by the dim glow from the lamp wick. He could smell a woman's perfume.

Then he became aware of his pain. It hurt everywhere. His head ached almost beyond bearing. It hurt even to move his eyeballs. His shoulder was on fire. His whole left arm was in agony. Scalding pain spread through his veins. To extend his fingers was to touch hot coals.

His next realisation came in a rush: a block of knowledge he didn't want, relayed by his memory of a single image. The practice yard. The moment before he'd lost consciousness. Uncontrolled power shooting away from his hand in a gold curtain of light. He had killed again.

No, no, no, oh no, please make it not be true, please make it all a dream, please, please, please . . .

'Are you awake?' A familiar voice at his side, responding to his stirring.

Hellesia. But he didn't want Hellesia. He didn't want anyone. He wanted to die. He wanted not to know.

Tarran? Tarran! Oh gods, Tarran, please, where are you? Did I hurt you?

The silence greeting his anguished call was as profound as the dark that had been his unconsciousness.

'Yes,' he said. Because in the end, you had to go on living. And suffering. And hating being yourself. Because in the end, there was nothing else you could do. 'Yes, I'm awake.' *Tarran? Please tell me you are all right . . .*

She rose to her feet and turned up the lamp. 'Are you hurting?'

He didn't reply.

'You were burned.' Her voice was gentle. Soothing. She knew what it was like to hurt. To be hurt. She'd been a slave.

'How – how many did I kill this time?'

His blunt query made her wince, but she answered just as bluntly. 'One. Lesgath Korden.'

He wasn't deceived. 'But—?'

'There were others who were injured.'

'Who?'

'A few broken bones and one fractured skull, but they'll all recover in time. Perradin was the only one badly hurt. They – they aren't sure if he will live.'

Perradin. Of all people. *Why?*

He shuddered. Pain lanced through him, intense agony that stopped thought, and he no longer knew if it was physical in origin, or a rip across his soul. Perradin had wanted him to say he was sick, unable to fight that day. Perradin.

Hellesia was remorseless. 'Little Serenelle Korden saved much of the class; she managed to get a ward up in time.'

He thought about that. 'She always was the best in the class at warding. Quick, too.' A prosaic statement of fact, delivered in a reasonable tone of voice; he was proud of that. As if the world hadn't fractured all over again. As if he wasn't to blame.

As if he hadn't hurt people he loved, all over again. He spared no grief for Lesgath, but *Perry* . . . Jahan and Jessah; Temellin – gods, was there never any end to the way he hurt those he cared about? And where was Tarran?

Please don't tell me I killed him too . . .

'I'll get one of the healers,' Hellesia said. 'That burn must be hurting you—'

'No.' He clutched at her, grabbing her hand. 'No. I don't want a healer. I don't want to see anyone.'

'The Illusa who is tending you asked me to call her the moment you woke. She said you would be in pain.'

'I don't care. I don't want to see anyone.'

She stood, indecisive.

'How long was I unconscious?'

'It happened yesterday. It's just before dawn now. I really should—'

'No. Hellesia, right now I want to be alone.'

Tarran, Tarran? Where are you? I really don't want to be alone . . . Please tell me you aren't hurt . . .

But one of the last things he remembered hearing had been Tarran's screaming. Tarran, who had lived with pain all his life, had screamed inside his head – and vanished like a candle flame snuffed in his fingertips.

Hellesia hesitated still. 'We have sent for your father and Jahan.'

'Good. Now go, please.' He wasn't able to stop the quaver in his voice this time.

She touched his hand. 'I'm sorry,' she whispered. She turned down the lamp again, then went out.

He lay in the dimly lit room, unmoving. And he remembered: Firgan. The elation of the man's triumph. Firgan had known his brother would die and hadn't cared. He had *known* Arrant's control would fail him. He had known what would happen. *How?* He thought back. Firgan's hand, clutching his shoulder. And now his shoulder hurt, as if it was burned. 'Did he somehow send power into me?' he whispered. 'So I had too much, and lost control?'

But that wasn't possible. If Firgan had sent that much power surging into him, he – Arrant – would have died on the spot. No one survived a direct blast of cabochon power of that magnitude.

And yet there was something Firgan had known that he didn't. Something. Inside himself, somewhere deep and dark with despair, he wept, for he had failed his father and his land. He'd lost control, just as he had lost control at the North Gate of Tyr when he was nine.

Tarran, if you are all right, please come . . .

There was no reply.

They came in the morning, of course. Healers to change his dressing and speed his healing and suppress his pain. Eris, his chamberlain, to cluck over him, bring him breakfast in bed and then coax him to eat a little of it.

And later, Korden – to condemn him.

He heard the commotion outside his room; people arguing. Then the door opened and Korden strode in, his grief radiating from him, unrestrained and wild. Hellesia clung to one arm, trying to hold him back; Eris clutched at the other, begging him to calm down. The blaze of his grief preceded him as he shook them both off and spoke to Arrant: 'You *killed my son*!'

Arrant froze in panic, sure his heart had stopped beating. What in all of Acheron could he possibly say to the father of someone he had slain?

Korden shrugged himself free of Eris and Hellesia, and strode to the bedside. His whole body shook with grief and rage. 'I *warned* Temellin about you. I warned him!' He shook a forefinger at Arrant, his speech thick with terrible emotion. 'I will see to it that you *never* do anything like this again. I will see to it that you will *never* become Mirager.' He shuddered, and regained some composure. 'You will appear before the Magoroth Council today,' he continued, 'in the first hour past midday. I am charging you with the misuse of Magor powers, and you must answer to that charge. You are also charged with the manslaughter of a fellow Magoroth, and will answer to that charge, too, before our peers. If you do not appear, you will be sentenced in your absence.'

Arrant couldn't move. No words came to him. He couldn't even say he was sorry. He hadn't sought Lesgath's death, but he regretted it more because of its consequences than because it grieved him. He had loathed Lesgath, loathed him deeply.

Only when the silence became embarrassing did he force words between his dry lips. 'I am sorry for your grief,' he said. 'I thought I had control. I didn't believe I would harm anyone, I truly didn't think I would. But Firgan put his hand on my shoulder and maybe somehow his power went into me. There's a burn mark there—'

'*What?*' Korden's rage was white-hot. 'You would blame another son of mine? How *dare* you!' His hands trembled, as though they ached to choke Arrant. 'Firgan tried desperately to stop you. Any power he used was aimed at halting you! If he had not done that, every child on that practice yard would be dead, in a shower of bloody rain.' His revulsion was complete. He stepped back from Arrant's pallet in repugnance. 'You don't even have the decency to accept the blame for what you've done. Firgan watched his brother burn. Alive. Burn until his eyes melted and his blood boiled. You are less than the leavings on a stable floor, Arrant Temellin. You will *never* have the option to harm anyone again. Today I will see to that.' With those words, he turned on his heel and left.

Arrant closed his eyes.

Hellesia and Eris exchanged worried glances. 'Find out if they can really do this in the Mirager's absence,' Hellesia said.

Eris nodded. 'They might not be able to get a quorum so quickly anyway.'

Hellesia came forward to stand at Arrant's bedside as Eris left, her face drawn with worry. 'They ought not to do this now. They ought to wait for your father's return.'

The quorum. He knew about that from his lessons. Half the number of Magor sword holders over the age of sixteen living less than a day's ride from Madrinya. 'Not so easy to raise a quorum so quickly,' he said. His voice sounded hard and frozen to his ears, a match to his insides. He couldn't let himself feel. To feel was pain. To feel was fear. No, terror. Terror that he had somehow killed Tarran. Terror that the Council was going to kill him. 'So many warriors are in the Mirage.'

'He sent word out yesterday. He seems to think he'll get the numbers,' Hellesia said.

Arrant wanted to ask: *What will the Council do?* but he knew she wouldn't know. She wasn't Magor.

Hellesia took hold of his hand. 'Temellin left you in the care of Magoria-jessah, but her son may not live. She will not be parted from his side.'

Gods, he was cold. 'I understand.' Jessah wouldn't want to see him anyway. He was the cause of Perry's injury. Ironic, that. Of all the people he had not wanted to harm, Perradin would have headed the list. 'Don't feel,' he told himself. To feel was too painful. Was there anyone else he could ask for help? In despair, he realised there probably wasn't. Many of the children of the senior Magoroth had been on that practice ground. They were not likely to view Arrant with anything but suspicion, or downright loathing.

'Will you be able to attend?' Hellesia asked. 'How do you feel?'

He shrugged. The healers had done their job well. The pain was manageable, the weakness surmountable. None of that mattered anyway, not to him. 'I'll be there.'

She nodded. 'Then rest now. I will go and find out as much as I can in the meantime. I'll ask Illuser-reftim, the librarian. He always seems to know what's going on.'

He lay quietly after she had gone, staring at the ceiling. Tarran still didn't answer his call, and Arrant's fear crawled into every thought and lay beneath them like a weight to drag him down.

'Firgan's won,' he thought. 'And I can't do anything about it. I don't even know how he knew I'd make such a mess of things. I don't know if any of it was his fault. I don't know what he did. Rest, Hellesia? I will never rest again, not really.'

He had never entered the compound of the Magoroth Council Pavilion. There had been no reason to do so; tradition decreed that only Magoroth over sixteen had free access to the building, and he was still short of his sixteenth anniversary day.

With Eris hovering at his side, he walked through the glorious colour of the gardens, poignantly aware of the perfume of the flowers and the joyousness of the birdsong, as if he was never going to smell or hear them again. He passed by a sundial carved with ancient runes, rescued, he had heard, from the ruins of the first pavilion. He skirted the fishponds brimming with inquisitive spout-nosed trout and arrived at the bottom of the broad stairs leading to the entrance doors. Two Magoroth waited for him. The first was Magoria-markess. He was glad when his cabochon didn't work because he was sure, from the expression on her face, that her disdain was hanging in the air like an unpleasant smell. The other guard was Perradin's eldest brother, Grevilyon Jahan, a Magori in his late twenties who had not long returned from a stint in the Mirage. Arrant had met him several times when he had come to see his brother in the Academy.

Arrant murmured, 'Thank you, Eris. You may return now.'

'I'll wait,' the man said.

Arrant opened his mouth to insist, but Eris's stare was implacable. Arrant nodded and mounted the stairs. Grevilyon stepped forward as soon as Arrant reached the top step.

'Welcome to the Hall of the Magoroth Council, Magori-arrant, Mirager-heir,' he said in formal greeting. He wasn't smiling. 'I will escort you to your place.'

They stepped inside the wide doorway, and he found himself in a large entry hall. People had gathered in unhappy groups, but his entrance was enough to stop all conversation. Arrant tried to ignore both the silence and the concentration of stares as he and Grevilyon started to walk across the hall in between the tense knots of people. He said quietly, 'Magori, I am deeply sorry for what has happened to Perry. Please tell me how he is.' In the silence that had followed his entrance, his voice echoed, clearly audible. He winced.

'He has a number of broken bones and, we believe, a lung torn by a rib. Some burns too. The injuries were severe, but we have not given up hope. He is strong and the healers do not leave his side.'

The cold came again, slithering. He said woodenly, 'Please convey my regrets to Magoria-jessah. I have known nothing but kindness from your family and it – it devastates me that I have done this to you all.' The words were too formal, he knew. Too cold. But he didn't know how to express the grief he felt. He didn't know that any words could *begin* to say what he felt.

'We know you didn't mean it,' Grevilyon said in little more than a whisper, but the words were edged with anger. 'That does not make it any easier to bear.' He looked at Arrant and the anger suddenly melted to sorrow. 'My mother dares not leave his side. And you should know that I will not vote to support you. I mean you no ill will, you understand; but I cannot think that you would make a good Mirager, not after this. I thought otherwise at first – especially when you took your Covenant vows. I'd never seen such pure untarnished power as I saw then. I like you, Arrant, but our next Mirager has to be someone who can control his power.'

Arrant nodded. There was a lump in his throat, too large to allow speech. Was the Council going to take a vote on his suitability as heir, then?

Wordlessly they crossed the space into the Meeting Hall. It lacked the marbled grandeur of a domed and pillared Tyranian public building, but was still astonishingly beautiful to Arrant's eyes. Polished adobe walls were studded with tiled niches containing busts of all those Magoroth killed during the Feast of the Shimmer Festival. 'Acheron's mists,' he thought, 'so many of them are children.' He'd known that, yet it wasn't until he saw their likenesses that the full extent of the tragedy became real. These children had been his parents' contemporaries. His father's sister was there somewhere. He wondered if there was a bust of their betrayer, Sarana's father, Solad. He assumed not.

The roof above was stone-arched, and a series of slits around the top of the walls angled in suffused sunlight so the terra-cotta roof tiles glowed. A bell hung from the central arch, but there was no mechanism to ring it.

The polished agate beneath Arrant's feet was stepped, which meant that everyone had a view of the stage at the front. A single stone lectern dominated the centre of the stage; behind it two tiers of stone steps provided benches for speakers awaiting their turn.

'Seat yourself on the bench,' Grevilyon said. 'There won't be long to wait. As soon as the shadow hits the hour on the sundial in the gardens, the Chamberlain of the hall will ring that bell.' He pointed upwards. 'You can stay seated, if you like, as you have been hurt. But take my advice and – if you can possibly do so – stand. It will look better if you stand to face your accusers.'

Arrant nodded. 'Who – who's in charge?'

'Magori-berrin is the Master of Proceedings.'

Berrin. Arrant had met him several times, but didn't know him well. He was a quiet, thoughtful man who had considerable stature simply because he was one of the original Ten. Arrant had a feeling that at least he would be fair.

'Grevilyon, if they find me guilty what is the penalty for killing another Magoroth by accident?'

'I – I don't know. They might ban you from using Magor power for the rest of your life. You'd have to relinquish your sword, I guess.'

He thought about that. He wouldn't contest either of those things. He didn't want to use his power again, ever, anyway.

He stared at the men and women now taking their seats in the hall. 'Might they banish me?' he asked.

Grevilyon shrugged uncomfortably. 'It's possible, I suppose. Just to make sure that the Mirage Makers don't bestow a Mirager's sword on you after Magori-temellin's death. They might think it wiser.'

He imagined Tarran saying, *Think of something else, you dolt*, and forced himself to look up at the curve of the arches over his head. Built by Kardi buildermasters he guessed; non-Magor who'd had the help of Magoroth power to lift and carve. Skilled architects and engineers had learned to soar with the help of the Magor. It interested him, how they had built those arches. He understood the geometry of them, he understood why they stayed up, but he desperately wanted to know how they had been built. The mechanics behind their construction.

He must ask Barret. Perhaps he could go to Tyr and learn how to build an aqueduct . . . He would enjoy that. He could still do something to be *proud* of, to leave behind when he died. He could still be a worthy man. He could try to forget that he had once been Magoroth. That he had killed and hurt and betrayed. *Oh, Tarran.*

The bell above his head swung, struck by a beam of Magor power to produce a sorrowing note, rung repeatedly like a Tyranian temple bell tolling for the dead. Arrant exchanged a glance with Grevilyon and stood to face the crowd.

He was glad he knew nothing of their emotions.

CHAPTER NINETEEN

'This is not right,' Magoria-ungar protested from behind the lectern. 'These events happened only yesterday morning. Feelings run high because so many of our children were injured or endangered.'

'Loyalty,' Arrant thought. 'She is loyal to her Mirager. But if she only knew it, I don't appreciate what she's trying to do. I want this over and done with. I want it finished before Temellin comes back, so that he doesn't have to sit through this hell.'

'Arrant's father is not here to guide him,' Ungar continued. 'The lad is injured and must still surely be in a state of shock. To bring him before this body at this time – in effect, to put him on trial – is not worthy of us. I beg you to consider postponing this session of the Council.'

As she sat down, Berrin said, 'Is there anyone else who would like to speak on the appropriateness of this matter?'

Korden rose from his place with his family in the front row. 'Yes, I would speak,' he said and went to stand at the lectern. He had the voice of an orator, and a tragic passion that brought tears to the soft-hearted in the audience. 'I am the aggrieved party here. My son is dead, at seventeen. I wish everyone who was present on the practice grounds yesterday to give their testimony while it is still fresh in their vision, unmarred by faulty memory. I was not there. I want to know what happened. And I wish to make sure it will never occur again.'

He waved a hand at Arrant without looking at him. 'It is my belief that this youth is a danger to us all. We must take steps to ensure that our children are safe. That they are safe *now*, not tomorrow or next month or next season. It is already too late for Lesgath. We need to act, not postpone. True, it is unfortunate that the Mirager is not here, but his presence should make no difference to the outcome, surely. He is one man, and it is the Council which will decide this matter.'

He tried to say something more, but emotions choked him. He returned to his seat and buried his head in his hands.

'I am not a matter,' Arrant thought. 'I am a person.' He raised his gaze to stare silently around the hall. 'I will not crumble. Not today. Not until I am alone and they cannot see.' Today he would show them what it was to be Temellin's heir and Sarana's son.

'If there are no others who wish to give their opinion, we will vote on this first,' said Berrin, scanning the hall for any other speaker. No one moved. 'All those in favour of holding this deliberation today, unsheathe your swords.'

Blades, spilling colour, rose into the air like the spears of an assembled phalanx. There was no need to count them. Everyone could see that Korden's plea had not gone unheeded.

Ungar gave Arrant a sorrowful shake of her head.

Arrant fingered the hilt of his sword, now tucked into its scabbard. His shoulder and arm throbbed, and it was an effort not to fidget to ease the ache.

'The glow of affirmation carries the motion,' Berrin said formally. 'Let us continue. We will first call Magori-firgan to speak on the events.'

Firgan took his place at the lectern. His account of the early events of the class that morning was, as far as Arrant remembered, accurate. He was calm, but his voice broke several times. Once, when he was referring to Lesgath, he actually had to stop speaking, as if he was too affected to go on. Arrant ground his teeth in silent contempt; he was certain that whatever Firgan felt, it wasn't grief for his younger brother.

In command of himself again, Firgan continued. 'I sometimes combine classes to give students, especially those about to have a test, a better idea of what happens in a real battle, where you can't be sure of the competence of your opponent. Arrant held his own against his first opponent, Grantel, but Grantel's physical strength won out in the end, so I decided to pit him against Lesgath, who is – was—' he paused, biting his lip. 'Who was closer to his height. However, I left Arrant on the sidelines for an hour. Many students benefit from observing.'

'That's ridiculous,' Arrant thought. He'd needed practice, not observation. Moreover, Lesgath had been nearly eighteen, and although not much taller, he'd certainly been more of a man in musculature and body frame than Arrant. From that point of view, the fight had not been even.

Once again Firgan seemed overcome with emotion. When he spoke, his voice was hoarse. 'I think that was a mistake. Lesgath was tired when he took on Arrant. Arrant, on the other hand, was rested. However, he seemed to have perfect control. I never dreamed—' He stopped again. 'I never dreamed anything would go wrong, but I did keep a close eye on the two of them. I knew the two lads did not get along. Most of you will have heard the rumours. But students need to realise that if you lose your temper, you probably lose the fight.'

He wiped a hand across his eyes and added in an almost inaudible murmur, 'I wish I could turn over the hourglass, and live the day again.'

Arrant just managed to stop a cynical curl of his lip. He was sure Firgan didn't want to change a thing. And yet he must be speaking the truth . . . 'Goddess,' he thought with distaste. 'The bastard actually would like to see it happen all over again. He enjoyed seeing his brother burn. He enjoyed seeing my pain.'

'We sympathise with your grief,' Berrin said. 'If you feel you would prefer to continue your account some other time—?'

'No, no. I shall go on.' He squared his shoulders and touched the outer corner of one eye with a fingertip. 'Lesgath kept taunting Arrant verbally. And then he hit Arrant with a pain-giving blast of power. Arrant was slow with his defence, and he was really hurt. And he went to retaliate.

'I knew something awful was about to happen. I shouted at Arrant. I can't remember exactly what. "No, don't!" Something like that. I drew my sword. I flung myself towards him and seized him by the shoulder. I should have been able to stop him. I was just the crack in a hair too late. By then he had swapped his sword to his right hand and sent a shaft of cabochon power towards – towards Lesgath.'

He was silent, and bowed his head, biting his lip.

Arrant tried to stand straight, to meet the accusing looks now fixed on him as heads turned from Firgan to him. It was hard. So Vortexdamned *hard*. He wanted to shout at Firgan, to say: 'How did you know I would lose control? How could you know? What did you do?' Instead he had to meet the blame-filled gaze of the Magoroth. He was glad he could not feel the scorn that must have been rampant in the hall.

After a moment, Firgan raised his head. 'I will never forget what happened next. Never. Gold exploded from Arrant. It rushed outwards in all directions. Such power! It was so wild and uncontrolled and – and *savage*. It mowed down my brother like a scythe in the hands of a madman. It sent students flying through the air to smash into the yard walls. Mirageless soul, I will remember the – the crunching sounds of bodies slammed against the adobe bricks as long as I live. Thank the Mirage for the instincts and swift response of my sister, or the carnage would have been unbelievably shocking, a match for the Shimmer Festival massacre. We owe her a debt of enormous gratitude. But alas, not even she could save her own brother. Or, perhaps, Perradin Jahan.'

There was a long silence before Berrin said, 'A question, if I may, Magori-firgan. Why were you unhurt?'

'Well, I could say it was because I was positioned behind Arrant, and therefore not in the direct path of that murderous blast. But, er, there is something else I should confess here, although you have probably all heard the rumour anyway.' He sounded rueful, even embarrassed. 'I suppose I should be ashamed to admit this, but I once placed my cabochon in his sword hilt. You see, he had a reputation for killing people by accident, and I was going to be teaching him Magoroth sword techniques. It may have been bad manners, but well, I *am* still alive.'

He cleared his throat. 'Possibly what happened is this: Arrant had been using his sword. It was filled with undischarged power. When he switched it to his right hand, he brought it back in a swing behind him. When everything went wrong, power leaped out of his sword as well as his cabochon, and most of the sword power hit me. That power was deflected back at him, through my cabochon, because I had protected myself by once holding his sword. I was gripping Arrant by the shoulder . . . and thus he was burned but I was unhurt. Arrant was lucky he didn't die, right then.'

Arrant froze, horrified. Everything Firgan said could have been true. It could have happened exactly that way.

Maybe Firgan had done nothing wrong at all. Maybe that

obscene triumph emanating from him in the practice yard was just delight that Arrant was making a mistake and losing control? 'Oh gods above,' he thought, 'it *was* all my fault! Tarran might be dead because of me. Perry too.'

He would have fallen just then if Grevilyon had not grabbed his arm and steadied him. Nausea threatened to conquer him as he stood there, attempting to remember the sequence of events. Everything was so muddled, so twisted by horror. His fault. His, not something Firgan did.

Berrin spoke, his tone subdued. 'Thank you for your honesty. Was it also true that Lesgath had held Arrant's sword, and Arrant knew this?'

'Arrant knew I had held his sword, of course. I would never have dreamed of taking such an action without telling the person concerned. It would have been unethical in the extreme to do otherwise. But to my knowledge, Lesgath never handled Arrant's sword. He certainly never did so in my presence, as I have heard Arrant asserts. And I find it highly unlikely that he took that action on his own. Now, of course, we will never know for sure, because he is dead.'

Firgan glanced at Arrant. 'I am sorry for you. I know that you didn't mean anyone to be hurt. But I beg of you, take steps to make sure this never happens again. Lesgath did not deserve to die at seventeen, on the threshold of his life. He was a Magoroth, and he was needed to defend this land. He – he was my brother, and our family is forever changed by what happened yesterday.'

Gretha started sobbing at that point, and Elvena hugged her, glowering sourly at Arrant.

Arrant hardly noticed. He was thinking furiously. Firgan couldn't utter an outright lie in front of an assembly of Magoroth without them knowing. So when he said Lesgath had not placed his hand in the hilt of Arrant's sword, he spoke the truth. The man must have swapped the swords in the racks around, so that Lesgath had picked up someone else's, thinking it was Arrant's. Firgan had deceived them both.

But why?

And then he understood, the realisation sickening. 'Sandblast him to Hades,' he thought. 'He wanted me to think I couldn't defend myself against Lesgath; he wanted Lesgath to think he was safe from me, which gave him the courage to taunt me. Firgan engineered me into believing Lesgath couldn't be hurt by my sword. When he saw me about to use my power, he thought I'd use my sword, believing in my heart it wouldn't harm Lesgath. He was wrong – I used my cabochon because I didn't want to hurt myself in the rebound of power, but in the end it didn't matter. I killed Lesgath anyway, probably because I couldn't handle both the cabochon power I was using and the sword power that was being channelled back into me through Firgan. Firgan gave me the plans and I followed them, fool that I was. And that ends any chance I ever had of being confirmed as Mirager-heir, so Firgan's got what he wanted.'

He turned his attention back to the lectern, where Firgan was now addressing Berrin. 'Magori, may I be seated? I—' He shook his head and rubbed a hand over his forehead. 'If there are any questions, later perhaps . . .' Without waiting for permission he stumbled to his seat, where he sat abruptly, dropping his head into his hands. His shoulders heaved. Korden slipped an arm around the shoulders of his eldest son who had all the appearance of a broken man, devastated by his grief.

'Hells,' Arrant thought, 'am I the only one here who can see his hypocrisy?' He took a deep breath, savouring the bitter irony. He had killed the wrong brother. Lesgath might have been a nasty bully, but Firgan was more than that. He was a man who would happily see his own brother dead – not because he stood in the way, but simply because he'd had the misfortune to be a piece that had to be sacrificed to achieve a victory in a game of power.

And the man had *won*.

A patter of conversation through the hall brought Berrin to the lectern, calling the hall to order and asking the next witness to step forward.

One by one they came up to give their account of events, most of them entering from outside because they were not yet old enough to be part of the Council. Some, like Vevi, were wounded. She had broken her arm and grazed her face. Her evidence was concise, given without glancing at him. Others, like Grantel, were unharmed and muddled in what they said. Some, like Bevran, tried to lessen Arrant's guilt in their telling. Others, like Yetemith, were virulent in their fury at him. The story they told was more or less the same as the one Firgan had recounted.

The only person whose testimony differed slightly was Serenelle, and that was because Berrin questioned her in a different way. 'You raised a ward and saved many people with the speed of your reaction and the strength of that warding. The Magoroth – no, all of Kardiastan – owe you a debt of gratitude, Serenelle Korden. We are deeply sorry that we have to question you at this time of your grief for your brother.'

'Thank you, Magori.' She sounded composed. The look she gave Arrant was more inquisitive than hostile. 'I am ready to tell you what I know.'

'I suppose the question that puzzles most of us here is this: how were you able to react so quickly? Were you expecting trouble?'

'Not precisely. Firgan said – this was before Arrant fought with Grantel – that there was always a possibility that Arrant's power may get out of control. So, just before each of the fights

Arrant was in, he asked me to wait and watch. If anything went wrong I was to fling up a ward. He said it was just a precaution. So I was watching. When Firgan shouted, I started to build the ward across the practice ground, between Arrant and the rest of us. Unfortunately, I didn't get it finished in time so a few people were either burned, or flung across the yard. Like Perry.'

'So we have Firgan's foresight to thank for the safety of most of those on the practice ground?'

'Hey, he couldn't have done it without me,' she said pertly. 'I can raise a ward faster than any other damn Magoroth you care to name.'

Arrant almost smiled. Although she didn't sound upset, let alone grief-stricken, there were times when he actually *liked* Serenelle.

She looked across at him. 'You owe me hugely, Arrant Temellin, for that warding. And don't you forget it.' Then she turned back to Berrin. 'It wasn't deliberate, you know. I saw his face before he passed out. He was appalled. He's just a complete daftbrain when it comes to Magor stuff.'

'Thank you, Magoria,' Berrin said. 'That will be all.' When she had left the podium, he turned to address Arrant. 'Magori, we have finished listening to the witnesses. You now have an opportunity to address the Council. Or you can ask someone else to do it on your behalf.'

Arrant took a deep breath. 'I'll speak for myself,' he said. He had an absurd flash of memory: his rhetoric classes with old Cominus back in Tyr. 'What would the old man think if he could see me now?' he wondered, as he stepped forward to take his place at the lectern.

It was good to be able to cling to the lectern-top; fatigue intensified the pain that ran through his body on a network of invisible pathways. The healers' pain-control was wearing off. As he spoke, he tried to push the physical hurt somewhere else so that it wouldn't sully the clarity of his mind.

'I didn't intend to hurt anyone,' he began, 'I swear. I thought I had control of my power and I had no idea that I would lose it. The only other time that happened, I was just nine years old. I – I deeply regret hurting my fellow students. I have no excuse, no explanation. I don't know why it happened. Nor do I want anyone else to speak on my behalf. There is nothing to be said. You can all sense the truth of my words.'

Berrin waited, but Arrant was silent. Berrin nodded. 'In that case, we will proceed with—'

'We *don't* know that he speaks the truth,' someone interrupted. Arrant sought the speaker, and found her seated behind Korden. Magoria-markess. 'We know his mother had the ability to tell lies without us being aware of her mendacity.'

Arrant stiffened. 'That is a rumour utterly without foundation,' he protested. 'She never lied.'

'She came among us pretending to be slave. Such a pretence – which she maintained for many, many days – is the ultimate deception, surely. And we *believed* her lies.'

'She never lied,' he reiterated. 'If she had, you would have recognised the untruth. She has no ability to disguise a lie from a Magor.'

'How would *you* know?' Markess asked, her bitterness as unpleasant in the air as the bile on her tongue.

'Please,' Berrin interrupted. 'Arrant's mother is not charged with anything here. It is Magori-arrant's shortcomings, or otherwise, that are the subject of this inquiry. And no one has offered a shred of evidence now, or in the past, that he can lie without us knowing it. If you have proof, then offer it. If not, sit down.' He turned towards Arrant. 'If what happened on the training ground yesterday is deemed by this Council to have been a deliberate act on your part, aimed at killing or injuring your fellow Magor, the penalty would be death. Are you quite sure you have nothing else to say?'

'Nothing. Except to repeat that it was an accident. I may not have liked Lesgath, but Perry is my best friend.'

'In that case, I shall put it to the Council for vote. If you believe Magori-arrant to be guilty of *deliberately* causing death and injury yesterday, please call colour into your sword. I repeat: guilty votes only, please.'

Arrant's heart pounded in his chest, unpleasantly evident. He expected to see the Korden family vote against him at least, and he assumed there would be others who would follow their lead.

He was wrong. Not a single sword, not even Firgan's, was unsheathed from its scabbard.

Berrin did not look surprised. 'Scribe, please note that the decision was unanimous: Magori-arrant is innocent of a deliberate attempt to kill or harm any Magor yesterday.

'Next we must decide what should be done, as Magori-arrant has admitted to being the sole cause of a Magoroth death, and several injuries. He has also admitted to being unable to control his cabochon power.' He cleared his throat before going on, and Arrant suspected he wasn't happy with what was coming.

'Berrin's known Papa all his life,' he thought. They had grown up together. Played together, studied together, fought together. And now Berrin has had to preside over this; yet another person being hurt by what had happened. Would it never end? Stricken, Arrant bowed his head.

'I have two recommendations before me,' Berrin continued, 'lodged prior to this meeting. The first is related to the Council's confirmation of the Magori-arrant as Mirager-heir on his next anniversary day. It has been proposed that this body vote to inform the Mirager that we will not favour the confirmation of Magori-arrant, because of his inability to control his cabochon, and that Mirager-temellin be advised to nominate another Mirager-heir as soon as possible. Magori-korden is the proposer and I yield the floor to him.'

Korden rose once again. He looked gaunt and strained, but there was no doubting his strength of purpose as he began to speak. 'We all know that a Mirager or Miragerin usually comes to that post because they are the eldest child of the previous Mirager. I would remind you that there have been exceptions in the past, where an heir has been deemed unsuitable by the Council, and the Mirager – governed by his promise to rule by consensus – has acquiesced, after which the next in line was appointed Mirager-heir.'

Arrant, still standing without the support of the lectern, interrupted. 'Hey, wait a moment. Surely it can't be, um, *appropriate* for you to bring this proposal forth. You are the next in line.' He surprised himself. That was *his* voice ringing out over the hall, clear and deep and authoritative? He stood rigid, trying not to droop with fatigue. Inwardly he quaked, aware of his youth and his inexperience and the frailty of his position, amazed at his own temerity. Was he mad? 'Oh, sweet Elysium,' he thought, 'I have to prevent Firgan becoming the Mirager-heir.' Temellin would expect it of him. It was time to apply all the rules about public speaking that he learned in his rhetoric classes.

He met Korden's gaze and refused to flinch before the man's pain. 'Your grief, Magori-korden, for which I accept responsibility, and for which I will bear the guilt for the rest of my life, excuses you. But nonetheless, you are next in line, and it ill becomes you to make a proposal that concerns the next heir.'

Both Berrin and Korden opened their mouths to speak, but Arrant held up his hand to stop them, even as he pitched his voice to override their words. 'I will make all that irrelevant, if you like. I'm not moondaft. I am aware of my inadequacies. It was the hope of both the Mirage Makers and myself that I would overcome my inability to manage my cabochon whenever I wanted. That has not happened, and our hopes have ended in a terrible tragedy for your family, and others. I agree with you, Magori-korden. It must not happen again. There will be no more attempts by me to use my cabochon. And as a Mirager can only be someone who can manage a Mirager's sword and bestow cabochons, I will relinquish my role as Mirager-heir right now. There can be no other decision open to me.'

A deathly hush had fallen over the hall. Every eye was fixed on Arrant. He had an idea that he had surprised them all, that they had expected him to fight for his position. But he had not finished. 'There is one thing, however, that I think should be quite clear to everyone,' he said. 'Mirager-temellin is not an old man and may yet have other heirs. He may also have grand-children – my children – able to take up a Mirager's sword one day. Moreover, he is not present. This is *not* the time to decide who will take my place as heir. Nor is it your place to recommend anyone.'

They wouldn't be doing it at all, if Temellin wasn't blind, he added to himself, unable to keep a rein on his inner bitter-ness. And who among them remembered that Sarana had a Mirager's sword and could rule in his stead? 'Your Mirager is very much alive and capable of leading this nation. As we argue here, he *fights* for us all. He battles the Ravage to save the Mirage Makers – so that your children and grandchildren will have Magor swords and cabochons. He battles to save Kardiastan. I may not yet be old enough to sit here as a member of this Council, but you can't tell me that it is *honourable* for you to debate the question of an heir while the present Mirager is absent fighting for you.'

'Well said!' someone called from the back of the hall, and

there was scattered applause. Ungar smiled; Grevilyon, and a handful of others whom Arrant recognised, nodded their agreement. It was all he could expect, he knew. Too many people had family members suffering because of the events of the day before. Wounds were fresh and raw, and he could not blame them.

Firgan stood up again. 'I'd like to argue the point,' he said, almost snarling.

Berrin nodded and gestured him to the podium.

'Really, Arrant made the point for me. We need to have a Mirager-heir *because* Temellin is fighting. What if he dies? And the likelihood of that is greater than most of our warriors because he is blind. I vote that we should decide on an heir now, just in case. Mirager-temellin can argue our decision when he returns.'

Ungar spoke again after Firgan, pointing out that all this could be discussed if and when the Mirager died, and to discuss it as if it was highly likely was bad-mannered to the extreme. After her cutting remarks, no one else rose to comment.

'Let's vote then,' said Berrin. 'Bearing in mind that Magori-arrant is refusing to be the Mirager-heir from this day, the question is this: should we in this assembly discuss the identity of the next Mirager-heir so that we can make our wishes known to the Mirager? All who feel that the discussion should continue, please show your sword colour.'

Once again, Arrant was surprised. Gretha and several of the Korden children, including Firgan, made moves to draw their swords but were stopped by a cutting gesture and a glower from Korden himself. No one else in the hall moved. Arrant felt overwhelming relief; he had bought his father a respite.

'Perhaps we should consider closing this meeting of the Council—' Berrin began.

'There is another proposal in your keeping,' Firgan protested, climbing to his feet once more, 'as you well know, Magori. And we should consider it, for it is surely urgent. How can we be satisfied with Magori-arrant's assertion that he will not use his power again? He has a gold cabochon in his palm and a Magor sword at his side. He is a Magoroth with power he cannot control, no matter how much he would like to. What guarantees can he possibly give us that we can believe? That *he* can believe? How do we know that in a moment's anger he will not raze this pavilion, or kill innocent people walking down a street quite by accident? He can't give us that assurance. He doesn't know himself what causes his problems.'

He met Arrant's stare and held it. 'You know I speak the truth, lad.'

The sick feeling inside Arrant suddenly magnified tenfold. 'Sandhells,' he thought, 'what is he planning now? I'm not Mirager-heir any more and it's *still* not enough for him?' Fear rippled through him in a rising tide.

Firgan turned from him to face the Council members. 'Are we going to risk losing more of our children?' he asked. He didn't sound impassioned, but heart-broken. 'I am a soldier, and I have seen too many battlefields. I never expected to find another here, within our pavilions, where we keep our precious children safe. Children flung through the air like sand on the wind. And yet that is what I saw yesterday: a battlefield strewn with bloodied, broken children. It was sheer luck and quick thinking that saved most from death and no more than a traumatic experience. My brother's charred, burned body, smoking on the sand . . .' His voice broke and he struggled to regain his composure. 'There is only one solution that offers us safety.

'Arrant's cabochon must be broken.'

CHAPTER TWENTY

Firgan's words stilled the hall. Then all present – except Arrant himself – were buffeted by the shock that echoed in the wake of those words. And every Magoroth clenched their left hand tight in horror, as they considered what it was to become non-Magor.

Never to know again the true closeness of Magor love and friendship. Never to know again the climax of love-making that came from the clasp of two cabochons. To lose the ability to curb pain and heal; not to sense others nor feel emotion as a physical presence, not be able to refine emotions into a potent form of communication. To give up the Magor sword and the security it provided. To lose the right to be addressed by title. To be no longer a member of the ruling class of the land, no longer accorded respect because you were a Magor warrior and had Magor talent.

Arrant saw their horror, but could not feel it. 'I have lived most of my life being ordinary,' he thought. 'It is not so very terrible, is it?'

Ungar was the first to move, the first to speak. She leaped to her feet. 'No! Anything would be better than that. Breaking cabochons was a Tyranian horror, inflicted on those of us they caught – a torture beyond bearing. And you would mutilate our Mirager's son in such a fashion? I will *never* permit that to be done in my name.'

Gretha scrambled up in a fury. 'Then do it in mine. I have lost a son because of this – this abomination of a Magoroth. How many more have to die before his warped power is gelded?'

'I could never face the Mirager again, if I voted for such a thing,' someone called from the back of the hall.

Berrin attempted to bring order to the room, and was ignored. 'Would destroying another Magor bring back the one we have lost?' someone else asked.

'My brother lies between life and death still,' Grevilyon said to Gretha, 'and I would never consider such a punishment justified. And neither would either of my parents.'

'Well, they're not here, are they?' Ryval shouted at him. 'And we are!' For once Myssa nodded, agreeing with her twin.

Voices were raised all the way around the hall, arguing with passion. Berrin held up his hand for silence, but the gesture had as much effect as a hand raised against the sands of the Shiver Barrens would have done.

Arrant listened, coldly detached, as if it wasn't him they were discussing. He thought the consensus was on Ungar's side. And his, he supposed. To crack a cabochon was too barbaric, and too reminiscent of the horrors of occupation and enslavement.

Arrant looked over at Berrin. 'Stop them,' he said. 'I wish to speak.'

Berrin angled his sword upwards and sent a beam of power to ring the bell under the roof. Even then, it was a few moments before the impassioned voices were reduced to a murmur. 'Magori-arrant wishes to address the Council,' Berrin said formally. 'But before he does, I would like to remind everyone that there is another possibility that might be considered before making any irrevocable decisions. Arrant could go into voluntary exile.'

Arrant gave a wry smile. 'And kill Tyranians by accident instead?' he asked.

'Or we could ward you here for the rest of your life,' Ryval said, his nastiness spilling over to reveal itself in the twist of his lips.

'Thank you for that kind thought, Ryval,' Arrant said, deliberately dispensing with the man's title. 'However, I do not think there is argument necessary here. I am willing to have my cabochon broken, as long as there is a way to do it without risking my life.'

Ungar was on her feet again, appalled. 'Arrant, you don't know what you are saying.'

'Yes, as a matter of fact I do.' Even to his own ears, he sounded surprised. 'Do you think I *want* to live the rest of my life worrying myself sick that I may kill innocent people because I can't help it? I thought I had found the way to control my power, but yesterday I discovered *it didn't work*. I might query Firgan's motives, but not his logic. I want this done. I want it done now, before my father returns to stop it, because stop it he will, if he can.'

He stepped up to the lectern so that he could hold tight to the top. He wanted to stop the trembling in his hands. His detachment had melted away into the realisation of what he was proposing, and he was scared. 'Let me have the courage to do this,' he thought.

'Arrant, I beg of you,' Ungar pleaded. 'Grevilyon, go fetch your mother —! Berrin, you are the most senior person here, stop this travesty, *now*. We must wait for Mirager-temellin's return.'

Even as Grevilyon left the hall to fetch Jessah, Arrant turned to Korden, who had not spoken for some time. He was sitting motionless, hunched over, staring at the floor with his forearms leaning on his knees and his hands dangling down. He looked up when Arrant spoke his name. There could be no mistaking his pain.

'My father always said you were a man of honour, Magori,' Arrant said, striving for formality in order to counter the terror that threatened to shred his ability to speak. 'I questioned that honour today, but in truth – of all men, it is you I would ask to do this for me. For both of us. Would you?'

There was a breathless hush in the hall. Even Ungar was rendered silent, her tears rolling down her cheeks, as they all waited for his answer. Slowly, Korden stood. He said heavily, 'It does need to be done. I am sorry, Arrant, but we both know it's true.'

'I know.' No matter what Firgan had done to precipitate or take advantage of what had happened on the practice ground, the fact remained: he, Arrant, had lost control of his power. Even with his brother in his head. And only the gods knew what he had done to Tarran.

Korden looked over at Berrin. 'Close this meeting,' he said. 'There is no need for a vote. Arrant knows what needs to be done and is man enough to accept it. We should honour him for that, and end this now.'

Korden turned his gaze on Ungar. 'Have one of the healers attend to us in the Mirager's room,' he ordered in a tone that allowed no refusal. 'And send Jessah in, if she can come.' He gestured to Arrant. 'Come, lad. Let's get this over and done with.'

Ungar choked, her dismay so potent even Arrant felt it. He turned away from her and joined Korden; together they walked the length of the hall between the now-silent gathering. One of the Magoroth stood. Then two or three others. Then the whole hall rose to its feet, in tribute to a youth who had, before their eyes and with the courage and integrity of a single decision, become a man they could respect.

Korden led him to a door at the side of the hall and together they entered a small room with a low table and a number of chairs. 'This is the Mirager's room,' he said. 'Where your father waits for the Council to assemble before he makes his entry.' He turned towards Arrant. 'He will never forgive me for this, you know.'

'I will explain.'

'Nonetheless, I lost a son yesterday. And today I lose a friend.' He shook his head in sorrow. 'I have been jealous of him most of my life, knowing he was Mirager, and I never would be. I felt deeply for Firgan, knowing he had the same battle of envy to fight. I thought he would be a better Mirager than you. Now I am not so sure. Now I have seen a fifteen-year-old lad put us all to shame with his nobility of spirit, and his courage. It is a tragedy that you were not granted control over your power, Arrant. A tragedy for Lesgath, yes, but also for you and this land. You would have made a fine ruler if you had been truly Magor. I grieve for you and Lesgath both, today.'

'That is – is generous of you. I think I understand now why my father has held you in such deep respect, Magori.' He looked down at his palm. 'How – how do we do this? You know, back in Tyrans I had a nurse with a shattered cabochon. A Theura once. She told me legionnaires crushed her cabochon with a heavy blow from a blacksmith's hammer while she was unconscious. In the process, they smashed her hand as well, breaking all the bones. And afterwards she couldn't mend herself, or halt the pain . . .'

Korden tried to reassure him. 'I have a Magor sword. There is no need of anything so crude or dangerous. The legionnaires had to use force because they had nothing else that would break a gem. Of course, leaking power often killed not only the soldiers who wielded the hammer, but also anyone standing in the vicinity. Magic escaping without control can be lethal, much as it was for Lesgath, I suppose. The Tyranians made slaves do it in the end. Not Kardi slaves, because they refused, preferring death for disobedience. To deform a Magor was anathema to them.' His eyes had the far-away look of a man recalling a distant past of abiding sadness. 'They were dark times, Arrant. So many heroes who died alone or suffered unsung – slaves who revered the Magor, and people like your nurse.'

'Can we be sure this is safe now?'

'If I use a thin, clean cut with my Magor sword, the power should leak out slowly enough to be contained. And contain it I shall. I'll build a ward. I'll attune it to you so that we can pull your hand out afterwards, and just leave the ward here with the leaked power within. It can dissipate over several days as the ward weakens.'

Arrant nodded. It was an effort to be so matter-of-fact, to resist the temptation to scream or run or cry – anything, rather than stand here and sound calm and rational.

Korden continued: 'The cut will be painful, but I'll place a pain block as soon as I can. You will feel weak and lose consciousness. The healer will keep an eye on you, to make sure you don't lose too much strength. When you wake, it – it will be as an ordinary man.'

Arrant nodded. 'I understand.'

'Are you sure? There can be no stepping back from this. Ever.'

'I know.'

'Are you ready now, or do you wish to wait for the healer?'

'Do it now, Magori. And feel no guilt. This should have been done a long time ago.' And he had another unwelcome thought: 'If it had, Papa wouldn't be blind and I wouldn't have hurt Tarran. Will I ever know if I have killed him?' A tear rolled down his cheek and he made no effort to wipe it away. Someone should cry for Tarran. His life should never be unsung.

Korden nodded. Arrant undid his scabbard and sword and laid it aside, knowing he would never wear it again. He knelt on the floor beside the low table, and placed his left hand, palm upwards, in the centre. Korden stood beside him, unsheathing his sword. The translucent blade filled with the gold of power. They waited, both calm and silent, while Korden built a ward, encompassing Arrant's hand and the space above the table. He strengthened it with incantations. Then he nodded to Arrant. 'Test it. Can you remove your hand?'

Arrant pulled his hand free and then thrust it back again. 'I am ready.'

Korden slipped his blade inside the ward, and used the cutting edge to draw a line – no wider than a hairline crack – the length of the cabochon. It began to leak colour. Gold. Beautiful flowing gold, rich in hue, vibrant in tone.

Arrant could not contain his gasp. The intensity of the loss made the blood drain from his face. His being was streaming away from him in a river of gold. All that he was, or could have been. His essence, his core, his Magorness; his integrity wrenched from his bones, stolen from his flesh, torn from his skin. Every drop of power was garnered at the price of an agony rooted so deep he thought it took his life as it flowed away from him.

He tried to call out. He tried to change his mind. To scream denial, to stop the tide. Tried to say just one word. Tried over and over. *No. No. No.* He opened his mouth to refuse, to plead – yet no sound came.

He had never felt such pain. He had never known it was *possible* to feel such agony. It was death. Not a quick death, but a slow eternity of dying. And he couldn't even scream.

In the end there was just a thought. 'Papa, I am sorry I cannot be an heir to be proud of . . . I am so very, very sorry.'

Goddess!

Ligea flew up the stairs, two at a time. As close to panic as she had ever been. Heedless of gaping servants. Swung around the newel post at the top. Flung open the door to her personal apartments. Scared the life out of Narjemah who was sitting in the atrium sewing. Grabbed up the Mirage clay in trembling hands, and waited, panting. Waited for the clay to change.

Narjemah came to her side, white-faced. 'The Mirager?' she whispered.

'I don't know. Gods, I don't *know*. Something awful. I felt as though someone ripped my heart out.'

The clay changed and Temellin's face appeared. He was smiling. 'No, not Temellin.' Appalled, she looked up at Narjemah. 'It must be Arrant. And Temellin doesn't even *know*.'

She drew her sword from its scabbard, and swapped it to her right hand to look at her cabochon. 'Will you help me—?'

Narjemah divined her intention immediately and grabbed her by the arm. 'No! Never. You are too far away. No essensa would ever be able to cross so far and then make it back to the body in time. You'd *die* out there. Die bodiless, fading away to nothing.'

'But I *must* know what happened.'

'Then go to Madrinya. Tyrans won't fall to pieces. You've had most of the highborn come and kiss the hem of your robe already. There's only Devros of the Lucii left, and Gev and Valorian and the Senate can handle him. In fact, it's time. It's time Ligea became Sarana, and went home.'

Ligea took a deep breath, calming herself. 'Ah, Narjemah, I don't know what's home any more. But yes, you are right. It's time I went to them both.' She slid the sword back into its scabbard. 'And I will have to bear the agony of the weeks of not knowing what happened until I get there. Oh, goddess, Narjemah, what if Arrant has *died*?'

The door to the Mirager's room in the Magoroth Pavilion burst open and Jessah rushed in. Her anoudain was crumpled and dirty. Her hair appeared not to have been combed in days. She looked from Arrant to Korden, aghast. Above the table was a pillar of gold, a scintillating, twisting gyre. The glowing intensity of it made her avert her face. She turned her shock on Korden. '*What have you done?*'

He looked up from where he was cradling Arrant's body, rocking him. 'Jess,' he said, his uncontrolled misery swamping her. 'I am glad you came.'

'What have you *done*?'

'What was necessary.' He brushed Arrant's hair away from his face. 'But there is such irony here. He could have been the greatest of us all. Look at his magic, Jess. *Look* at it.' He gazed at the twisting colour. 'Have you ever seen anything so beautiful? So pure?' He turned back to Arrant, and gently touched his face. 'The greatest of us all – if only he could have controlled what he had. That power killed my son, Jess. I have made sure it will never kill again. Ironic, isn't it, that something so radiant, in a lad so brave, could kill my Lesgath so wantonly.'

She looked up at the warded magic. 'Mirageless soul. You – you cut his cabochon?'

'You should be glad. It hurt your son.'

'*Glad*? Never! *Sands* but you are sick, Korden. Is – is he going to die?'

He shook his head. 'No. And perhaps that is his tragedy.'

She crossed the room to take up Arrant's left hand. The cabochon was just colourless glass in his hand, with a crack running lengthways down its centre. 'No,' she said, and the word was a sob in her throat. 'I'm not glad. Mirageless souls, Korden, he was in my care. Poor, poor lad! And how do I tell Temellin this?'

'I don't know. Arrant killed my Lesgath, but I think what I've done to him is far worse. I have made the greatest Magoroth ever born so . . . so very *ordinary*.' He bent his head, and for the first time since Lesgath had died, he truly wept.

CHAPTER TWENTY-ONE

'Papa, if you are going to stay in Madrinya, then so am I. And that's the end of it. No more discussion. I really will *not* return to Asufa and Theura-viska. You've been ill, and you need someone to look after you.'

Garis looked across at Samia and stifled a sigh. He had no idea how he was going to manage her for the next few years. It wasn't that she was wilful exactly, or even disobedient. Most of the time she was everything he could have asked for in a daughter: dutiful, kind, loving, intelligent, thoughtful – until she got an idea into her head that nothing could dislodge. Like a kitten, he thought. All fluffy and adorable, until the moment it dug its claws in.

'Asufa has the Healers' Academy.' His last line of defence, and he'd already used it. A number of times.

He patted the neck of his shleth. They were ambling down the paveway into the vale of Madrinya as they chatted, on the final stage of their journey, and his leg ached. Not even Samia's healing had been able to fully repair the damage it had suffered. The city was in sight, tight-packed houses jostling one another, the odd-shaped blocks of adjoining buildings separated by a web of narrow streets. And beyond, edging the lake shining in the sun below, the belt of trees. It had been a labour of love to replant that woodland after the Tyranians had gone.

He was still saying that all she was going to do was *visit* her aunt, but he knew she had made up her mind before they'd left Asufa that she was staying as long as he did. And who knew how long that would be? His recuperation had delayed his coming to Madrinya to guard Arrant, but Temellin had indicated he was still expecting trouble. As the time for Arrant's confirmation drew closer, so Firgan would be more desperate to find ways to discredit him.

A ripple of anticipation ran up Garis's spine. He had been so bored with his convalescence, and his duties as administrator of Asufa had not helped. Administrator! Hells, how Brand would have laughed. They'd spent ten years dodging a hundred different ways of dying, in various vassal states and provinces of the Exaltarchy – all for Garis to end up shoving his seal into a ball of warmed wax on yet another document?

'Well?' Samia asked. 'Aren't you going to say all the other things you usually say next?'

He obliged. 'You want to be a healer. The Academy for healers is in Asufa. That's why Temellin sent me there in the first place.'

She gave the answer she always did. 'Papa, I am already a healer.' But then she added something extra. 'I am a better healer than any of my teachers. By rights, *I* should be teaching *them.*'

'Damn it,' he thought, 'that's probably true, too.' Aloud, he said, 'There are other things to learn.'

'Yes, and I can learn them at the Academy in Madrinya. In fact, I need to study some of the original books on healing, the ones the Mirage Makers gave to Miragerin-sarana. I'm sure that the copyists made mistakes in the anatomy diagrams.'

'You realise I will be spending a lot of my time with Arrant. Last time you met, you weren't happy being around him.'

'No, but I was younger then, and I didn't know how to handle the terrible pain he was in. I'm better at shutting that sort of thing out now. I have to be,' she added complacently, 'as I am far too good at feeling it. If I couldn't build walls around myself when I need to, I would be moondaft by now. No, Papa; make up your mind to it. I am staying in Madrinya for as long as you are.'

He grimaced. 'It's all my fault. I should never have taken you everywhere with me when you were a child. It made you a darn sight too fond of travel and change.'

'It made me resourceful too. Don't forget that. Did the Mirager give you any idea of what you are supposed to be protecting Arrant from?'

'Korden's sons, I gather. Especially the youngest and the oldest.'

'Ah. You'll have to be diplomatic, then. Difficult,' she added with a cheeky grin.

He made a face. She knew him far too well.

They continued to chat as they rode on into the city, but when they passed through the outlying streets, Samia fell into a quiet silence and her hands fidgeted restlessly at her reins. The shleth responded to her mood, and one of its feeding arms reached out to pinch Garis's mount. 'Samia, do pay attention,' he admonished. 'Your mount is misbehaving.'

She didn't appear to hear him. 'There's something wrong,' she said. 'You said Mirager-temellin wouldn't be here – well, he is, and he's terribly upset. So are lots of people. Lots and lots. It's *awful*. Papa – can't you feel it?'

But as always, she had sensed things first. 'Someone's dead?' he asked.

'I think so. And more.'

More? Fear eroded the edges of his heart.

*   *   *

Samia ran past the servant who was escorting them and reached Arrant's bedroom first. She did not bother to wait for an answer to her knock. She and Garis already knew who was inside: Temellin, Arrant, Hellesia, Jessah, Jahan and an Illuser whom Garis didn't know. She marched in, and went straight to the pallet where Arrant lay unconscious.

Only Temellin observed the protocols of greeting, and he was terse. 'Garis, Illusa-samia. I am glad you came. I wish it could have been sooner.' His haunted gaze returned to his son. 'As you can see.'

'What happened?' Garis asked. In truth, he was shocked. Arrant felt all *wrong*. And he had not seen Temellin in such a state since the day he'd thought Sarana was dying. His grief was entangled with rage and horror and a compulsion to do something about it that he was only just suppressing.

Samia provided him with the answer. She held up Arrant's left hand, and showed her father the gemstone there. A lengthwise crack, too fine and straight to have been an accident, ran down the middle. It looked as if someone had rolled the cutting edge of a Magor sword along it. All hope Garis had held that this might have a happy ending plummeted.

The tragedy had already been played out and there was no way to change it.

'Oh, my mirageless soul,' he whispered. 'Who did that?'

With the exception of the healer and Arrant himself, they all moved to the sitting room next door. It was Temellin who recounted most of it, with some contribution from Jessah. It was a sad and bitter recital. Garis and Samia exchanged a glance; the tale was even worse than either of them could have thought possible.

'And Perradin?' Garis asked Jessah. 'Is he all right?'

'It was touch and go for a while, but the healers — and his

own powers – pulled him through. Another day or two and we won't be able to keep him on his pallet.'

'He tells the same story?'

She nodded. 'He was able to give us more detail of the events that led up to it, though. He – he is wild to see Arrant. To tell him that he's fine.'

'When did all this happen?'

Temellin answered. 'Eight days ago. Jessah sent for me the moment she learned Perradin was hurt and I arrived back yesterday. Arrant hasn't regained total consciousness since Korden cut his cabochon. He will rouse himself to take liquids, but other than that . . .' His words trailed off and it was a moment before he had enough composure to continue. 'He didn't deserve this.'

Garis looked away, struggling to ignore the intensity of the emotions that swirled around the Mirager.

'He is healing,' Samia said. 'I can wake him, if you like. His body is in shock. What happened was just too – too traumatic. Sometimes not being here is the best way to cope.' That last bit was just quoting her teachers, but that didn't make it any less true.

Temellin nodded. He fixed his sightless gaze on her. 'Samia, I had personal proof of your healing skills when you were barely eleven years old. I believe what little sight I have is evidence of that. What is your assessment?'

She hesitated and glanced at her father, not wanting to say the obvious. In the end, Temellin said it for her. 'I know he's not Magor any more, which means he won't heal as fast or as – as thoroughly as we do.'

She nodded, relieved to hear he had no unrealistic expectations. 'I think I could help heal his body. I – I don't know how he will, um, mend his, his *spirit*, though.'

Temellin rose and went to the window. 'Let him have

another night of peace. Tomorrow morning you can rouse him. He needs to eat, if nothing else. I have sent for Sarana to come,' he added, staring blankly out into the gathering dusk. 'She might be able to help.'

'Have you seen Korden yet?' Garis asked.

'No. I have been too angry.' He turned back to face them all. 'I will say this: I will never allow any of the Kordens to be Mirager-heir while I am alive. More than that, I will do my level best to see to it that whoever succeeds me does not bear the Korden name. To that end, I have decided to appoint Sarana as Mirager-heir.'

For an instant no one reacted. Then Garis flashed a smile and let loose his approval for Temellin to feel. 'You think the Council will allow that?' he asked. 'After all, you are supposed to have consensus on your major decisions . . .'

'I think this will be the one time that I can make such a decision about Sarana and have them endorse it,' Temellin said quietly. 'It will be a fight, I know. But in this I will succeed, and there will be enough sympathy for me to carry the vote, I think. I will extract Korden's promise to support her.'

Garis looked disbelieving. 'Korden would do that?'

'Either that, or have me ban him from this pavilion for the rest of his life. If he wants me to listen to his advice in the future, he has to offer this concession. Above all, Korden needs to feel empowered. Being my adviser in the past has given him that.'

Garis was dubious. 'Still—'

'The Kordens did not come out of this whole affair well,' Jahan said. 'Firgan came across as self-serving.'

Jessah nodded. 'Arrant himself changed the way people felt. Apparently he was magnificent. You would have been so proud of him, Temel.'

'I am.' He shook his head in distress. 'There should have

been another way out. There should have been *something*. Korden should have counselled Arrant to *wait*. He was my closest friend once; but now – now my closest friends are right here, in this room.'

Samia ignored the pleased embarrassment of her elders that skipped around the room, and changed the subject. 'Why did Firgan want Arrant and Lesgath to think the sword Lesgath had held was Arrant's when it wasn't?'

They all turned to look at her. Temellin frowned. 'I've been wondering that too. The only explanation that makes any sense is that he wanted Lesgath to feel secure enough to goad Arrant – without him actually *being* secure. He wanted Arrant to kill him.'

'That's daft,' Samia said.

Garis glared at her. 'Don't be rude, Sam.'

'No, she's right,' Temellin said. 'It *is* daft. Arrant would never have used his sword against Lesgath. He knew any power that hit that youth would just come straight back at him! And if it was lethal, then Arrant would die, not Lesgath. Arrant's not an idiot, so why would Firgan think he was? There's something we still don't understand about this.'

'Arrant thought it was his fault,' Samia said. A tear ran down her cheek. 'That's why he allowed Korden to cut his cabochon. He didn't want to hurt people any more.' She bit her lip, trying not to cry. 'That's about the bravest thing I've ever heard of.'

'I think you are right,' Temellin said softly. 'It was very brave.'

Later that evening, in the quiet of the apartment they had been given in the pavilion, Samia brought up the same topic with Garis. 'There's something missing,' she said. 'Arrant couldn't call up his power at will, it's true, but only once – when he was nine – did he actually *lose* control to the extent of hurting anyone. That's right, isn't it?'

He nodded.

'Firgan couldn't have thought that Arrant was likely to lose control again. So what was he planning? It just doesn't make sense, Papa!'

'Things often don't,' he pointed out.

She glowered at him. 'Be serious!'

'I am. Possibly Firgan's plan was never carried out. He might have schemed to do something on the day of the test. Perhaps Arrant losing control had nothing to do with Firgan's plan. It was just a tragedy. That's evidently what Arrant thought – otherwise he would never have allowed Korden to do this to him.'

'I'm going to get to the bottom of this.'

'Sweetheart, there are some things you can't fix, you know. And sometimes stirring things up can make matters worse.'

'I don't see how things could be *worse*,' she grumbled. 'Papa, what will happen now? I mean, Arrant . . .' She went to put her arms around her father and lean her head on his chest, as if she was a child once more, and a hug could take away the worry. 'What will he do? He – he's not a Magor any more. When I took his hand, there was this horrible *emptiness*. It was like he was missing part of himself. As if his essensa was gone.'

She shivered in his arms. Her horror tendrilled around him, telling him more than he wanted to know. He wanted to protect her, shield her from all the grief that crouched in waiting in her life. He took a deep breath. 'I won't hide the truth from you, Sam. During the war, the Tyranians did this often, especially in the early years. They knew it devastated a Magor, so they did it a lot. They broke cabochons, and turned Magor into slaves, forcing them into the worst sort of work. Most of them killed themselves within weeks of losing their power.'

The anguish of realisation widened her eyes. 'You think you're going to have to guard him from – from himself?'

'I might, yes.'

She shook her head. 'Arrant won't kill himself,' she said with certainty. 'He has courage to match any warrior, anywhere.'

'He will need more than battle courage,' Garis said.

Tarran? Are you there?

No answer. He had the idea that he had been calling his brother in his sleep. For hours. Without answer. Wearily he opened his eyes, knowing the reality waiting for him contained more pain than he knew how to handle.

The first person he saw was Temellin, and he was alone. 'Papa,' he said. Temellin's hand groped for his. Their two cabochons clinked against each other, an empty sound. Temellin's grip tightened.

Arrant said, stumbling after the right words, 'Being non-Magor – it doesn't matter to me, well, um, at least not as much as you think. I mean, I've never been a whole Magor, not really. I've hardly ever been able to do all the things that you do without thinking. So I won't miss it. Honest.'

'That's not the whole truth, is it, though?' Temellin asked after a short pause.

'I – well, maybe not. I wanted to please you. I wanted to be the kind of Mirager-heir you'd be proud of. And I was beginning to think it might happen, because of Tarran. I thought – I thought everything might be all right in the end. But now I've disappointed you. And that *matters*.'

'*Disappointed* me? Dry hells, Arrant, I've never been more proud of you than I am right now. And what matters is you. That you are all right. That you can cope with this. That you can build another life where you will be happy.'

Arrant looked down at his cabochon. At the crack that now sliced through it lengthways. 'I'm all right,' he said. 'It doesn't hurt. I don't feel any different. And part of me always wanted to be ordinary. It's *easier* to be ordinary.' So why did he have that odd feeling of being incomplete? Yes, it might be easier, but it was also – he groped for the word – unsatisfactory. He looked up. 'But there are things that matter more than how I am. Perry? Can you tell me if Perry is all right?'

'Perradin is fine, already back on his feet and asking to see you. So are all the others who were injured. Lesgath was the only real casualty.'

Relief flowed through him in a cleansing flood.

'What about Tarran? Was he with you when all this happened?' Temellin asked.

'Yes. He disappeared, and I haven't heard from him since. I call him – but there's nothing there. I don't know whether it's because I've changed or – or because he died. Last time I lost control because he was pulled back to the Mirage. But it didn't happen that way this time. I lost control, and he screamed. Then he disappeared.'

Temellin sat motionless. Finally he said, 'There's a young lad due to collect his Magoroth sword soon. I'll ask him to ask the Mirage Makers about Tarran.'

Arrant nodded. Patience. He would have to be patient.

'And I've sent word to your mother. She'll be here soon.'

'Surely not! I mean, what about Tyrans?'

'This time you will come first,' Temellin replied, as if he already knew it for a fact. 'You'll see. Besides, the worst of the rebellion there is over. In her last letter, she said she was working out some compromise with the highborn who wanted slavery brought back, in the form of tax relief for those who employ large numbers of labourers.'

'Really? She won't have liked having to do that.'

'No, but she has learned to compromise. Most rulers do, I think.' He smiled. 'The Magoroth Council has just compromised – they have agreed to your mother being the new Mirager-heir.'

Arrant's eyes widened. 'They *approved* it?'

'This morning. It was not exactly unanimous. About one-third of those present voted against it, and a number abstained. But she is the rightful Miragerin and she already possesses a Mirager's sword. There is nothing much they can do about that, except grumble, and hope that I live a long healthy life.'

'But she's not even here.'

'She will be, soon, I promise. Don't worry about it, Arrant. As we both know, your mother is quite capable of looking after herself. Firgan will have his hands full if he wants to take her on.'

He smiled at Arrant and Arrant tried to smile back as he drifted into exhausted sleep.

When Arrant woke next, the face he saw bending over him was vaguely familiar, but he couldn't immediately put a name to the owner of it. A girl. Thirteen or so, and she had her cabochon held against the ruins of his own. A healer, then.

'That won't do any good,' he mumbled.

'You'd be surprised,' she said, and held his hand up so he could see his own cabochon. It glowed softly gold.

He snatched his hand away, and was surprised to realise how weak he felt. 'What did you do?' he asked, furious. 'I don't *want* it to work any more.'

'Well, it's not really working,' she said. 'I was just sending you some healing power and that seemed to be the best way to do it. It makes your gem glow, though, even though my power is red, not gold. Odd, isn't it? I hadn't expected that.' She frowned, puzzled, then continued, 'If I don't hold my cabochon to yours, my healing power will not be as effective.' She took his hand back and her hold was firm. 'Lie still.'

It was too much of an effort to struggle, so he lay back and felt the power trickle into him. There was nothing of his own rising to meet it, but then, there often wouldn't have been in the past, either.

He stared at her, trying to place where he had seen her before. For her age, the strength of her power was surprising, especially as she was only an Illusa. She didn't blush or giggle when he stared at her; she held his gaze, amused. That was enough to tell him exactly who she was. The freckles across her nose confirmed it. 'Ah,' he said.

'Well,' she asked, 'have you worked it out?'

'Samia,' he said. 'You've changed.' She had filled out – gone from being a child to the beginnings of womanhood. 'You looked more like a Sam last time I saw you.' His smile flashed, but was quickly gone. 'Your father is here?'

'Yes. He's going to be your bodyguard once you are up and about. I think he's hoping Firgan will try something.'

'He won't. Not now I'm not standing in his way. In fact, I don't need a bodyguard any more.'

'No? Well, we'll see. Perry said to tell you that he is not allowed out yet, which is driving him crazy, because he wants to see you.'

'I'd like to see him too. To say sorry.' He took a deep breath. 'I didn't think I could have borne it if he had been—'

'Well, he wasn't. I've seen him and he won't even have much of a scar. And what there is, across his cheek, he's actually quite proud of. He reckons he looks like a real warrior now, even though it was a burn, rather than a cut. Which reminds me. What happened to your shoulder, Arrant?'

He shrugged his left shoulder to see if it still hurt. It did. 'Firgan said it was my sword power being flung back at me, channelled through him. It was just my bad luck that he happened to be gripping my shoulder at the time.'

'A Magor is not supposed to be hurt by their own power,' she protested.

'No, that's true. But they also say that you can be killed by your own Magoroth sword if you use it against someone who has held it.' He shrugged. 'A paradox. But then, nothing about my power has ever been normal. Power did channel through me – I felt it go down my arm, burning all the way. Felt like I'd been chopped by an axe. Hades, I recall that.' His mouth went dry as he remembered. That awful moment in time when everything went wrong and he knew he couldn't undo what was happening . . .

'Tell me about it. As much as you can remember.'

'Why? It's not something I particularly want to talk about. Or remember.'

'I think you should. Because something happened out there that doesn't make sense, and I think you ought to think about it.'

He sighed, recalling that Samia could be as irritating as a stone lodged in your sandal. 'Nothing about my cabochon power has ever made sense, Sam. My mother thought it might have had something to do with all the things that happened to her when she was pregnant with me. Not even the Mirage Makers know why I am the way I am. Was. The way I was. They thought that I was missing the connection between the power and the means to control it.'

She gave him a wistful smile. 'I'd really like to know what happened. Then maybe I can help you heal better. You know healing is not so quick for you now that you aren't Magor.'

He found he wanted to please her, and was surprised. Why should it matter so much? He mustn't become too fond of her. Or any Magor. He wasn't one of them any more, and never would be. If he wanted a girl now, he'd have to look elsewhere.

'I think you probably know most of it already,' he said. 'But if you want my point of view, here it is. As far as I can remember.' He closed his eyes to conjure up the scene once more, and began to describe everything he could recall.

When he had finished, she looked thoughtful, but didn't comment.

'What is it?' he asked.

'Well, I still don't understand how you hurt your shoulder. It's deeply burned.'

'I lost control. My cabochon mowed down Perry and the others in front of me. My sword power channelled through Firgan and out of his cabochon, burning me.' He snorted. 'He probably enjoyed that too. It's no big mystery, Sam. I should count myself lucky I wasn't killed. I suppose that's because I had powered my sword down for the practice fight. There was nothing much there.'

'Yet it made a horrible burn. You're contradicting yourself.'

'Maybe Firgan added a bit of his own power. Wouldn't put it past him.'

'But it's not the only odd thing,' she persisted. 'Why did Firgan give you the impression Lesgath had put his cabochon to your sword hilt when he obviously hadn't? Did Lesgath know he hadn't, or was he deceived too? And why? Arrant, you don't think Firgan could be somehow to *blame* for all this, do you?'

He said slowly, 'I think he was planning something, possibly for the next day, during the tests. When it happened this way, he was delighted.'

'Except that anything he was planning must have involved assuming that you are a total idiot, daft enough to use sword power against Lesgath, knowing you'd be hit by the backlash. Shleth droppings!'

'Samia, it doesn't matter. None of it matters any more.' And yet . . . he remembered that moment when he'd felt Firgan's triumph.

'What do you mean? Of course it matters.'

'No, it doesn't. My mother is going to be Mirager-heir. She

and my father have years to sort out who will follow them. Maybe they can even have other children. She's not *that* old for a Magoria. Firgan will never be Mirager. And that's all I really care about.'

She was silent, so he added, 'You shouldn't even feel sorry for me, you know. I don't *mind* being non-Magor. It's better than being Magoroth and knowing that I could kill my best friend. Or you. Or anyone. Quite by accident.'

A tear trickled down her cheek.

He stared at her in astonishment. She'd cry for him?

'But what will you *do*?' she asked.

'I am going to go back to Tyr,' he said. He hadn't given his future much thought, yet the idea came to him fully formed and obvious. 'I shall study architecture.'

It was her turn to be astonished.

'I'm lucky, Samia. I know how to be ordinary,' he said.

She thought about that, then nodded. 'What happened to Tarran?'

'What do you mean?' he asked cautiously.

'I know he helped you control your power. I can keep secrets, so Father tells me everything. I pester him until he does. Anyway, you don't have to worry. I am far too sensible to be a tell-tattle.'

'Big-headed for a little brat, aren't you?'

'Papa thinks I'm perfect.'

'Little does he know.'

'Tell me about Tarran.'

He meant to avoid the question; to refuse to answer, but something in her earnest expression stopped him. It wasn't curiosity that drove her, but desire to help. And suddenly, he wanted to tell her. He wanted to share the burden. And so he told her everything, from the time he was a child visiting Ordensa, to the horrible moment when Tarran began screaming in his head as Lesgath tumbled through the air, burning.

When he'd finished, she said, 'But that is so – so *sad*. All of it. Tarran suffering. And you. Oh, Arrant, you were probably the strongest Magor there ever was; if only we could have solved the problem of how to make the right connection between your mind and that power, the way you did when Tarran was in your head.'

'"If only". They are pathetic words, Samia, because we can never go back. And I *did* have Tarran in my head this time – and look what happened!'

She was silent, and another couple of tears rolled down her cheeks.

He saw them, and felt guilty. 'I shouldn't have told you. Now I have made you miserable too.'

'I am glad you shared it. You haven't felt him since your cabochon was cut?'

'Nothing since my magic went out of control in the practice yard. The next person who goes to get their Magoroth sword will be able to tell us what happened to him. Father has already arranged that.'

'It must be terrible not knowing.'

He nodded. His ignorance of Tarran's fate eroded any chance he had of peace. He felt as if half his life had been shorn away, and he was left half a man – and it wasn't only his lack of Magor power that made him feel that way.

She stood up, releasing his hand. 'You need your rest. And I've pestered you enough.' She didn't wait for him to reply, but skipped out of the room, suddenly a child again. He couldn't make up his mind whether he liked her enormously, or whether she was the most annoying brat he'd ever met. 'Now I know what it must be like to have a little sister,' he thought.

* * *

He didn't see her again until the next day, when she took her position in the continuous line of healers who came throughout the day. He had complained to Temellin, saying he really wasn't ill enough to warrant such attention, but Temellin's reply was stern: 'These healers are the reason you feel as well as you do, and don't you forget it.' Chastened, he submitted with as much good grace as he could muster to the entry of yet another taciturn Illuser who took his hand and concentrated over his work.

He brightened, though, when it was Samia's turn. The moment she came into the room, he felt happier without any good reason that he could see. She was bossy, she scolded, she talked far too much, she treated him as if *he* was *her* younger brother – yet he cheered up the moment she was around.

'I've had a trim idea, if you'll listen,' she announced. '*I* think it's trim anyway.'

'Not something that's going to make me feel an awful fool because I didn't think of it first, I hope.'

'Oh, most boys your age are awful fools,' she said. 'I'm not sure why. Look at Perradin and Bevran and—' He glared at her and she subsided. 'Anyway, here's my idea. When a cabochon is shattered, or when we use up all our power, the gem goes almost clear. I checked with the healer who saw you first: he said when he first saw yours, it was colourless, like clear quartz. Then, as you recovered, it recovered some of its colour, just as anyone's does as they build up power again.'

He looked down at his hand and snorted. 'This is just a pale reflection of what it should be. Back in Tyrans, I had a nurse, a Theura once. Hers was shattered by legionnaires. It was pale green; a pretty shade, but never that lovely deep emerald colour it should have been. She had no power. None. Ever.'

'No, and I don't suppose you will either. The cut is there, and nothing will change that – but you were born with power, and every time a Magor uses up that power, it's renewed. Remember, the gem just magnifies what the individual Magor feeds it. In other words, you are still producing power. I think a cut cabochon would probably still work – but it can't, because the power leaks out.'

He stared back at his hand. 'You're saying I *still* have power?' He regarded his palm in revulsion. It was obvious when he thought about it. Gods in Elysium, what did he have to *do* to get rid of something he didn't want? Aloud he said, and his voice held a note of desperation, 'No amount of potential is going to amount to much now, is it? So what's your bright idea?'

'I can build a ward around your hand tonight. I'll stretch it tight over your cabochon and attach it to your bed, with your hand trapped that way. I know wards are hardly my strongest skill, but if it's just a tiny one, I think I can make it tough enough to stop your power leaking out temporarily.'

'But why would you want to do that?' He stared at her in genuine puzzlement.

She rolled her eyes. 'Preserve me from the stupidity of sprouts! To give you enough power to call Tarran and talk to him, of course. After all, don't you think it's possible Tarran might be just as worried about you as you are about him?'

'Oh. *Oh!*' He thought about that. It might just work. For a while.

But what if he lost control again? He didn't know why his magic had flown away from him in all directions out there on the practice ground. What if it happened again, here, in the confines of the bedroom? Of course it wouldn't be much, but it might be enough to hurt Samia. Or Tarran yet again . . .

'No,' he said flatly. 'No. I have no idea if I can control any power at all. I will not put myself in a position where it can happen again. *Never*. Understand?'

She pulled a face. 'Oh, all right. And it was *such* a good idea, too.'

After she had gone, he tried once more to speak to Tarran, but the inside of his mind was his alone.

And that was the true horror of the breaking of his cabochon.

CHAPTER TWENTY-TWO

Just a few more days and she'd be in Madrinya. She'd hold Temellin in her arms once more. She'd see Arrant. How much he must have grown in two – no, almost three – years. A youth on the edge of manhood. Indeed, his next anniversary day was the age of manhood in most of the known world.

If he was alive. She had left Tyr before receiving any message, and she still didn't know what had happened. That ghastly feeling of knowing someone she loved had been somehow torn, but not knowing exactly how – or even being positive who: it haunted her dreams as well as every waking moment.

The news she'd heard at the wayhouses on the paveway from Ordensa was unsettling rather than tragic. Unfortunately, it had also been garbled, with every traveller having a different tale. Arrant was ill. No, he wasn't, but he was no longer Mirager-heir, Korden was. No, that wasn't true. The Mirager-heir's cabochon had burst and killed people. No, that was shleth tripe. He'd been tried by Council for killing Korden with his sword.

Knowing she wouldn't have the real story until she reached Madrinya, she tried to relax.

When she rode into one of the wayhouses north of Asufa, after asking in vain for some accurate news, she used the baths and went to her room, intending to sleep early as she wanted to ride a double journey the next day; two days' ride in one ... She had to know, blast it.

She dozed, only to be woken not much later by agitated voices. *Trouble*. She knew the sound of it, the feel of it. Emotions seeped through the wall. The wayhouse was awash with alarm and grief and shock. *Vortexdamn*. She listened, then rose and dressed, and by the time the knock came at her door, she was ready for it.

'Magoria?'

The wayhousekeeper. He didn't know who she was, and she hadn't given her name, but the fact that she was a Magoria was enough. This kind of trouble was Magor business. 'What is it?' she asked, although she had already heard the gist. A strange wind. A dust-storm. People slaughtered in a vale like chickens for a feast. And no one to blame for it. Magic, someone said. A Magor murderer, another postulated. No, numina, it had to be numina, those strange spirits that no one ever saw, but that everyone thought existed nonetheless.

One part of her didn't want to deal with this, not now, but this was Magor business, and she was Magoroth. She sat in the wayhouse refectory and listened to the stories, and promised to tell the Mirager of all the tellers had seen. Not numina, but beasts leaving the Mirage on the wind. She recognised the descriptions. The Ravage was on the move.

He was on the road, waiting for her. He'd felt her coming and had ridden out, alone, to meet her. In the distance Madrinya huddled, glowing in the soft light of sunset, but he was a mile or two outside the last of the houses. The feeling of him gleamed as steady as a lamp in a still room. The essence of him hadn't changed. He was Temellin, Mirager of Kardiastan, who loved her. She'd seen him last when Arrant was five, and he'd been standing on the shore in Ordensa, watching the

Platterfish sail out of the harbour. Ten years ago, ten years of separation, yet now even a few more moments seemed too long to wait. She urged the shleth into a last burst of speed.

And at last she was tumbling off her mount and into his embrace. She didn't need to ask if her son was alive, she felt that much in him. But the rest? She felt that too: his pain, his grief, his anxiety. His reluctance to tell her what it was that had torn her soul in two.

'Whatever it is,' she said, her first words, 'we will survive it, and go on. *Tell me.*'

Arrant woke, knowing that she was there in his room. And feeling for too brief a moment that he was a child again, and the arms that reached out to him would make everything all right, the way they had when he was very young. She held and rocked him and brushed the hair away from his forehead before he managed to sit up straight and give the appearance of being someone on the threshold of adulthood.

'It's good to see you,' he said.

'I am so, so sorry,' she said. 'You didn't deserve this.'

'Has Father told you everything?'

'Yes. Everything. Including everything about your brother, and your power. I should have believed you concerning Tarran. I – I can't apologise for doing that to him, though. It was the only way I had to save him.'

'He knows. He has the Mirage Makers' memories of everything – of who his mother was and what she did, and what happened the day she died. He grew up knowing. It bothered me more than him. He is proud to be a Mirage Maker. I might have blamed you, but he never did.'

She took his hand and looked at the cut along his cabochon. 'I can understand why you allowed this. Better, I think, than your father does. We both know there is a world beyond being Magor, don't we? You must go and find it, Arrant. Find a way to be happy. To be the best you can be. You have so much to give.'

'I thought of going back to Tyr, to learn how to build aqueducts for Kardiastan. It's absurd to be so limited by water resources when there is all that snowmelt from the Alps going to waste.'

She laughed. 'That is a very Tyranian answer.'

He looked sheepish. 'It is, isn't it? But then part of me is still Tyranian, I swear. Tell me everything. How is Gev? And Narjemah? What did you do about Devros?'

They talked till dawn, catching up on the missing years, with an easy camaraderie he could not remember ever having in the past. 'I am older,' he thought. 'And we have much in common – we are both haunted by our different guilt.' And haunted by the same tragedy too: Brand's death.

'Will you come back to Tyr with me?' he asked, as the sun came up on a new day.

She shook her head. 'No. As of this moment, the last Exaltarch is no more than someone for historians to argue about. Now Temellin needs me. And I need him. I'm sorry, Arrant, I am abandoning you yet again, aren't I?'

He shook his head. 'No. The other way around this time. It's me who's leaving.'

'Well, I *am* stealing a position that's rightfully yours.'

'Watch your back,' he warned, and he wasn't joking. 'Firgan wants to be the next Mirager a lot more than either you or I do, and he has no scruples about how he gets there.'

'Oh, I'm pretty experienced with devious schemers. Rathrox Ligatan was a good example and I was a willing pupil.' She stood up and yawned. 'I must go; I have kept you up all night. Don't worry about us, Arrant. You go and build your aqueducts. Pick up the threads of a new life.'

He nodded and smiled. New threads for the weaving of a future of his own patterning: he liked the idea of that. He would be the architect of a new Kardiastan, a land where everyone had water piped to their house. Nothing romantic in that, perhaps, but a worthy ambition nonetheless.

It was odd, but the two people who made the most fuss about his decision to leave Kardiastan were Serenelle and Samia. When he was up and about again, Samia cornered him in a quiet corner of the garden, and enumerated a whole list of things he ought to be doing instead, which included finding a way to mend his cabochon, discovering why it didn't work in the first place, investigating if Firgan really had engineered Lesgath's death somehow, and working out a way to banish the whole Korden family to the islands off the west coast of Inge or somewhere equally remote. He didn't know whether to be amused or exasperated.

Serenelle was even more blunt when she found him packing up some of his belongings left in the Academy classroom just prior to his departure. 'You're running away,' she said.

He shrugged. 'No point in staying. I don't belong here any more.'

'You let him win.'

He didn't have to ask whom she meant. 'He didn't win.'

'You know he did. And worse is coming, you'll see. He'll be the next Mirager, and your parents will be dead before their time.'

'My parents can look after themselves. They're good at that.'

'I hope they are better than you are.'

'Why does it worry you, Serenelle?' He was genuinely curious. 'I would have thought you'd be glad if Firgan became Mirager. He's your brother.'

'And what do you think it's *like* having a brother like him, you fool?' She stamped her foot at him in frustration. 'Mirage preserve me from shleth-brained sprouts!'

'If Firgan bothers you, go to your father.'

This time she rolled her eyes. 'No father wants to acknowledge that his heir is a murderer. Least of all mine. Do you think he'd ever credit the idea that his precious firstborn is guilty of fratricide?'

He was shocked that she spoke so casually of Firgan having a deliberate role in Lesgath's death, astonished that she had even considered the possibility of it. While he was still trying to think of something to say, she took a step closer and reached out to take hold of both sides of his bolero. Then, even as he wondered what she was up to, she had pulled him close and kissed him full on the lips. He was so unprepared, he went cross-eyed trying to look her in the eye.

Then other parts of his body reacted to her curves pressed against him and he found himself kissing her back with an ardour that came from nowhere he recognised. Just when he'd decided that the sensations he was feeling were very pleasant indeed, she stepped away from him.

'That,' she said, 'was just to show you what you could have had, if you'd kept your wits about you. I don't know exactly what Firgan did, but I do know that he made a fool of you, Arrant Temellin. And I know that you wrecked my life as well as your own when you allowed your cabochon to be destroyed by my idiot of a father.'

With that, she turned on her heel and left him.

He felt a fool. He'd kissed Serenelle and enjoyed it, but he was far from sure he liked her, and damned sure he didn't trust her.

PART THREE

FRIENDS, FOES AND LOVERS

CHAPTER TWENTY-THREE

In the valley of the River Arteus, which flowed from the Alps to join the River Tyr near Getria, a man hauled himself up the flimsy scaffolding ladders to the highest point on the stone arch of a half-built bridge. His movements were as deft as a spider on its web, and on arriving at the top, he strolled casually over the freshly laid stonework to within a finger's breadth of the edge. He was now further above the ground than the roof of the tallest building in Tyr. Until the keystone was slipped into place, the only thing that held up the arch – and him – was a makeshift wooden mould, yet the height worried him not at all.

The bridge workmen called him Araneolus, 'little *spider*'. He wasn't that little, being rangy rather than short, and muscular with it, too – a man couldn't spend much of his days on the network of scaffolding without building muscle – but they thought the name suited his fearlessness and agility. Besides, they found the similarity between Araneolus and his real name, Arrant, amusing.

Once he had been an Exaltarch's son, but the workmen didn't consider that of any importance. There was no Exaltarch now; the last one – a woman, would you believe? – had vanished one day after addressing the Senate and telling them they didn't need an emperor any more. What was important to those who built the aqueduct was that they now had a bridge builder who knew what he was doing, who worked alongside them, who wasn't too uppity to haul on a rope or pass a pail, who cared if one of the labourers was hurt, and who saw to it that they were paid on time. They mocked him to his face, and he would grin amiably at their rough wit, but in the company of others they referred to him as Architectus, builder-master, and they didn't give that title lightly.

A stonemason, awaiting the arrival of a carved block of stone from below, greeted him with a grin. 'Right on schedule, Master Araneolus. The last keystone.'

'Looks as if you'll get your bonus, Licinius! Start the winch and let's get that thing up here.'

The stonemason bellowed, the workers started to turn the winch, the rope squeaked across the pulleys of the wooden crane. Arrant felt a deep satisfaction. Maybe he couldn't help out with Magor power, but he could build a fine bridge spanning a river valley. They'd be laying the channel for the aqueduct across it soon, and water would flow from the mountains down to Getria.

'The most beautiful bridge in Tyrans,' he told himself. 'And when it is finished . . .' He looked over at the mountains, where the aqueduct would collect pure spring water. The Alps, barrier between him and Kardiastan, between him and what was left of the Mirage, between him and his brother. So near – and so impossibly far. Perhaps one day, it would be time to go home. But not yet.

When he had left Kardiastan, he'd just turned sixteen. Now he was twenty. Four years, studying and working and building. And living without the people who loved him best.

At least he knew Tarran had survived. Before he'd left Kardiastan, a young Magoroth sent into the Shiver Barrens had brought back a message from the Mirage Makers: *He lives, but cannot find you. He was hurt, but has recovered.* The terror dammed up inside of him melted away with the news. Tarran lived! And doubtless it was the lack of colour in Arrant's cabochon that prevented contact.

He should have been happy.

If anyone had asked him, he would in fact have said he *was* happy. He was doing something he had often dreamed about, yet never thought would be within his reach. He had the joy of seeing the simple elegance of one of his bridge designs become reality. He was young, yet had the respect of his teachers and his artisans and his workmen in ways that had nothing to do with being the son of the last Exaltarch or the son of the present Mirager.

The truth was, though, that he could not remember the last time he had been completely happy, unworried by his fears that the Ravage would win untrammelled by the burdens of the past trailing after him like a clogged plough dragging behind an ox.

Worse, his brother's absence from his life was a constant ache. And it wasn't just Tarran who was absent. He missed his friends: Perry with his sturdy, unquestioning support; Bevran with his funny face; Vevi with her bossy ways; Samia, pertly irritating and always so annoyingly *right*. There were even times when he would have given anything to see Serenelle, whom he didn't understand at all.

He, who had never had a family life, found he missed it with an intense longing. It was four years since he had seen either of his parents. He missed Temellin with a sorrow that lingered, in spite of frequent letters. And he longed to see his mother, to talk to her. To tell her about the things only she would understand: how Gevenan had come to see him, how Arcadim was now the Rebiarch, how the Senate was struggling to stop the highborn families from circumventing the anti-slavery laws by indenturing the poor and then forcing them to work off the debt.

'Hey, Araneolus!'

Arrant broke free of his reverie and peered over the edge of the arch. The winchman supervising the raising of the keystone had his hands cupped around his mouth. 'Someone here to see you!'

Arrant waved to signify he'd heard and scanned the people below. Carpenters, masons, labourers, surveyors, a water-boy – and a man wearing a riding cloak, sliding down from his mount. From his *shleth*. A second shleth was being used as a pack animal.

Oh gods, Arrant thought, *please don't let this be bad news.*

He made for the topmost ladder, calling to the mason as he went. 'Licinius, seems I have to go down. The honour of placing the last keystone is yours.'

He more than earned his right to his nickname by the speed with which he reached the ground. '*Garis*?' he asked as jumped from the bottom rung. 'What are you doing here? Is everything all right back in Kardiastan?'

For a moment Garis looked at him blankly. Then he stepped forward, submitting to Arrant's hug with an incredulous grin on his face. 'Mirageless soul – I scarcely recognised you. You feel different. And you've grown. Filled out. Shiver the sands, you're taller than I am.'

Arrant grinned in turn; Garis was not a tall man. 'It happens. But you haven't answered my question: is everything all right?'

'Everyone's fine, but I have something to tell you. In private.'

'Then let's go to my tent.' He informed the mason master where he was going, and the two men picked their way through the construction site. 'I suppose my parents told you where to find me?' he asked as they dodged around a cart unloading more stone blocks from the quarry.

'Yes. Building a bridge across the Arteus, Temellin said. Which didn't mean a thing to me. I had to ride to Getria first, to ask for directions.' He glanced over his shoulder to where the aqueduct stood, clad in its scaffolding. 'Temellin would like your bridge. He's proud of you, of what you're doing, you know.'

'Is he? At last I've found something I can do well, huh? It's a pity he can't actually *see* it.' There was an awkward silence. 'Sorry,' he added, sighing. 'That was an utterly tasteless remark. Sometimes I wallow in self-pity, as unattractive as it must be.' He flashed a smile at Garis. 'I am delighted to see you, really! I've missed you.' He'd also missed Sam, although he wasn't about to admit that. She'd written the occasional letter, without much news, but always including some funny facet of her life as a student healer. He invariably ended up laughing as he read them.

With Garis leading his shleths, they left the work site between the rows of stacked stones ready for the building of the aqueduct channel, and headed upriver. When they rounded the first bend, Arrant indicated the largest tent in the encampment on the banks ahead. 'Beautiful spot, isn't it? I swim in the river every evening, and the kingfishers are so used to me that they hang around to catch the fish I scare in their direction.' He called to a boy carrying a basket of onions from the store tent to the kitchen area. 'Hey, Senesces! Take these beasts and get someone to unsaddle and water them, will you? And then bring the packs to my tent, and some wine and something to eat, as well.'

Senesces gaped at the shleths and took the reins with nervous reluctance. 'Will they bite?' he asked, wide-eyed.

'Not even a nip,' Garis said airily, slapping down a mischievous feeding arm.

Arrant grinned and shook his head in mock despair as he drew back the flap of his tent to allow them to enter. 'Slip your sandals off, you barbarian. You're in Tyrans, you know, and even a tent has refinements here.'

'Oh, Tyranian niceties now, eh?' Garis asked as he removed his footwear. The floor was strewn with reed-woven mats, smooth to the feet. The interior was capacious, but even so a large table, spread with scrolls, architectural designs, styli, rulers and callipers, took up most of the available space. A cot with Arrant's bedding was pushed into a corner, clothing hampers underneath. Several upright chairs, a number of stools and a bronze washbowl on a carved stand made up the remainder of the furniture.

'Have a wash and take a seat,' Arrant said.

'You live well,' Garis remarked as he dried himself after rinsing his face and hands. 'Better than an officer in an army camp, anyway.'

Arrant shrugged. 'Better than my pay as bridge builder allows. I have an allowance Sarana arranged for me, which old Arcadim deals out every month. Did you ever meet him? Sarana's moneymaster. He never did go back to Assoria, as he used to say he would. Whinges like the wind all the time, then sends me small luxuries he buys with his own money – and bills her for.' He laughed. 'She always pays. I think he's trying to tell her something, but I'm not quite sure what. Her personal fortune is huge now, you know. The allowance is ridiculously high, so I use most of it to give the workers bonuses if they keep on schedule.'

He dropped into a chair and waved Garis into the seat opposite. His voice sobered as he asked, 'Tell me, are the – the Mirage Makers still alive?' His mouth went suddenly dry as he waited for the reply. *Tarran, don't you dare have died on me, please . . .*

'Yes, just. They are down to an area about fifty Exaltarch miles long, bordering the last of the rakes.'

Arrant paled. The original length of the Mirage had been close to five hundred miles, surely, and the width around two hundred. 'And how wide?' he asked in a whisper.

There was a long silence before Garis replied. 'Half a mile, no more.'

'*Gods.*'

'It's much worse than when you left, Arrant. What we do does help a little, but most say that all we are doing is delaying the inevitable. Others are more optimistic, and think we can save that small area. Every so often a Ravage beast turns up south of the First Rake, usually dead. Almost like a reminder not to be too complacent, to remember that sooner or later we'll be fighting on our farms for the safety of our vales and in our streets for the lives of our townsfolk.'

It was a while before Arrant could speak. No one had told him by letter that it was as bad as that. Then he asked, his voice gruff, 'Tarran?'

'No news. I'm sorry.'

'I'll come back immediately. My sword skills will be useful even if my power isn't. And it's time I saw the Mirage.' Time he saw Tarran. Before he died.

He stopped speaking when Senesces entered with the wine, followed by several camp boys bearing an array of dishes and Garis's packs. Arrant swept the scrolls on the table up to one end, and washed his hands as the food was laid out.

'Pull up your chair,' he said as the servants left. 'Let me see, we have bread, cheese, honey cakes, cold baked wood-possum and quail and those shrivelled things wrapped in vine leaves are stuffed dormice, I think. Crunch them up, bones and all. I have a good camp cook. He's always trying to feed me.' He poured out two goblets of wine and handed one to Garis.

'I had another reason for coming. Did you know that Samia never gave up trying to find out how Firgan was involved in what happened to you?'

'I did tell her it didn't matter.'

Garis snorted. 'And when has Samia ever taken any notice of what you or I said? I don't know how you explained why you lost control of your power while fighting Lesgath, but she never believed you had the right of it. Then one day she stumbled on something that the others had forgotten.' He rubbed his forehead ruefully at the memory. 'Did she ever scold them over that! The girl's becoming a terrible shrew.'

Arrant was not deceived. Garis's tone was one of fond indulgence. 'So, what did they forget?' he asked.

'That Firgan had been in the library, researching things. Remember? Once she found that out, she was in the library every day, hunting for whatever it was he discovered. She was certain there must have been something, and I think she was right.' He cradled his goblet and met Arrant's gaze over the rim. 'She found a short passage in one of the books that the Mirage Makers originally gave to Sarana, something buried deep in a discussion of battle techniques. Explaining how a Magor can place his cabochon directly onto the skin of another Magor and send his power through that person, without killing him, to discharge out through that person's cabochon. It was mentioned as a method of creating a force greater than the two separate powers. Painful to the conduit person, though. And not controllable by either party.'

Arrant stilled. Shock dug claws into him, dragged out his memories in its talons. His right hand involuntarily flew to his shoulder. His fingers touched the burn puckering his skin there. 'No,' he whispered. 'Don't say it. I don't want to hear it.' But he did. He had to know.

And Garis was relentless anyway. 'It was mentioned as

something to try only in extremity, not just because the mesh of power formed was uncontrollable, but because it was *especially* dangerous to anyone in the vicinity if *either* person involved in delivering it was a Magoroth. It doesn't even mention what might happen if both of them are.'

Arrant swallowed. For a moment he was back on the practice ground. A wave of gold roiling outwards, pain flaring through his body, people falling and tumbling like chaff before the winnow.

He licked dry lips. Rage began to well up from some place deep within. 'Can – can Firgan have done this accidentally?'

'No. You'd be dead if that was the case. Without special conjurations from the initiator, a surge of cabochon power through someone's body would kill them. He didn't want you dead, Arrant. He wanted you blamed for something you didn't do.'

For a moment Arrant couldn't move. Then he clamped a hand across his mouth, abruptly jumped up and ran from the tent. He just reached the privacy of the bushes along the riverbank before he threw up everything he had eaten that day. Afterwards, he leaned his forehead against the trunk of a tree, his body shuddering.

Garis came after him a moment later, to lay an arm around his shoulders.

'The murdering bastard,' Arrant muttered. 'He really did kill his own brother deliberately. And he made a fool of me. I did indeed take the blame.' Nausea uncurled inside him in waves. He pushed himself away from the tree with his forearm and turned his head to look at Garis. 'I volunteered to have my powers taken from me, because of him. I castrated myself. I made myself less than I had been, less than my potential. I removed myself from the line of succession. And I cut myself off from Tarran forever. How Firgan must have laughed at me. Shades of hell, one day I will make him pay. It will be my hand that sends him to oblivion. I swear it.'

'He must have laughed at us all. Come, let's go back to the tent.' As they walked, he added, 'You can't blame yourself for Firgan's crimes, you know. You didn't do this; he did.'

So caught up in a ferment of emotions, Arrant hardly heard the words. 'Fools are easily fooled. I kept thinking he was going to goad me into attacking Lesgath, even though I knew there were several things about that scenario that didn't make sense.'

'It could have been his back-up plan,' Garis replied as they re-entered the tent. 'A soldier like him wouldn't have aimed all his spears at the same place, after all. The trouble was that we didn't have that last piece of the puzzle – the bit Samia found that made sense of his main thrust. How could we know exactly what he intended without that? And I suppose another reason we underestimated him was this: it's hard for decent people to imagine anyone being vile enough to kill their own brother, not because he was a threat or a rival, or even because he was in the way, but simply because he made a handy instrument to eliminate someone else from the running. That's about as evil as you can get.'

He pushed Arrant back into his chair and shoved the goblet of wine into his hand. 'Drink this. Firgan did make one mistake, though. It never occurred to him that you would voluntarily give up your Magorness. Your bravery, your sacrifice – coupled with Korden's inability to wait for Temellin to return – turned most of those in the Council Hall that day against the Korden family, in spite of Lesgath's death. Firgan has found it hard to regain the respect he had previously. People saw a side of him they didn't much like.'

Arrant gulped some wine.

Garis added, 'From what I hear, people went into that hall wanting your head delivered to them on a spear, only to come out admiring your courage while condemning Korden for being precipitate and Firgan for being vindictive and greedy for power.'

Arrant drank deeply. 'We can't prove a thing, can we? We can't prove Firgan read that passage, or that he acted on it if he did read it. Knowing it's possible – probable, even – doesn't *change* anything, Garis. Temellin can't charge him, or even accuse him. He'd just refuse to answer and behave as if he had been deeply insulted.'

Garis persisted. 'We know he'll kill anyone at all if he doesn't get what he wants. *Anyone*. Think about that for a moment.' He rose to go to his packs. He undid the ties on one of them and unearthed a long parcel wrapped in cloth, which he handed to Arrant.

Silently, Arrant unwound the cloth and took out the contents. He already knew what it was. His Magoroth sword and scabbard.

'I thought this was supposed to have been given back to the Mirage Makers? Anyway, I'm not entitled to wear it,' he said. 'What possible reason can Temellin have for sending it to me?'

'I think he wanted to point out that, although you may not be able to use Magoroth power, you were born a Magoroth and part of you will always be Magoroth. He wants you to use it as a blade, if Kardiastan comes under attack. We want you to return.'

Arrant rose and went to stand in the tent opening, still holding the sword. He could see the soaring elegance of the aqueduct arch above the trees. His design. His bridge across the River Atreus. 'Beautiful, isn't it? I dreamed of returning to Kardiastan as a famous architect, not as a failed Magoroth with an empty sword coming to fight a final battle.'

'You father thought you'd want to be there.'

'He was right.'

'Your mother wanted you to stay here.'

'Mothers always want their sons to be safe.'

'Sam sent you a message. She lives in Madrinya now.'

'Oh?'

'She said I had to get the wording exactly right, so here it is, exactly as she said it. "Tell Arrant that no man should die without ever seeing his brother."'

Arrant ran a hand through his hair and turned to face Garis once more, shaking his head in wry amusement.

'I know,' Garis agreed. 'She's like a damned grass seed stuck in your trousers. Never lets anyone get too comfortable.'

'Trouble is she has a habit of being infuriatingly right.'

'Just like your mother.'

'Exactly. They aren't related, are they?'

'Distantly, yes.'

'I have another reason to come home, you know.'

'Firgan?'

Arrant smiled. 'Exactly.'

CHAPTER TWENTY-FOUR

In a vale famous for its cotton-growing, a cotton farmer named Brix hefted another basket of bolls into the hopper and felt a quiet satisfaction. A good harvest this year. A good omen, what with him and his wife, Faretha, about to be parents for the first time. He thought of her and the swell of her belly, and smiled. He'd married well, and he knew it. The best spinner in the valley, and a darn fine cook too. She'd make a good mother ... His thoughts wandered on as he turned to fetch another full basket.

Until he saw the cloud.

Brown-red. Moving faster than any cloud he'd ever seen. Devouring the sky like a lake pike after minnows. Wind blasted at him out of nowhere, filled with grit. He only just tied down the hopper lid in time to prevent the cotton being scooped out and scattered across the vale.

He started to run for the house, to warn Faretha to coop up the hens and close the doors and windows. He didn't like the look of this. He liked the stench even less. Sandhells, he'd never smelled anything that bad before.

He was still running when he heard a sound, as if something had dropped out of the sky behind him. He whirled, but saw only a child standing on the pathway. He knew her, but she belonged on the other side of the valley. 'Sweetheart,' he said, 'where did you spring from? You shouldn't be out in this wind. Where's your mama?' The cloud was above them now, blocking the sunlight. 'Never mind,' he said, 'no time for that. Come into the house. We'll look for your mama later.'

The child extended her hands and he picked her up into his arms. Her body was stiff, her clothing rough under his fingers. As he turned back towards the farmhouse, the smell was intense, choking. She leaned into him, her button nose rubbing against the stubble of his chin, the pink bud of her mouth opening into a smile in the moment just before her fangs tore out his cheek and her slavering tongue whipped around his to rip it out through the hole she had just made in his face.

In the farmhouse, Faretha noticed the cloud through the window, even as she heard the wind howling around the corners of the outhouses. Quickly she shuttered the windows and ran to fetch the clothes she'd left drying on the berry bushes. On the way back to the house, with the wind whipping her anoudain skirting up around her face and her arms full of washing, she heard the door slam. She paused, wondering how to open it, only to realise her husband was coming up the path. She laughed. 'Lovely – you can open the door for me.' Her eyes sparkled at him over the top of her washing.

He stared at her, his face as blank as new wax on a tablet. The wind pushed him towards her in a blast of dust and leaves, whirling him so that his feet hardly seemed to touch the ground. When he reached her, the gale died to a whisper. He swept the clothes out of her arms, scattering them unheeded to the ground. His gaze fell to the curve of her body where her baby kicked. She faltered. 'Brix –? What's wrong?'

He put his hand to the swelling of the child. She wanted to run. Knew she should run, but he was her husband. He loved her, she would have staked her life on that. And she loved him.

He curved his hands and the eagle-sharp talons that she'd thought were fingers drove into her body.

It took her a long time to die, watching with uncomprehending eyes while her husband ate their unborn child.

'You're daft.'

'No, I'm not. *You're* the one that's daft. You've been discussing what to do about Firgan with his *sister*. Are you out of your mind?'

'Arrant, you *know* you want to talk to Tarran, and this is the only way to do it. And now you know that what caused your loss of control had nothing to do with you, you can do it without fear.'

Samia had waylaid him while he was raiding the fig tree in one of the Mirager's Pavilion gardens, and now she stood, her hands on her hips, glaring at him belligerently from the other side of the sundial. 'And to think I spent so much time trying to help you in Madrinya while you were running off to Tyr.'

'Help me? How was it going to help me to tell me that what I did was all for *nothing*? That Tarran and I didn't lose control of my power after all? That I threw away any chance I had to be a proper Magoroth because I was stupid enough to be duped? And why, under all the wide blue skies, have you been friendly with Serenelle, of all people, while I've been gone?'

She thumped her hand down on the sundial, narrowly missing the bronze gnomon casting its shadow across the dial. 'Arrant, she's *scared* of Firgan. He *killed* Lesgath, remember? Maybe she's next.' Her chest heaved as she took a deep breath and calmed. It took physical effort for him not to let his gaze linger on the swell of her bodice as she continued: 'She's been helpful. She was the one who kept goading me to find out how Firgan did it. She was so sure, just as I was, that he must have been responsible, and she wouldn't give up. Anyway, you've got a cheek to say I shouldn't be friendly with her. You're the one who kissed her.'

He stared at her, mortified. 'How do you know that?'

'She told me. How else?'

He felt his neck going hot and red. 'That was years ago.' To buy himself some breathing space, he took a bite of the fig in his hand, cursing himself for sounding so feeble.

Samia raised her eyebrows.

He stared at her, baffled, and wondered if it had been such a good idea to come home after all. In Tyrans people had looked up to him and called him buildermaster; here everyone was trying to tell him what to do, without even asking his opinion first. He'd been back two days and he'd spent a remarkable amount of time arguing with someone or other, mostly about how to regain his powers.

Sarana wanted all the healers to be called, to see if they could mend his cabochon permanently. Temellin wanted to try to give him another cabochon – in his right hand this time, although that had never been done before – so that he could power his sword again. Perry wanted him to spend all his time in the library, looking for solutions in the old texts. Vevi and Serenelle – another unlikely alliance, he thought incredulously – wanted him to work out some way to ward his cabochon to keep his power inside, even though everyone knew wards attached to a living creature, man or animal, never worked because the moment they moved, they left the ward behind. Hades only knew *why*.

And now Samia. Only she wanted to go one step further. She wanted to put her cabochon over his and use her direct healing power to seal his cabochon temporarily. 'I think my seal will last a few hours,' she said. 'Long enough for your power to build up a bit. In the end the gold will be strong enough to break through my red, but until that happens you could call to Tarran. My seal is better than a ward, because you won't have to keep immobile while your power builds. And with a ward, we'd have to remove it for you to use the magic – and then the power would start pouring out, so it would be quickly lost. Maybe before you had a chance to use it.'

He almost choked on the fig. 'Listen to yourself! My power breaking through your red? Sam, *I don't want to hurt anyone.* And if power pours out of a cut the length of my cabochon, that's exactly what I will do. Hurt someone. I won't do it.' He thought he'd won the argument.

He should have known better.

That night they had dinner together: his parents, Garis and Samia, and himself. At first, no one mentioned his cabochon. They spoke of the Mirage, and of Tyr. They talked of his studies, and of how he wanted to build aqueducts in Kardiastan.

'Why should people have to cart water up from the lake?' he asked, unaware how his enthusiasm lit up his eyes and tinged his voice. 'It's laborious and expensive. Why should people have to spend so much time waiting at the wells to draw a single jar? With an aqueduct, there is water available all the time – clean water.'

'Where would you get it from? The lake?' Sarana asked.

'No, no. Already people are saying the lake levels have dropped from when they were children. We are drawing too much as the city grows, and polluting it with our waste. I want to bring water in from the mountains northwest of the Asida paveway. There will be some source of underground water in the foothills. I'd have to survey it, of course, but I imagine the line would be less than a hundred miles and I think the incline will decrease—'

'One hundred *miles*?' Temellin's face swung in his direction. 'And how do you expect to pay for an aqueduct that long?'

'Less than one hundred. Although I did wonder about building an underground drain as well to carry the waste water out of the city, rather than dumping it in the lake. We could sell the rights to the clean water, keeping the price cheaper than the water sellers can bring water up from the lake. That way, the aqueduct will eventually pay for itself. In the meantime, Mother has enough money to invest in the scheme if she wants to. Otherwise, I'll go to the Assorian moneymasters.'

Sarana looked up from her wine. 'Of course I'll invest if you think it's viable. It would be wonderful to have a bath without worrying about whether I was being extravagant with water.' She smiled at him and he knew she was remembering, as he was, the luxury of the Exaltarch's palace. After a childhood spent either on a farm or in the stark stone Stronghold in the foothills of the Alps, he'd always appreciated the baths in Tyr.

'An aqueduct sounds like a worthy project,' Temellin agreed. 'But surely there are others who can do the preliminary surveys? I'd rather you worked at finding a way to regain your power.'

Arrant frowned, annoyed. Would no one see that he had another way to contribute to the prosperity of Kardiastan? He had a skill, and knew how to use it . . . 'Why? I still wouldn't be able to use it properly even if I did regain it.'

'Declaring Sarana Mirager-heir was just a way of buying time,' his father said. 'She and I are almost the same age; there has to be someone to follow us. And if it's not you, then we really don't have a choice but to look at Korden's family. And there's not one of them that is unflawed, thanks to their unbalanced upbringing. Gretha is a singularly stupid woman, and Korden was an exacting and unsympathetic father, hardly the kind of man to make up for her deficiencies.'

'Father, even if someone can mend my cabochon, I'll only be back where I used to be: with a cabochon that often doesn't work. And no one is going to trust me until we can prove

Firgan killed his brother. Which is impossible unless you can force him to answer questions about it in public.'

'There's no legal way I can force him without evidence to back up an accusation.'

There was another long silence that Arrant couldn't interpret. Then Sarana said, 'I think we must look to the next generation for an heir.'

Arrant brightened. 'Am I going to have a brother or sister then?'

She laughed. 'No, although I wouldn't be averse to that solution if it happened. No, I was thinking of *your* line.'

'Ah, Arrant,' said Garis, grinning, 'it seems we have a matchmaking mama about to start a campaign. Watch out, lad, there's no more dangerous species on earth. But who would have thought? *Sarana*, of all people. She'll soon be drawing up a list of all the eligible gold-cabochoned girls of a suitable age and looking them over like a shleth merchant at the stockyards.'

Samia squirmed uncomfortably and closed her left hand in her lap, hiding her red gemstone in an involuntary gesture. Arrant noticed and hurriedly looked away.

'Shut up, Garis,' Sarana said amiably and tossed a grape at him.

He caught it, grinning, and wondered aloud if being a grandmother mellowed a woman.

'Arrant,' Samia said, leaning forward to speak to him privately while their parents bickered amiably, 'if you can spare time from your courtship of sundry Magorias, I would like to see the Phalanx Swirls. I thought of riding out tomorrow. Would you like to come with me?'

He stared at her blankly. 'What are they?'

'One of the new desert patternings. It's not far; an hour and a half by shleth.' She smiled up at him, her eyes full of mischief. 'It might be good to get out of the city.'

The temptation was overwhelming. 'I'd love to. I'll meet you in the stables – when?'

She smiled in delight and so transformed her face that his breath caught. 'Immediately after breakfast?' she asked.

He nodded his agreement, and when he went to his pallet that night, he was mulling over just when she had altered from a gawky skinny child with freckles to an eighteen-year-old woman who could halt his breathing. He wasn't even sure why, because she wasn't really beautiful. Not like Elvena. Or even Serenelle.

But it was another complication. His parents obviously wanted him to marry someone with a gold cabochon to beget a more suitable heir. And he didn't want to involve himself with *any* Magor woman. It wouldn't have been fair to her. He may not have had first-hand experience of a Magor coupling, but he had been told that it held an intensity of physical and emotional pleasure not available to a Magor if their partner was non-Magor. And what Magor woman would want to deny herself that?

'Oh, Samia,' he thought. 'We shouldn't tread this path.' And then: 'But oh, it is hard not to take the first step down a road so alluring.'

He deliberately breakfasted early the next morning to avoid his parents, and was down in the stables before Samia. He was chatting to one of the stableboys about shleth bloodlines, when a familiar voice drawled from behind him, 'Looking for work in the stables now, are we?'

Firgan.

He whipped around, his fury rising in his throat. The man waved the stableboy away, and the lad left without a second thought.

Firgan smiled.

Arrant gritted his teeth. How *dare* he? 'How did you get in here?'

'What guard on the gate is going to stop Firgan Korden when he says he has an arrangement to see the previous Mirager-heir in the stables? I happened to be walking by and felt your presence. A handy ability that, I've always thought. To know where people are – your friends, or your enemies . . .'

The sod. 'You're not welcome here. Get out.'

'I just wanted to make clear to you, Arrant, that I don't like you coming back to Madrinya. I don't know what you're up to, but if I were you, I'd think very seriously of returning to Tyr. Because if you believe the end of the Mirage Makers bestowing cabochons means a cabochonless man has a chance to be Mirager one day, we-e-ll . . .' He dropped his voice to a whisper and leaned forward. 'I would rethink. I'll see you dead first.'

'Like your brother,' Arrant said. 'Pleasant fellow, aren't you? Just go away, Firgan. You put a foot wrong, and we'll bring you before the Council on murder charges. You killed Lesgath and we know it.'

Firgan gave an easy smile and stepped still closer, so that he was whispering into Arrant's ear. 'You can't prove a thing. And no one will be able to prove your death was murder, either. But I'm a generous sort of fellow at heart. Leave, and nothing will happen to you.'

'Prove it? Perhaps not. But we can put you in a position where you'd have to refuse to answer questions about your brother's death. Which might start people wondering, don't you think?'

'You'd never dare. I would act righteously indignant, and refuse to answer such insulting insinuations. And you'd be the ones with muck on your faces.'

'Shall we try it and see?'

'Last warning. Arrogant. Go back to Tyr.'

'No, Firgan. The last warning comes from me. Threaten any of us again, and I'll see *you* dead. You're not talking to a youth half your age any more. I've grown up. I'm looking you straight in the eye now, or haven't you noticed?' He shot a hand out and seized Firgan's left wrist, bending it so that the cabochon pointed at Firgan's chest. At the same time, he threw the man backwards against the stable wall. 'You can feel the strength there, can't you? You can't always hide behind your Magor power, like a child sneaking under the skirting of his mother's anoudain.'

Firgan lashed out in a fury, and for a moment they wrestled in a brutal embrace. Arrant slammed Firgan's head against the wall. Firgan tried to knee Arrant in the groin, but didn't have enough room for any real leverage. In the meantime, Arrant head-butted Firgan on the nose, which started to bleed. Firgan roared and stamped down hard on the bones of Arrant's sandalled foot.

'*What* is going on here?' a voice bellowed from the doorway. 'No one brawls in my stables! And I don't give a turd's stink who you are, either.'

Arrant separated himself from Firgan's grip and turned to face the irate stablemaster, Barrid, who had plunged a pail into the water trough while he was yelling. He pulled it out, slopping water, and held it ready to throw as he glared at them.

'I guess we don't want to be doused like a pair of scrapping cats, do we, Arrant?' Firgan drawled, dabbing at his bleeding nose with the edge of his bolero. 'Just a friendly bit of sparring, Barrid, that's all.' He nodded pleasantly and left the stable.

'Sorry, Barrid,' Arrant said. 'I've, er, come to get a couple of mounts for Magoria-samia and myself. We are riding for the Phalanx Swirls this morning.'

The stablemaster snorted.

*   *   *

After enduring his monosyllabic conversation for some time as they rode, Samia finally said in exasperation, 'Arrant, what in the world is wrong with you this morning? You're as mumpish as a shleth who missed out on the mating season. And there's blood on your collar.'

He laughed. '*Mumpish*?'

'Mumpish! And it means the way you are feeling at the moment,' she added, forestalling his next question.

'You made that up.'

'Tell me what's the matter.'

He knew better now than to try to avoid answering Samia. 'I just met Firgan, who threatened to kill me. And that's quite enough to make anyone feel, er, *mumpish*. And I hope you can't read *all* my emotions. That would be far too embarrassing.'

'For a healer, reading emotions is considered a good thing. It makes our job that much easier. You, however, are mostly unreadable.'

'Mostly?'

'Well, unpredictable, compared to the rest of us. Sometimes not a whiff of emotion, and then wham! You hit us with a passion so strong, everybody shuts up. Your mother says that her Altani friend, Brand, was like that, too.' She put her head on one side and regarded him thoughtfully. 'That unpredictability tends to keep people off balance. Never quite sure what will happen next. I like it.'

Once again she had deflated his protest, leaving him with nothing to say, so he tried to change the subject. 'How do we find these Phalanx Swirls?'

'I was given excellent directions, and the turn-off from the paveway is marked. Now, let's get back to the question of a threat from Firgan.'

'He'll lose interest once he realises all I am doing is building an aqueduct.' His inner voice added, 'I hope. No, that's a lie. I don't hope so at all. I'm hoping the bastard will give me an excuse to kill him. Vortexdamn, I'm as bloodthirsty as the next warrior after all.'

The look Samia gave him bordered on open disbelief but she let the subject drop. 'Look, the last of the city houses. Let's gallop.'

From a small hill, they looked down on a flat depression about half a mile long. Tall thin rocks thrust up out of the sands, their surfaces pitted and roughened by wind and sand. And around the base of each, coloured grains had built up a giant artwork filling the vale with circles and swirls of red and mauve and grey and ochre and rust.

'Oh!' Samia said. 'That is superb.'

Arrant sat still on his mount. It was like a mosaic, but something in its inherent splendour sent a touch of cold down his spine. 'How long has it been here?' he asked.

'No one knows exactly. The vale is hidden and the track has only been here since someone stumbled across the patterning a month or two back, and brought others to see.'

He rode down the slope to the edge of the first swirl. There he dismounted and knelt. He slid his cupped hand into the sand and let it sieve through his fingers.

'Is there something the matter?' Samia asked, riding up.

He stood, filled with sadness. 'Oh, Sam, this used to be part of the Mirage. It's been brought here by the winds.'

'How can you tell?' she asked as she dismounted.

'I'm not sure. I can – I can feel it has a connection to Tarran.'

'Oh.' She looked aghast. 'I'm sorry.' She walked away, perhaps to give him time to compose himself, perhaps because she didn't want him to see how upset she was.

'Hey, you're vandalising an artwork,' he said, trying to regain their light-heartedness. 'Look at your footprints!'

But she wasn't listening. She had knelt down and was prodding cautiously with a fingertip at something lying half buried in the sand. Then she shuddered and pulled a face. He joined her to look. It had been a large creature once, at least as big as a Tyranian goat. Except it didn't seem to be all there. 'Something must have been eating it,' he said. 'There are no bones.' All that remained was a dried-up pile of sinew and skin and scales. 'I don't like it. It doesn't feel right. Let's leave it alone.' She stood and pulled him away.

'It's just a dead animal.' But even as he said the words, he knew it wasn't. It was the remains of a Ravage beast. And they were just a few miles from Madrinya. His heart pounded, his mouth went dry.

'You know what it is,' she said flatly. She turned to lead her mount back up the slope to where the spreading branches of a solitary thorn tree offered shade. She tied her mount to the trunk and emptied the saddlebags. She'd brought a mat, and food and drink for a picnic. As she laid out the things, she asked, 'If the Mirage Makers die, my father says all the Ravage creatures will come streaming out of the Mirage on the wind.'

He nodded. 'The winds apparently come every night now, cold air from the mountains drawn in to the heat of the Ravage sores. But we can fight them when – if – the time comes. The beasts cannot live long outside of their sores, we know that. It won't mean the end of Kardiastan, just – just a bad time for us all.' He added abruptly, 'You're right. I have to go and see the Mirage. I have to see Tarran in case—' In case he dies.

'I'm sorry,' she said as he joined her on the mat. 'I didn't mean to make you sad by bringing you here.'

'Then I shan't *be* sad,' he promised. 'This looks good. And I am hungry.'

She reached out and took his left hand in hers. 'You are going to have to eat with one hand.'

He stared at her, not understanding.

'Because I am going to hold your hand, cabochon to cabochon, and repair the cut. It will probably take half an hour or so. After which I shall ride back down to the inn along the paveway. I'll wait for you there.' She raised her other hand to forestall his protest. 'Think of this as an experiment. There's nobody here to hurt. We are out in the middle of nowhere. If something goes wrong, the worst thing you could do would be to blast a pile of sand into a spectacular whirlwind.'

'I thought it was an artwork.'

She ignored that. 'I estimate you will have to wait a couple of hours for your power to build up sufficiently for you to be able to call Tarran. Please, Arrant. Do this. Do it for your brother if you won't do it for me or for yourself.'

He shook his head, but more in exasperation than negation. 'You planned this. You never give up, do you?'

'Not often. Not with people I care about.'

He lifted his right hand and put a finger to her lips. 'Don't care too much, Sam.' It was all he dared say.

She just smiled and held out the loaf of bread. 'Shall I hold and you cut, or you hold and I cut?'

Almost everything she had brought necessitated two hands to unwrap or open, cut or peel; tasks that now had to be shared. Peeling an orange resulted in juice all over her anoudain; opening the small earthenware jar of olives squirted oil down his bolero and sleeve. Every misadventure sent her into peals of laughter and, swamped by her sense of fun, he was helpless. By the end of the half-hour, his sadness was unremembered. And he knew he was three parts in love.

It was she who sobered first. 'I've finished. The crack in your cabochon is filled.'

She unclasped his hand. The cut was now a thin blood-red line in the gem, with fine webs of scarlet spreading into the tiniest of hairline fissures he hadn't even known were there. 'It's pretty,' he said, and laughed. 'If nothing else, I have the prettiest cabochon in the land.'

As she bent to look, her hair brushed his lips. He drew back sharply, overwhelmed by longing for something he could never have. 'It's time you left,' he said and faced his cabochon away from her. 'If something were to go wrong—'

'All right,' she said and scrambled to her feet. 'You will remember to bring back the rest of the picnic things, won't you?'

He shivered, waiting there. The air was still, and the day pleasantly warm, yet he shivered. He wanted Samia there beside him. He wanted to touch her. He wanted to see her smile at him again. He wanted so much to love her. And he had no right to want anything when he had so little to give.

Fiercely he turned his gaze back to his cabochon, and concentrated. Nothing happened for a long time. Then, after almost an hour, he thought the pale gold may have deepened a little. He had no power he could discern – his far-sensing wasn't working – but that was nothing new. Just because his power wasn't leaking out any more didn't mean he could use what there was.

He waited another half-hour and thought about the carcass in the Swirls. It smelled wrong. It had no proper skeleton. Had it once been mostly illusion? Built of nightmares, not bone? A Ravage beast. *And they were two hundred miles from the Mirage.* Perhaps Madrinya had been lucky that the beast had ended up in the Swirls, and not, say, in the Madrinyan marketplace on a busy day.

Tarran, it's me. Can you hear me? Are you there?

And something slipped into his mind and huddled there. It was scrunched up, folded in on itself, barely alive. He couldn't even recognise it.

Tarran? Tarran, is that you?

It couldn't be; not this thing, this twist of life that lay there in his mind, unspeaking, unshaped, unresponsive. This, his vibrant, laughing brother? Yet he was touched with a familiarity, a tenuous feeling of connection. His brother, what was left of him.

He forced the horror down. Contained his despair where only he would find it. And did the only thing he could; he enveloped the scrap of life crouching in his mind with his caring. He turned every thought inwards, to love and heal. And because his brother was there, his magic worked. The mind within his own began to open, to unfold like a crushed bud struggling to peel back its wounded casing in order to bloom.

Tarran, I'm here; you're safe.

And then, softly, he added, *I love you.*

Had he ever uttered those words before? He couldn't remember, and was ashamed. He'd taken for granted that Tarran knew he was loved. And he probably had known; he had inhabited a corner of Arrant's thoughts at times, after all. But it wasn't the same. Arrant should have said the words.

He wound his love tight, swaddling his brother, pouring all the power he had into the healing embrace of his mind. 'I love you, Tarran,' he said aloud, and held his breath, waiting for a reply.

And Tarran responded. He unfurled, the bud opening. *Arrant? Is that really you?* No more than a thready whisper of thought.

Arrant breathed again. 'It's me.'

I knew you'd find a way to find me. I knew it. The bud opened a little more. Strengthened. Stretched.

'What can I do to help?'

Just be.

Arrant quietened, turned inwards, lending his strength. His power. Time passed. The shadow of the tree lessened as the sun climbed in the cloudless sky. And gradually the bud blossomed.

Let me in, Arrant. Show me what happened. Show me who did this to us. The person who sent that blast through you that seared me so, that sent me flying back to the Mirage – who was it?

'Firgan, Korden's oldest son. Were you hurt?'

The surge of power scrambled my thoughts. I couldn't even remember who I was for days. And then when I did, I couldn't get back to you. I – I thought you'd died. That hurt, Arrant. I never knew what grief was till then. Not really. I thought I'd never speak to you again. If that young Magori had not come, I'd just be so much sand blowing in the wind by now. But he told me you were alive. Knowing that made all the difference. Tell me what happened.

To save time, Arrant lowered all his barriers and let his brother roam freely through his memory.

When Tarran spoke again, it was to offer practical advice. *The Mirage Makers know of no way to repair your cabochon. And trying to give you another will not succeed. The best that can be done is what Samia has done.*

'When her seal breaks, what then?'

Have faith in her. She knows her own power. The seal will slowly fade, not break. Your loss of power will be a gradual leak. In fact, it's already happening. Take a look.

He glanced down. A faint golden glow had spread across his hand, to trickle between his fingers. His power, drifting away into the air. 'And when it's all gone? Will you be able to stay in my head?'

I don't see why not. But once I leave, I won't be able to come unless you allow her to do the same thing again. When you have

*no power in your cabochon, I cannot sense you all the way from
the Mirage. I could not find you, Arrant. It was terrible . . .*

'Tarran, how—?'

A pause, but Tarran knew exactly what Arrant could not
say. *I don't think we'll see the beginning of another year. What
the Magor are doing helps – but nothing can stop the Ravage.
Nothing. Only the intervention of the Magor has kept us alive
as long as this. I'm frightened, Arrant. I don't want to – to not
be. The others are caught up in the fighting; they don't have time
to – to think about what it all means. But everything feels
unfinished for me . . . As though if I die I would take the world
with me, instead of leaving it behind. Does that make sense?*

'It's guilt,' Arrant thought. Tarran had been supposed to save
the world, or the Mirage anyway. He'd carried the burden of
that all his life, yet never found an answer. No wonder it all
seemed unfinished.

Some of us have died, Tarran added. *They just became too
tired and – ceased to live. And there have been several recently
who – who disappeared. That's never happened before. It's hard
for us to separate one Mirage Maker from another, but I knew
the essensa of one of them well. She was one of the most ancient,
and rather absent-minded. I called her Flower. She loved flowers.
She always did the flowers. Skies, Arrant, what happened to her?
Did she disappear on the wind?*

'I want to show you something.' Arrant walked down to the
Swirls again, and indicated the carcass. 'What does that look
like to you?'

*I can tell you what it smells like. A Ravage beast. But there's
no Ravage sore.*

'And we are two or three hundred miles from the Mirage.'

The winds grow stronger as we weaken.

They were both silent, taking in that thought.

Arrant walked back to the mat. The serrated edge of his

terror sharpened his thoughts. The Ravage – his *nightmares*, damn it – leaving the remains of the Mirage on the wind . . .

To destroy Kardiastan. And a Mirage Maker had just gone missing.

Tarran, who had been continuing to sort through the memories Arrant had opened up to him, suddenly laughed. *Hey*, he said, *what did I tell you! You have a weakness for long legs. That Samia really has you panting like a shleth on heat, hasn't she?*

'It's just as well you don't have a body, brother, or I'd thump you on the nose. You keep your mind on your own affairs, and stop rooting around in my personal memories, thank you very much.' Carefully, he shut up the private part of his mind.

Spoilsport. Ooooh, your memories would light a fire all by themselves. Why haven't you done anything about it?

'Tarran,' he growled, 'I'll stuff your memories full of pallet cotton if you aren't careful. None of that is ever any of your business.'

She's coming back, his brother said smugly. *This should be interesting.*

Arrant's heart sank. Tarran was right. His positioning abilities indicated Samia was riding their way. Confound it, he had his brother back, and the first thing he did was tease.

You said you loved me, Tarran hastened to point out. *I heard you. Several times.*

'I lost my mind there for a bit, that's all. I was worried about your invisible hide.'

Lost more than your mind, I think, where the lovely Samia is concerned.

'Manure sweepings! Hankering after a roll on the pallet is *not* the same as losing one's heart.'

That's true. I remember how your eyes used to pop out of your head every time you saw Elvena Korden. You used to positively salivate. But this feels different.

'Of course it's different. Samia is a friend. And I am a lot older.'

Ah. And that explains everything?

'Oh, shut up.'

Go and eat something, brother. Not surprising with so much magic leaking out that you feel hungry. It will put you in a better temper if you eat.

'Huh! You just want to enjoy the sensations on my tastebuds.'

Inside his mind, Tarran was grinning. And Arrant had to admit it felt good to have him there, even if it meant he was being laughed at.

Samia tied up her mount and came to sit next to him.

'You weren't supposed to come back,' he scolded.

'I worried too much. Couldn't stand it any longer.' She took his hand to look at his cabochon. 'Oh, it's leaking all over the place.'

His heart started to thump and he silently cursed Tarran for putting ideas into his head.

Rubbish. Wasn't me put the thoughts there. They were already in evidence, as thick and rich as cream on cow's milk.

'Yes, it is,' Arrant said in answer to Samia. 'No problem, though. It's just a bit at a time.'

'Did he come?'

'Yes. He's still here. And thank you, Sam, for everything. I should have listened to you a lot earlier.'

'You should *always* listen to me. Would you like me to renew my seal?'

'Yes, please,' he replied more graciously. 'Tarran says he thinks it won't break. So nothing too drastic ought to happen.'

'Good.' She smiled into his eyes. 'Well met, Tarran.'

Well met, Samia. I used to know your parents when they were young. Arrant, you are salivating again. Calm down, boy.

'He says well met. And wants you to know that he knew your parents when they were young. Well, he means that he has memories of them then.'

Her smile widened. 'You'll have to tell me all about them. Well, about my mother, anyway. I never knew her.'

She was fun. And pretty. She used to have the same effect on your father as you do on Arrant.

'He says she was fun. And pretty.'

And what about the rest?

If you think I am translating that, you're got the brains of a senile gorclak.

'So people tell me,' Samia said, sighing. 'You'll have to tell me everything.'

Oh, I will, if I can calm Arrant down long enough to be coherent. His heart is doing a dance in his chest at the moment simply because you are holding his hand.

'He will, but, um, not – not now,' Arrant said, desperate to maintain his equilibrium. *Shut up, Tarran.*

This is fun.

'Oh – all right,' Samia said. 'So, what now? Can I keep mending your cabochon for you after today?'

Yes, what now, Arrant? Can I stay a while? A day or two? I – I need the rest.

'Yes. Of course,' he said, not sure who he was answering. 'I – I don't know what to do. Tarran says they are all very weak.'

Samia looked stricken. 'Oh, Tarran, I'm so *sorry*.'

Yeah, well so am I. Can't do much about it though.

'You could stay with me.'

'Why would I want to do that?' Samia asked, puzzled.

'Not you; Tarran. He could stay in my head if – if the other Mirage Makers . . .'

Oh sure. You'd love being two people for the rest of your life.

'It would be better than mourning you the rest of my life.'

'What is he saying?' she asked.

Stop right there, Arrant. It's not going to happen. I'm a Mirage Maker. I live and die with them. And that's final. Now let's change the subject.

'He says he won't.'

Arrant, you have to do something about Firgan.

Like what? 'He's also changing the subject.'

Kill him?

Oh, sure. As much as I'd like to, I don't want to be dragged up before the Magoroth Council again, or worse still, the Hall of Justice, on charges of murdering a war hero.

'Stop it, you two. You are cutting me out,' Samia complained, digging Arrant in the ribs.

'Sorry.'

No one would know it was you if you used your power. After all, who would think you could kill when your cabochon is cracked open? But we could with me here. You tell Samia, and see what she thinks.

Arrant threw up his hands. 'Tarran here just came up with the bright idea of killing Firgan. Which is odd, because he is usually not in favour of randomly murdering people.'

True, but this is Firgan. If someone doesn't kill him, then he will go after our father, and your mother.

'Someone should certainly do it,' she agreed emphatically, 'after what he did.'

'Not you too. Gods, is everyone here bent on wholesale slaughter? Tarran, the Mirage Makers don't approve of murder, surely?' He glared at Samia. 'Any more than healers usually do.'

Not usually. It's against the Covenant.

'Of course they don't,' Samia said. 'And neither do we. The proper thing to do would be to try him before the Magoroth Council for murdering his brother. But we all know we couldn't prove a thing. And that's not just why he ought to die. He ought to die because otherwise your parents are in danger, and you, and one day he is going to end up being Mirager if nobody does anything. He threatened you only this morning, Arrant.'

See? Tarran crowed. *The woman has sense. As well as luscious legs.*

'Oh gods, stop it, the two of you. I'll admit it. I want to kill the bastard. But it's one thing to think about it and another to do it in cold blood and that's final. Sam, let's go back to Madrinya. I need to tell my parents what Tarran says about the Mirage Makers.'

She pulled a face. 'I suppose you're right. As much as I feel like punching Firgan Korden on his supercilious pointed nose.'

Arrant chuckled. 'His nose is rather sharp, isn't it?' He picked up the mat and began to fold it up.

'There's one thing you have to make up your mind to accept, though, Arrant,' she said, watching him. 'You will be the next Mirager-heir, after your mother. There's no alternative.'

And whether you have a working cabochon or not will be irrelevant by then, Tarran added. *When the Mirage Makers die, the Magor begin to dwindle in number too.*

'What did he say?' Samia asked, seeing Arrant frown.

'Sweet Elysium, you two are going to send me crazy,' he replied, 'dragging me to and fro like a shuttle across a loom.'

In truth, for the moment, his heart sang. He was Magor again. Samia was smiling at him. Best of all, Tarran was safe. Not for very long perhaps, and maybe none of it would last, but for now, he savoured every grain of time running through the hourglass.

CHAPTER TWENTY-FIVE

'We have to bring Firgan before the Council.'

Temellin strode back and forth across the room, turning with uncanny accuracy just before he bumped into the walls at either end. Easy enough, Arrant supposed, with the wall fountains. Fish still swam in a dish on the table too, and the lizard Arrant had trained to stay in the pile of wood near the fireplace was still there. A cage of finches hung at the door to the bedroom. He wondered who now cared for them all, and whether people thought it strange that the Mirager had kept the pets around once Arrant had left for Tyrans.

He switched his attention to his mother, seated by the window watching Temellin's pacing with concern. 'I don't see how we can prove anything against Firgan,' she said.

'Arrant has just told us he was threatened with death. Isn't the word of the son of the Mirager good enough?' Temellin's rage was suppressed in his voice, but not in the emotion he released for them all to feel.

Sarana raised an eyebrow and waved a hand around at Jessah, Garis and Samia. 'In this room, certainly. In the Council? What do you think, dear?' Her tone was mild, without any of the sarcasm she was capable of dispensing, but it stopped his restless pacing.

'I know, I know. But I *don't know what to do*. And that's a hard thing to admit. I can't just murder him. I'm not very good at that sort of thing.'

'I am,' she said. 'I'll do it if you want.'

The words were stark and brutal, and it wasn't quite a lie, but Arrant felt her innate distaste. *She has no stomach for an execution either*, he thought. *She has been glad to leave all that behind*.

'Not a good idea,' Jessah said hastily, trying unsuccessfully to hide her shock. 'People would talk, and if the slightest blame came our way, Temellin's position would be threatened.'

'Especially as there is already talk about Kardiastan being led by a blind man who can't work out how to stop the Ravage, eh?' Temellin asked.

'Firgan's rumours,' Garis said.

Sarana looked annoyed. 'Not to mention the rest of his twisted family. And, unfortunately, there are so damned many of them.'

Temellin dropped into the chair next to her. 'I cannot countenance murder. I am the Mirager and I have sworn to uphold governance by consensus. I *will* follow the law. And so will the rest of you.' He laid a hand on Sarana's arm. 'I will not tolerate anyone else to break it, either.'

'All right,' she said, apparently unfazed. 'I thought you'd say that.'

'We will just have to lay a snare for Firgan,' Garis said.

'He'll see through anything too obvious,' Jessah warned. 'That man is as devious as a trapdoor spider.'

'I'm an expert at deviousness,' Sarana said. 'I was taught by the very best web-spinners.'

'Everybody give it some thought,' Temellin said. 'Unfortunately, we have to keep fighting the Ravage in the meantime and we will all have to take our turns there.'

Arrant looked up happily. Was he about to see the Mirage for the first time?

Not a hope, Tarran said. *You'll see.*

'Except Arrant, of course. His power is too unpredictable when Tarran is not around.'

Told you.

'Garis,' Temellin continued, 'when you are not tackling the Ravage, you are back on bodyguard duty for Arrant. Alternate with Jessah. I'll send Firgan – and other members of that damn brood – out to the Mirage as often as I can. Arrant, I want you to go ahead with the aqueduct project. I want to allay Firgan's suspicions. I don't want him, or anyone else outside this room, to know you have your cabochon power back yet, so keep away from all the Magor. As far as everyone is concerned, you are just a non-Magor buildermaster.'

Arrant nodded, his delight at the idea of building an aqueduct warring with his disappointment at not being able to go to the Mirage. *I want to see you*, he told Tarran, *in person.*

I'd rather you didn't. I wouldn't want you to remember me the way things are there now.

Temellin hesitated. 'I wonder if it would be better for you not to leave your cabochon sealed when Tarran is with you to decrease the chances any of the Magor will notice?'

'And leave him defenceless?' Sarana asked. 'No. Arrant has been without reliable power long enough. And now that he can sometimes have perfect control, you want to take it away from him? Over my dead body!' She glared at Temellin even though he couldn't see the expression.

'You're right. That was a ridiculous suggestion.'

'Insensitive,' Sarana said.

He threw his hands up in the air in surrender. 'Insensitive. My apologies, Arrant.'

He sent out his regret to Arrant – who managed to return

a feeling of amused sympathy of the kind one man gave to another in the face of the incomprehensibility of women — only to have both his mother and Samia glare at him in turn. *Hey*, he thought, *I could get good at this emotion-sending*.

And upset half the population in the process, Tarran pointed out. *Tact, brother, tact*.

They settled into a routine. Each evening, at his request, Tarran returned to the Mirage to take his place among the Mirage Makers. Each morning, Samia came to seal Arrant's cabochon so that he could call Tarran back again. That way Tarran could rest and maintain his strength. Tarran gleefully said he did it because he knew how much Arrant enjoyed Samia holding his hand for half an hour every morning, but Arrant ignored that.

He began planning the aqueduct. He despatched surveyors to map the route, arranged the financing and spent part of most days working with the engineers and masons and builders of Madrinya, maintaining a conspicuous presence away from the pavilions in order to lull Firgan into thinking he was harmless. He wore a fingerless glove on his left hand, and Garis fostered a rumour that the Mirager's son hated to talk about his Magor disability.

And all the while, Arrant tried to devise a plan to trap Firgan into a mistake that would condemn him in the eyes of the Magoroth. 'I have to be the bait,' Arrant said to Tarran and Samia as they sat and chatted over breakfast in his sitting room one morning. 'It's the only way we can do this. Pretending I am not Magor, hiding the fact that I have power in my cabochon, that's not the way to have Firgan act precipitously. I have to be a bait worth eating. We need to make Firgan think I will be made heir to Sarana. It might be a good idea if he was to find out I had my cabochon mended. Tarran agrees with me.'

'So do I.'

'You do?'

Maybe she likes the idea of you being the worm on a hook, Tarran suggested. *Can you try some of that honeyed porridge stuff over there? It smells delicious.*

Arrant ignored him.

'Yes, I do,' she said. 'I prefer us to be in control of the situation, rather than Firgan. We need to plant some misinformation so that Firgan thinks he found out all by himself.'

'You're good friends with Serenelle. Tell her in confidence and she'll pass it on.'

Samia pursed her lips in annoyance and glared.

Just about curled your eyelashes that time, Tarran said. *And no, I don't want boiled eggs. They are boring. If you don't want porridge, then take some of those pomegranate fritters.*

Arrant rolled his eyes, but reached for the fritters.

'Don't you roll your eyes at me, Arrant Temellin,' Samia snapped. 'Serenelle would *not* pass along *anything* I said to Firgan. She hates the man.'

Thanks a lot, Tarran.

Unfair! I didn't roll your eyes.

'She's a Korden, Samia, and not a particularly nice person anyway. Her loyalty is to her family. She's also scared of Firgan. She'd pass along the information and have a good laugh with her brother over your naivety. Try it and see.'

'I will,' she snapped. 'And you'll be the one to see that nothing happens. You know *nothing* about women.'

Tarran laughed. *You can say that again.*

Arrant winced and dropped his head into his hands. Sometimes he thought the two of them would drive him insane. 'I think,' he said, carefully neutral, 'we ought to talk to my father about this first. But he has just left for the Mirage.'

He discussed the question with his mother later that morning, only to find her reluctant to think of using him as a lure. 'Arrant,' she said, her tone troubled, 'there are two wonderful things in my life at the moment; one of them is my relationship with your father, and the second is you. I have a marked reluctance to endanger either.'

'That's richly ironic, coming from someone who made a career out of throwing herself from one dangerous situation to another.'

'Ah, but I was a Magoroth living among the non-Magor. A Magoroth with a cabochon I could rely on. You are neither of those things. It's very brave of you, Arrant, but I'd rather we find another, safer way of doing this.'

'That is such a motherly thing to say,' Arrant complained.

She laughed. 'It is, isn't it?' She sobered. 'I've just had a report in from one of the northern vales. I'm going to investigate. I should be away about eight or nine days.'

'Ravage beasts?' he asked.

'Looks like it. But this time a lot of people seem to have died, which is why I want to look into it myself.'

He gave a quick frown. 'Sounds bad.'

'I've not been mothered for a long time,' he grumbled to Tarran afterwards. 'And she forgets I am twenty. Besides, she's not just my mother, she's Ligea Gayed, too. And laying a trap is what Ligea would have done.'

You'll be more vulnerable once I die, Tarran said in reflection. *Your cabochon will go back to being unreliable. We have to do something soon, while I am still in your head and helping you control your power.*

'Do you know anything about this vale she's gone to see?'

No, but the winds have been especially bad. Maybe we've been losing a lot of Ravage beasts. It's hard to tell.

'I'll work out something then,' Arrant said, 'with Sam. How many—' He choked on the words, and had to complete the question silently. *How many months, Tarran?*

One or two.
Arrant felt as if he'd been punched in the stomach.

The valemaster took Sarana to the drying racks of their cotton shed, where they had laid out the dead. 'It's been fourteen days, but we wanted to show the Magoroth before we buried them,' he explained in a wooden voice. 'We want to know what killed them, and if it will happen again. We all moved out of the vale. We want to know if it is safe to return.'

The dry air had kept the bodies in a good state of preservation and the stench of their rot was nothing more than a slight sourishness in Sarana's nostrils. The Ravage smell was worse. She forced herself to walk up and down the rows of bodies. Looking – for what? Clues to the way they died? Hardly. That was obvious. Most had died because their hearts – or their livers, or their kidneys – had been ripped from their bodies. They died because they had been torn to pieces. More than one hundred people.

'Funny thing is that most of them weren't eaten,' the valemaster told her. Not once did he look at the bodies. He kept his eyes fixed on the floor. 'Nothing was missing, like.'

'Most?' she asked, trying not to show how shaken she was.

He took her to the end of the racks. 'We think these two people were the first,' he said. He still didn't look at them. 'Brixatim and his wife Faretha. Faretha was about to drop a young'un any day.' There was a long pause, then he added, 'My first grandchild.'

She looked. And looked.

'Sweet Elysium,' she thought, 'war is bad enough, but this is sick . . .' Her stomach heaved. 'Oh, hells. Gev, you'd never believe this, but the Exaltarch, veteran of years of battle, is having trouble keeping food in her stomach.' She clamped a hand firmly over her mouth and nose and studied the bodies.

Something had gorged on the contents of Brixatim's chest, crunching his ribs to get at the organs, hollowing him out like a ground squirrel making a meal of a melon. And something had eaten Faretha's baby out of its womb. Except for the tiny head. That, they had left behind.

'What would do this, Magoria?' the valemaster asked, looking at her briefly. 'How can we find out?'

She was astonished. 'No one *saw* what did this?'

He shook his head. 'Everything was hidden under clouds of choking red dust for hours. Most of us just stayed indoors. When it cleared, this is what we found.'

He turned his misery-filled eyes on her. 'Magoria, what could kill one hundred and twenty-six people in a couple of hours and then vanish?'

'This was done by Ravage beasts,' she replied, the grimness of her own voice unpleasant to her ears. 'I can tell that much by the smell. And some beasts remain in the village somewhere. The stench is still here. It won't take me long to find them. They might even be dead by now; they find it hard to live away from Ravage sores.'

'And if they are alive? You can kill them?' he asked.

'I can kill them.'

In the end she found only one beast. Which was just as well, because it was unexpectedly difficult to kill. It was hidden in the roof space of a house where the whole family had been slaughtered. She located it using her sense of smell, and her Magor positioning powers. 'Keep away until this is done,' she told the valemaster and the men with him.

'We can help,' he protested. 'Magoria, Faretha was my daughter—'

'That was an order,' she said quietly. 'These beasts are best killed by Magoroth power.'

He nodded unhappily and ushered the others away.

She waited until everyone had gone, then she stepped back inside, gagging on the stench. She aimed her sword at the boards under the roof, and sent a blast of Magor gold upwards. The wood disintegrated and someone came tumbling down to land on the floor in front of her.

It was Temellin. He scrambled to his feet, and quirked a smile at her. A slightly younger Temellin than the one she was used to, but just as handsome. Just as desirable. Still with a head of hair that he could never quite keep tidily tied back, although there were streaks of grey in it now.

He didn't speak and neither did she. She melted a hole through his chest instead. Impossibly, he kept moving towards her. His eyes pleaded, loving, his hand outstretched asking her to reach for him, to hold him. To cradle him while he died. His lips moved, mouthing words of love. And she ploughed another beam into his face, melting his eyes, his face, his brains.

And then he wasn't Temellin, but a Ravage beast, with claws like an eagle's talons and teeth a handspan long, with scales and a long thin snout like a gharial of the Altani Delta. She struck again and again, burning and burning until there was nothing left. Nothing left of it, nothing left of her sword power.

And when she was done she stepped outside and waited for the valemen to come. She was shaking. Her hands, her body, all shaking. Not believing what had happened. A Ravage beast had made an illusion. But only Mirage Makers could make illusions become real. Only Mirage Makers could make illusions do anything.

'Vortexdamn, Temellin,' she muttered, 'you'd better be alive and well, or I'm as good as moondaft for the rest of my life.'

Elvena pouted, then frowned. 'But I don't *want* to marry Firgan.'

Her mother, who was examining several lengths of silk from Corsene, took no notice. 'You have to, dear. We need to keep the power in the family, and he is going to be Mirager one day. Do you like the blue, Elvie? It is such a pretty colour, even though the weave is not so fine. Bring the lamp closer, Serenelle, so we can see better.'

'It doesn't suit her,' Serenelle said. 'And you shouldn't frown like that, Elvie; you'll get wrinkles and then no one will want to marry you, including Firgan. And I wouldn't be happy then, because he'd want to marry me instead. And I utterly refuse to.'

'Don't be silly,' Elvena said. 'You're far too young for Firgan.'

'And you are far too stupid. Come to think of it, maybe that's why he wants to marry you. And unfortunately, I am not actually too young to marry. Or have you not realised I am over twenty?'

Gretha, her mind still occupied with the silks, scolded, 'Girls, girls! Behave.'

'I don't understand how he can ever be Mirager,' Elvena said. 'That Tyranian bitch is Mirager-heir.'

'She's as old as the Mirager. She could easily die first,' Gretha said complacently.

'And if she doesn't, doubtless Firgan will help her along,' Serenelle added.

Gretha looked at her, appalled. 'Serenelle, how can you say such a thing! I should make you wipe your mouth out with salt.'

'Like that's going to change the truth,' Serenelle muttered. Sometimes she could hardly believe how stupid the other members of her family were. With the exception of her eldest brother, of course, and he was just plain evil.

'He's coming up the stairs right now, so you had better keep your mouth shut,' Elvena told her.

She was right, and by the time Firgan entered the room, they were talking quietly about the merits of the different lengths of cloth.

'I like the blue,' he said. 'That will do for your wedding dress, Elvena. I have set the date, by the way. First day of Cornucopia. The month of fecundity – what could be more appropriate?' He came forward and kissed her lightly on the cheek. 'Now run along to bed, both of you. I want to talk to Serenelle.'

Gretha and Elvena obediently bundled up the lengths of silk and left the room. Firgan watched them go, smiling slightly. By the time he turned his attention back to where Serenelle had been lounging on a divan, she had warded herself in the corner of the room, using her sword and conjurations.

'I heard what you said,' he told her, and took two steps towards her ward.

'Eavesdropping on your own family, Firgan? Nice.'

'Just as well I did, it seems.' He took another step closer.

'And just what did you hear—?' she asked politely, proud of how steady her voice remained.

'You mentioned I might help the Tyranian bitch to die.'

'So? What of it?'

'It's dangerous to speak so casually of murder, Serenelle. I wouldn't want anyone outside my family to hear that kind of talk. Do you understand me?'

'Perfectly.'

'No, I don't think you do.' He stepped closer still, until he was almost touching the ward. 'I've been watching you the past few days. Your emotions reek of secrets you're keeping.'

'I am of an age to have secrets I want to keep from my brother.'

'True. And I don't give a damn about who you're sleeping with, or not usually. But something has you sweating every time I look at you. And I want to know what secret it is that

makes you so damned scared of a loving brother, m'dear.'
Casually he reached through the ward and cupped her chin in
a powerful grip.

She squealed in shock.

'Did you really think that I would not have put my hand
to the sword hilt of every member of this family?' He slipped
his left hand around to the back of her head, where he twisted
it into her hair. His grip tightened as he stepped through the
ward and brought his face down towards hers, as if he meant
to kiss her. She tried to wriggle away, but he was a fighting
man, all muscle and sinew. He hauled her up into his embrace,
pinning her arms between their bodies and turning her
cabochon so that it pressed hard against her diaphragm. She
shuddered as he brushed his tongue along her lips and then
nibbled her earlobe.

He whispered into her ear, 'You think you are so clever,
Serenelle, but you're just as stupid as the rest of them. You
shouldn't have used your sword to build the ward. A cabochon warding might have kept me out for a while.'

She struggled, even knowing it was futile. His arms were
like iron; the rock-hard muscles of his thighs pressed her hard
to the wall. 'You'll hurt yourself,' he said, his smile mocking.
'Tell me, what is it that you have been keeping from me?'

'Mirage help me,' she thought, 'why does no one come?
Can't they feel my panic?' She knew the answer, even as she
asked the question. The only person who would have come to
her aid was her father, and he was away accompanying a young
Magoroth relative who had gone to pick up her Magor sword
in the Shiver Barrens.

He pulled back on her hair so that she had to keep her face
upturned to his. He ran his mouth over her cheek, her nose,
her eyes, her ear, nuzzling. Licking away the perspiration of
her fear. 'Tell me, little sister. *Tell me.*'

She smelled her own terror. She tasted the bile rising in her throat.

Then he released her hair and gripped her face in both hands instead. He ran his thumbs up to the corners of her eyes and pressed down softly. 'You know what we used to do to legionnaire prisoners during the war, Serenelle? For fun?' He kissed her eyelids, his voice dropping to a murmur. 'We used to gouge out their eyes with our thumbs. A bloody business. How they used to scream. There was a man in my cohort who used to eat them. The eyeballs, I mean. Raw. What shall I do with yours? String them on a chain around my neck? Such pretty brown irises. Your best feature, I've always thought.'

Gently, he increased the pressure at the corners of her eyes.

'You can't do that,' she said, trying to believe her own words. 'No one would forgive you. Even Papa would turn against you. You'd never become Mirager.' His thumbs made circles on her skin, unpleasantly firm against the edge of her eyelids.

'Hmm. Possibly you are right,' he conceded, but he increased the pressure enough to move from discomfort to pain. Her eyes watered. 'So I'll make a little bargain with you. If you tell me what you are so desperately trying to keep from me, I won't blind you this way when I *am* Mirager. I have a very long memory, Serenelle, and I don't forgive. Ever. And never doubt that I will be Mirager. Sooner than you think.'

'Skies,' she thought. 'He'd do it too. He killed Lesgath.' Her courage drained from her, leaving her limp and clammy. 'All right,' she whispered. 'I'll tell you. It was Samia – she confided in me, about her and Arrant. She is using her healing power to seal his cabochon, and he can build up his power every time she does it. They aim to establish him as Sarana's heir.'

'And that's all you have to tell me?'

'That's all.' Her truth wafted between them as tangible as perfume.

'Does he have control of his power?'

'I – I didn't ask and she didn't say.'

He released her and stepped away. She leaned weakly back against the wall. Her knees were trembling and she could not have stood without support. Blood trickled from one of her eyes. Slowly she slid down the wall until she was sitting on the floor.

'Damn him,' she thought. 'I hate him. I hate him so much.'

She quelled the desire to kill him with her cabochon. She'd never succeed, and the price of failure was too terrible to contemplate. She tucked her hands under the skirting of her anoudain so he wouldn't see how they trembled.

'Not a word about this,' he said. 'Or you'll be the victim of a mysterious murder one day soon.' With that he was gone.

She sat there where she was, unmoving, shrunken, as if he'd sucked something from her, and left her no more than a husk. How could she ever find the courage, in that hollow shell she'd become, to tell anyone the truth about him?

Then she thought of Arrant. How handsome he was now that he had grown. What a fool she'd been! There'd been a time when he could have been hers for the taking, but she'd been too proud. She'd wanted a man who was a proper Magoroth, not someone struggling with a deformity. She'd admired his courage, but not enough to recognise its nobility. And she'd walked away. Now Samia had him, and the way he looked at the Illusa was enough to tell Serenelle there was no going back. Angrily, she brushed away her tears.

Sands, she had to warn him. Or tell her father. But Firgan would kill her . . .

She was still there, on the floor, when the lamp burned out. She was still there when her father came home. She heard the servant let him in the main door. His emotions arrived before he did, a dark gout of depression, defeat, fear. She recognised them all; they were hers too. Something terrible had happened.

He entered the room and sought her in the gloom by tracing her despair. Yet he didn't go straight to her. He sank down onto the divan and wearily reclined there before he spoke. 'Come, little one,' he said, patting the cushion beside him. 'We'll tell each other what's the matter.'

She rose and went to him, to cry against his chest.

CHAPTER TWENTY-SIX

There can't be a better way to start the day than holding hands with a pretty Illusa over breakfast in your apartment every morning.

Arrant flushed, tried to hide his heightened colour from Samia, and failed.

She hazarded a guess. 'Tarran has arrived? Sometimes I wonder just what he says to you.'

'So do I,' he said with feeling. However, he thought he'd caught the undercurrents of fatigue and despair and fear in his brother, and so the stab of dread in his own guts was savage. Gods knew, it was damnably difficult. Every day Tarran arrived, he seemed weaker than the day before, although never as bad as that first day at the Swirls.

Rest, he said gently. *Everything here is fine. Father's here – he came in yesterday.*

Samia pushed her plate aside with her free hand, then used it to prop up her chin while she watched Arrant eat. 'Well met, Tarran. I am enjoying watching your brother devour food. Even breakfast is a small banquet. I wish I could eat as much, but if I did, I'd be as fat as a pregnant gorclak.'

'It's all a by-product of leaking power. I have to replace the energy I lose somehow. But I wouldn't advise cracking your cabochon just so you can make a glutton of yourself.' Arrant helped himself to more olive oil. He poured it over his bread, added some honey and pine nuts and ate the result.

'That's disgusting,' she said, screwing up her nose.

'You're just jealous.'

'Absolutely. Now, about laying a trap. I told Serenelle about the return of your powers. I don't for a minute think it will work, but I thought I'd better warn you. Just in case.'

He grinned at her. 'Having second thoughts about her, are you?'

'Not at—'

A knock at the door interrupted her.

'It's Eris,' Arrant said, puzzled that his chamberlain was so early. The man always came to clear the dishes at the end of an hour, and Arrant could have set his water clock by his punctuality. 'Come in!' he called.

As Eris entered, the Council Hall Pavilion bell began to toll, the reverberations loud in the still morning air. A gong somewhere in the Mirager's Pavilion took up the warning. Samia jumped up, turning over her chair.

'What's happening?' Arrant asked Eris as he scrambled to his feet.

Agitated, the man flapped his hands. 'I don't rightly know, Magori. Nothing is normal this morning. The Magoria-sarana came back very late last night, and so did Magori-korden. The two of them have been closeted with the Mirager for a couple of hours this morning. Now they have all moved over to the Council Hall. Korden took two young Magoroth to the Shiver Barrens to get their swords, you may remember. I think it has something to do with that.'

Arrant nodded, frowning. *Tarran, do you know anything about this?*

Things have been – bad, Arrant. The fighting is too intense for us to think of anything else. And the storms are getting worse.

Storms?

The winds. When Arrant was silent, Tarran added, *It won't be long now.*

Arrant headed for the door after Samia, but then turned back to rummage under his pallet platform. He drew out the package there, still wrapped, just as it had been when Garis had given it to him in Tyrans.

Slowly, he unwound the cloth.

The bell was a signal that there was to be a meeting in the Council Hall of the neighbouring pavilion, so that's where he headed. In the distance, they could hear the bells of Magor households tolling to pass the message all over the city.

Samia argued with Arrant all the way to the hall. 'If your father wanted you there, he would have called you,' she pointed out with her usual impeccable logic as they traversed the gardens. 'And why have you brought your Magoroth sword? You are supposed to be keeping your Magorness a secret.'

'Well that's rich coming for someone who told Serenelle all about it. Not that I mind. I'm fed up with all the hiding,' he replied. 'At the moment, I *am* a Magoroth. And I don't care who knows it. I'm going in. I'll tell you all about it afterwards, I promise.'

She caught at his arm as they arrived at the foot of the main steps to the hall. 'You know your father doesn't want Firgan to know—'

He stopped to look at her. 'Samia, I have a genius for doing the wrong thing at the wrong time. I know that. But time is running out for the Mirage Makers. And therefore for us, too. Tarran has been saying for years that their end is coming soon. Well, their idea of soon and our idea of soon are usually two different things and we've sort of got used to that. We've almost convinced ourselves that the end won't happen yet a while;

it'll always be just one more crisis. But we can't say that any more. Now "soon" means just that. And I can't hide myself away and watch it happen. I have to try to find a way to . . . I don't know. Do something that might postpone the inevitable. Just . . . *something*.'

She was silent, but she released his arm. He smiled at her, trying to be comforting, but she looked more resigned than comforted – and not a little put out because, as an Illusa, she could not go in with him. He turned and marched on up to the guard at the top of the steps. It was Perradin.

He flushed when he saw Arrant, his expression appalled and his embarrassment leaking. 'Oh, sands – Arrant, I can't let you in. Standing orders, you know. Everyone past this door has to show colour in their sword. Or be specifically granted exemption. I can send someone to ask—'

'No need,' Arrant said with a smile, sliding his sword out of its scabbard. It filled with glowing gold.

Perradin's jaw sagged. 'Isn't that impossible?' he asked.

'Evidently not,' Arrant said drily.

Perradin's face lit up. 'Welcome back,' he said, and held out his left hand. Arrant switched his sword over to clasp cabochons with him. Perradin's emotion was untarnished pleasure. 'I'm looking forward to hearing how you did that, Arrant. In detail.'

Arrant grinned at him. 'Soon, I promise.'

Behind him, Samia winced and shook her head, but Arrant didn't see. He sheathed his sword and marched through the doors into the entrance hall, where he threaded his way between the waiting groups of people, heading for the door to the Mirager's room. Conversation stopped as he passed, then resumed with renewed intensity as they saw his sword and felt his leaking of Magoroth power. Emotion filled the hall, and it was mixed. Surprise, shock, annoyance, delight, acceptance – it was all there.

Sometimes I'd rather not know, he told Tarran.

Once outside the room, he hesitated. His cabochon burned at the memory of what had happened behind that door. He flexed his hand, trying to accept the memories without flinching. *You with me, Tarran?* he asked.

Not going anywhere else. Father is going to skin you alive, though.

There was no guard outside the Mirager's door, but he remained where he was anyway. Temellin, Sarana, Korden. And Firgan. *Damn. What the Ravage hells is he doing here?* All of them had their emotions carefully muted. He could have enhanced his hearing to listen in, but if ever anything had been instilled in him since he had arrived in Kardiastan, it was the sacredness of privacy. He could have knocked, or entered without knocking, but he refrained.

He waited.

A moment later his father opened the door. 'Firgan started to bristle like a cat under threat the moment he sensed your power,' Temellin said softly. 'Couldn't you have waited? Sarana was going to see you before the Council meeting, to speak to Tarran. However, I suppose it is too late to change things now. Come on in.'

Arrant smiled at his mother as he entered, then looked past her to Korden and said, 'Well met, Magori.' It was the first time they'd spoken since he had returned from Tyrans.

'Well met,' Korden replied, but there was no pleasure in the greeting. He looked old and tired and shrunken. The creases of abnormal fatigue dragged the expression on his face into a parody of its normal hauteur. His eyes reflected something akin to horror.

Firgan was furious and did not try to hide it. 'Did you have an exemption to be here?' He stared hard at Arrant's left hand.

'No,' Arrant said, sounding cheerfully unconcerned. 'I didn't need it.' He grinned and held up his palm. The cabochon throbbed with rich colour. Firgan stared, but Korden didn't even notice.

'How the hells did that happen?' Firgan asked, his fury spilling over into the room, resonating in his voice.

'Both Korden and Sarana have bad news,' Temellin said, ignoring Firgan and speaking directly to Arrant. 'The Mirage Makers did not appear when the last two candidates went to the Shiver Barrens to receive their swords.'

The words exploded in Arrant's head, stark and unexpected in spite of the warning Eris had given. He felt Tarran's shock slicing across his thoughts. *Ravaged hells*, he asked his brother, *you didn't know they were there?*

No. We didn't.

Someone had come to the edge of the Shiver Barrens to obtain their Magor sword and the Mirage Makers *had not felt them*. The implications were searing.

'That has never happened before,' Temellin said. 'Never, in all our history.'

Tarran?

Shiverdamn, Arrant, what can I say? We didn't feel them.

It was an effort to speak, to unstick his tongue from the roof of his mouth. 'The Mirage Makers never felt them arrive.' *Can you rectify this?*

Tarran's answer was strangely formal and Arrant repeated the words exactly as Tarran said them. 'The Mirage Makers no longer have the strength to manifest themselves in the Shiver Barrens. There will be no more Magoroth swords.'

Temellin sat motionless, not speaking, for a long time. No one else broke the silence either. There was little anyone *could* say. When at last Temellin roused himself from his thoughts, his voice was harsh with grief. 'We will inform the Council,' he said.

Korden looked up then. 'All that we have done – the battles, the deaths – it has been for nothing. The Mirage is dying.' He sounded defeated. Almost uninterested.

'Not for nothing,' Sarana said. 'We have delayed the inevitable. Delayed it by years, perhaps.'

That's true, Tarran said. *But the delay is almost over.*

Korden continued. 'No one else will have a Mirager's sword after you two have gone. Then no more cabochons. And finally no more Magor. We've failed our people, Temellin.' His voice wavered as if he had suddenly sunk into old age.

Arrant stared. The man was only five years older than Temellin.

'Perhaps there was nothing we could have done,' Temellin said gently. 'After all, the Mirage Makers themselves thought it would be my other son who would make the difference.'

'Pinar died for nothing,' Firgan said, his voice harsh. 'Her son was sacrificed for nothing. In all probability, Ligea misinterpreted what was required—'

Temellin changed in an instant. They all felt it: the transformation into a man as dangerous to his enemies as a predator to its prey. '*Sarana* saw the same vision I did, Firgan. There was no room for misinterpretation. For some reason, Pinar's son has not been able to do what they hoped; that's all.'

'You have one flawed son; perhaps the other was too.'

Told you once he was as nasty as a Ravage beast, Tarran said.

Korden winced and lowered his gaze.

He's ashamed, Arrant said, noticing. *He's finally ashamed of his son.*

'Get out of my room,' Temellin said, his voice dropping several registers to a note that made Arrant shiver, 'before Sarana and I show you the real power of a Mirager's sword and teach you a little respect.'

Firgan stood up, shrugged and headed for the door. Just

before he exited, he added, 'If you want my respect, then tell us how to save the Mirage. But then, I suppose that's too much to expect of a blind man and a Tyranian compeer bitch.' He closed the door behind him with more force than necessary.

Sarana fixed Korden with a hard stare. 'And this is the man you want as the next Mirager, Korden? You'd better think again.'

Korden, upset, wouldn't look at her as he answered. 'He is devastated. His grief makes him tactless. This is a tragic day for us, after all.' Then realising he was making excuses for something inexcusable, he bowed his head, and followed his son out.

Sarana snorted. '"Tactless". I am glad he explained that. I would never have known.'

'I almost killed Firgan, right then,' Temellin said, shaking his head. 'He'll never know how close he came to death. Arrant, go and see if Korden gets to his seat all right, will you? And then ask a healer to look at him. I don't think he is at all well.'

Arrant nodded and did as he was asked. When he stepped outside, it was to find that Firgan had already disappeared into the main hall. Korden, though, leaned against the hall doorway, sweat trickling down his cheeks and neck.

Arrant went to him and touched his shoulder. 'Magori? Are you all right?'

The look Korden turned on him was terrible. His mouth worked but no words came out. His emotions had slipped free, but were muddled and senseless, like a child's babbling.

He's ill, Tarran said. *Really ill.*

Ryval strode towards them, preceded by a wave of dislike and red-hot rage. 'What's the matter with him? *What have you done to my father?*'

Before Arrant could answer, Korden roused himself enough to shake a finger at Ryval. 'He's a viper, your brother. A murderer! Did you know too – did you? Maybe *all* of you are vipers. Turning on your own family. Lesgath, oh, my son. And my little Serenewaaaa . . .' Half of his face went slack, slurring the words into nonsense. One of his legs collapsed under him and Arrant only just managed to catch him before he fell. Gently, he lowered Korden to the floor.

'*Ware*, Tarran said. *Firgan*.

Ryval was still gaping at his father, caught unawares by his accusations, and it was Firgan now who was raging at Arrant, ordering him away. Arrant stood and backed off, glad enough to go. People milled around, offering healing help. Gretha came, trailed by Elvena, Serenelle and several of her other children, only to wring her hands in useless lament. More and more people crowded into the passage.

Arrant turned away, intending to tell his parents what was happening, but Serenelle blocked his way.

'It's bad, isn't it?' she asked quietly.

He glanced over to where people were lifting Korden up. He nodded. 'In his brain, I think. He's paralysed. He's not dead, though.' Not yet.

She took a deep breath. 'Firgan's going to kill you. He knows your parents want you to be the Miragerin's heir.'

'You told him?'

She nodded. 'I'm sorry.'

'He threatened you.' It wasn't a question.

'I'm not very brave, Arrant.'

She turned and began to walk away but he called after her. 'Serenelle.'

She stopped and looked back.

'Your father knows Firgan murdered Lesgath. Was it you who told him?'

She nodded.

'Firgan will guess it was you.'

She gave a slight smile and gestured to where her father was being borne away. 'He was my only protection. I gambled when I told him the truth about Firgan, and I just lost.'

'Go to the Mirager's Pavilion. Right now. Ask for Hellesia. Tell her I said you were to be given a room in the Mirager's apartments. And stay there.'

She stared, then nodded, adding softly, 'Samia is a lucky woman.'

People pushed between them, and someone asked him what had happened, grabbing him by the arm. By the time he had answered and freed himself, Serenelle had gone.

He returned to the Mirager's room with the news. Temellin disappeared to see if there was anything he could do for Korden, and to delay the meeting.

Sarana watched him go, and said soberly, 'It looks as if we have to contemplate a near future with Firgan as the head of the Korden family.'

Arrant nodded and tried not to think about that. 'I still haven't heard your news.'

'Ravage hells, there's never just *one* grain of sand under the saddle, is there? That northern vale I went to – Arrant, as far as I could discover, it had been attacked by a single Ravage beast. Yet over a hundred people were killed.'

He stared at her, appalled. 'That's not possible, surely. Not with just *one* beast.'

'I could not find any other. And this one was different. It used illusion. I killed it, but not before it had taken Temellin's form.'

'That's not possible surely!'

'We don't understand it. I think it must have stolen something from the Mirage Makers – the ability to create an illusion. And it could *move*. Independently, free of any Ravage sore. I keep imagining thousands of them with those abilities, arriving on the wind, showing us things that aren't real. Killing for the pleasure of it, and then consuming us. Arrant, I had comforted myself with the thought that we could handle the Ravage beasts if they left the Mirage when the Mirage Makers died. It wouldn't be pleasant, but Kardiastan would survive. And so would the Magor. But that thing I killed? Even though I knew it couldn't be Temellin, it *looked* like him. The Magor can't see through illusions! We can't ward against *seeing* illusions. A few thousand of those could wipe us from the face of the earth. They could obliterate all life in Kardiastan. And you know what that whole incident smacked of to me, as a military planner? A scouting foray. An attempt to see what could be done in a new arena of war. And it was Vortexdamned successful. One creature, more than a hundred dead, and it was still alive fourteen days after it arrived. I suspect the only reason it wasn't even more successful was because everyone fled the vale.'

He went cold all over, just thinking of it. Human malice and jealousy and cruelty let loose on the world, with the skills of an illusionist and the appetite of the Ravage. His mouth went dry as he suddenly realised what she had done. 'Ocrastes' balls – it looked like Father? And you killed it? How did you know it *wasn't* him?'

She chuckled, but there was little humour there. 'The illusory Temellin wasn't blind. And it was too young. The beast obviously hadn't seen him recently. But you know what the really scary thing was? *It knew who I was.* It knew the connection between Temel and me. Is Tarran still with you? Can he tell us anything?'

Flower, Tarran whispered. *She went missing about that time . . .*

The blackness of Tarran's misery made it hard for Arrant to think. 'Shit. Sandhells, Tarran – no Mirage Maker would do what happened there, would they?'

Of course not. That's unthinkable. There is no way Flower would help a Ravage beast.

'Could she be forced to?'

How? Hells, Arrant, there's nothing you can tell us about suffering that we do not already know. What torture could force her?

Arrant sucked in a breath and tried not to think about the hell Tarran had lived with every day of his life. 'All right then, could her powers be stolen from her?'

Impossible. They are integral to us, just as no one can steal your cabochon and use it.

'What about if she was somehow separated from you? What then?'

How could she be separated from – But Tarran didn't finish. Couldn't finish. He knew the answer, and so did Arrant.

'The wind,' Arrant explained to Sarana, who had been trying to follow the one-sided conversation. 'There was a Mirage Maker. She could have been swept away by the wind. Too suddenly and too far away for them to be able to sense her in their weakened state. But Tarran doesn't understand how she could have been, um, subverted.'

Sarana paled. 'No! Don't tell me I killed a Mirage Maker. Please don't tell me that. Without the illusion, it looked like a Ravage beast!'

Tarran was silent in Arrant's mind for a long time before he managed to say in an anguished whisper, *We are losing our hold on everything inside the Mirage. The Ravage beasts, the land itself, and now ourselves . . . Skies, what is to become of you after we are gone?*

'The only solution is to stop you dying,' Arrant replied. 'Why has only one of you been swept away so far? Maybe they aren't trying to—' This time he was the one who stopped, unable to go on. His mind focused down to a pinprick thought, shutting

Tarran out, shutting out everything around him – his mother, the room, the morning's events. He took the thought and fed it, rounded it, moulded it, turned it this way and that to find the holes, the fallacies, the bits that wouldn't fit.

Tarran and Sarana waited. Just then Temellin came back into the room and the bell started tolling again.

'Oh, my pickled hells,' Arrant said softly, addressing them all. 'We've been looking at this the wrong way around. The Ravage doesn't want to *kill* the Mirage Makers.'

Tarran snorted. *Well, they've been giving a damn good imitation.*

'No. What you said once before was true. They can't do without you. They are part of you – kill you, and they kill themselves. They don't want to *destroy* you. They want to *become* you.' Terror lapped at him, ripples of it coming from some inner place to break inside his mind and race his heart.

'Mother, you *did* kill the missing Mirage Maker. I'm sorry, but she was the Ravage beast. The Ravage beast was her. Hells, why did none of us this see this earlier? It's so obvious! Tarran, they want to make the Mirage Makers so weak you can no longer keep yourselves separate from them. *They want to force you to let them back in.* They want you to become whole again. Only this time, they – all that is bad about humanity – have multiplied. *They* will be in command, not the gentle essensa of a Mirage Maker.' He looked at his parents. 'The missing Mirage Maker was called Flower. She was old and frail and harmless, a lover of flowers – and look what she became.'

Poor, poor Flower. I – I was the one who called her that. And I thought of her as female, although she might not have been. When I was little, I gave names to all the ones I could differentiate; it was easier to see them as separate entities that way . . . He paused. *I guess there are times when I am very human, after all.* He added, despairing, *Do you think she knew what she did?*

He couldn't lie. He didn't know how, not to Tarran. 'How could she not? She was taken over by a Ravage beast which was then able to use her powers of movement – and illusion.'

'Not very well, perhaps,' Sarana said. 'But if it'd had time to practice? Oh, Tarran, it chewed a baby out of its mother's womb. It fed on people. What if – what if they bring you all to the brink of death and then seize your wills, your minds, and ride you on the winds into Kardiastan? Into Madrinya? To feed on us . . .' Temellin held out his cabochoned hand to her, and she clasped it in her own.

Tears trickled down Arrant's cheeks, but they weren't his. He allowed them to fall unchecked.

They were all silent for a long while. Then Tarran started to speak and Arrant softly repeated the words for the benefit of his parents. *The way we expected to die was to be consumed by the Ravage. We kept the heart of what we were inviolate. We thought no Mirage Maker could be torn from our unity, from our core. Our Mirage illusions – they are being destroyed, but they are just our – our vestments. Our adornment, our extension of self. They are not our soul, not our essensa. We had held on to that, or we thought we had. But perhaps you are right. That is the part of us they really want. They wish to become us, and change our Mirage to their vision of the world.*

Their vision of the world. A mirage that was not eccentric, but vile. Illusions that were nightmares beyond imagining, where men could run but never escape, where children were eaten and people driven mad with terror.

'Mirageless soul,' Temellin said, his emotions savage in the air. 'Think of what it would mean. A Ravage instead of a Mirage. Or many scattered Ravages. And within each, Ravage beasts with Mirage Maker power and the will to use it. Going where they want using the wind, guiding it with Mirage Maker skills. Breaking out from behind the Shiver Barrens to conquer us all. They could do anything. Why stop at Kardiastan?'

Another silence while they digested that, then Sarana murmured, 'It was hard for me to kill it even though all my senses told me it wasn't Temellin. How much harder for common folk to kill something that looks like their wife or child or mother?'

'The permutations are endless,' Temellin said. 'What if they use an illusion of, say, a flock of four-winged fisher birds? Or a melon vine? Or a broom? No one is going to expect to be ripped apart by their kitchen broom.'

Arrant sat unmoving. His nightmares, real. He couldn't speak. He hadn't wanted to be right.

'Tarran, how many Mirage Makers are there?' Temellin asked.

I don't know. I've never counted them. It would be hard to tell anyway. Many have sort of blurred into one another and are never found apart. In one sense, none of us are ever entirely apart, not even me when I am with you. There are always connections.

Arrant repeated the words aloud, then asked, 'Hundreds, then?'

Skies, no. More than that. Many thousands.

Arrant blinked and wondered, as he repeated the answer aloud, why that surprised him. He didn't have to think about why it terrified him.

The bell continued to ring, calling everyone back for the meeting, but none of them moved.

'I don't like the Ravage connection to you, Arrant,' Sarana said. She came forward to lay a hand on his arm in emphasis of her concern. 'I've been thinking about those Ravage dreams of yours. What if they were Ravage sent – deliberately?'

'Why would they want to do that?' Temellin asked.

'Because there is something about me that scares them,' Arrant said. 'They want to frighten me into staying away.'

Sarana gave him a sharp look and her unease permeated the room. 'This already occurred to you?'

He nodded. 'But I have no idea why I should be a danger to them. None.'

'Because of your fraternal connection to Tarran? The Ravage has known about you ever since you were an essensa. And I can tell you right now, I don't want you going anywhere near the Mirage.'

Behind her, his father was nodding in agreement. Arrant felt a sharp disappointment and didn't bother to hide it.

'Hells,' she said, 'I've got to get used to feeling your emotions. I don't know whether to be delighted I can, or to tell you not to be cheeky.'

He refused to be diverted. 'If they are frightened of me, then I should go there. Anything that scares them should definitely be pursued.' The fear inside him tightened as he added to Tarran, *I hope she's wrong.*

'Not until we work out what it is about you that scares them,' Sarana said firmly.

And just how often is your mother wrong? Tarran asked.

Arrant's next thought was chilling. Maybe it was better if she wasn't wrong. If the Ravage feared him, then there was something about him that would spell the end of the Ravage. Maybe he was the only hope for their future. Maybe he would have to become a Mirage Maker to defeat them, forfeiting his physical self. The thought left him hollow with terror, as if he'd been gutted.

It's not that bad being a Mirage Maker, Tarran protested, offended.

Sorry. It's just, um, oh, never mind. I can't even begin to explain. 'So what do we do?' he asked.

'We will have to prepare for the end of the Mirage, for a start,' Temellin said.

'Better that we prevent the death of the Mirage Makers in the first place,' Arrant said, the edge of anger in his voice matched by loosed emotion.

'He is my son too,' Temellin replied, chiding him gently for the unspoken criticism. 'I never forgot what it means to speak of the death of the Mirage Makers and the vanishing of the Mirage. Never.' He ran a hand over his head, dislodging the thong that tied back his hair so that an unruly lock flopped over his forehead. 'I don't know what to say to you, Tarran. We will go on fighting. All of us, I promise you. We won't give up, until there's not one of us alive.'

The bell stopped tolling and the last reverberation died away into the silence.

'Time for the meeting,' Temellin said, and rose to his feet.

Arrant dodged Samia after the Council meeting finished. He felt guilty about it, but just then he couldn't bear the thought of having to relate the details of that turbulent session. It had been horrible to watch. The shock, the protests, the arguments. The endless circular discussions. The blaming. Firgan using the opportunity to question Temellin's competence and Sarana's influence, ranting how his noble father had sacrificed his health attempting to bring a more responsible governance to the Mirager's rule.

The only admirable thing had been Temellin's demeanour throughout. He'd calmed, cajoled and reassured long past the moment when a lesser man would have lost his temper. If he'd felt despair, he had not shown it. For Arrant, watching his father being buffeted by the emotions of the assembly had been hard. And so, afterwards, when he'd seen Samia demanding to know what had happened from Perradin, he had taken the opportunity to sneak past her. He wanted to talk to Tarran, trying not to think how every moment they had was precious, and how few moments could be left to them. That Tarran would soon be gone from the world seemed impossible. That acerbic, witty brother of his? His sharp inquiring mind erased, never to make Arrant laugh again? *Let's get across to the Mirager's garden*, he said. *We can be quiet there.*

Tarran was silent as Arrant walked, but the moment they had entered the confines of the garden he said, *Arrant, I'm going back.*

'Now?'

Yes. Um, say goodbye to Papa.

'Acheron's mists! You don't intend to come back?'

No. I don't know. Probably not. I'm sorry, Arrant. I don't like leaving you powerless, but that will happen anyway, and soon. We – the Mirage Makers – have got to think of a way to kill ourselves. And quickly. Before the Ravage makes us too weak to resist it. It's not going to be easy. The only way we have to die is to starve ourselves of energy – and that would make us weak and vulnerable and they would take us over anyway. I don't know what we are going to do.

'Wait, Tarran—'

I've got to get back there. He gave a dry laugh. *I don't need to be strong any more. I have to die, and to do that I have to be weak. Silly, huh? I've been doing the wrong thing all along.* His grief trailed through Arrant's mind. His fear of dying underlaid every word he uttered, the poignancy only emphasised by his attempts to suppress it.

'Don't you dare go before I tell you what I have to.' Arrant said fiercely. 'Listen, if the Ravage has been sending me dreams all my life to scare me away, then it's because I have the power to defeat them, and they know it.'

Brother, that is all conjecture. Very likely they just took a dislike to your sense of humour. And for sure they don't like your parentage. Arrant, it takes energy to listen for you – don't expect me to hear.

'I'm sure I'm right!'

Tarran's next words were gently said. *If you ever find out what it is they fear, come to us. Stand on the Fifth Rake and call my name. Part of us will hear and if I still live, I will come. Full life, brother. I will never forget you.*

Arrant's thoughts went blank. This was too sudden, too abrupt, too shocking. He wanted to say so much, but nothing would come to him.

I know it all, Tarran said. *I have felt it. You don't have to say it. We have loved, you and I.*

And he was gone.

CHAPTER TWENTY-SEVEN

'He's *gone*?'

Samia stared at him in consternation. She had come to him that morning not knowing that Tarran had vanished from his mind the day before. He nodded in reply and sketched in all that she did not know, finishing with, 'I've tried calling to him, but he won't answer. Which is a nuisance because Father wants to know whether it's possible to interpose an army between the Mirage Makers and the Ravage beasts, to physically separate them to give the Mirage Makers time enough to die. And if that's possible, he wants to know how long they'd need, um, before they'd die.'

'But – but wouldn't that mean the death of our army?'

He nodded again. 'Yes, probably. It's either that, or every living Kardi. Imagine it, Sam. Illusions that are *real*. Not the harmless craziness that you were used to when you lived in the Mirage. These new illusions will be a darkness, a Mirage in which – no matter where we look – we will face things beyond the horror of our imaginations.' The creatures of his dreams. 'And they will be real.'

She looked sick and he knew she was thinking of her father. 'Mirage help us, we have to work out why the Ravage fears you.'

'I know.' But his thought, which he kept to himself, was bleak: 'Something tells me I may have to die to make this right.'

'Your connection to Tarran has got to be at the top of the list. Together the two of you are certainly stronger than anyone I know.'

'Yet hardly powerful enough to kill a whole sea of Ravage beasts.' He touched the Quyr necklet. 'I also have this. It gives me a connection to my mounts. Especially to shleths. And it worked well when we were under the Shiver Barrens. In the end, it was what saved my father and me because I could sense where the shleths were.'

'Is that how you did that?' she asked, interested. 'I'm not sure if that is relevant, though. Nor am I certain we should assume just because you have dreams about the Ravage that they sent them. Or, if they did, that they sent them for a reason. It may have just been sheer malice.'

'Either way my parents won't let me go to the Mirage yet, especially now that Tarran's not around and my power is as unpredictable as ever.' He looked at his nearly colourless cabochon. 'They keep on saying: later, later. It's driving me sand crazy.'

'They think the Ravage will target you.'

'Yes. Father sent Firgan back last night, did you know that? He was furious, but he went. Oh, and I was right about Serenelle. She did tell him about me having cabochon power again, and my parents wanting me to be Sarana's heir. But only because he coerced her. So in a way, you were right too.'

'Oh! Well, I suppose you made that redundant anyway, when you powered up your sword yesterday to get into the Council Hall.'

'Don't remind me. Gods, Father ripped strips off me over that last night. How on earth does he make me feel thirteen again so easily? It's ridiculous. But what's worrying me is that

I can't find Serenelle. I told her to go to the Mirager's Pavilion, but she didn't arrive.'

'But you said Firgan has left for the Mirage?'

'Serenelle was already missing by the time he left.'

She didn't reply. She didn't need to; her anxiety was there in the line of her brow and the hunch of her shoulders.

'Oh, sands take it, Samia. I feel so – so *frustrated*.'

She came to stand close to him, and took his hand. 'I know. I feel I want to stop the water clocks and halt the hourglasses and keep everything the way it is,' she whispered. 'Because what comes next is going to be too catastrophic.'

'Sam,' he said, 'I may not have seen the Mirage, but I do know the Ravage. It's one thing to try to kill the beasts one at a time. But to attempt to drive a force between each Ravage sore and each unsullied piece of the Mirage? The beasts will unify to shred us all.'

They stared at each other, momentarily immobilised and silenced by the proximity of disaster, by the intimate approach of death; for their parents, their friends, and ultimately themselves.

'I can't stop thinking of Tarran,' he said. 'He has to die, or he will come on the wind to kill us. Do you think he'd know what he did? I do. I think his mind would still be alive there, somewhere inside a Ravage beast, as he tore us to pieces.'

She faltered. 'If they are just human failings, why are they so very bad?'

'They are human failings that have been allowed to grow and fester in Ravage sores for hundreds of years, separated from the, um, the *moderation* of human virtues. The Mirage Makers didn't try to change them, or soften them; they just tried to keep them encapsulated. We are all going to pay for their mistake, Samia.'

In answer, she reached across and held his hand. 'Whatever we do, Arrant, promise me we'll do it together.'

He stared at her, nonplussed.

Her plea took on urgency. 'I'm a healer; I don't fight. And without Tarran, you won't have much control over your power. To keep what you do have, you will need me to heal your cabochon from time to time. My father, your parents – they are warriors. They won't have time for us. And I don't want to die alone. I don't want to *be* alone, without a friend who cares. Promise, Arrant – no matter what happens, we'll be together.'

Her bottom lip trembled, and he could no more have refused her anything than he could have stopped time by refusing to invert an hourglass. 'I don't want to be alone either,' he said simply. He hesitated, desperately wanting to take her into his arms and kiss her, but he delayed too long and the moment passed.

'You're thinking of going to the Mirage, aren't you?' she said. 'Tonight. Without telling anyone.'

He nodded. 'Am I so obvious?'

'I'm coming with you.'

When he hesitated again, she cocked her head, her whole stance daring him to patronise her by refusing.

'You wretch, Sam!' he said. 'I am blessed if I understand how you can say so much by not saying a word.'

'And you don't even need a cabochon to know. What time do we leave?'

Garis had once told Arrant that the stones of the Ordensa paveway had been cemented with blood. He'd meant it figuratively, referring to the hundreds of slaves who had died in the rush to have the road completed as quickly as possible and the numerous Tyrians – overseers, engineers and legionnaires alike – who had fallen to Magor attack as they built their wayhouses and forced the paving across the drylands from vale to vale.

The first time he had ridden it, Arrant had been moved by

the thought of what this road had cost in human life; now, as they left the city behind long before sunrise, there was so much more to concern him. His fear for his brother yawed in his stomach, and the idea that everything depended on him, on some unknown factor that made the Ravage fear him, was there to sicken him as well. He had felt the claws of hate digging into his dreaming soul. And now his responsibility for Samia's safety touched everything he did. But he had promised her . . . and he needed her.

Gods, Garis was going to be *furious* when he found out.

He fingered his necklet, trying to take comfort from the warmth of the runes. Darkness lightened into pale sky and silhouette; the eroded remains of Tyranian grave stele materialised out of the blackness of the night, thrusting up from the sand to line the way like sentinels for the buried dead the invaders had left behind. He glanced across at Samia, and caught the glimpse of her smile in the first light of dawn.

How long before his departure came to his father's ears? He calculated: several hours yet before Eris came to wake him. He'd be surprised that Arrant wasn't there, but not alarmed. He would just assume he had gone to his father to work on the problems besetting them. It could be hours before anyone realised he was missing.

Samia would be another matter. When they walked the shleths he asked, 'Did you leave a note for your father?'

'Of course.'

'What did you say?'

'Just that I was with you and not to worry. Of course he will.'

'I want to ride as continuously as we can.'

She rubbed her thigh meaningfully. 'Ouch.'

'I'm afraid so. We'll change shleths at every wayhouse or livery.'

'Have you enough money? That will cost.'

'I shall bill the Mirager.'

She laughed. 'You disobey your father and then get him to pay for it? I like the way your mind works, Arrant Temellin.'

'And I like the way your body moves,' he said silently, and then cursed to himself. Why did his mind always turn to things like that? He forced himself to think about what they were doing.

Someone would be sent after them. Garis, probably. Arrant would certainly refuse to return. The Mirage – Tarran – was running out of time.

Fear, fatigue, jingling harness, the rise and fall of a mount; pursuit behind, the unknown ahead. The glorious freedom of the road narrowed by the confines of the task undertaken; the tension that never relaxed its hold ... He knew it all. He'd ridden this path before as a child. Only, this time he was in charge.

Paveway wayhouses with accommodation were a day's ride apart, interspersed with livery stables. They made the first wayhouse in time for lunch, thanks to the quality of their shleths. He doubted that they would be able to maintain that speed for the next leg of the journey because the pavilion-pampered beasts were swapped for wayhouse sluggards with mouths as tough as the maw on a clam. Worse, his new mount had the gait of an overweight goose. Samia's had feeding arms that hung out of the neck grooves and flapped as if the beast had flight in mind.

'I feel ridiculous riding this,' she muttered, as they rode out of the wayhouse gate.

'I know it looks silly, but the stablehand did say it was a comfortable mount. Come, we have to ride faster, or your father will be breathing down my neck, and I am none too sure how I can look him in the eye and tell him, yes, I do indeed intend to take his daughter into what is probably the most dangerous place in the known world right now.'

'Just tell him I wouldn't take no for an answer. Then he'll be all sympathetic.' She smiled at him.

'*Gods*,' he thought, '*I love her.*'

Garis woke that morning, knowing something was wrong.

The night before, Temellin had suggested that he stay in the Mirager's Pavilion, but he had refused and made his way back to his sister-in-law's villa where, he hoped, Samia was long asleep. It was well past midnight when he entered the house, and he would have loved to have peeked into her room and tucked her in, as he had done when she was a child. He passed her door regretting she was too old for that now, and wondered where all the precious years of childhood had gone.

At least they would have breakfast together, because who knew when they would see each other again? His last thoughts as he went to sleep that night were about how to persuade her to stay in Madrinya even though, as a healer, her talents would be invaluable in the battle with the Ravage. Maybe he didn't have the right to stop her. Perhaps people would die if she wasn't there. But, oh, his mirageless soul – what if she were the one to die? How would he ever forgive himself?

When he woke before dawn, he knew she was gone. Always the first thing he did in the morning was to seek her out with his positioning powers. And she wasn't there.

Within a quarter of an hour he was flinging open the doors to Sarana and Temellin's room in the Mirager's Pavilion. They were both still asleep in the same bed. Sarana was half sprawled on top of the covers. She wasn't wearing anything.

They both woke and moved at the same time – and they

both did the same thing. They reached for their swords hanging from the wall above the bedhead, only halting the instinctive move to arm themselves once their senses told them who had intruded.

Sarana grabbed for a sheet to cover herself instead. 'Vortexdamn it, Garis – do you make a habit of walking in on me when I'm naked?'

'Twice in twenty years is not a habit,' he said. 'And you still look ravishing.'

'He's done this before?' Temellin asked her, scowling.

Garis refused to allow himself to be diverted. 'Listen, you two, Arrant and Samia are missing.'

'What do you mean, missing?' Sarana asked, flinging off the covers to get up. 'Turn your back, you barbarian. Did no one ever teach you to knock?'

He looked away. 'She left a note to say they were together, and I suspect they have gone to the Mirage.'

'Blast the lad,' Temellin muttered. 'And that girl of yours, too. She ought to have known better. Garis, go after them. You too, Sarana.'

'What about all the arrangements that have to be made?' Garis asked, turning around to face them again even though Sarana was only half-dressed. He didn't notice. 'You gave me enough orders yesterday to keep me occupied for a month. *And* asked them all to be done today.' He swallowed, hating himself for saying the words. 'We are going to a battle that means everything. Our children are – are precious to us, but—' He halted, unable to betray Samia by saying the obvious. She wasn't as important as the nation. She was only one person.

Temellin's reply was calm and measured. 'We need to know, urgently, the answer to those two questions I had for Tarran. Arrant obviously has not been able to contact Tarran from afar, and they have gone to do it from the last rake. It's now your job to keep him safe. What you do about Samia is your business. Is that clear?' Temellin asked.

'Er – yes. Of course,' Garis replied. He suddenly felt he ought to be standing spear-haft straight, saluting like a Tyranian soldier. Damn it, how could the man do that with just a few choice words?

But Temellin hadn't finished. 'And need I remind you that Firgan is out there somewhere? Those two children of ours will be riding as if the winds of the Vortex are on their tails. They'll catch the bastard up. If you want to put personal considerations aside, Garis, just remind yourself that the nation needs Arrant alive to speak to Tarran and it's doubtful if Firgan will let a little fact like that bother him.'

Garis went pale. He had forgotten Firgan. 'Right,' he said.

Sarana, in the meantime, had gone to the door and given orders to one of the servants. Now she was gathering a few things together and stuffing them into a pack. 'Go down to the kitchens, Garis, and get us both something to eat and drink. I'll meet you at the stables in a quarter of an hour.'

He nodded. 'Full life,' he said to Temellin, and suddenly the words of farewell seemed poignantly final.

'Indeed, I hope so,' Temellin replied. 'Do not fail me, Garis.' They both knew he was not speaking of the answers he required of Tarran.

As soon as Garis closed the door behind him, Temellin held out his left hand to Sarana. She placed her cabochon against his. They knew they might never meet again, and this hand-clasp, this simple giving of love through a touch, might be the last time for them.

'When we met, I thought I had only days to live,' he said, knowing she would know what he was talking about. 'I had no choice except death. And then you gave me back my Mirager's sword. Every moment since then has been a bonus

I never thought I would have. I don't know that we will live through this. I do not expect to. But I do know what I owe you. And I do know that I am the luckiest man who ever lived.'

She stepped into his arms. 'It seems so long ago that I came to take you to Tyr in chains. Gods, we have both been so lucky, Tem. I have regretted much – but never have I regretted knowing you.'

He bowed his head into her hair. 'Save him, Sarana. Kardiastan needs him. He is our future. Both of them are.'

By the time they had reached the second wayhouse, it was close to midnight. Neither of them had spoken for several hours. Arrant didn't need to feel Samia's pain to know it existed, even though she must have been healing herself as they rode. No longer used to spending long days in the saddle, he was sore all over and his misery was exacerbated by any lack of contact with Tarran. Whenever he reached out to him there was no reply, not a whisper. His brother was gone as if he'd never existed as anything but a figment of his imagination.

In his place, terror swirled. And endless, unanswerable questions. He couldn't understand how he could make a difference to the Ravage. Not even with Tarran in his mind.

When they saw the lamp on the gate of the wayhouse ahead of them, he said, with a relief that he felt all the way to his sandalled feet, 'We'll stay here for the rest of the night.'

Her reaction was unexpected. She halted her shleth and he heard her gasp. He couldn't see her face in the darkness, but he felt her raw consternation. 'Oh, sweet hells, you can't feel him, can you?'

'Who?'

'Firgan! He's there – in the wayhouse.'

They exchanged a look, even though there was little to see in the gloom. He should have thought of that. By travelling so far in one day, they had caught up with the man. 'Vortexdamn him to Hades,' he said. 'We can't just ride on. We have to change mounts. And I am so confoundedly tired I'm going to fall off the shleth any moment.'

'If I were to dismount, I don't think I could get back on again,' she admitted. 'But Arrant, this is *Firgan*. He mustn't find out you are on this road without guards. If he knows you are here, he will kill you. Maybe not in the wayhouse, but what about in an ambush along the way tomorrow? We are at a disadvantage, too. You can't feel him coming and I'm not warrior.'

'He's probably sound asleep right now. In which case he wouldn't sense either of us. Not even if we rode down there and took a room for the night.'

'True – but he'd know in the morning.'

He thought about that. 'Would he? I mean, most Magor don't bother to do a scan of the area around themselves on a continual basis. Why should they, unless they're expecting attack? What if we stay in our rooms until after he has left . . . or if we leave earlier than he does? Would he ever know we were there?'

'And then what? We'll end up being together at the next wayhouse tomorrow night.'

'Confound it, Sam, do you have to think of *everything*?'

'I'm a woman,' she said.

'Another time I shall argue the logic of that, but not now. I am too tired. We are going to ride down to the wayhouse. We are going to take a room. One room. We will barricade ourselves in. And we'll worry about the consequences tomorrow. Right now, you know what? I don't care.'

'I am quite sure that tomorrow I will think a pallet for the night is an awful reason to risk dying,' she said, 'but right now – I don't care either. Let's go.'

They continued on to the wayhouse and woke the gatekeeper

to let them in, then roused the stableboy to take care of their mounts and the wayhousekeeper to give them a room. The latter eyed them sympathetically and promised them hot baths in the morning. Arrant told him who he was, and the man couldn't quite hide a smirk when he asked for only one room. 'Remember,' he said sternly, 'that the baths are segregated. This is a respectable house.'

The nightmares came in all their wretched vividness: he woke once thinking the skin was hanging from his face in bloodied strips. He lay on the pallet, shrunken with fear, bedcovers wet with sweat, still feeling the raking talons of Ravage beasts tearing the flesh of his cheeks, hearing their inhuman laughter . . . knowing that for Tarran such horror was reality.

His thoughts spiralled in tortured questioning, without finding answers. Mirageless soul, he'd once thought he hadn't wanted to live in a world without Tarran; well, it looked as if he wouldn't. They'd both be dead. And so, perhaps, would everyone else. The scope of the disaster was beyond imagining.

Eventually he drifted off to sleep again.

When he woke in the morning, it seemed far too soon. He raised himself up on one elbow. The night before, Samia had said – as she collapsed fully dressed on the pallet, 'I have never ached so much in all my life.' Now, when he looked across at her, she was still lying on top of the covers, with her head under the pillow.

He groaned as his own body registered its protest at being made to ride so long and hard, covering a normal two days' ride in one. At least he was still alive. Firgan had not run a Magoroth sword through his insides during the course of the night. He had pushed his pallet platform against the door of the room before collapsing, and as far as he knew, no one had tried to enter.

He sat upright, wincing. 'Sam,' he hissed. 'Wake up.'

She stirred, opened an eye – and moaned.

'I need to know where Firgan is.'

There was a long silence. And then, 'He's gone. At least, he's not in the building.'

'Let's hope he never sensed our presence. I'll go and see what the wayhousekeeper says.'

'Ask him about those hot baths.'

The news was good. Firgan had ridden off about an hour earlier – and the baths were ready. 'He said he would bring our breakfast into the baths,' Arrant told Samia. 'I asked him if Firgan had spoken to him about us, and he said no. We may have been lucky . . .'

As he lay in the hot water a little later, watching a servant deposit a tray of still-warm bread and goat's cheese for his breakfast, he felt deeply grateful that not only had the Tyranians brought the idea of baths and piped water to the wayhouses of Kardiastan, but that the Kardis had learned to value them. He began to feel the ache of over-used muscles subside.

When he returned to the room, Samia was already there, brushing her damp hair. 'I feel human once more,' she said. 'So what do we do now? If we head off up the paveway, we'll only meet Firgan again, at the next wayhouse.'

'I have to go on,' he said. 'No matter what. I shall leave at midday, arrive late – and hope that he is asleep again. I can't let my fear of that man stop me from getting to Tarran.'

'Then we will leave together,' she said. She sounded matter-of-fact. 'Would you like me to do a bit of healing on those muscles of yours?'

He knew enough about healing to be aware that muscle aches were normally treated by applying healing hands close to the point of trouble – and where his muscles ached most were in his thighs and buttocks. 'Er, no,' he said.

'I'm a healer, Arrant. I've seen everything there is to see.'

'Not on me, you haven't.'

'Oh yes, I have,' she said. 'You just weren't conscious.'

'Samia, I don't think it would be a good idea.' He could feel the flush that started on his neck spread to his face.

She put her head to one side and regarded him with serious eyes. 'Have you ever loved a woman, Arrant? Physically, I mean.'

He felt as if all the important bits of him were suddenly too large for his skin. His answer, a strangled no, didn't sound as insouciant as he'd hoped.

She said, 'Neither have I. Loved a man, I mean.'

'Skies, you've only just turned eighteen. Loads of time yet.' He knew he must sound ridiculously hearty, like an uncle trying to give advice to a favourite niece.

'Well that's just it, isn't it? We might not have loads of time. We might not have any time at all.'

She was looking straight at him, and his heart wouldn't stop thundering. He searched for the right words and ended up sounding as though he thought he'd been insulted. 'You want to bed me just to find out what it's like in case you might get killed soon?'

She uttered an exasperated grunt through gritted teeth. 'You are *such* a shlethhead. No, you dolt, I'm asking because I want to. In fact, right at this moment, with you standing there with your hair still wet, I can't think of anything I'd rather do than have you kiss me. If you want to.'

'If you knew how much—' He cleared his throat. 'And it has *nothing* to do with maybe dying sometime this month.'

'Then what in all of the wide blue skies are you waiting for?'

'Um, I'm not sure. For me to decide whether I can believe my luck? For you to change your mind?'

She started laughing and took his hand. 'Idiot. Are you so shleth-brained you don't know how I feel about you?'

'Ah – yes, I guess so. You'll have to explain it. In detail.'

She raised her lips to his, and started her explanation without saying a word.

He might have known he would make an utter muck of things. He tried too hard, it all happened much too fast, and in the end his cabochon didn't oblige at the crucial moment either. It sputtered like a guttering candle and gave off a few ineffectual sparks that were just plain silly and did nothing for either of them. Under all those circumstances, it was hardly any wonder that Samia's cabochon remained entirely quiescent.

After it was all over, she separated herself from him, lay quietly for a moment and then asked in a puzzled fashion, without any suggestion of blame or criticism, 'That can't be all there is to it, can it?'

He said involuntarily, 'Vortex, I hope not!'

They looked at each other, simultaneously started to giggle and then fell back into each other's arms, their laughter full-throated and contagious.

A little later they tried again. This time, more relaxed, everything seemed to come right. And – for once – his cabochon did all the right things as well.

Afterwards, she nibbled at his earlobe. 'Now that was more like it.'

'Ah, Tarran,' he thought, 'you would approve of the way I feel . . .'

They held each other and talked, lovers' nonsense to keep the world at bay for a little longer, and after a while, both fell asleep.

The next thing Arrant knew there was a knock at the door.

'Who is it?' Samia asked sleepily.

Whoever it was took that for an invitation, opened the door and stepped in. They both sat up, clutching desperately for the covers. Belatedly, Arrant grabbed for his sword as well. Sarana's lessons in survival could never be quite forgotten, even in the most embarrassing of situations, even as he was cursing his stupidity for having forgotten to bar the door in the first place, and Samia was stuttering her awareness of the intruders.

'P – Papa?'

'Oh gods,' Arrant moaned, 'Mother.'

Sarana stared at them both from the doorway, Garis at her shoulder, and for once both of them were nonplussed. 'I think,' Sarana said at last, 'we had better come back once they are dressed.' As she turned to go, she added, still speaking to Garis, 'You really do make a habit of this kind of thing, don't you?'

'It's all your fault,' Garis said as they left.

Samia and Arrant exchanged a glance as the door closed once more. 'I think,' Arrant said, 'that the best part of today is definitely behind us.'

'He's always liked you, you know.'

'I wonder if he still does?' He stood up and began to search through the bedding for his clothes. 'I know I've always liked him. I owe him more than I can say.'

She handed him his trousers. 'Arrant, I'll be very angry with you if you're not still alive at the end of all this, you know. I want to know how this relationship of ours is going to develop.'

He grinned and kissed her. She kissed him back and the idea that she seemed to like it still managed to amaze him. He wished he could let her feel the way he felt through his cabochon, but even though she had sealed the crack again, it wasn't being obliging.

'It's strange,' she said as she dressed. 'We could all be dead in a few days' time, but Papa is worrying about the two of us. I felt his concern. He thinks you're going to walk away, going to have to walk away from me because I'm only an Illuser. He thinks that I – that we'll both be hurt if we go on.'

'Samia, unless Tarran is with me, I'm not a Magoroth, not really. And if I'm not a Magoroth, I can't be Mirager, and if I'm not Mirager, nobody's really going to care who I . . . take to my pallet. Or who I love. Or marry. Quite apart from that, I'm going to make my own damn choice anyway. So if I ever walk away, it will be for our reasons – yours and mine – not other people's.'

She smiled, trying to cover her sadness, knowing they were talking about a future that they would probably never have. 'That's good enough for me.'

CHAPTER TWENTY-EIGHT

A quarter of an hour later they met in the atrium. As was usual in that part of Kardiastan, the daylight hours were searingly hot; only the vines grown across the open space of the courtyard and the cool splash of the central fountain made the noonday temperature bearable. Hidden somewhere in the thick foliage a mellowbird called monotonously. 'We could be back in Tyrans,' Arrant thought. There was still not much about wayhouses in Kardiastan that was Kardi.

He felt an intense embarrassment. If there was one thing worse than your mother walking in on your first experience with a girl, it had to be to find her accompanied by the girl's father. As he and Samia walked up to join them, he held her hand tightly. He had no idea what he was going to say.

His mother pre-empted him. 'We owe you both an apology. We were worried, and the wayhousekeeper had just told us that Firgan had been here – we didn't know what we would find when we opened that door.'

'And that's all the apology you two are going to get,' Garis growled. 'What on earth were you thinking of, racing off like that when we are in the middle of a crisis?'

'Irrelevant, Garis, at the moment,' Sarana said. She was using her quiet, firm voice of authority. Arrant knew it well; when she spoke like that, discussion tended to die an immediate death.

Garis threw up his hands, but he subsided.

'I have already sent a messenger back to your father,' Sarana continued, speaking to Arrant, 'to tell him you are both fine. Now, have you managed to talk to Tarran?'

He shook his head. 'He still doesn't answer. He did warn me that he wouldn't hear.'

'Then you will ride on to the Barrens with me tomorrow. You still need to ask Tarran those questions. Garis can take Samia back to Tyr. I will mend your cabochon when needed.'

'No,' Samia said.

Sarana raised an eyebrow. She wasn't used to being so baldly contradicted.

'Arrant and I don't want to be parted,' Samia explained. 'Not now. Not the way things are with the Ravage.'

Sarana tilted her head, considering. 'Your problem, Garis,' she said at last. 'Your daughter. Good luck.'

'Samia,' Garis said, 'you aren't a warrior.'

'No. I'm a *healer*. Now tell me I am not needed.'

Father and daughter glared at each other. Arrant thought of intervening, and then decided that Samia was quite capable of arguing her own future. In those two sentences, she had summed up the essence of her purpose. She was needed. And yes, it would be dangerous for her. Arrant knew that none of them could stop her. Or, in fact, should. Garis turned away, and the look on his face was one Arrant hoped never to see again. Intense fear, tearing grief, pride – strong emotions in a painful blend.

Sarana evidently felt his capitulation because she said, 'Garis and I aren't in any state to ride on today. We will wait for dawn tomorrow. Right now, I am going to take a bath and bless the Tyranian plumbing. Show me where the baths are, Arrant.' She laid a hand on his arm and as she guided him away, she bent her head to say in his ear, 'Father-daughter talk is in order, I think, and we are unwanted.' As he led her through the atrium to the baths, she added, 'You made a good choice there, Arrant.'

He smiled faintly and said, 'And she probably made a poor one.'

She wrenched him around to face her, suddenly fierce. 'No, she didn't. I am so proud of you. And so is your father. He's as angry as a bee in a bottle, of course, over this mad trip of yours, but admiring nonetheless.'

'It's moondaft, even I know that. But I had to do it anyway. If I am going to die, then it's going to be searching for the chance to win. As for Samia, well, I made her a promise that we'd be together, no matter what. I'm glad you came, though. I was worried that Firgan would stop us before we ever reached the Mirage. Mother, do you think we could try to reach the Three Wells Wayhouse tomorrow? Two days' ride in one again? Even if it does mean catching up with Firgan.'

She sent him a speaking look, and rubbed her backside. 'Well, I'm not worried about Firgan. My *comfort*, however, is another thing . . .'

Late in the evening of the next day, they rode – sore, tired and dusty – into the wayhouse, to find Firgan in the common hall. He wasn't alone; he was drinking with a group of fifty or so Magor who were on their way back to Madrinya after their period of duty at Raker's Camp on the Fifth Rake. Sarana eyed him with a wistful rapacity, wondering if she dared kill him without Temellin's permission.

'Just what we needed,' Garis muttered under his breath. Aloud, he said heartily, 'Why, Firgan, such a pleasant surprise. I would have thought you would have retired to your pallet by now. However, I am glad to see you have stayed up to welcome the Miragerin.'

Firgan's face darkened. 'She's no—' Under the threat of four pairs of eyes, all reflecting an intolerance of insult, he changed what he had been going to say and said smoothly, 'Of course. Although I cannot imagine what you are all doing here, arriving so late, too. Are you all going to fight the Ravage? Even young Arrant here?'

'That's right,' Garis said. 'There has been another development since you left.' He raised his voice to make it obvious he was including all the other Magor in the conversation. 'Listen, everyone. The Mirager-heir, Miragerin-sarana, has something to say to you all.'

The thought of the hot bath she had just ordered from the wayhousekeeper beckoned, but Sarana pushed away the temptation. 'Goddess, but this is depressingly familiar,' she thought. 'And I was foolish enough to think I had left pre-battle orations behind me?' Aloud, she said, 'I'm afraid I have bad news. Those of you who thought you were on your way back to Madrinya will have to turn around. The final battle for the Mirage Makers is about to begin.' She held up a hand to stop the murmurs of protest. 'This is not something that any of us have a choice about.' She fixed her gaze on Firgan. 'It seems that the Ravage intends to take over the Mirage Makers, not kill them—'

Firgan tried to corner her alone afterwards, but Sarana refused to cooperate. She brushed by him, urging Arrant along with her. 'Lesson,' she said in her son's ear as they walked away, 'when a man like that wants to talk to you alone, it's because he thinks he has a way of unsettling you. Don't give him the opportunity. We don't need to hear his poison.'

'Can't we do something? I'd like to murder him on his pallet.'

'So would I, but let him go fight the Ravage instead. He's needed there.'

'Do we have to ride the rest of the way with him?'

'In the morning I'm going to order him, in front of the other soldiers, to leave first with the men. I'm the Mirager-heir; he will have to do as I say,' she said cheerfully. 'Rank has its advantages sometimes. Now go and join Samia over in the corner there – you need as much time as possible with her.'

He had no idea how much it hurt her to say that; she coveted his time too, but knew it was no longer hers to command. She went to eat with the Magor, and her dread as she thought of the days to come was as cold as hoarfrost on winter-bare trees.

Firgan and the other Magor rode out before daybreak, but not before Firgan had managed to corner Arrant in the latrines. There were plenty of other people around coming and going, so Arrant wasn't worried about his safety, but given what Sarana had said to him the previous evening, he regretted his inability to escape the confrontation.

'I have something to show you,' Firgan said. He put his hand into his belt pouch and extracted a marble vial. He removed the stopper and poured a handful of what looked like sand into his palm. Arrant stared at it, mesmerised. Casually Firgan tipped his hand over the latrine hole, and the grains tumbled down in a stream of gold. They sparkled in the light of the oil lamps as if they had a life of their own, twisting and glittering on their way to oblivion in the wayhouse's drainage system. A few grains hit the polished marble of the latrine seat with a sharp sound.

Not sand then. More like stone grit. Arrant looked at it blankly. 'Very pretty,' he said tonelessly. 'What game are we playing now, Firgan?'

Firgan bent to whisper in his ear. 'The last of Serenelle,' he said. He smiled. 'Watch that lovely lady of yours. The next time the powdered gem could be red. For no better reason than that it would hurt you.'

He turned on his heel and left, leaving the vial behind.

Arrant, shocked almost beyond thought, steadied himself against the wall. He stared at the few grains still on the latrine seat. They winked at him; gold fire clung to their shattered facets as if clinging to the last moments of life.

Serenelle?

He dampened a fingertip and picked up the grains, then rolled them down to nestle against the glow of his cabochon. And felt her, the remnant of her, pulse through his body.

He stared, hating, in the direction Firgan had taken. The man had carried around the remains of his sister's cabochon just to mock him. 'Oh, Serenelle, I'm so sorry.'

Carefully he placed the grains back in the vial and put it in his belt pouch. 'One day soon, Firgan. I swear it.'

Pale-faced, he joined the others in the stables. Firgan and the Magor warriors had already left. The keeper of the wayhouse came to talk to them as they readied their mounts. A worried frown furrowed a face that age had already creased as generously as folds had pleated the rakes. 'Miragerin,' he said, addressing Sarana, 'you heading for the Shiver Barrens or down the paveway to Asufa?'

Arrant looked up, not liking the fearful note in the man's tone. 'Ravage hells, what now?' he muttered.

Sarana slung her saddlebags across the shleth the stableboy was holding for her. 'We go to the Mirage,' she said.

'I'd postpone the journey, if I were you.'

She looked at him in surprise. 'Why?'

'Look. That's between you and the First Rake.' He waved a hand in the direction of the stable gateway.

They all turned to stare through the entrance in the wayhouse wall. The day was already hot, with a dry, ovenlike heat that held no moisture. The sun had just risen, but the sky ahead was an eerie brown, moving like the waves of an ocean made restless by unseen currents.

'Clouds?' Samia asked, awed. 'In Kardiastan?'

Arrant swore. Clouds? They weren't clouds. Turbulent smoke from Ocrastes' war-forge, an eruption from the bowels of the ground, perhaps, but nothing as tame as storm clouds. It was the Ravage on the move. This was part of the land that the Mirage Makers had kept bound with their magic, this was the foundation on which they had built their crazy, wonderful, humour-filled world . . . and it was blowing away in the wind.

The wayhousekeeper said, 'It's something that's been happening more often over the past half month: winds, great winds filled with dust, coming out of the Mirage. No, more than just wind. Storms. They form in the Mirage every so often, during the night, and start to move with the dawn – a great wave that bears down on us full of driving, choking dust. The Magor warriors here last night? They called them ravage-gales.'

'Have you seen anything – anything *unusual* within the cloud of sand?' Garis asked.

The wayhousekeeper waved towards the cloud in the sky. 'Isn't that unusual enough for you? Don't ride out in this. You may not reach the rakes. This one looks worse than usual. It may last for hours.'

'I have to go,' Arrant said. His voice sounded harsh and cold to his ears. 'There's no choice, not for me.' Perhaps the storm was another attempt to keep him away. He took the shleth reins out of the stableboy's hands and prepared to mount.

Garis shrugged. 'Applies to the rest of us, too,' he said.

The wayhousekeeper nodded. 'What is happening out there is Magor business at that, and only the Magor can stop it. But you will need something more than what you have. Wait.' He turned to the stableboys. 'Belcallin – you go get all the straining cloths we have from the kitchens. And you, Marcar, get four empty nosebags.' As they ran to obey he turned back to say, 'The nosebags will give the mounts a chance to breathe if you run into the dust. I don't want them choking to death. And the linen you can use for yourselves. Stretch it over your nose and mouth.'

'Did Magori-firgan know this dust cloud was out there when the others started off this morning?' Sarana asked.

He shook his head. 'They left while it was still dark. Perhaps they'll turn around now that they see it.'

Perhaps. But Arrant didn't think so. Hells, the man had killed Serenelle and cut out her cabochon. His own sister. The shock of it was still raw, his rage still bitter, his regret still heavy.

For the first three hours along the road, the air hung still and thick and the land was hushed, as if every living thing was quiet with dread. Nothing sang or chirped or moved; the shleths and their four riders might have been the only living things abroad in the world. Then the wind began, unnaturally hot. Skin dried out like parchment left in the sun. The shleths tossed their heads and grizzled in the back of their throats, unhappy noises of animals made fearful because something was wrong with the world.

Ahead, billows of liver-brown loomed, tumefying in slow motion, an amorphous being swallowing the sky. Arrant kept a tight rein on his emotions. This was no natural windstorm, blowing just because the Mirage Makers had lost their hold on the land beyond the Shiver Barrens. This was Ravage-caused. He shivered. This was the advance guard, seeking them out. Seeking him.

And one day soon, even if the Mirage Makers starved themselves into oblivion, the creatures of the Ravage would ride that wind into Kardiastan. All of them, trying to live on Kardis the way they had lived on the Mirage. And if the Mirage Makers didn't manage to commit suicide, then it would be Tarran and his kind who looked out of those Ravage eyes with rapacious hunger.

The wind blasted into his face as he marshalled enough courage just to ride on. 'I am going to die out there,' he thought, saddened. 'I am leading Samia to her death.'

He thought those things, and yet still rode on. The weight on his shoulders was almost more than he could bear, but he made sure none of the others saw how it burdened him. And through it all, he remembered Firgan and the stream of golden dust trickling through his fingers.

Of that, he told no one. It was between him and Firgan. And Firgan was somewhere up ahead.

CHAPTER TWENTY-NINE

The road they now used headed northwest, a single file path heading up into the outer line of stony hills that paralleled the rakes. Time and countless feet had sliced the zigzag track deep into the steep slope. Once they began the climb, much of the brown cloud was blocked from view by the hill itself; Samia could even pretend for a while that there was nothing unusual in the sky, nothing sweeping down on them from the Mirage.

Until she caught an unpleasant whiff of rot. She looked over her shoulder at Arrant. He smiled encouragement, but she sensed the lie residing in the optimism of the curve of his lips. 'He must surely be just as frightened as I am,' she thought, 'even though I can never sense his fear. How does he hide it so well?'

Past him she glimpsed Sarana and Garis. They had fallen behind, and were about to turn the sharp bend of the zigzag below. Sarana's mount had proved to have a hatred of steep slopes and had slowed to a dismal crawl. Earlier, Garis had been cracking jokes about ageing arthritic joints and matching mounts to riders, and Sarana had used some choice words to describe what she would do to the wayhousekeeper next time she saw him. Now they worried the slowness of the beast would kill them.

Samia turned to face forward again, and her shleth plodded stoically on. Her thoughts returned to Arrant. 'I do love him, although sometimes I'm not sure why. He's not amazingly handsome like Grevilyon Jahan. He's not dark and dangerous and intriguing like I used to think Firgan was. He's not witty, like Bevran, or endearing like poor tangle-footed Perry.'

He was just quietly brave. 'I think that must be it,' she pondered. 'Inconspicuous courage, the kind of bravery that is breathtaking because he always knows what the cost is. Even when he left for Tyrans, it wasn't in defeat. It was with a plan to return and make Kardiastan a better place.' She glanced back again. He was dropping behind, wanting perhaps to talk to Garis and Sarana. He waved her on.

She remembered the litheness of his body, the muscular strength of his arms and thighs, the charm of his smile that always seemed to catch her unawares with its suddenness – and she grinned at her self-deception. 'Stop fooling yourself, Sam. He may not be as handsome as Grevilyon, but you find him irresistible anyway.'

By the time she reached the underlip of the crest, she was dwelling pleasurably on her memories of the night before – until the quiet of the steep-sided valley was overwhelmed by a rushing roar of wind. She looked up. The brown cloud glowered down on her from the sky like a living thing. A gale swept before it, barrelling straight at her, gathering dust, ripping bushes out of the ground and bowling pebbles like tors in a game of hopsquares.

The skin of her body tautened in terror. She had a flicker of time in which to react, to work out a way to save herself from the onslaught. Paralysing terror snatched that splinter of possibility from her.

But not from the shleth. It reared. The digits of a feeding arm clawed around her lower leg. A savage yank tore her from the saddle. She sailed through the air, one hand still desperately clutching the reins. She slammed into the ground. In its eagerness to escape, the shleth planted a paw on her stomach. She yelped and let go of the reins. The animal took off faster than she would have thought any shleth, let alone a wayhouse beast, could move.

And she was flat on her back in the middle of a sandstorm bad enough to make a Magor-made tempest seem like ripples on bathwater. She wanted to scream for Arrant, but had no breath to spare.

The ground was shaking. She raised her head – and knew she was dead. The top of the hillside shuddered. A rockslide beginning. A slip of dust here, a few stones there. A deep rumble in the heart of the earth, matching the wrench of the ripped land above. And she was in its path. Her fingers dug into soil as she scrabbled for purchase to lever herself up. Boulders shifted above her head. Bile – fear? – moved to her throat, burning. She struggled to overcome the jolting of her fall. To command her jangled body. Just to *stand* . . .

A twist of wind whirled along the ridge. At its centre, unmoving in the midst of movement, a scaled, many-limbed body. Its shining eyes locked on hers. It drooled, then its gaze slid over her, to rove on in search of other prey.

She thrust out her hand to build a ward. Knowing she was too late. The creature's eyes lit up with glee, but it wasn't looking at her. Not her; *Arrant*. The first of the boulders heading her way exploded in a shower of light. Golden light. The shards sprinkled her, stinging. Arrant's power? Or perhaps her father's. Or Sarana's. More boulders on the way, though. She'd be flattened . . .

At last her legs answered her. She scrambled upright and terror took command of her body. She darted away through the swirls of sand and grit, leaping after her shleth.

A voice roared at her from behind. 'Mount up!'

Creeping cats, dubblup. On a wayhouse sluggard? The man

was mad! She didn't turn to look, but tensed as she raced headlong.

A shower of dust and rock hit her legs. Somehow she managed to keep her feet amid rolling pebbles. She heard another boulder explode and saw the flash of gold that had caused it.

The head of Arrant's shleth drew level on her left side and then eased in front. But the beast wasn't cooperating. It should have had its feeding arm down, ready for her to plant her right foot on its palm between the clutching digits. Instead, its arm was firmly slotted into the groove on its neck. She raced on, arms pumping, legs leaping anything in her way.

'Blast,' she thought, 'how long can I keep this pace up?'

Arrant, white-faced, leaned forward over the shleth's neck and jabbed at its arm with his shleth prod. Reluctantly, the beast brought its palm into position. '*Now!*' Arrant screamed at her, and reached down with his right arm.

Lessons learned from a dozen falls and countless bruises. Hand, foot, hand. Timing was everything. She grabbed his hand with hers, took one skip then – hauled up by Arrant – hoisted her right foot onto the waiting shleth feeding arm. She snatched at the back of his saddle with her left hand and was half-vaulted by the shleth, half-pulled by Arrant up into the saddle behind him, all without the shleth missing a pawbeat. She'd done it often enough in foolish play, but this was the first time in earnest, with a wind beating at them all, with dust in her eyes and dirt choking her throat. And on a mount that neither of them knew. How the sandhells had he done that? Persuaded a strange beast to do all the right things at the right time? Did he *talk* the language of his mounts?

His necklet, of course.

She put one arm around his waist and buried her head into his back to escape the dirt-laden wind. She fumbled in her belt pouch and extracted the piece of linen the wayhouse-keeper had given her. She tied it over his nose and mouth. Only then did she risk a look behind.

And saw the whole hillside on the move, tumbling, roaring, gushing into the valley. Rocks, boulders, scrubby trees, earth – all pouring like water. Somewhere beyond were Garis and Sarana. Rasping gasps spasmed her throat. Terror or dust; she could no longer tell. She was unable to see if Garis and Sarana had survived, unable to see them at all.

The shleth galloped on through a shower of earth. Arrant turned his head to look up at the cloud. A gold beam pierced the murk, coming somewhere from behind. The twist of it hit something and exploded. Flesh and blood and bones and green muck swirled out in all directions. Arrant ducked as something hit his face. Blood showered them both.

More soil and rocks thundered down, but the shleth had carried them beyond their path. Samia watched over her shoulder while the cascade of earth and stone engulfed torn limbs and unidentifiable pieces of something alien that had once been living, and buried them mercifully deep. The noise changed from thundering earth on the move to the whine of the wind and an occasional soft slither of unstable ground. And then a howl reverberated around the valley.

Shivers cascaded down her spine. 'What was that?' Her voice shook. She was caught up in terror and didn't know how to escape.

'Ravage beasts. There's more of them inside the ravage-gale,' he shouted. 'We have to keep going.'

She knew what he was saying. They couldn't do anything. They were cut off from Sarana and Garis by the landslide, an enormous slip of earth and rock that looked as if it would continue on its way down to the bottom of the valley if anyone so much as sneezed. Sarana and Garis, if they were even alive, would not be following on their heels.

'One of them sent that final blast of Magor power,' Arrant said, as if he'd read her thoughts.

She took a deep breath and began to calm down.

He added, 'We'll go on and try to pick up the road ahead somewhere.'

The air was thick with scurries of dust and heavy with an indescribable stench of rot. There was no way they could see where they were going, so Arrant gave the shleth its head. They had to hope it wouldn't carry them over an edge. The animal trotted on, its long neck pushed out in front like a spear, with the fingers on its feeding arms trying to shelter its eyes from the bombardment of dust.

Afterwards, Samia couldn't have said how long it was before they stopped. They'd gone uphill first, then the slope of the land had altered and the shleth had gained enough momentum and energy to gallop. The wind lessened, the air cleared. Breathing became tolerable again. Gradually the animal tired and came to a halt, panting, its head hanging low. Arrant slid from its back, unwinding the linen from his face and unslinging his waterskin. He uncapped it and handed it to the animal, which snatched it from him and drank deeply. Afterwards it didn't want to relinquish the skin, and they tussled for it. In the end Arrant was forced to pull it out of its fingers. 'After a run like that, you mustn't drink too much, you stupid lump of wool. You'll bloat up like a dead pig.'

He handed it up to Samia.

She took it but didn't drink. 'That,' she said, still shaking, 'was the most ridiculous, idiotic, totally *insane* thing I have ever seen anyone do. You should have gone back the other way, to Sarana and Garis. You were closer to them. You would have been safe. Mirage take it, Arrant, you could have ended up *under* all those boulders. And what made you think I'd ever mounted a shleth that way before? I might have pulled you off. And this is a wayhouse hack anyway. How could you possibly know it knew what to do?'

'Of course you would have done that before. Being a girl never stopped you from doing anything, I'll bet.'

'Sweet hells, though, how could you be sure the shleth would let us do it? It all depended on its feeding arm, and it almost failed you.'

'Most wayhouse beasts were riding hacks for someone else once. I just gambled that it would remember . . .' He shrugged. 'I was wrong, as it turned out. It didn't remember. But I have a way with my mounts.' He fingered his necklet.

Her anger drained away. 'You saved my life.'

'Can you feel our parents?'

She enhanced her hearing. 'Nothing,' she said. 'We're probably too far away for Illusos power to pick up anything. They blasted that creature to bits, and one of them was alive to make a ward. I felt it. Maybe they could make it strong enough to—' To stop an avalanche of boulders and earth from flattening them.

They both turned to look back the way they had come. Or rather, the way they thought they had come. It was impossible to be sure any more. No path was visible anywhere. Even the recent paw prints of the shleth had vanished under the sand scurrying to and fro, chased by the remnants of the wind.

'We can't go back the way we came,' Arrant said. 'The landslip will be too unstable to cross, even if we could find it again. Trouble is, I haven't a clue where we are. Not on the road, certainly.'

'And we've lost my shleth, too. Perhaps you'd better start finding something good to say again, Arrant, before I start crying.'

'Um, we have my waterskin, my sword, the contents of my saddlebags. Er, containing a change of clothes. That's helpful.

Just what I need, to save my life. But there's also some food and a bag of oranges the wayhousekeeper gave me. Oh, and grain for the shleth. And his nosebag.'

'I have my waterskin too. Plus the contents of my belt pouch – a comb and some other useless stuff. But that's about all. And although we are separated from your mother and my father, we probably aren't cut off from Firgan. Oh, and just in case it has escaped your notice,' she added, waving a hand at the sky where another long billow of brown loomed ahead of them, 'in a few minutes' time we are going to be in the middle of an even worse sandstorm. Ravage-gale. Whatever. That's between us and the rakes, isn't it?'

He glanced at the position of the sun and nodded. 'I'm afraid so,' he said, managing to sound cheerful. She suspected that was for her benefit because as he gathered up the reins again, he said, 'We only have one way to go, Sam, and that's in the general direction of the First Rake.'

'I think we had better walk that poor beast, rather than ride it,' she said, trying to be cheerful in turn. 'It looks as if it has had the stuffing knocked out of it.'

He glanced at the sky again and dragged in a startled breath. The turbulence had come much closer in just the moment they had spent talking, towering over them in dark bulges. The wind sharpened once more and sand grains flicked against their skin. 'Ouch,' he said. 'It's like being pulled backwards through a thornbush. Let's use the linen again, and I'll put the nosebag on the shleth.'

Hoping to interpose the animal's bulk between them and the direction of the gale, they walked alongside the shleth, but the wind was too strong, its direction too unpredictable, the sand it contained too blinding. When Arrant finally shouted that they couldn't continue like this, Samia nodded in relieved agreement.

The moment he halted the shleth, it dropped down into a slight depression in front of a low rock, curled into a ball and tucked its face under its arms – but not before it had given them both a reproachful look.

'That,' Samia said, 'would have frizzled our wool if we were fellow shleths.'

'Get down next to him,' he said. He drew his sword and looked at it. There was a faint splutter of power as his cabochon slid into the hollow on the hilt, and then nothing, even though her latest seal still held. He flung himself down as a sudden gust of wind threatened to send him aloft, puffed along with his cloak as a sail. Even crouched beside her, he was having trouble keeping his cloak clutched around him. She giggled. He pulled a face at her and asked, 'Do you think you could raise a ward for us all?'

She nodded, aware that he was embarrassed. An Illusos cabochon ward was a poor thing in comparison to what he ought to have been able to do with his sword. She began the conjurations, keeping the area small, just enough for the shleth and the two of them. The smaller the area, the longer she would be able to maintain it. They hunched with their backs against the animal and their feet drawn up in front.

After the choking, stinging vortex outside, the peace inside her ward was blissful. The gale still howled and battered, but it couldn't penetrate the wall. Arrant twitched back his hood, scattering dust.

She resisted the temptation to run a hand through his hair and dug her waterskin out of her saddlebags instead. She took a drink and offered the skin to him. She said. 'That thing in the wind back there. My father or Sarana killed it.'

He nodded and took a sip. 'More than one.'

'The first one looked at me. Its eyes met mine – but it wasn't looking for me. Then it saw you.' But she couldn't go on. She couldn't tell him what she had seen there. Glee. A hungry joy that it had found what it sought.

'It was hunting me.' It was a question, she knew, but his tone was flat.

She nodded. 'That's what it looked like. And the rockslide – I thought it was caused by the wind at first. But it wasn't really, was it? The creatures did it.'

Reluctantly, he nodded. 'Sam, I think I am finally face to face with an evil that I have been fleeing from all my life, from the time I was an essensa inside the Ravage, before I was born. My dreams have been haunted by those creatures since I was a toddling brat, too young to understand. Something – something happened when I was in the Ravage. They tasted me. Learned something about me then. The question is: what?'

'Your connection to Tarran?'

'Something more than that.' He shook his head in puzzlement. 'I think I could be a great bridge builder one day, even perhaps the designer of the loveliest aqueduct arcades ever constructed. But a Magor warrior capable of ravaging the Ravage even with Tarran in my head? I don't think so.'

'How can you be sure of that?'

'I have felt Ravage strength via those dreams. Besides, Tarran knows what it would take to defeat the Ravage, and it's not us. They are vile, they are strong and there are too many of them, believe me.'

'Yet they have tried to scare you. Kill you even.'

'Yes. And not just then, either. I think they were responsible for what happened when I received my sword. They made sure the Mirage Makers in the Shiver Barrens were pulled away in a hurry.' He dribbled some dust through his fingers. 'I have a confession to make. I wouldn't have brought you here if I hadn't decided that the Ravage does indeed – for some mysterious reason – fear me. Which doesn't necessarily mean that it has reason to, of course. Samia, I am more than three parts in love with you. Give me another hour or two, and it will be all four parts. No, what am I saying? It's already all four parts. Head over heels and any way you want. And yet I fetched you here, because I needed someone to seal my cabochon. I weighed up your wellbeing against that of Kardiastan, and you lost.'

She opened her mouth to say something, but he had already ploughed on. 'If this is a mistake, I don't think I could live with the outcome. If you die, then so do I.'

'Oh, well, that's a great comfort, Arrant. You certainly have a genius for unorthodox declarations of love. "Hey, Sam, I adore you. Oh, and by the way, why don't you come and get killed with me?"'

'I never was much of a one for poetry,' he said with a sheepish smile, and then added with brutal honesty, 'I'd do it again, you know. No matter how much I love you. I believe, somewhere deep inside, that there is one chance, one way the Ravage can be defeated. And it has something to do with me. I knew I'd never find out what, if I stayed in Madrinya.'

She took his hand and squeezed it. 'You worry far too much. You did right. This is larger than both of us, and we both know it. I will do my part, if this damnable wind will let us do anything at all. And I want you to remember one thing: I *chose* to come; I chose to die out here, if dying is what's needed. If the Ravage gets as far as Madrinya, riding on the backs of enslaved Mirage Makers, we all die anyway. You aren't sacrificing me.' She paused, then adopted a mock-dramatic pose, palm flat to her heart, head thrown back, eyes cast upwards. 'Self-sacrifice of a pure young maiden for her country—'

'Maiden? *What* maiden?' he interrupted, grinning.

She bent forward and kissed him hard on the lips.

*   *   *

The wind worsened. The force of it buckled the ward. The protected area grew smaller as the sides and top sagged; sand drifted in. Arrant watched as Samia went through the conjurations again, then looked at her handiwork critically. 'It's not doing so well this time,' she admitted. 'Illusos wards are really not made to withstand a continuous battering like this.'

He tried to call on his cabochon power, but it remained quiescent. 'Skies, Sam – I don't know what I think I am doing. What can I do when my power is so unreliable? Bash the Ravage over the head with a dead sword?'

'I have a horrible idea our problem is more immediate. This ward is not going to last, and I'm not sure how much longer I can keep mending it.' She looked down at her cabochon. The colour had dimmed from its original bright crimson. 'You know, Arrant, I thought we'd die fighting in what's left of the Mirage, and I'd sort of resigned myself to that. But now I'm not too sure that we're going to live long enough to get there.'

He thought, 'Sweet Elysium, she's right.' The ward was bending alarmingly; he could feel it pressing into his side. Dirt silted in underneath to cover their feet. He couldn't see anything outside; they were looking into a vicious murk of whirling brown. He slipped an arm around her shoulders. He meant it as a gesture of comfort for her, but even under these circumstances, the feel of her body against his was enticing. He ruthlessly quelled the urge to do something about it.

The ward gave an audible creak and a blast of dust-laden air whirled in. Her skin was bronzed by the colour of the light that filtered through the dust and sand around them; she was lovely and he told her so.

'You're moondaft,' she said, but he enjoyed the smile she gave him. 'Let's talk about something else.'

'I like talking about you. Let's start at the beginning. Where were you born?' he asked.

'Altan. We were there because Papa and Brand were helping the rebellion against Tyrans. We left after my mother died, and went to live in Cormel for a while. Then Gaya.'

'What happened to your mother?' He remembered something Garis had once said to him. A tragedy summed up in a few words: *I was responsible for the death of my wife and my unborn child because I did something foolish.*

'She died while giving birth to my little sister.'

'But your father blames himself. Why?'

'He told you that? Yes, he does. We were in the Delta at the time. You've been there, haven't you? You'll remember what it was like. All those reed islands with the narrow waterpaths between, like a maze. We lived in one of the rebel strongholds on an island. But for some reason, Papa decided it wasn't safe there and moved us to another island. He was wrong. The legionnaires attacked our new refuge, my mother went into labour. We were cut off from help. Papa and some of his friends tried to get us out, but the legionnaires saw us. There was fighting, the boat overturned. Papa grabbed me and swam to the closest island. Brand was the better swimmer, even though he had a withered arm, so he took Mama. Papa said you knew him.'

His heart beat uncomfortably fast. 'Yes.'

'Well, he saved Mama, but they were separated from Papa and me. By then she was very weak. She gave birth on the beach, but the baby was dead and she bled to death because Brand didn't have the healing power to save her. Papa blames himself for making the wrong decisions. For not keeping her safe in the first place. For taking me and letting her go with Brand instead of the other way around.'

'Do you remember all that?'

She shook her head. 'No, not really. Just some vague recollection of fighting and blood and being in the water. I kept thinking Mama would come back. But she never did – and gradually I forgot her. Isn't that sad? Not to remember someone who loved me so much once. But your father told me something that was beautiful. He said I am what I am, because she was there for those first two years of my life. I've held on to that thought ever since.'

'He said that?'

'Yes. He understands things about people. He's very proud of you, you know. And you aren't nearly as proud of yourself as you should be.'

He thought about that. 'There was a time when I was ashamed of my lack of power, I'll admit. But not now, because I don't think it's my fault. It's just the way I was born. Like you having freckles on your nose.' He grinned at her. 'I used to blame myself for lots of things. I've got over it, mostly. The adult me can finally forgive the child of nine and the youth of thirteen that I was.'

'So what bothers you now?' she asked, searching his face with eyes that were far too knowing. 'You have a dark place inside you still, Arrant. I'm a healer. I feel it.'

'I allowed myself to be castrated of power by Korden because I thought I was at fault. I gave up, you see. And one shouldn't ever do that. You have to pick yourself up and go on. That's what Father did when he was blinded. I betrayed him the day I let Korden have his way. I betrayed Kardiastan too. I allowed Firgan a vile victory. The only excuse I have is that I didn't know it at the time. One day soon I will remedy that, if the Ravage gives me a chance. But I think the thing that bothers me most is that I know there's a way Tarran and I ought to be able to save the Mirage Makers. And we have failed to find it.'

A trickle of sand dribbled on his trousers and he brushed it away as he strove to regain composure, to repair the dam holding back the memories that still had the power to well up and choke him.

There was a long silence before she spoke. When she did, it was with prosaic triteness. 'Life – life's not easy sometimes, is it?'

He looked at her, then at the sand battering against her ward, heaping up against the barrier of it, then at the trembling shleth looking at him with a miserable, fearing gaze, then back at her dusty face and sand-filled hair and reddened, gritty eyes. 'You may be right,' he agreed solemnly, his face bland, his tone overly polite.

And simultaneously, they started to laugh.

An hour later the wind died.

Her ward had held.

When the ravage-gale finished, they headed northwest, knowing that sooner or later they would hit the First Rake. 'We'll take it in turns to ride,' Arrant said. 'You go first.'

She smiled slightly as she took the reins.

'What's amusing you now?' he asked.

'Ah, I see the Miragerin's influence in you all the time. She has taught you well.'

'Taught me to do what?'

'Treat me as an equal,' she said, 'not as some fool girl who has to be coddled.'

'You aren't equal,' he grumbled. 'You're a darn sight better at most things. You should coddle me.'

'About as much chance of that as milking a shleth. Which way is northwest?'

He looked at his shadow and the position of the sun and pointed.

'I'm glad you always seem to know that sort of thing.'

'I had the best astronomer in Tyr as one of my teachers. Our problem will be the terrain. It looks rugged, to put it mildly. We must be miles off the road. And I don't even know if it is to the west or east of us.'

'You don't think my shleth could have survived the sand-storm, do you?'

'As much chance as you'd have of milking it,' he said.

About half an hour further on, as they were discussing what to do when they reached the First Rake, he had to take back those words. The ground erupted in front of them, and her shleth emerged from the heaped-up sand.

Samia yelped in momentary panic. '*Skies*! I'll be sandblasted.' She drew in a calming breath. 'Um, sorry. I thought it must be a Ravage beast. Arrant, it *buried* itself.'

'They are born under the sand,' he reminded her, grabbing the reins before the animal could bolt again. 'Anyway, that's a big relief. We have your pack back, not to mention everything in the saddlebags.' He didn't have to say what relieved him most: she could now cross the Shiver Barrens with him. She could keep his cabochon mended.

They camped beneath the stars that night, huddled together for warmth under the cold desert sky. They made makeshift hobbles for the shleths out of the bridles and the nosebags and turned them loose for the night in a depression where water had seeped to the surface and plants grew in abundance. They boiled more water and rationed their food carefully, and Samia – with Arrant's help as a beater – killed a pair of ground squirrels with her power. Lighting a fire to cook them was no problem when she had a working cabochon, and the colour had soon returned to hers. The squirrels were tough and taste-less, but oddly satisfying, perhaps because it had been their own efforts that produced the meal.

'An interlude,' Arrant thought as they sat by the fire that night, surprised at his own ability to be happy when he was with Samia. 'It won't last, but as sure as the sands are dry, it's good.'

CHAPTER THIRTY

'Anything?' Garis asked her.

Sarana, who had been using her far-sensing, shook her head and sat down again. Around her the camp on the First Rake bustled. Servants groomed mounts or cooked the evening meal. Magor warriors cleaned their weaponry or found more entertaining ways to wait for the dark, for the coming of the frost. Men wagered on the progress of two scorpions battling with pincered claws and curled tails; further away others listened to a man playing a lute. The smell of burning shleth pats sifted through the still air.

'No.' She was trying to keep the anxiety under control, but it wormed into every corner of her thoughts. 'You and I were lucky. Lucky not to have been killed. Lucky to have survived the ravage-gale. Lucky to find the road again. We are strong in power and we had good wards. They had nothing!'

'Not nothing,' he said. 'Samia is an Illusa. She can make a cabochon ward. And if I have learned anything in this life, it's not to underestimate that daughter of mine. Or, in fact, that son of yours.'

'Nobody has found them, and we have men scouring the land in all directions. Every one of them a Magor with an ability to far-sense.'

'And a huge area of steep gullies and eroded hills to cover. Come on, Sarana – how far can you far-sense? Half a mile if you're lucky?'

'More if there's a wind to carry sound.'

'Which there hasn't been for two days. We still haven't found all of the men who were with Firgan, either. Or Firgan himself. My guess is this: Samia and Arrant arrived at the First Rake a day before we did, because we had to backtrack and go around the landslip. They started across the Shiver Barrens the moment the frost formed. In fact, you *know* that's what they would have done if they got that far. Arrant was desperate to get to Tarran. That night there would have been no one looking for tracks, because we were still on our way here and no one knew they were missing.'

She grimaced. 'Yes, you're right, of course. I agree – we'd best ride on tonight to the Second Rake, and try to find them somewhere along the Fifth Rake later. And I guess I should be glad that he knows how to head north and not walk in a circle.'

He nodded, and tried to hide his bleakness from her. As usual, he wasn't successful. She always could sense him. 'Spit it out, Garis,' she said.

It was a while before he replied, and when he did, the words belied his usual optimism. 'Sarana – the truth is there's no hope for any of us. We have failed. We failed the Mirage Makers, and ourselves, and Kardiastan. We were always so intent on ridding our land of the Tyranians, we didn't give enough thought to our real enemy. We never even thought the Ravage *was* our enemy, but just the foe of the Mirage Makers. At first, we were all too young to understand, and we were raised without the guidance of older Magoroth. Too much was expected of us, and we failed.'

'Acheron's mists! Just because you're worried sick about Samia is no reason to give up.' She glared at him, wondering why his uncharacteristic pessimism galvanised her. 'She'd deliver a lecture that'd leave you skinless if she heard you say that.'

Unexpectedly, he laughed. 'You're right. Skies, Sarana, you sounded so much like Brand then.'

'Did I?'

They exchanged a look, remembering.

'I miss him still,' Garis said.

'So do I,' she said, softening. 'Goddess, so do I.'

Firgan straggled into the camp on the First Rake late that night. He had ten of the Magor with him, all he could collect of the group that had started out from the wayhouse several days before. Some he had saved by brutally bullying them into using a collective ward to keep out the wind, the sand and the Ravage beasts looking for hell-knew-what in Kardiastan. Others of the band had panicked and tried to run their shleths for safety. Some of those, the ones who had regained their senses in time to ward themselves, he'd found alive. Others he had buried out there. Bloody fools.

It would all become part of the Firgan legend, he knew. If there was one thing he did well, it was look after his men. He was *proud* of that. Always had been. Proud of being a war leader who never let his men down, as long as they were committed to following him. His reputation had taken a battering lately; it had been time to repair the damage. And Firgan knew he had made a good start. The tale of his leadership would be all over camp before the last man rolled into his pallet that night. He gave a haggard smile in the direction of someone who asked after his welfare, and slid off his mount.

'Oh, bit of a rough ride,' he said, and then raised his voice a little. 'But we can take it, eh, men?'

There was a sprinkling of laughter. He relinquished his reins to one of the servants and called for some wine for everyone in his party.

Someone said, 'Ah, Firgan! Good to see you – we were worried sick you wouldn't make it through. Especially after the Mirager came in and said he hadn't met you on the way.'

'The Mirager is here?' he asked, and hid his annoyance. 'I didn't see him on the track.'

'He's not here any more. He came just before sunset, cross country. There's a landslip on the road. He and the Miragerin and Magori-garis rode out as soon as the frost was thick enough. They are looking for their children – they are still missing after the ravage-gale.'

One of Firgan's eyebrows shot up. 'Are they indeed?' He shook his head in a gesture of resigned sorrow. 'That lad of the Mirager's shouldn't be allowed out on his own. Did Temellin bring the whole army?'

'A cohort came in today, but that's all so far. The rest are clearing the track. They'll be here in a day or two. What's it all about, Magori? We heard tell they expect the Ravage to take over the Mirage Makers.'

'I think the Mirager and his Tyranian consort have been listening too much to Arrant. But parents always want to believe the best of their offspring, don't they? Sad story, really. He's a little twisted since his cabochon was cut. Couldn't take it, poor lad.' He clapped the man who had asked the question on the back. 'I don't think we need worry about being attacked by the Mirage Makers, do you?' He grinned around the circle of men who had gathered to listen. 'Since when have we been scared of pretty illusions anyway? Now, where's that wineskin gone!'

Several people laughed and someone handed him the skin that had been doing the rounds. Firgan ignored the rest of the conversation, thoughts turbulent. Garis's daughter and that piss-weak Arrant – if they were still alive – were out there somewhere without protection. He'd never have a better opportunity to get rid of the lad once and for all. And he wouldn't mind killing the girl as well, especially as it would upset Arrant. She had the loveliest legs he'd ever seen on a woman. He hid a grin just thinking about how he could deal with her when he found the two of them. He'd always found resistance added spice to any encounter.

The problem would be to find them.

The hunt would be a gamble, but one worth taking. East or west? In the Shiver Barrens or still to the south of the First Rake? Ahead of him, or behind? Think. Process of elimination. Arrant badly wanted to get to the Mirage. So he was more likely to be ahead, rather than behind, and in the Shiver Barrens, rather than not.

But Sarana and Garis would have had people searching the edge of the frost every night for footprints. And they hadn't found them, obviously. Was the boy stupid enough to have gotten himself lost getting to the rake? Firgan doubted it. He'd been well taught – the little bastard had told him that much himself – and his teachers would have covered astronomy and navigation by the stars. Rule out being lost. So, what?

Dead, perhaps? Possible. They might have had no more than a puny Illusos ward. Easily broken. They might have panicked the way some of the soldiers had. Possible, but he couldn't assume that. No, let's say he lived, and yet hadn't arrived at the First Rake. Why not?

Not dead, not lost – just slow. The terrain. Not so easy if you couldn't find the track, and Mirage knows, it had been buried under dust an arm-length deep in places. So Arrant and Samia might have lost the path and had to backtrack each time they found their way blocked by a ravine or a gully or a cliff.

'Now that's a clue there,' he thought. The terrain to the west was flatter. The terrain to the east was more rugged.

Firgan smiled. He would look east, and he would hunt himself a Tyranian-raised bastard. It was an off-chance, he knew that, but you had to make your own luck.

After that, it would be Sarana's turn. Somewhere, sometime. Firgan was only in his thirties. He had time, and he could be patient. And he *would* be Mirager-heir. And once he was, well, he had no intention of waiting for that blind man to die of old age.

They stood by the shleth on top of the First Rake and looked out over the Shiver Barrens. It was already late in the afternoon, and the sands were cooling. The dance had gentled; the grains wove languorous designs a few inches high, strands criss-crossing each other like patterns on a loom. Their song matched the sleepy torpor of the movement.

'It's like a lullaby,' Samia said, 'singing a child to sleep. It's hard not to think they are alive, isn't it?'

He shuddered, remembering. 'Sentient, perhaps,' he said harshly. 'But uncaring for all that.'

'Maybe not. They could be like the Mirage Makers were in the past, harming us just because they did not understand human needs.'

Her words discomforted him, niggling like grit in the eye, although he wasn't sure why. 'Possibly.'

'Why do they seem to be confined by the rakes? I mean, they can move. They could just roll on up and over the rake to join the sands in the next portion of the Barrens. Or escape altogether – end up in Madrinya. Yet they don't. They don't even get caught up in the wind – or the ravage-gales.'

'You are thinking they are like grains of ordinary sand. But these form an entity, each grain seeking to stay close to the whole.' When she looked puzzled, he added, 'Think of them as being more like water than sand. The ocean doesn't crawl up out of the depths and just keep on going when it hits the land. A wave breaks on the slope of the beach, then flows back to join the ocean. Oh, a storm wind may push it a bit further inland than normal, but it always strives to return to the whole, to the body of the sea.'

Her face cleared. 'Ah. That's a good analogy. It makes sense now. Do we cross tonight?'

His answer was an unequivocal 'yes'. They had spent three days wandering around trying to find a way through the ravines to the First Rake. Wasted days.

'Do we have enough feed for the mounts?' she asked.

They had been grazing the animals, rather than using the wayhouse grain, but it took four nights to cross the Barrens. 'We are a bit short.' His words sounded wooden, a result of his refusal to let her hear his anxiety. 'I've been collecting water beans in the soaks, and we could give them most of our food.'

'Arrant, why don't we try to find the end of the road? We'd be able to replenish our supplies from the storage bins there. Besides, Papa and the Miragerin could be there. Even if they weren't, there'd be others.'

'It could take us several days to find the camp. More, unless you can pinpoint which direction we should travel in. Is the end of the road that way' – he pointed to the east down the length of the rake – 'or that?' He looked to the west, his gaze following the long line of the rock until it disappeared on the horizon. 'Each rake is hundreds of miles long. Sam, can you sense anyone? Hear anyone?'

She shook her head. 'But I thought you could tell where we are from the night sky?'

'Well, I can tell what direction to travel in, but I don't know where we started from. We might have crossed the track without seeing it during the ravage-gale. And then we were forced into so many diversions because of the gullies and rockslides . . .' He shrugged. 'I got us to the rake, but I don't know how far to the east or west of the track. I want to cross here, Sam. I don't have the luxury of time.'

'Tarran's still not answering?'

'Nothing. I have to get to the last rake and call for him.' And then what? A miracle? The only thing he knew for certain was that he was damned if he'd give up.

He'd heard all the tales throughout his years in the Academy. Everyone always talked of the dangers of the Shiver Barrens crossing, of the way a slight mistake in direction could result in death, of how cabochon powers didn't work there, of how this or that Magoroth had died when they'd been thrown and abandoned by their shleth, of how many Tyranian legionnaires had tried the crossing and never returned.

No one had ever told him how beautiful the Barrens were. He'd seen them before from the First Rake, of course, but he'd never set foot on their frozen surface. He'd never been far out on that expanse of white frost glistening in the starlight, never listened to the utter silence, never seen the immensity of untouched sparkle stretching away from him in all directions, never felt the lingering magic of something in the air – of songs not quite heard, of love not quite realised, of happiness not quite attained. And yet, it was lonely out here, and deadly.

He wasn't worried about being lost in the darkness. His Magoroth sword may have been no help, but he could read the stars and a plain of frost held no fears just because it was trackless.

Nonetheless, hours after they started, the sight of the Second Rake ahead – blood-red and ancient against a purple dawn sky – melted the fear of dying that had lain in his gut all night.

He glanced at Samia. Skies, but she was beautiful. Graceful. Courageous. Everything about her seemed to promise a future. *I will find a way to make sure she has one. I must.*

They didn't talk much. He concentrated on the careful pacing of the journey so as not to tire their mounts. And he thought about what lay ahead. He couldn't be sure the Mirage Makers were still holding the Ravage beasts at bay, although he had a feeling he would know the moment the battle was lost. If Tarran was taken over by the Ravage, the monster he became would seek Arrant out. To gloat, to show him the twisted remnant of his still living brother, to reside in his own mind and – what? Drive him crazy with illusion? Kill him outright?

He would know if the Mirage Makers lost the battle, of that he was certain.

The long, hot day spent resting on the rake was a mix of pleasure and frustration, discomfort and fear. Pleasure because he was with Samia. Frustration in the constant painful rasp of not knowing if Tarran and Garis and Sarana were alive. Discomfort because they were hungry and the heat – as Samia put it – was hot enough for a curl-feathered hen to lay hard-boiled eggs. Fear because there had been another Ravage-gale early in the morning, carrying yet another Ravage beast, hunting them.

It must have been controlling the gale, at least in part, because the cloud dropped down low when the creature saw them, and the beast tumbled out. It meant to fall at his feet, he was sure, but it misjudged its forward momentum and fell instead into the edge of the singing sands. The sand grains were merciless. They attacked from all sides, like a hungry school of fish, each after the same morsel of food. They thrashed and boiled and ripped the beast to shreds, the frenzy spreading through the sands in a turbulent wave.

Arrant and Samia stood on the rake, and watched in grim fascination until it was all over.

'It wasn't like that when you and the Mirager were under the sands,' Samia said. 'It can't have been. You would both have died.'

'Maybe because Temellin and I are human.'

'Or because that beast was not.'

'Perhaps.' He touched his necklet. It was uncomfortably hot. He felt the runes move along his skin, as if they had left the stone to touch him. When he saw Samia watching him, he said, 'I wondered once if the necklet was trying to tell me the words of the song of the Shiver Barrens, the way it tries to tell me what my mounts are thinking. Trouble is, it speaks a tongue I don't understand.'

She glanced back at where the Ravage beast had been. The sand danced on, as if there had never been anything there. 'I'm not sure I'd want to know.' She paused, then added, 'People only become evil when they don't listen to the good that's within them. You are right. The Mirage Makers should never have tried to separate one from the other. Arrant, there's no way their goodness could curb the evil of the Ravage if they were reunited, is there?'

'Once that might have worked, but not now. Come, let's try to sleep.'

But a day spent dozing and waiting for nightfall seemed endless. Restful sleep evaded him.

Samia's severed head presented to him on clawed hands covered in gore, blood streaming from her eyes, her toothless, tongueless mouth opening to dribble entrails while the Ravage laughed ...

Dreams? These weren't dreams. They were promises – and more.

Her breasts cut and diced and stuffed into his mouth while she screamed and pleaded and the Ravage beasts giggled as they played with her body, their talons tearing and probing and violating—

While he slept the agony was real; the blood was wet in his mouth, on his chin, the taste of it on his tongue. *The teeth ripped open his belly, the intestines spilled. They forced him to run, trailing his innards behind him over the frost, leaving a bloody furrow behind while Samia vomited and vomited and her vomit was full of baby Ravage beasts that crawled to feed . . .*

He smelled the vileness of their Ravage glee in his nostrils as he woke, rocked in Samia's arms, her cool hand stroking his head. Her healing empathy seeped into him with her touch to banish the horror.

Yet, as always, the respite was only temporary. Worse, her healer's empathy and her cabochon made his torture her own; he would feel the tears on her cheeks, he would see the horror within the compassion of her gaze. They clutched each other in wordless consolation.

After the second night of the journey, their spirits weakened, and the shleths grew more irritable. The third night of riding was even worse. The steady pace, essential if they were to arrive before dawn and the melt of the frozen surface, disintegrated into a shambling run, interspersed with a dragging walk that broke the frozen surface and set free a line of dancing sand behind them. Whenever Arrant looked back he could see it, marking their path like dust behind a galloping horse, until the sands succumbed to the cold and fell back to the surface.

They barely made the safety of the Fourth Rake. The sun was already perched on the horizon, misshapen by rising mist to the shape of a huge red water-filled bladder. The cavorting sand grains, lit by the dawn, were fire-sparks of crimson and scarlet and carmine under the feet of their mounts.

'Cabochon be thanked,' Samia said as she slid down from the saddle. 'One more night. Will we make it?'

'Yes, of course we will.' He knelt and broke the ice on a pool of water for the shleths to drink. 'We have no choice. The distance between the Fourth and Fifth Rakes is narrower than the others. Or so I have been told. We still have a handful of grain left. And we can give the shleths the rest of our food, if you think you can go a day without anything. Once on the Fifth Rake, Tarran can tell us where to find Raker's Camp.' But the prosaic voice of reason told him that the animals were weary and starving and that they had never had the strength of pavilion hacks in the first place.

She tried to smile. 'A choice between not eating at all for a day or two, or rubbed raw, skinned and then choked with a throatful of sand? Hardly a difficult decision, Arrant. I'll starve. For a week if you like.'

'We'll make it,' he said, smiling to cheer her, but he knew there was more determination than certainty in his words.

He lay awake a long time that day. Fear skipped across his mind. Fear of sleeping. Fear of the Shiver Barrens. Memories. The feel of sand against his skin . . . Grains wriggling into his nose, shredding the skin inside. Pushing under his cuticles, forcing their way into his flesh in trails of fiery pain. Trickling into his ears to thunder against his eardrums. Edging under his bleeding eyelids to scratch his eyeballs.

Blinding his father.

And even if they crossed the Barrens successfully, he was going to face the Ravage for the first time in reality, and this time it would be no dream from which he could wake.

Arrant glanced over his shoulder, but couldn't see the rake behind. The sky was beginning to lighten, yet when he looked forward, he couldn't see the one ahead, either. They were halfway. Perhaps. And he knew then – with crushing certainty – that they weren't going to make it. Not with these shleths. His mount was already faltering beneath him, and only kept its feet because he asked it to, because his necklet warmed at his throat and he and the animal were attuned to each other. He had slowed the pace, but still it fumbled. The shleth would die for him, if he asked that of it.

'Arrant.'

He turned his head to look at her. Samia. Gods, how he loved her. Her courage, her calmness – her smile. Even now she could smile, the curve of her lips gentle with love, though her tone was taut with warning. 'Stop a moment.'

He halted his shleth and so did she.

'Someone is following us.'

He felt a surge of hope and looked behind, but it was too dark to see anyone, even against the white of the frost. He couldn't hear anything either, but his shleth was pricking up its ears and had swung its head back as if it sensed something, or someone, behind.

'Arrant, I'm not sure it's someone who will help. It could be Firgan. I keep getting a wisp of – of a pursuer. A man hunting.'

His hope plummeted as fast as it had been born. 'Only one person?'

'I don't know. Still too far back to tell.'

He concentrated, using the power of his necklet. 'Two shleths.' One person with a pack animal? Or two people without? 'Sam, if it is Firgan, no matter what – keep riding. You understand? If one of us can escape, he dare not kill the other. Just ride. Get help.' Useless to tell her that her shleth would not make it. She knew it. But they had to try. No matter what, they must never give up, not until the last breath. He'd learned that lesson.

She nodded.

He followed, pushing his fear away, trying to gather all the strands together to give him the truest picture of their situation. They were not on the usual route across the Barrens. If they had been, they would have seen signs of others by now. But they had seen nothing, not even the mark of camp fires on the rakes. They were miles either to the west or east of the usual route. So whoever was behind them was unlikely to be a Magor warrior on his way to the Fifth Rake and the Mirage. This had to be someone looking for them. Anything else would have been too great a coincidence. Someone had spent the day on the same rake as they had. After sunset, perhaps he – or she – had looked for their footprints on the frost. And found them.

Sarana? Garis? Firgan? Or someone else? No way to know for sure, but Samia's far-sensing had made her uneasy. If it was Firgan, there could only be one reason – and it wasn't concern for their wellbeing. Yet if Firgan attacked them now, out here on the Shiver Barrens, he would have little advantage. His cabochon wouldn't work here, any more than Arrant's, or Samia's. His sword would be no more than a cutting blade. But Firgan had a soldier's experience. And possibly a faster, better-fed mount. He might not even be riding a wayhouse beast, not if he'd found the First Rake camp, and he would never have started out without enough food for it, and a spare mount as well, carrying extra supplies. Firgan would have the speed to catch up with them.

But would the man really try to kill him? He'd have to kill Samia as well . . . He'd threatened to do it, although that might just have been to frighten Arrant. 'Can't rely on that, though,' he thought. 'Maybe he can be persuaded into helping us in exchange for – what? My promise to leave Kardiastan?'

No. Firgan would never believe that.

There would be no bargaining. If it was Firgan riding after them, it was for one reason only: to make sure Arrant would never be Mirager-heir.

Arrant grimaced and called for Tarran. No answer.

'He's closer,' Samia said. 'I think it's Firgan.'

'If it is, you keep riding!' he yelled, hoping his urgency would impress itself on her. 'No matter what. It's our only chance.'

He looked back over his shoulder and saw the shape behind him. A man on a shleth, a pack beast on a lead behind. Arrant's mount was striving to please his rider, but still it slowed, its exhaustion palpable.

Samia was slightly ahead and to Arrant's right, when the follower drew level on Arrant's left. Arrant looked across. It was just light enough now for him to recognise features. Firgan, without a doubt.

Damn him to a mirageless hell.

CHAPTER THIRTY-ONE

Firgan dropped the lead to his pack animal and smiled. Arrant was glad he couldn't feel the emotions that went with that smile.

'Ride on, Sam,' he thought, 'please ride on. Don't look behind. Not now, not ever.'

When the man pulled his Magor sword free of its scabbard, Arrant hauled on the reins to swerve his mount. Firgan moved with him, stirrup to stirrup. And jabbed the sword, not at Arrant, but at his shleth. Arrant dragged back hard on the reins. The animal, indignant, propped as abruptly as it could. Firgan overran them and the blade did not connect. Arrant turned them away still further, dug in his heels and headed off in another direction. Away from Samia.

Once again Firgan moved with him. Arrant drew his own sword, but a wayhouse shleth was no battle mount, and it was too tired and too weak anyway. Firgan caught up. This time it was Arrant's sword that deflected the lunging blade.

On his third pass, Firgan slammed the edge of his sword across the rump of Arrant's mount. It screamed, the horrible sound of an animal in pain, and stumbled. As Arrant tried to hold it up, Firgan swerved in again and slashed his blade into the delicate throat area at the base of the shleth's neck.

Blood spurted, and their forward momentum whipped it back to shower Arrant. The shleth crumpled under him. Far to the left, Samia's mount faltered at the scream and Arrant saw her white face through the pre-dawn gloom, peering in his direction. He wanted to shout at her to keep going, but he was already falling, tumbling with his beast, trying to kick his feet free of the stirrups.

He hit the ground and the shleth came down on top of him. For one terrible moment, he thought he'd died. He couldn't breathe. His chest felt crushed. His arms were paralysed. Red blurs billowed in his mind. Terror that wasn't his wrapped around his thoughts, squeezing everything else out. He felt pain that didn't belong to him. And the runes at his neck warmed against his skin. He was sensing the dying of the shleth.

It struggled to its feet and stood, head drooping, blood pumping from its neck. The alien emotions weakened, and Arrant could breathe again. His arms and legs moved, the terror – not his – faded into lassitude and vanished. His body ached, one big bruise, but nothing seemed broken. He groaned and rose on one knee.

He stared, and saw certain death: the animal's, and his own. The blood splashed down to melt the white of the frost; dancing sands escaped and jiggled upwards, washed red with blood. They looked so harmless. A wave of fury broke in his mind, his own anger.

The shleth collapsed once more. Arrant looked around for Samia, but the gloom ahead had swallowed her. He thought, 'Keep going, please . . . just keep going.' He groped for his sword and his hand closed on the hilt.

Firgan, still mounted, backed his shleth away to a safe distance. 'I don't think that's necessary,' he said softly. 'You can't harm me with that, Arrant.'

'Maybe I can,' Arrant thought. 'Magor magic doesn't work here, remember, Firgan? Maybe this is the only place in the world where I can use the edge of this blade to cut you open . . .' Good reasoning or just a wild hope? He had no way of knowing. For some reason he remembered Favonius. The way the legionnaire had died, asking not to be killed by cabochon power.

'Let me die on your sword then,' he said aloud. 'Give me that much. Or are you so much of a coward you won't even take your chance with an inexperienced bridge builder who has only a blade you have neutered by your hold?'

Firgan laughed again. 'So, boy, you are that frightened of the sands, are you? And with good cause, I imagine, having tasted their bite. And having seen your father humbled to become the crippled old blind man that he is.'

'I am not a boy and my father is neither old, nor blind, nor crippled, Firgan. Wisdom can never be blind. Do you think we don't know how you killed Lesgath? Do you think no one will realise you killed Serenelle? Do you really dream that you will ever step into Temellin's sandals as Mirager? It will not happen. Even if you strike me down here, now, it will never happen. I know who is crippled here: the man whose soul is so twisted that he would kill his sister, betray his own brother, his own kind, his land. Come, Firgan, show me you can kill me. Prove yourself a warrior. It's the only thing you *are* good at, after all.' To himself, he added, 'Keep riding, Sam. I'll give you time if I can.'

Firgan smiled, mocking. 'Throw me your knife, Arrant. And then I'll fight you.'

Arrant hesitated, his desperation a cold grip ever tightening its grasp in his chest. He reached into his belt and drew out his dagger. It wasn't much of a fighting weapon anyway, more designed for slicing a hunk of bread than killing a man. He tossed it at the feet of Firgan's mount. 'There, does that even it up, you treacherous piece of muck?' As if the man didn't have his own dagger tucked away somewhere.

Firgan gave a command to his mount, which then picked up the dagger with its feeding arm and handed it to him. 'Not to even up the battle, Arrant,' he said. 'This is just to make sure you have no way of killing yourself. You see, I want to know that you die at the hands of the Shiver Barrens during the course of the coming day. You and your pretty little healer. In the most excruciating way possible. Goodbye, Arrant. Enjoy the next few hours. I am sure you will have time to do so.'

He turned his mount around, looking for his pack animal. And it galloped out of the darkness, passing them both into the grey dawn light ahead. And there was someone on its back. *Samia.*

Arrant laughed out loud. 'Skies, Sam, I love you, you foolish, brave, wonderful woman . . .'

Firgan scowled, dug in his heels and took off after her.

'Keep riding, you can do it on that animal. Don't stop. Don't come back. Just keep riding, Sam, please . . .' But his unspoken words were agonised. Something told him she wouldn't heed, even had she heard them.

'Promise, Arrant,' she'd pleaded, 'promise no matter what happens, we'll be together.'

'No!' he screamed. 'Don't come back!' And he started to run after them, his bruising forgotten, legs taking huge strides, arms pumping, sandals scrunching and slipping on the frozen ground.

He could keep them in sight. The sky was brightening and he could see the jagged horizon ahead: an outline of tortured rock marking the border between the Barrens and whatever now lay beyond it. An hour's ride away, perhaps. And in less than an hour, the sun would be cresting the horizon. A little later, there would be enough heat to start the sands dancing. She could make it if she rode on, easily. She had a well-fed, well-bred mount.

And she was already turning the animal in a wide circle to come back for him.

'Oh gods, Sam. Don't. Please. No matter what you do, you can't save me. Firgan will stop you. He'll kill you. Your only chance is the rake and other people.'

He ran on until he could run no more. Until he had to halt, chest heaving. Near his feet, a bone had broken free of the frost-encrusted sand: a shleth rib-bone. Someone else's mount; someone else who had fallen within sight of safety. The ache in his heart seemed infinite.

Then someone tapped him on the shoulder.

He yelped and leaped away in fright, his hand flying to his sword hilt as he whirled. And came face to face with Samia's abandoned shleth, scratching at him with a feeding arm. Its rheumy eyes regarded him sorrowfully. If Arrant had been paying any attention to anyone but Samia, its wheezing alone would have alerted him to its presence long before. It panted asthmatically, each breath more gasp than inhalation, each exhale a cloud on the cold air.

'Oh hells,' he said aloud, reaching up to pat the beast on the nose. 'If I were to mount you, I think you'd collapse under me. You're not going to make it to the rake any more than I will.'

The beast snuffled at him, its nose twitching at his tunic where the blood from its stablemate stained the cloth. And Arrant felt its grief clutching at him in a surge of pain.

He looked down at his cabochon. It was colourless and quiescent, even though Sam had sealed it before they had left the last rake. His Magor power was not working. And anyway, it should never have told him what an animal was feeling. It had to be his necklet. Quyriot magic. The necklet hummed and the runes shivered against his neck. It had saved him last time . . .

The Quyriot smuggler had told his mother, *There's stone magic in the runes. Wear those beads and he'll always understand the beast he rides.*

He looked away again to where Samia was racing back to him. Firgan had turned as well and would cut her off easily. He stared at Firgan. The vastness of his ache to stop the man overwhelmed him – but the necklet had no interest in men. He switched his focus from man to mount. And the runes at his neck *burned*. He ignored the pain. His mind sang with something ancient and rudimentary and feral. He felt the shleth's mind and spoke to it. Ordered it to come. *Compelled* it. Ancient Quyriot magic flowed. The Shiver Barrens recognised it and allowed it to pass.

Firgan cursed and battled his mount. It reared and fought him. Unaware, Samia came riding up to Arrant and held out a hand to him. 'We've a better chance with two of us on this beast than if you mount that poor fellow I was riding.'

He took her hand and pulled himself up behind her. 'Take me to Firgan,' he said.

'What?'

'Don't worry. He's no great danger to us at the moment, and I need his shleth. We'll not make it, else.'

She turned the mount and urged it to where Firgan and his shleth were dancing in a circle as man and beast struggled for ascendancy. He doubted Samia intended to stop though; she was heading for the Fifth Rake beyond.

'Drop me off near Firgan and you head straight for the rake,' he yelled in her ear.

Her reluctance expressed itself in the rigidness of her back. '*Why?*'

'I'll explain later.'

'I won't go without you.'

'I'll be right behind you, I promise.' When she opened her mouth to object, he said, 'Sam, you are a healer. I don't want you to be a party to what happens here. Stop here – this is close enough.'

She pulled up and he slid to the ground. They were still at a respectable distance from Firgan. She said, 'Arrant Temellin, I'll *never* forgive you if—'

He grinned at her and slapped the shleth on the rump. It took off towards the rake without waiting for her signal and he urged it on with his new-found power.

'You dare—' she called over her shoulder. But she had stopped hauling on the reins, knowing she was beaten.

Arrant urged the sorry beast from the wayhouse to follow her. He then turned his attention to Firgan, whose mount propped without warning, then reared. As it pawed the air, it reached back with its feeding arm, grabbed Firgan's hand and yanked him out of the saddle. He crashed hard to the ground and the shleth gave a satisfied shake of its neck and trotted over to Arrant. He reached up and patted its head, crooning words of delighted praise in its ear before he mounted.

Once up on its back, he turned to where Firgan was staggering to his feet, his face murderous with the rage that overlaid his bewilderment.

'Get off my shleth!' Firgan roared.

Arrant smiled. 'You can't be serious, surely.' Then his smile died as the enormity of what he was about to do seized him. To kill a man was not an occasion to be smiling. 'Firgan, it ends here. Justice for a man who would murder his brother as part of some larger plan for his power-hungry self, and then his sister because she had the courage to tell her father. You have my knife. I suggest you use it. There at least, I have more compassion than you had for me.'

'You're going to *leave* me here?' The man was incredulous, as if he had trouble believing that this could happen to *him*. Outraged, he leaped towards Arrant across the frosted earth.

Arrant danced the shleth away. 'Yes. Why not? You were doing the same thing to me.'

Firgan halted. 'Come now, I was just joking. You didn't really think I would leave you here, did you? I just wanted to frighten you a bit. To extract your promise to let me be Mirager-heir, that's all. And I never killed Serenelle. Or Lesgath. I just wanted you to think I had.'

Arrant gaped at the brazen audacity of the man. 'Dry hells, Firgan, just how stupid do you think I am?' He edged the shleth away again as Firgan crept a little closer. 'I'm not a sadistic man, and I wouldn't leave you here if I thought there was any other way to do this. It's a cruel, miserable death. But if I try to help you, you'll kill me. And Samia too. And Kardiastan will suffer.'

'Let's fight it out like men. The two of us, two daggers seeing how you can't use your sword against me – and the winner kills the other and takes the shleth. A quick death.'

Arrant shook his head. 'You are certain you'd win, aren't you? And it's true I don't have battle experience. But I *was* well trained, and I'm the not the puny youth I used to be, either. I could give you a fight. But too much hangs on my winning. I have to put Kardiastan and the Mirage Makers first. Sorry, Firgan.'

He turned the shleth and started towards the rake at a trot. He sneaked a look behind, just to make sure that Firgan wasn't trying to throw a blade at him, but the Magori just stood there, the astonishment of disbelief at his predicament written all over his face. Then he started running after Arrant. Not sprinting, but a fast loping run.

Arrant could have gone faster, but he didn't. He paced the shleth so that they kept the same distance ahead of Firgan, just out of range of an effective knife throw. The rake ahead grew larger as the minutes passed and, inexorably, Firgan began to slow. When he was sure the man was not just pretending to tire, Arrant slowed too. He kept a watch on the sky, on the brightness to the east where the sun would soon rise. Even riding a quality shleth, he would be cutting it fine.

He took no joy from what he was doing, but he did not falter either. He knew exactly what outcome he wanted and nothing was going to change it; not guilt, nor second thoughts, nor misplaced compassion. 'I matter,' he thought. 'Sam matters. Tarran matters. You, Firgan, do not.'

Within a quarter of the run of an hourglass, Firgan was labouring, his face flushed and sweating, his stride shortened. He shouted after Arrant, begging him to stop. The sun sent its first rays racing across the Barrens. The rake cast shadows that ran for miles and then began to recede as the red ball of dawn slid along the horizon, lifting itself higher each time Arrant looked. The first rents appeared in the frost, little melt lines that ran like cracks in an eggshell, radiating out from where the shleth's paws broke the crust. The grains began to dance. They wriggled out of the fissures, sluggishly rolling this way and that.

As the sun rose, the frost succumbed, melting into a dampness that quickly vanished. Beneath the feet of the shleth the sands began to move as they dried, trickling in little runnels like water, or shifting in sheets like parchment in the wind, or rippling like the still water of a pond ruffled by a breeze.

Firgan staggered after him, still shouting. 'No, wait, please—' Arrant halted and waited for him to catch up. As soon as he did, he urged his mount on. Firgan yelled after him. 'There's nothing noble about this, Arrant. Fight me like a man!'

Arrant glanced over his shoulder, but didn't stop. Firgan ran again. The grains rose around his feet, occasionally as high as his knees. His movements became laboured, as if he ran through water. The shleth slowed too, the sand shifting beneath its feet, and it had to use the balled digits of its feeding arms as an added set of legs. With a body clad in thick wool, however, it wasn't bothered by the pain of the quickening dance around its legs.

Firgan, however, fell. And rose again, ran again, only to fall a second time. And a third. And a fourth. And then stayed down, exhausted, kneeling on the ground panting, defeated. This time he lacked the strength to raise his head above the level of the whirling, singing sands. The grains attacked him with savage ferocity. They clawed into his eyes, his nose, his mouth, his ears. They crept under his clothes, entering every crevice. Arrant remembered the horror of it . . .

He rode back and dismounted. Walked up to the man, ignoring the grains creeping under his own clothes. Firgan stared at him, his terrified eyes showing a glimmer of hope. The rake was close. So close. Two of them on shlethback might make it. Or—

Or he could use the chance to kill Arrant. Arrant read his intention in the glint of anticipation in his eyes.

'My knife, Firgan, or I ride away.'

The man fumbled at his belt and held out the dagger, hilt first. 'Please,' he whispered. 'Anything, anything.' Blood ran down his face and neck.

Arrant stepped forward, and Firgan, still kneeling, flipped the knife over to grab the hilt. And lunged upwards. But there was no speed there, not any more. He staggered as he threw himself forward, as he tried to stand. Arrant avoided him easily.

Firgan collapsed to his knees again. The dagger dropped from his hand. Arrant snatched it up before it hit the ground.

Firgan fumbled blindly in his clothing for his own knife, couldn't find it, and began to cry, sobs of hopeless frustration. The grains battered at his face and ran down his neck under his clothing.

Arrant, still standing, shuddered, even though his own face and shoulders were above the level the grains had reached. He stepped behind Firgan, and wrenched his chin upwards with one hand. Quickly, cleanly, he slit the man's throat with a deep, savage cut.

Warm blood spilled. The last look on Firgan's face was one of befuddled astonishment.

'Nothing very noble about that, Firgan, I know,' Arrant told the dying man as he dropped his hold and Firgan fell, his head flopping uselessly on his neck, his laboured breathing dragging his own blood into his lungs. 'But then, there's nothing noble about being a fool, either.'

He remounted and urged the shleth away. 'Everything you've got,' he whispered in its ear. He didn't look back, not once. Around them the moving sands glittered in the morning light: purple, with silver flashes as they turned. Cabochon, but it was pretty! Pretty, and so apparently harmless.

And overlaying it all: the song. When he'd sat and listened to it with Samia at his side, he'd thought it beautiful, that wordless melody of the Shiver Barrens. Now it was a dirge, sung for Firgan, but also in anticipation of his own death if he didn't reach the rake in time.

Thoughts jumbled in his mind. 'Mirage help me. Keep Tarran alive. Let Samia live. Let Sarana and Garis still be alive and unhurt. Show me some way that I can stop what is happening there, to the Mirage Makers. Show me why the Ravage fears me.'

He kept his eyes on the rake ahead and refused to think of the man he'd left behind, soaking the sand with his blood;

refused to think of a body excoriated with the flesh shredded from it and spun out into the dance.

He could no longer see Samia. He hoped that was because she was already there on the rake, safe. How much further? A tenth of an hourglass? Less? The shleth floundered as the grains reached its underbelly. Arrant hitched his feet up higher, touched his necklet and spoke to the beast, projecting his admiration, his encouragement.

The smell of blood on his clothes was overpowering. It reminded him of other times he didn't want to remember. Of Sarana hugging Brand to her breast as he died, of a sword in his hand stained red with Favonius's blood, of flesh raining from the sky the day he'd thought he'd slaughtered the whole world. And of Firgan, dead by now, behind him.

Too many deaths.

The song of the Shiver Barrens thrummed on.

Why wouldn't Magor powers work in the Shiver Barrens? The Mirage Makers never had any difficulty with their powers here: they could stop the sand from hurting the Magoroth, they wound their song into the dance, they called up their visions and their mirages, they brought forth the Magoroth swords. Yet the Magor couldn't raise a wrinkle of power out of a cabochon. Why not? Then there was Quyriot magic. It was even stronger inside the Barrens than it had ever been elsewhere.

Tarran, if you hear me, come. You could save me with your Mirage Maker's power. I'm not sure I know how to save myself.

The irony dredged up a laugh from deep within him. He'd come to save Tarran, and here he was calling on his brother to rescue him. His head ached, his eyes were gritty and sore, his throat dry and painful, his bruises throbbed. Muscles screamed out their pain.

He was probably as much use to Tarran as a hole in the

bottom of a boat, but he reached the rake alive just before the surface of the Shiver Barrens leaped into its full frenzied dance.

Samia flung herself at him the moment he dismounted, almost knocking him over. 'You, you, *block*-headed bollard of a man! Don't you ever, *ever*, do that to me again. Just an instant – an instant! That's all you had left. Oh, sands, Arrant, I thought I had lost you and I've never told you all the things I wanted to say . . .'

He smiled, enjoying the feel of her arms tight around him. 'Um, like the fact that I'm a block-headed – *what* was it you called me? *Bollard*?'

'I love you, you horrible man. Don't you ever do that to me again.'

'Say that again.'

'I love you. And you're horrible.'

'I love you, too. And you are quite, quite wonderful. You saved my life back there. Gods, Sam, stealing his shleth!' He bowed his head close to hers and closed his eyes. He wanted to promise her the world, and he couldn't even promise himself another sunset.

Behind them the wayhouse shleth dragged itself out of the Shiver Barrens and onto the rake. Its thick wool had saved it from the worst the sands could do, but it looked a picture of misery anyway. Its nose was bleeding and it gave a series of non-stop sneezes as it tried to clear its nasal passages.

'Oh, you poor thing,' Samia said, and rushed to show it a pool of water in the rocks, and to feed it grain from Firgan's saddlebags.

Arrant's amusement faded as he turned at last to look down on what had once been the Mirage, spread out before him at a lower level on the other side of the rake. His first glimpse of what his brother had become.

He was appalled. He tried to feel glad that the Mirage Makers still lived, that indeed Tarran must be alive, but there was no joy in the scene below him. He sank to his knees, hand over his mouth and nose to block the smell. But nothing, nothing could shut out the stink of evil or the reek of rampant malfeasance gleefully running wild. Nothing anyone had said had prepared him for this. His own nightmares had not prepared him for this.

Oh, Tarran, I'm so sorry. I'm so, so sorry.

There was a sea of murky greenish brown stretching to the far horizon. A grey scum oozed greasily across its surface; the liquid beneath was thick and foetid and corrosive. And warm. A shimmer of heat had already formed across the sludge to shiver the air above it. Occasional green bubbles rose to the surface to sit, glistening in foul humps, before they burst. Every now and then something living heaved itself up out of the depths to break through the scum and he had a glimpse of the creatures he'd fought in his nightmares.

He had thought he'd known them. He was wrong.

To see the reality of them had him gagging on bile – sweet cabochon, was this really what Tarran had lived with all these years? This disease eating away at his body? His cheerful, bantering brother had suffered the cruelty of these malicious scaled monsters with their baneful gleaming eyes?

He felt them reach out with their hatred, their loathing. They wanted him dead in the worst possible way; they wanted to tear into him with their serrated teeth and sharpened claws; they wanted to consume him alive and listen to his screams. They wanted him to die knowing he was defeated and the world was devoid of hope.

In this midden, Rathrox Ligatan and Firgan Korden would have been banned as saints.

And yet, in the midst of all this, there was beauty and an element of purity; not goodness exactly, but a droll mixture of good sense and zany humour: the Mirage. The Mirage Makers' creation, their physical manifestation. It survived as a series of islands thrust up out of that foul sea, pathetic patches of courage and colour linked by strands of coloured ribbon held up above the muck by what appeared to be flying fish skeletons with furry wings. The islands had covered themselves in flowers. They were dying in agony, being submerged in a sea of pain, and they covered themselves with an absurd blanket of singing blossoms made of living butterflies and bright petals.

Arrant knelt there, agonised.

Tarran, brother, I see you—

There was a pause before Tarran came, as if he couldn't believe he'd heard the call, as if he'd had to gather strength out of nowhere to answer it. He hauled himself into Arrant's head, his weakness smudging the sharpness of Arrant's mind. And the edge of hope in his words cut Arrant to the core. *You have found out why the Ravage fears you?*

'No. I just had to come.'

Oh, Vortex, you fool. You curl-feathered fool. And Samia too? Are you moondaft?

'How could I do otherwise? *You* always came when I needed you.'

I don't need you, Arrant.

'No? Then how come you're crying?'

They're your confounded eyes, you shleth-head. But they were his tears as much as they were Arrant's, and they both knew it. *Arrant, we are still trying to find a way to die without giving the Ravage a chance to seize us. That way you'll all be safe at least.*

'Father wants to know two things: if we can interpose our forces, a whole army of Magor and non-Magor, between you and the Ravage would that give you a chance to – well, to escape or die. And if that is possible, then he wants to know how long you would need. How long we'd have to hold them off. He is bringing every Magor in the country here, as well as ordinary soldiers.'

I don't think that's possible, I really don't. You wouldn't survive long enough.

'Oh, Tarran, if we don't try, we are going to die anyway. Killed by the Ravage using the Mirage Makers' illusions and mobility. And not just us, but the whole of Kardiastan. And who knows where after that? If we Magor can stop the Ravage by dying here, then we must do so. We all know that.'

Wait.

The silence that followed carried no possibility of a joyous outcome. Tarran was discussing the proposal with the other Mirage Makers, and whatever they decided, whatever they thought was possible, it would end in tragedy.

Behind him, while he waited, he heard Samia moving around attending to the shleths. She must have been seething with questions, but she didn't disturb him. This was his time; his and Tarran's.

When Tarran spoke again, he seemed subdued. The words he spoke did not sound like his. They reached into something much more ancient, into the other part of his greater whole.

The Mirager's plan would not meet with success. However, there is another possibility. We Mirage Makers could all congregate in one place, and the Magor could build a ward around us, the tightest, strongest ward that has ever been built. It has to last three days.

Arrant blanched. 'Three *days*?' The difficulty of building a ward as strong and as large as that was daunting. But to maintain it for three whole days?

'You think the Ravage will die if it is cut off from you for that long?'

No. The Ravage could go on living in their sores for months, years perhaps. And they could leave on the wind, to torment your people. The ward is to kill us. To block everything that is life-giving from us. The sun, warmth, water, light. We must be enclosed in darkness and cold. Such a ward can only be built and maintained if the Magor give all that they have, in unity of purpose.

The Ravage will try to stop you. Many of you will die, perhaps all. Perhaps you will not succeed. Some beasts will choose to leave on the winds before the warding is complete and they will feed where they can. And you should be warned – more of us have been torn from our entity. Nineteen so far. Soon, there will be more Ravage beasts with Mirage Maker powers among you. You will have to fight them.

If you are successful, there will a future. We salute you all for your intended sacrifice, you, who will be the last of the Magor.

Through a blur of tears, Arrant saw part of one of the islands crumble. It slid into the sea and disappeared; its agony hit Arrant like the backwash of a boat, wave after wave of it, channelled through Tarran. He began to shake, but he said aloud, calling out to his brother, 'No, not yet. I haven't finished. I refuse to give up. Tarran, we've got to think of something. There has to be a better way. There has to! And anyway, I'm not going to let my brother die: if there's no way out, none at all, then you must come to me. Permanently.'

Don't be bloody daft. His brother was alone; the larger entity had retreated. *How can you go around with a Mirage Maker inside your head for the rest of your life? It'd drive you crazy.* He paused. *Crazier.*

'It's better than you being bloody dead.'

No, it's not. You don't know what the inside of your head's like. Oh, Vortex, Arrant, I know what you're saying, but I won't do it. Not ever, so don't even think it.

'Then what about you all moving to another place? You

came here from all over Kardiastan – why not leave that sea of muck here and move yourselves elsewhere?'

Do you think we wouldn't have done that if we could have? The Ravage wouldn't let us leave without it. It'd just come with us. It's part of us. Or perhaps it's the other way around now: we are part of it. Arrant, I must go.

'Not yet. What if we built the ward, and then you left? Couldn't you leave them behind then?'

If there's a ward, we couldn't pass through it to go anywhere, he pointed out. *If there is no ward, then the Ravage beasts would leave with us.*

'Tarran, there *must* be a reason the Ravage fears me.' He was frantic, yet knew he had nothing to offer.

Cracks appeared across another of the islands and the Ravage crept forward, insinuating itself into the openings, its glee palpable. The heat intensified; Arrant could feel it rising from the surface of the sea. And once again he felt the wash of pain from the Mirage Makers. Behind him he felt Samia wince. She had felt it too. Without turning around he held out his hand, and she came to take it, kneeling beside him, leaning into him, hiding her face against his chest.

'He's with me now,' he told her.

'Well met, Tarran. We have been worried about you,' she whispered, looking into Arrant's eyes as though she searched for his brother there.

I hope – I hope we can give you both a future. He was silent a moment, then added, *Vortexdamn, Arrant, I'm sorry. I just don't see what you can do. It's no use plunging into that sea of sleaze over there waving your sword, even with me in your head, because it wouldn't accomplish anything but your death. The creatures of the Ravage can't be wiped out that way. The Magor have tried it, remember. We will all gather here by tomorrow morning. Be ready to ward us.*

'Which way is Raker's Camp?'

To your left. A few miles along. He hesitated. *Arrant, brother—*

But whatever it was he was going to say he couldn't voice. Instead, he sent a touch of love, and gratitude, and sorrow: his farewell. And then he was gone, and Arrant knew Tarran meant it to be final.

He knelt there, grieving, Samia clinging to him, unable to offer any panacea as he told her all the Mirage Makers had said.

Somewhere inside him he knew there was an answer, but he couldn't find it, and because of his failure, a world was dying.

He had no tears, yet felt that he wept.

CHAPTER THIRTY-TWO

'Arrant? Samia?'

It was the last voice he had expected, and yet the one he had unconsciously most wanted to hear. He scrambled to his feet and turned, Samia beside him. Temellin was mounted on a shleth, and he'd ridden, not out of the Shiver Barrens, which were already impassable in the heat, but from the east, along the rake.

'*Father?*' he asked, unbelieving. 'And you're alone? Sweet Elysium – what are you *doing*?'

'Looking for you.' He slid down from his mount and waited for Arrant to come to him.

They embraced, and Arrant was surprised by the fierceness of the hug. 'You were worried?' he asked. 'I didn't know you even knew we were in trouble. Have you seen Mother and Garis? Are they all right? There was a landslide—'

'They're fine. They're asleep back there. They were looking for you all last night.' His sightless eyes moved towards Samia. 'Well met, Samia. Garis is frantic. You had better get your shleth and go to find him and tell him you are in one piece.'

'Well met, Magori-temellin. We were worried about them, too. Where is he?'

'Just ride straight down the rake that way.' He pointed the

way he had come. 'We camped there this morning. About three miles along. Tell them to join us here. We'll head back to Raker's Camp.'

Arrant unfolded his anxiety for them to feel. 'Will she be all right alone? I mean – is it safe? The Ravage—'

'They don't leave the sores unless there's a wind, and you can tell when that's coming. Just don't go close to the edge, because they can snatch the unwary.'

Samia patted Arrant on the arm. 'I won't take any more foolish risks, I promise.' She kissed him lightly on the cheek. 'Skies, what did you do to your neck? It looks as if you burned it. You need healing.'

He touched one of the places where the runes had seared his skin and, wincing, he removed the necklet. 'Quyriot magic. Perhaps, Father, you could do something—? I am aching all over, come to think of it. I fell off my shleth. Sam, go put your father out of his misery. And my mother too, if it comes to that.'

He watched her go, riding one of Firgan's mounts, and tried desperately to hide his emotions. She looked back over her shoulder, a look of pure mischief, so he suspected he had not been too successful.

Temellin touched his neck with the glow of his cabochon. He was sucking in his cheeks in an attempt not to laugh.

'I'm broadcasting my emotions, aren't I?' Arrant asked, annoyed with himself.

'You love her. No shame in telling everyone.'

'You don't mind? Because she is not Magoroth . . .'

'Mind? I am delighted! The daughter of one of my closest friends, a healer of note, and a memorable woman in her own right – I owe her what little I have of my sight, you know. You could not have made a better choice. I married once for Magoroth reasons, and the only good thing to come out of that was Tarran. If we live through this, you marry whom you will, and be happy. Arrant, is – is he still there?'

Arrant nodded. 'Not with me, but out there, yes. He hurts, Father. And I know there must be a way to do something. I just can't work out what it is.' The tragedy of his failure tore at him. He looked down at his cabochon. Samia's seal was tight and gleamed crimson against the gold. 'I have a message for you, from the Mirage Makers. The answer to your questions.'

He related again all the Mirage Makers and Tarran had told him, then added, 'There is a possibility we can defeat it this way, Father. But the cost is going to be so high and we will have problems with those nineteen Mirage Makers who are now Ravage beasts.' He paused. 'You aren't angry with me for leaving Madrinya, are you?'

'I was scared for you, not angry. I understand your need to be with Tarran. And now you have given us a road to success, of a kind. Be proud of that. And be careful. If those beasts see an opportunity to kill you, they'll seize it.'

'I know. I feel their hate. How far is Raker's Camp, by the way?'

Temellin pointed in the opposite direction to the way Samia had gone. 'About six miles that way. I shall go to tell them in a minute what you've just told me. We will gather here by tomorrow morning.'

'I'll go with you.'

'No – you wait here for the others. You mother won't be happy until she sees you.'

'It's dangerous for you. The rock is uneven. You could fall.'

'My shleth can see and it knows I rely on it. I've trained a number of them to travel without guidance from me, and this one's the best of the lot. I keep it at Raker's Camp for whenever I'm here. It's used to me riding the rake. Besides, I can feel the Ravage. Better than I used to be able to, in fact. A man with Magor powers is never really blind.' He made a gesture of dismissal. 'But enough of that. Come, it's getting hot here. Let's go and find a spot of shade and talk for a bit while I fix that burn of yours. It may be our last chance for private conversation in quite a while.'

As they walked further away from the Ravage and what was left of the Mirage, to where an outcrop of rock still cast shadow, Temellin said, 'Oh – one thing you probably don't know. Serenelle Korden: she was found dead in the woods along the lake. Murdered, someone had cut out her cabochon.'

'Firgan. He told me he'd done it.'

'Mirageless hells! He *told* you that? Is he mad?'

'I suspect he thought I would not live long enough to testify to it. But as it turned out, he's the one who's dead.'

Temellin was silenced for a long moment. Then, 'You came across Firgan, and Firgan's *dead?*' They reached a patch of shade and Arrant guided him to a place where they could sit under an overhang. His father's healing touch continued, but it was some time before he spoke again. 'Arrant, I have to say you impress me.'

Of all the things Arrant might have expected his father to say, that had not been on the list. He ran a hand through his hair. 'Well, Samia had a lot to do with it, too. He tried to kill us both out there in the Shiver Barrens. We stole his shleths. I sent Samia away first, then I slit his throat. It wasn't particularly heroic.'

'Dead is dead, and being heroic is stupid if you fail. However, I don't think I would tell anyone about it, if I were you. Firgan's mounts turned up on the rake without him, that's enough.' He paused and then added, 'I'm glad he's dead. That can't have been easy, though it was well done.'

Arrant nodded, but took no pride in taking a life, not even Firgan's.

'What can you see out there now?' Temellin asked.

'A string of islands, along the edge of the rake, none of them larger than, say, the Council Hall back in the pavilions. They are connected by ribbons. Held up by, um, things with wings.'

'Last time I was here it was chains made of beads that floated below clouds of thistledown. I am almost glad I can't see it like this, because it means I will always remember it the way it used to be. Perhaps, perhaps there is a time for all things to die, even the Mirage. And the Magor.'

'I don't believe that,' Arrant said. 'Death is for individuals, not for the legacy we should leave behind us for those who come after.'

'Wise words. We won't give up, Arrant, not while there is a single breath left in us. Do you want me to go on with the healing?'

Arrant touched his neck. 'No. It's much better, thank you. But I know now why the Quyriot horsemen have collars on their tunics. Y'know, I always was good with horses and I loved riding. People said I was a natural, but no one thought anything of it. It was hardly strange; I was practically brought up on the back of a horse. No one thought my talent was special.' He handed the necklet to Temellin to feel. 'Such a little thing – I could have stopped wearing it long ago. Sarana wanted me to. If I had, you and I both would have died in the Shiver Barrens. Or Samia and I would have died today. Instead it gave me the power to make Firgan's mount obey me, not him.'

'Little things that count,' Temellin agreed, fingering the runes. 'It's often the way. Sarana helped the Quyriots before you were born, and that's why you were gifted with this. How could she ever have known how much would ride on it? The line between life and death can be a thin one.' He gave a half smile.

'I think I'll put it back on again. Just in case.' Arrant thought of Brand as he did up the clasp. A finger's width to the right or left and he might not have died. A heartbeat slower, and Sarana would have been the one stabbed in the throat.

Temellin continued: 'If Sarana had taken another week to get to Kardiastan back in the very beginning, I would have already been dead. If she hadn't later quite innocently fitted her cabochon into my sword hilt, she would have died with you unborn. Did she ever tell about the time I tried to impale her with my sword?'

He shook his head. 'Tarran mentioned it once though.'

'I meant to kill her. Because I thought she had betrayed me and my pride was hurt. And you would have died with her. Twenty years later and I still get this awful sick feeling in my stomach when I think about it. I wake up in the night and I see that blade heading towards her, and I break out in a cold sweat. *That's* the story I should have told you that day you first came to Madrinya, when you spoke of your adolescent foolishness that forced her to face Rathrox defenceless and brought Brand to his death. I was luckier than you were, that's all. And she was luckier then, than Brand was later. But instead of showing you that what you did was human, and utterly forgivable, I played the martyred, forbearing parent.' He shook his head, remembering. 'Never doubt that I loved you then, Arrant, as I do now. Never doubt that sending you back to Tyrans with Sarana when you were five was the most difficult thing I've ever had to do. I could hardly bear to look at you, knowing that I wouldn't see you again for years, that I would never know your childhood. I thought I was doing it for the best.

'Maybe I was wrong. It seems that in some ways Sarana didn't have much more success with being a mother than I had as a father. Between us, we contrived to make you miserable and uncertain. And yet here you are, a man for any father to take pride in. And since the day Korden broke your cabochon, there are many who agree with me when I say you will make a fine Mirager one day.' He added sadly, 'As for your lack of power, it seems that the ability to make cabochons is not one that will be possible for the next Mirager anyway.' He reached out and clasped Arrant's cabochon to his own. 'I wish you could sense right now all I feel about you. About both my sons. No father could ask for more than I have.'

Arrant was unable to reply, but knew he didn't have to.

He watched as his father rode away towards the Raker's Camp, and part of him grieved. Possibly neither of them would survive what was to come. All Temellin had said, just before he mounted his shleth, was, 'Madrinya needs your aqueduct, Arrant. Life must go on.' The words he had not said resonated also. 'Survive. You are my son, our future. I need you to survive.'

'I want to do more than survive,' Arrant thought as he settled down to wait for the others. The heat was intense now, yet it wasn't even mid-morning. The reek of the Ravage was thick in the hot air, almost too much to breathe. He sent his thoughts questing out after Tarran, but there was no reply.

He thought, 'I want victory.'

He was torn; he couldn't bear to look at the Mirage with its fragile, absurd loveliness being swamped by such vileness, yet if he turned away he was tortured by the idea of what was happening to it. To Tarran. The horror of his brother's situation flickered around the edges of every thought, just when he would have preferred to concentrate on the new contentment – no, the new *serenity* – that his conversation with Temellin had given him.

He also had to acknowledge the finality that their conversation had implied. 'Sometimes,' he muttered, 'a relationship is *supposed* to have unfinished ends. Is it too much to ask that we all come through this alive and go back to having misunderstandings and differences of opinion? Why must someone always *die*?'

A child's question for an adult world, and he had to laugh at himself for the naivety of his wishes.

There were going to be many deaths. Tarran's certainly. Possibly his own, or Samia's or his parents' – or all of them. They were about to embark on a battle that would make the bloodbath at Tyr's North Gate look like nothing more than a skirmish. And life always seemed more than just valuable when you were about to lose it; it was beyond price.

He turned his back on the Ravage and climbed the short distance to the crest of the rake. The sands of the Shiver Barrens were already at the height of their dance and the flashing of their grains as they turned and caught the light made his eyes ache. They battered at the rocky barrier that bordered them, as though it was a dam they sought to breach. Idly – anything to take his mind off the hell behind him – he wondered if they would ever succeed. Perhaps in another thousand years or so they would have etched away the stone, to tumble and twist their way into . . . into . . . whatever was left. Just as the sea eventually crumbled a rocky coastline.

Why wouldn't Magor power work in the Barrens when Mirage Maker magic could?

Because Magor power was closer to its human base? Get your thinking straight, Arrant. The Mirage Makers had once been human-like, but the aeons had changed them. They had tried to rid themselves of their human basis, they'd disposed of their human bodies and built something else, they'd changed themselves into the Mirage. And the human traits they couldn't change: the badness, the baseness, the evil – call it what you will – that they had tried to encapsulate.

Human faults. The Ravage was made of human faults. It was more human than the Mirage Makers themselves.

Magor power, human-based, didn't work in the Shiver Barrens.

Mirage Makers' power did.

The Ravage was more human than anything else.

The Shiver Barrens had savagely attacked and slaughtered a Ravage beast.

The Shiver Barrens killed humans with their relentless battering. *But they didn't hurt the Mirage Makers.*

He turned, running, drawing his sword, bellowing, 'Tarran, get your backside over here!' He put everything he had into that cry: all the rage, the hope, the frustrated longing to do something that counted.

And Tarran came. And through his despair, his pain, his weakness – still he was able to joke. *I don't have a backside to move*, he said. *I've never thought I was missing much either. From what I've seen of backsides they're prone to all kinds of ailments, more trouble than they're worth and no use for anything other than sitting on. Arrant, this had better be good.*

'Of course it's good,' he said and opened up his thoughts to his brother.

For a moment Tarran was puzzled. *Vortex, Arrant, can't you ever get any order into your thinking? You have the mind of a deranged centipede trying to decide which leg to move first! Ah, I see your point. Oh, my mirageless soul. I see your point . . .*

'Worth trying?'

He struggled for a moment, torn between hope and restraint. *Oh, yes. I'll be a shleth's backside – the fellow can think after all.*

'It won't harm you Mirage Makers?'

No, no. I shouldn't think so. And if it does – well, what does it matter? We'll be dead, which is what we are trying to do to ourselves anyway.

'Right. We'll wait for Garis and Sarana and Sam.'

I – I think it would be better if we didn't wait at all, Arrant. We are close to losing out here. We lost another Mirage Maker a moment ago.

'Lost?'

A Ravage beast absorbed him. That makes twenty. Another Ravage beast with the talent of an illusionist. Start now, brother. Before we lose more of us. Find the narrowest, lowest part of the rake. And I hope you are right in your assertion that the Barrens have the same properties as water.

Arrant pointed to a spot about two hundred paces away to the east. 'There, I think. It's only about, what, twenty paces wide?' He strode off in that direction and positioned himself on the crest. The Shiver Barrens were clearly at a higher level than the Mirage. Any channel he dug to connect the two would slope down towards the Mirage.

You think it will pour itself, like water?

'Yes, I believe so. A cascade. We know they dance in the heat, just as waves dance in wind, and I don't believe they can flow uphill any more than water can. We have to give them a slope, even if it's not a very steep one.'

Then let's try it.

Arrant drew his sword out of its scabbard, and it jumped joyously in his hand, flaming with light. He had to struggle even to hold it, as it was fuelled by the sudden passion of Tarran's last hope.

What are you doing? Tarran asked as the weapon skidded in a sideways swipe and almost removed Arrant's kneecap. *You'd better get it under control, brother, before you decapitate yourself. I'd hate to think what that would do to your thought processes.*

'Sweet Elysium! Listen!' Arrant hissed at him. He could not believe what he was hearing. Voices in the air, whispering voices, repeating the same words over and over. *Free us, free us, free us . . .* He'd heard those voices before, but they had never made sense. He stood motionless, gripping the sword, his jaw sagging open.

I'll be Ravage blasted. Tarran's amazement was a blaze across Arrant's mind. *It's the Shiver Barrens. It's the song of the Shiver Barrens.*

'They are using *words*?' He could hear them, and yet still couldn't believe it. 'Sweet cabochon. It *is* them. I can understand them.' It wasn't that the song had changed, but rather that the two of them had attained the ability to understand it. 'Why now?'

With breathless wonder, Tarran said, *This is the first time we've been within range of them while I was in your head and your sword was in your hand!*

'And with my necklet around my neck.'

Sands, yes. The necklet, the sword and the two of us.

The song swirled and twisted, swelled and faded and skirled, following the patterns the skeins of sand wove in the air. *Free us to serve you, free us, Mirage Maker, free us ...*

'I'll be Vortexdamned,' Arrant said weakly. They'd thought it just a pretty melody, and all the time the sands had been trying to communicate.

Free us to serve you, Mirage Maker, free us, we can help you, free us ...

Tarran laughed. *Who would have thought it? We were deaf to its messages. I wonder what else it's been saying?*

'Sweet hells, *this* is why the Ravage has worked so hard to keep me away from here, frightening me with its dreams! It was afraid that together we'd be able to hear the song of the Shiver Barrens – and be able to do something about it. That we'd *know* what to do about it.' On the heels of soaring joy came the sadder thought of how different things might have been if only Tarran had entered his head the day he had first received his sword.

They knew, Tarran said, realising it for the first time. *They knew and kept me away that day with their attacks. It must have been something they sensed in us from the time I became a Mirage Maker and you had the necklet given you at birth. They've known since you were born.*

Arrant didn't reply. There was no point in agonising over what might have been.

We have another chance now, Tarran murmured, comforting him. *Is this the spot?*

'This is it. Well, shall I free them?'

Do it.

Arrant put both hands to the hilt of his sword and steadied it. Then he aimed the point at the rocky barrier separating Shiver Barrens and Ravage, choosing the place where the crest was lowest. The sword released a stream of power. And he almost fell over backwards, flattened by the force that spun out of the blade. He'd never seen anyone produce anything like this before. A band of light, a pulsating stream of writhing power – it hit the rock in a shower of yellow sparks and everything there melted into a molten stream. He took a flying leap out of the way as liquid red-gold magma flowed towards the Ravage. He watched it go, mesmerised by its terrible destructive beauty, until it poured away into the khaki ooze of the sea. The Ravage boiled, and then erupted in a spout of sludge and slime. A fractured scream followed the eruption into the air. An instant later steam billowed out in a hissing whoosh of sound.

I'll be a wingless butterfly, Tarran said, awed. *Did we do that?*

'Hells, Foran always did say I might have had more power than I could handle.'

He directed the power of the sword back at the rock once again, this time taking more care to stand well clear of the resulting flow of molten colour. 'Tarran,' he asked a moment later in irritation, 'what are you doing?' His brother was jiggling around in his mind, making it hard for him to concentrate.

Hey, he said, *this is my life we're saving, you know. Allow me the privilege of excitement, will you?*

Arrant found himself grinning, and it wasn't him that had put the smile there. He went about the job of melting a channel between Barrens and Ravage with a joyous sense of accomplishment, fuelled by Tarran's exuberance.

Arrant, Tarran said a little later, suddenly sober, *would you mind turning around for a moment and having a look behind you?*

Arrant did as he asked, and drew in a sharp breath of dismay. Ravage creatures were climbing towards him out of the sea of muck they had created. They were scrambling over the rock on their loathsome bodies, ponderously dragging and sliding and humping their way, leaving slime trails, globs of mucus and smears of purulence behind them. Out of the ooze they lived in they were clumsy things, flopping about like fish on the shore, but Arrant didn't doubt for a moment that they were dangerous. They propelled themselves up the slope with flippers and claws and coils and hooks, their eyes burning with red-rimmed loathing. Fortunately their progress, while steady, was slow. They bellowed their distress and pain and suffering.

You can walk faster than they can crawl, Tarran reassured him.

Yet, even as he kept a wary eye on what was happening, he saw the exodus of the Ravage spread up and down the rake in both directions. His heart plunged. In one direction, Temellin was riding towards Raker's Camp. In the other, Samia and Garis and Sarana would have started on their way towards him. As far as the eye could see, the Ravage beasts were leaving the sea of muck. He could walk faster than they could crawl – but there was nowhere to go.

'Oh, *shit*,' he whispered.

*   *   *

They'll die, Tarran said. *They can't live out of their liquid.*

'I'm not exactly seeing them keel over, am I?'

Give them time.

'Have I got time?'

Tarran was silent.

'Right now, I don't think they care. As long as they can tear me to pieces first. And what about Father and the others –?' He didn't stop pouring power at the rock, and the molten river widened, catching some of the creatures and melting them into nothingness.

They are Magor, Tarran said, looking for a way to comfort them both. *They can fight.*

Arrant kept his next thought to himself: 'Temellin is alone and blind.'

At least it looks as if we're doing the right thing, doesn't it? Tarran remarked. *Otherwise, why would they bother to kill themselves by coming after you?*

'Yeah, thanks. I'll remember you said that as I get minced up into Ravage food.'

He continued to blast the rock and Tarran kept swivelling his eyes at the progress of the foul parade scrabbling towards him, until Arrant told him crossly to stop that and allow him the control of his own body.

Sorry, he said, contrite. *It's just that I'm very fond of you, and it upsets me to think of you as dinner for one of those things. That black worm-like creature appears to be winning the race, doesn't it? Keep an eye on it, Arrant. It can wriggle faster than the rest—*

'I will, I promise.'

When the time comes, don't cut them. You'll either have to burn or melt them to make them stay down.

'*I know, I know.*' He didn't want to be forced to divide the power of the sword between the job in hand and a slimy parade of murderous chimeras. He concentrated on the rock, until it became clear that he had to do something to stop the tide of monsters inching their way closer. A blast from the sword then sent them reeling back, a bloodied mass of limbs and pus and high-pitched screams.

The respite was temporary. More clambered out of the dross to take their place, each more hideous than the last, their determination undiminished. Even as he turned his back on them, he could hear the scrape of claws behind him, the snapping jaws, the rattling scales, the grinding teeth: the sounds of their single-minded progression.

'How long do you think my cabochon power is going to last at this rate?' he asked Tarran, worried. He had been expecting to blast the rock into pieces, not melt it, and the amount of power his blade produced scared him even as he rejoiced in it. 'Are you, um, augmenting this somehow, Tarran?'

Er, well, sort of. We are burning up the extraneous bits of the Mirage. The flowers and stuff. And channelling the power from that through me to you.

'You might have told me.'

I didn't want to scare you.

'Now whatever gave you the idea that I would be scared of a beam of gold light powerful enough to melt rock?'

He ignored the Ravage creatures and looked at his handiwork. He aimed to make the channel about ten paces wide. Fortunately, with the level of the Barrens so much higher than that of the Ravage sea, the channel didn't have to be very deep. He left a thin barrier of rock in place next to the Barrens, and concentrated on gouging a channel between this and the Ravage. The first part was easy because the molten rock rolled down the slope without any encouragement. As he dug deeper, the rate of flow slowed, and he had to urge it along by keeping it almost vaporously hot. The steam where magma hit Ravage liquid billowed into a cloud.

Beneath the steaming vapour, the sea of ooze bubbled and boiled and thrashed. The keening of the creatures it sheltered became a single sound of anguish; had Arrant not known of their remorseless desire to cause pain themselves, he might have felt sorry for them. As it was, he didn't even bother to block out the sound. They had tortured the Mirage Makers for generations and he had no compassion for them.

The sword became easier to handle. He wasn't sure if that was a good sign, suspecting that it was more amenable because his cabochon was no longer able to power it to the same extent. He could feel himself tiring. Sweat ran from his body to splash on the rocks. Even Tarran had quietened. Did that mean the Mirage Makers too were being drained? He didn't dare to ask.

Time to blast the slimy bastards again, Tarran said. *Damn it, Arrant, is there no end to the things?*

'You know them better than I do,' Arrant said, burning another line of them to charcoal. 'You tell me.'

Line after line emerged from the flux, scrabbled over the bodies of those that had gone before, dragged themselves towards him filled with their mindless lust for his flesh. He alternated between killing them and digging into the red rock of the rake.

And then at last – the final thin barrier that divided Barrens from Mirage. One last golden beam and the task was done. He stood to the side of the sloping channel he had created and waited. At first nothing happened. The last of the molten rock moved sluggishly past, leaving a coating behind that cooled and congealed as smooth as glass. Then the first of the grains of sand danced through as if delighting in their expanded horizons. Most of them were immediately fused into the still molten sides and bottom, but there were countless more to follow them. And follow they did, still singing. *Free us, free us, free us . . .*

'Vortexdamn,' he wondered, 'what are they?'

The heat of the channel, the beckoning heat of the Ravage beyond, seemed to increase the frenzy of their movement. They quickened their dance, tumbling and wheeling their way, flashing their colours, aided by the downward slope and the heat. *Free us, free us, we can help you . . .*

Gradually the channel was coated with a lining of sand, and the grains that followed the first waves were able to pass on, to tumble their way down into the Ravage, a river of dancing sands.

Arrant watched, breathless with anxiety. If this didn't work, he was dead. He began to doubt. The sea was too vast, the sand too pathetic a trickle. The grains sank into the scum and disappeared, still singing. And the Ravage had an unlimited number of beasts to throw at him, too many for his power to outlast. Worse, some of those that he thought he had destroyed pulled themselves together again, reassembling their burned parts, not always correctly. Suppurating green flesh sometimes coated the outside, foul-smelling innards protruded, limbs were grotesquely attached.

Persistent little devils, Tarran muttered. *Human follies are not easily vanquished, are they?*

More sand danced through the gap Arrant had made, all the grains travelling in the same direction. They seemed so eager to move. Their song was no longer the gentle melodic lullaby that had once charmed him, nor was it the repeated request for freedom. It had quickened, become more frenetic, almost delirious, the words running into one another and no longer intelligible.

'What are they?' Arrant asked. 'Tarran, what are the Shiver Barrens?'

Haven't the faintest idea, he said cheerfully. *All these years, and we thought they were just sands that danced in the heat.*

'They must have had some connection with the people who made my necklet.'

Who were doubtless the same folk who carved the runes into the rock beneath the Mirage. We'll probably never know more than we do right now, though. One thing I can say, these sands don't like humanity much. Perhaps their whole dance was aimed at protecting us – the Mirage – from human intrusion. Although I'm blessed if I know why they should want to help us. He thought for a moment and added, *Perhaps it's just a natural affinity of one form of magic creator for another form. Indeed, we have always felt a certain attraction to them. It's why we settled here in the first place. Whenever we have projected ourselves into the Barrens we have felt . . . welcomed.*

The grains moved faster still, streaking, pouring through the air like a stream over a waterfall, their colours blurring in the movement, their song becoming a whine. Arrant looked out over the Barrens, and gasped. The whole area, right to the far horizon near the Fourth Rake, seemed to be moving inexorably towards him, a heaving, tumbling flood of sand, all of it jostling to reach the one small break in the barrier of the Fifth Rake, the breach in the dam that had confined them.

'Vortexdamn,' he said, swallowing. 'I hope we don't regret this.'

He looked anxiously along the rake, searching for Sarana or Samia or Garis. And in the other direction for Temellin. But there was no sign of any of them. His heart thudded sickeningly. If they died now – no, that would be too dreadful an irony. Fate could not be so unkind, surely. And even as he quelled the thought, he acknowledged the truth: fate could indeed be that unkind. Or worse.

He turned to look back at the Ravage. In the area touched by the flow of sand, the ooze was frothing: a fan-shaped delta of bubbles and turmoil spreading outwards, marking the surface of the Ravage like the muddy floodwaters of a river pushing out into the sea. Ravage creatures heaved and thrashed and screamed on the surface and then disappeared in whirlpools of putrescence. The smell was still nauseating, still suffocating. He gagged.

Arrant, careful, Tarran warned, directing his attention towards several of the creatures that were trying to circle him so they could attack from the rear.

He aimed his sword and a weak stream of gold wavered forth to hit the first of the beasts. It yelped in pain – and kept on coming. The gold flickered, dimmed, then vanished. He swapped the weapon into his other hand and looked at his cabochon. It was dulled and lifeless.

'Well, that's it,' he said, trying to sound philosophical, but his fear of dying, of being dismembered and eaten, almost stopped his thoughts. 'There won't be any more power until we've both had a day or two's rest. And Samia will have to repair it again, too.' He looked at the nightmarish animals edging their way towards him. He tried to draw breath, but the stench had him choking. He didn't seem to be able to drag in enough fresh air.

The touch of Tarran's love was in his mind, together with his anguish. *The blade's still sharp*, he said. *Perhaps that will be enough. Separate out the pieces. Throw them into the Shiver Barrens.*

Arrant refrained from mentioning that he felt as weak as a newly hatched shleth. Tarran didn't need to be told. He knew.

He stepped forward and lopped off the head of the nearest beast; it rolled away and he kicked it into the channel, but the creature refused to die. It flopped sightlessly in front of him, swiping the air with serrated arms and sharp-honed talons. Weakness swept Arrant like a sudden fever; he staggered and fell to his knees.

Vaguely he heard Tarran's anguished, *Oh, Mirage save us, not now, Arrant!* and then he was toppling sideways. With the last vestige of strength, he rolled away from the Ravage creatures. Tarran bounced around in his mind even as claws scrabbled a pace away from his ear. A sick lip-smacking sound slurped somewhere close by. The snap of jaws . . .

He struggled up. He seemed to be eyeball to eyeball with the closest Ravage beast. It took a swipe at him with a talon that was a handspan long. He leaned back, mercifully out of range, and groped for his sword. Tarran gasped directions, until Arrant's hand closed around the hilt and he swept the blade across to remove the claw and an arm or two from the dross-covered body.

He clambered to his feet.

He had his back to the channel of flowing sands. In front of him, a semi-circle of furious brutish faces, their hungry eyes relishing his flesh, a hideous carpet of living obscenities: hundreds of them. There was no way he could destroy them all.

He accepted then that he was going to die.

Half-heartedly he lopped off the nearest groping limbs and spared a glance towards the islands of the Mirage. The sands of the Shiver Barrens were still pouring through the channel he'd cut, sweeping the grains that had preceded them further out into the Ravage sea to envelop and conquer it in a tide of colour. Dead bodies of Ravage beasts floated here and there, gradually being shredded by the dancing sands. But as more sands barrelled in from behind they created waves, and the waves passed into the Ravage liquid, washing it ahead.

He watched, appalled, as wave after wave of poison slapped against the islands of the Mirage. The ribbons and the flowers had all gone. The islands were unadorned now. Humps, protruding above a poisonous sea. Around the edges, they crumbled and slipped and were swallowed up, diminished like children's sandcastles being swamped by an incoming tide.

Ironical, eh? Tarran said, and the ache in his words spoke of a lifetime not fully realised, of the time he might have had. *It's mostly just Mirage that's dying, but the Ravage will get to the heart of us soon.*

Arrant saw at a glance what he meant. The Shiver Barrens were going to win their battle. They were going to pour every grain of sand they had available, the whole band of dancing sands between the Fourth and the Fifth Rake, into that sea of purulence until they had shredded every Ravage creature and suffocated every Ravage sore in their own vast ocean of sand. Not even the setting of the sun would stop them because the Ravage heat alone would be enough to keep them moving, to draw them on. But in their enthusiasm, in their unbridled, unreasoning desire to help, they were going to be the death of the Mirage Makers and their Mirage. They were forcing the Ravage into deep-troughed swells that were going to swamp the islands before the first of the Shiver Barrens could get to them.

'Oh cabochon, I'm sorry,' Arrant said. *I'm so sorry.*

This will save Kardiastan. The Ravage dies, here, today, with us both. Resigned, sad, accepting. *We did well, brother.*

'We did, didn't we?'

Even the warriors at Raker's Camp will be singing our praises. Imagine that, Arrant. Epics recited around the fire at night of Arrant and Tarran, heroes of Kardiastan.

He laughed, wondering if it might one day be true. 'I'd rather be alive,' he said, and then fell silent as he was forced to deal with another oncoming wave of Ravage beasts. The effort of it left him gasping. When he could speak again, he asked, 'Do you know anything about Father? About any of them?'

No, I'm sorry. We are too weak to feel anyone. He hesitated, reluctant to say what was in his mind. *Arrant—*

'Yes?'

I think I belong with them. The Mirage Makers. Do you mind?

He minded; he minded terribly. It took all he had to hide his horror of a lonely death. But he knew Tarran was right: his brother belonged with the Mirage Makers, with his own kind. He had lived with them all his life. They were his real family. He was *part* of them. 'I love you, Tarran,' he said. 'Cabochon, you don't know how much.' Tears blurred away the reality of the horrors he faced.

I think I do, Tarran said softly. *I love you too. Your mind's a muddled cesspit of idiocy sometimes – but I wouldn't change a single witless inanity of it. Go, and die well, brother. Wade into those bastards and give 'em a taste of perdition!*

And he was gone.

Arrant faced that mass of hate and mindless bloodlust alone.

CHAPTER THIRTY-THREE

The Miragerin was fretting. As they rode towards Arrant and Temellin, she asked Samia for the third time, 'You are *sure* he was all right?'

Samia, half-amused by Sarana's anxiety, hid a smile. 'Positive. He had a fall from the shleth, and the necklet burned his neck a little, but he was fine. Really.' To think there had been a time when she'd been scared of meeting Sarana Solad. She'd heard all the stories: a woman who had been a ruthless agent of the Exaltarchy, then a great Magoroth warrior who had turned back an invasion single-handedly, then a rebel leader who had terrorised the legions, then a visionary ruler of Tyrans. Some called her a leader of genius, others a power-hungry Magoria. It depended on which tale you believed. But now that Samia was getting to know her, it turned out that she was also a mother worried about her son, and a woman anxious about the man she loved. 'I like her,' Samia thought.

'And Firgan's dead?' Garis asked.

She turned to him, wondering what to say. She had skimmed that part, thinking it was Arrant's story to tell – or not. 'Magori-firgan's two shleths came back to the rake,' she said neutrally, 'but he didn't.'

Garis and Sarana exchanged glances over her head.

'Idiot,' she thought. 'As if you can fool either of these two.'

'That's odd,' her father said, and it took her a moment to realise he was not referring to Firgan or his shleths. He was staring at what had once been the Mirage. 'There's a sudden upsurge in activity along the, um, shoreline.'

She turned her head to look. It did resemble a shore, but the sea beyond was a sore in the landscape. And he was probably going to die there. Arrant too.

Her breath speeded up, her skin went clammy. 'Don't think about it,' she told herself.

Then she saw what her father meant. Where the Ravage sore met the rake, there was a line of seething monsters in the shallows. And they were scrabbling to haul themselves up on the rock.

'Ocrastes' balls,' Garis muttered, and that in itself was an indication of his shock. He didn't usually swear by Tyranian gods. In fact he usually didn't curse at all, at least not in front of Samia.

Dread grabbed at her throat and wouldn't let go.

'Let's get to Temellin and Arrant as fast as we can,' Sarana said, slapping her shleth prod down on the shoulder of her mount. It leaped forward in immediate obedience.

It was tough to gallop along the rake. The rock, at a time in the far distant past, had been crumpled or carved by forces impossible to imagine. There were folds and pinnacles and dips and peaks, all of which should have been negotiated carefully rather than galloped across, but Sarana rode with reckless speed.

Her impatience was contagious. 'If she fears, then there is reason,' Samia thought, and her own terror trembled behind the fragile veneer of her healer's composure as she followed.

The line of Ravage beasts edged their way up from the sea. Each time she looked, they had progressed higher, far too many for a handful of people – trapped between the Shiver Barrens and what had been the Mirage – to hold at bay. The sun was high in the sky; nightfall, when they could escape to the south, was still half a day distant. She tried to calculate the speed of the Ravage creatures compared to the length of the daylight hours. And concluded, with cold certainty, that time was on the side of the Ravage.

Sarana was in the lead when they reached Arrant. Samia saw the Miragerin bring her shleth to an abrupt halt, still short of where he stood. Only when she and Garis galloped up to her side did they see why Sarana had stopped. A river blocked their way. Only there was no water – it was a river of sand, flowing Shiver Barrens sand. They were on one bank and Arrant was on the opposite side. The sands between raced towards the Ravage sea. The sound as they passed was no gentle song, but a whine like the furious hum of wasps from a disturbed nest, a sound of deadly intent. It raised the hairs on the back of her neck.

For a sliver of time none of them moved or spoke. Arrant didn't even know they were there. He had his back to them, and to the river. He was fighting desperately for his life, and he was losing. There was little power left in his sword. The beasts had moved much further up the rake on his side of the river than on theirs, and they had cornered him.

Sarana had drawn her sword, and Garis drew his too, but both of them hesitated. Samia knew why. The river was about ten paces wide. They couldn't stand too close to the edge for fear the sides would crumble. Arrant was at least a pace away from the edge on his side. Twelve paces separating them altogether. Most of the creatures were another couple of paces further back. Fourteen paces, which was beyond the normal limit of Magoroth sword power. The beam from Samia's Illuser cabochon wouldn't even reach that far.

Sarana tried anyway. A gold beam shot across the river. It sliced into one of the closest creatures, which then toppled. They all watched, horrified, while it rose again in two pieces.

Arrant looked back over his shoulder. 'You trying to double my trouble?' he shouted. There were burns and cuts all over him. His clothing was holed, rotted by whatever had splashed it. 'Roast them before you cut them up!'

'Gods, he can *still* joke?' Samia thought, anguished.

Sarana shouted back. 'We'll use a whirlwind!' She let the colour in her sword build up again. 'I can't feel Temellin,' she murmured. 'I can't feel him anywhere.' Samia read her despair in the air, as cold as winter wind.

Some time earlier and with grim determination, Arrant had decided he was not going to give up without a battle that would surely have gone down in history, if there had been anyone to see it. He laughed at the thought, with a strange, poignant happiness, as if he had sloughed off many unwanted burdens and rejoiced at his final freedom.

Tarran was gone and there were no choices any more, and no uncertainties. He slashed and hacked and stabbed. He lopped heads and sliced open bellies; he cleaved skulls and gouged out eyes; he slit throats and severed limbs. Then he heaved the pieces into the flow of the Shiver Barrens. He stamped on those foul things, squelching them underfoot and then kicking them into the river of sand, shuddering as their ooze squished up between his toes and over his sandals. He was sprayed with their liquids and splashed with their blood. He was burned and lacerated, ripped and gashed. Those he didn't tip into the sands, dragged their hacked parts together again into bizzare parodies of their real selves.

The intense heat sucked the fluids away from his suppurating body. His tongue was swollen in his mouth, his lips were cracked and bleeding; thirst was twisting his insides with added pain. There might have been water in the rock pools, but he could not get to it.

He retched, breathing in the stink. The smell burned in the dryness of his throat. He felt their hatred, their glee. These beasts had condemned themselves to ultimate death by leaving the fluid that protected them. The kin they'd left behind were fighting a futile battle, but they sensed Arrant's defeat. Their maws slobbered in triumph, their blood-shot eyes gleamed with exultation.

His shoulders were knotted with pain, his clothes tattered, his skin covered with raw and bleeding patches. He was close to the limits of his endurance; of any man's endurance, surely. He had done his best and his was the larger victory, not theirs – and so he could yet laugh.

And then he was bathed in a faint gold light.

He knew what it was. Cabochon light. He felt the gentle touch of its magic caress him, then pass on, to gain enough intensity to cut a Ravage beast in two. Which then reassembled itself. He brandished his gore-drenched sword at the wriggling mass of bodies in front of him and looked over his shoulder. His mother, Garis and Sam.

There was nothing they could do to help him. Perhaps there was nothing they could do to help themselves, although they did at least have Magor power. He was so, so tired. He thought he made a joke, but didn't know whether what he said was funny.

He heard his mother shout back something about creating a whirlwind.

'Don't – don't watch. There's nothing you can do,' he said aloud, hoping the others had enhanced their hearing, because he no longer had the strength to shout.

A creature leaped to grab his arm, teeth sinking into his flesh, grating on bone. The pain was searing.

He saw the whirlwind come spinning past him, cutting a swathe through the milling beasts, whisking them up into the air, tossing them into the Shiver Barrens river. But those that remained took no notice.

He tried to lop off the head of the beast that held him, but lacked the strength. He chopped at it instead, weak strokes that did nothing but open up cuts the beast did not appear to feel.

The whirlwind crept closer, trying to gather in the creatures that dragged their tortured bodies towards him. He felt the wind tear at him, whipping his hair across his face. He had long since lost the thong that kept it tied back. With one last thrust of his blade, he dislodged the beast that had clung to his arm. Blood dripped, sending the nearest creatures into a frenzy of teeth-snapping. His sword arm sagged. He no longer had the strength to hold it up.

The whirlwind came closer. The spinning wall of it was studded with beasts now. The roar of it was a solid sound in his ears. He struggled for clarity of thought, and wondered if he'd be spun off his feet. He sank down to his knees, driven by weakness and the knowledge that he should keep low. But the move brought his throat that much closer to the teeth and claws of his attackers.

The wind reached out and plucked his sword from his weakened grasp.

He turned his head to look over his shoulder, to see once more three of the people he loved most in the world. Saw them through a haze of blood and pain. Garis and Sarana were pouring all they had into the whirlwind.

'I love you all—' he whispered, and something slammed into his chest. Dug its claws into his flesh. Under the impact, he began to fall backwards, into the Shiver Barrens.

He thought, 'Better to die in the sands than to feed the Ravage.' He heard Samia scream.

He fell, but never hit bottom.

It was like falling into a torrent of stormwater. He hit the sand, was whirled downwards and then rose again to find himself being shot forward inside the rush of sand grains. The twisted creature that had hooked its claws into his chest was torn away. Flipped upside-down, then right-side-up, head above the torrent and snatching a breath, he was submerged again and choking on sand, then skimmed along the ground like a fallen rider dragged behind a runaway horse – he had no control. Clothes and skin burned away every time he touched rock. He was flayed, bruised and finally thrust once more to the surface, a pummelled wreck. It all happened so fast that the pain hadn't yet managed to catch up.

He emerged in the midst of a slaughter somewhere inside what had once been the Mirage, amazed to find himself still alive and borne along on the sands rather than battered by them. Grains entering his nose and mouth arrived more by accident than malice or design. The Shiver Barrens, he surmised, had more important enemies in mind than one poor ruin of a human being.

The Ravage creatures clawed and bit and gnashed, to no avail. Their attackers were as ferocious as a swarm of maddened hornets, yet were no more than spinning sand grains slashing their prey with honed edges. The beasts tried to shrink away, but the Shiver Barrens spun whirlpools around each trapped victim, scoring them remorselessly until they were peeled open, layer after layer, and their blood and ichor was whirled out of them.

Arrant was terrified of being sucked into one of these deadly gyrations, but was at the mercy of the unpredictable currents within the sands; it was all he could do to keep his head up. Borne to the crest of a swell, he saw in the distance the remains of the Mirage – pathetically little left now; just a few separate huddles of wilted flowers and flesh-coloured mounds already awash with the liquid of the Ravage, each of these embattled isles hardly larger than his bedroom back in Madrinya. And then he was down in the trough, trying to swim in sand to avoid a splash of greenish blood and pus that was another Ravage creature in its death throes.

A moment later he crested a wave again and glimpsed the shore where he had made his stand against the Ravage beasts. Sarana, Samia and Garis had retreated to the crest of the rake. They scanned the sea of sand. Looking for him. He was too weak to attract their attention, but Sarana, her sight enhanced, saw him anyway.

He was being swept away from them, towards the Mirage, towards where Tarran was dying. 'Perhaps the two of us can die together, after all,' he thought.

And then he was sucked under by a violent eddy, dragged down, scraped along the ground and tumbled. He struggled, unable to breathe without inhaling sand. Tried to push his way up to the surface – tried so hard . . .

Back on the rake, Sarana cursed. 'I *won't* lose him,' she said. 'I won't.'

'If you go into that, you'll die,' Garis warned. 'And if Temellin has already died along the rake somewhere, then your sword might be the last Mirager's blade we'll ever have. We need you, Sarana. You can't risk yourself.'

She turned on him in a fury. 'And I need *them*!' She took a calming breath. 'Garis, there is always one last thing one can try. There's always *something*.'

Temellin almost made it.

Because he could not see, his first intimation that there was something wrong came from his positioning powers. He was always aware of the Ravage creatures in their sea of muck, aching to get at him. One part of him kept them in mind, no matter what else he was doing. He knew, then, the moment they left the sea and crawled up onto the rake, even though their action seemed inexplicable. Slow the creatures may have been, but he felt them as far as his senses reached.

He reined in his mount and considered his options. He was still much closer to Arrant than he was to Raker's Camp. He could turn back, help his son if he needed it, and be helped in return. On the other hand, it was essential that the Magoroth in the camp knew what they had to do . . .

'Sarana and Garis are there for Arrant,' he decided. 'I'll ride on.'

In the end, all he could do was rely on his mount because he could neither see nor feel the folds of the rock. He did force the shleth to find a way over the crest of the rake to the Shiver Barrens side. Away from the proximity of the beasts, the animal calmed and bore him on. He pushed it as fast as it would travel, but it was too experienced and wily to endanger itself on the uneven terrain.

They might have made it if they hadn't reached an area, about three miles from the camp, where the rock bordering the Shiver Barrens was too rough and steep to cross and they were forced back to the Mirage side. By then the Ravage beasts were well up on the rock and wild to find prey. The shleth panicked and tried to bolt. Temellin did his best to calm it, did his best to guide it away from the attackers – but how much could a blind man do when he could not see much more than the difference between rock and sky? He used his sword power to create a whirlwind, and for a time he was able to blast a clear passage for them through the lines of waiting predators.

They might have made it, if the shleth's instincts had not let it down. It entered a narrow defile between two arms of rock – thirty paces along, it proved to be a dead end. Temellin had to dismount and edge the beast backwards until it could be turned. By then the entrance to the defile was blocked with Ravage creatures.

He still had power, he could still create a whirlwind, but there were so many of them. By the time he had cleared a way free of the defile, his cabochon colour was dimming. He mounted again but the shleth was edgy, baulking at every movement, reaching back to pinch Temellin's legs and thighs in its unhappy fear.

When he felt his power fading, he knew both he and his mount were doomed. Beasts brought the shleth down, clawing and ripping its legs to shreds, and then leaping to tear out its throat. Temellin managed to scrabble away, to back up against a wall of rock. His sword had no colour now, but he still had a little sensing power left. While that remained he could use his blade, he could defend himself.

'I promise you,' he snarled at the beasts, 'this won't be easy.'

Arrant's first thought on waking was: 'So there is an afterward.' And then: 'But I'm glad the priestesses of Tyrans are wrong about the nature of it.' Then the pain arrived, and he thought perhaps he was indeed in Acheron. Or Hades. Or worse.

Yet what he was looking at was no Vortex of the Dead sweeping him down to Acheron, no whirlpool of the sad-eyed deceased serving out their time for their sins before they were allowed to rest. He was lying on his back looking up through a funnel, and his first impression – before the onslaught of the agony – was one of peace and silence. He was in a globe of still air. Outside, the sands of the Shiver Barrens blurred past in a Ravage sea. The funnel-neck led straight up to the surface. A moment later he decided that he was in fact breathing and could not therefore be dead after all.

And then he saw her. Sarana. She was outside the globe, a strangely ethereal naked figure that seemed to lack substance.

She smiled and held up her cabochon. He was uncomprehending. He could see right through her. The sands of the Barrens swept through her, apparently unfelt. He frowned, wondering if he was dead after all. Or dreaming.

She indicated her cabochon again and he saw that it seemed to have been split. Realisation came. And the pain, waves of it to leave him gasping.

She was an essensa. She had split her cabochon using her own sword to release her spirit self. And, he guessed, used her positioning powers to find him. Then she'd built a ward, the globe, around him, extended it up to the surface so that air could flow in. Temellin had done it for her once; now she did it for her son.

He wasn't dead, not yet. But he felt he'd been skinned alive. Between the moans he couldn't hold back, he said, 'I'm blessed if I know how you're going to get me out of this one.'

She gave him a look that seemed to say she didn't know how he'd ever managed to get *into* this one, then pointed behind her. Garis was there too, also in essensa form, and looking far from happy.

Arrant breathed in quick gasps, trying to hold down the pain enough to enable him to think. He had no idea what they intended and they had no way of telling him. Essensas could not speak, or in fact move anything in their environment. They passed through the solid, or the solid passed through them.

Garis, as far as he could see, was building another ward, extending it out from the globe into a long box-like tunnel that shut out the whirling sand grains.

And that was when Arrant understood. They were going to take it in turns to build wards, one after the other, all the way to the shore, like locks on a Tyranian river.

'Yes,' he whispered. 'I can see what you intend to do. I'm not going to be any use to you though, you know. My cabochon is drained.'

Sarana nodded and walked her fingers through the air.

'Well,' he said, 'I don't know about walking exactly, but I think I could manage a crawl.'

She nodded and smiled encouragement. There was no joy there, though.

He answered the unspoken questioning in her eyes. 'He rode back towards Raker's Camp. Before the beasts came out of the sea.'

She nodded, accepting that he did not know Temellin's fate, and looked away. Perhaps she wanted to hide her pain. Or perhaps she could not bear to see his.

Garis completed his ward and the two of them opened a door between the warded areas. He crawled from one into the other, each movement a lancing rawness that swallowed every thought, that made existence seem undesirable. Garis closed the ward behind him and the first globe collapsed as Sarana floated away to build another in front of Garis's.

And so he dragged his flayed body from one warded area to another, to lie sheltered within each for a blessed moment in time before he had to move again. And through it all, Garis and Sarana drifted unperturbed by the sandstorm that whirled through them.

Something bothered him about that. He tried to concentrate. Anything was better than allowing the pain to swamp him.

Of course. This was the Shiver Barrens now and you weren't supposed to be able to use Magor magic in the Barrens. The Barrens ate Magor magic. He wanted to ask how the wards were possible, but then realised he knew the answer. The presence of the Mirage Makers held the Shiver Barrens power at bay, just as they always had. Which meant Tarran was still alive. For now.

Tarran? Tarran are you there?

No answer.

Vortexdamn, he had to move again . . .

CHAPTER THIRTY-FOUR

Arrant crawled out of the sea of sand. The two essensas winked back into the bodies lying on the rock. Garis groaned. Sarana rolled over and used her right hand to pull her swordblade from her left palm, where it had been driven through her cabochon. Then she did the same for Garis.

Dead Ravage beasts were heaped up around them like stacked carcasses in a slaughterhouse. One functioning part of his head noted the unlikelihood that the four of them had killed so many. It was surreal. 'Who killed them all?' he asked.

'They just died,' Samia said. She was holding his hand, tight. Waves rippled through him, dimming the pain. 'Up and down the shore, everywhere. Possibly because they were too long out of the Ravage sore,' she said. 'For a long while new ones kept crawling over the dead to get at us. Then they stopped coming because there weren't any more new ones to come. The Shiver Barrens had killed them.'

'All the Ravage beasts are dead?'

'There are more still out there, in the sea, but they are cut off from us now by a wide band of the dancing sands.'

He tried to focus on her. 'You're beautiful,' he croaked. He was beginning to feel better, and blessed her healing. 'Feels good,' he said. A moment later it felt even better, when she lifted his head into her lap.

He asked for water, and it was Sarana who offered him a waterskin. He drank greedily from it, rejoicing in how wonderful a simple drink could be. When he handed the waterskin back, she took his free hand. Her eyes were flooded deep with pain.

'Father?' he asked.

'He didn't come back,' she said.

And then he remembered the rest. He struggled to rise, desperate to see past Samia to the Mirage.

'The Mirage Makers are still alive,' Samia said, and propped him up against her so he could see over the sea of sand. It had spread wider and wider, fanning out as it went, but it still hadn't reached the Mirage. The edges of the fan boiled and bubbled with thrashing bodies. The waves created travelled outwards in concentric rings.

The flowers had all gone, and so had the islands. Instead there was a single finger of rock pointing skywards like a sign of hope. Behind it the sky was blood-red with the setting sun.

'That's them?' he asked.

She nodded. 'They managed to join the islands together, what was left of them, by floating one to the other on top of the sea, and then they changed themselves into that.'

'That's *all*?'

'I think so,' she whispered. 'I don't know if they all made it.'

While he watched, he saw the base of the rock crumble as a wave of Ravage liquid hit; the pinnacle was suddenly lower. A Mirage Maker lost? Or just more of the Mirage? He had no way of telling. His hope vacillated. He murmured helplessly, 'They still may not survive.' It would be a race between their ability to maintain themselves and the speed with which the sands could reach them.

She didn't answer but held him a little tighter.

Next to them, Garis groaned and stirred. 'Vortexdamn it, Sarana, that's the most tiring thing I've ever had to do. Blessed if I know how you managed to get yourself halfway across Kardiastan like that all those years ago.'

'I had help, if you remember.'

It took Arrant a moment to realise that she meant him.

'Well, don't anybody ask *me* to do it twice in a lifetime.' Garis sat up groggily and examined his cabochon with care. There was no sign of a split, no mark to indicate it had been pierced by his own sword. A cut that had been so catastrophic to Arrant when performed by another's blade, left no trace when made by the point of one's own weapon. Apparently reassured, Garis looked out across the Ravage and then back at Arrant. 'By all that's holy, m'lad, when you decide to gain control of your cabochon, you don't believe in half measures, do you? Gouge out a canyon, rearrange a few of Kardiastan's topographical features, shift an entire desert, arouse the ire of a few thousand ravening beasts—'

'Tarran and I decided it was worth the risk. We thought it would work.' He watched the Mirage and saw the rock tower slip a little lower into the ooze. 'Looks like we were wrong.' That was Tarran dying, there. And he couldn't help him.

Garis stood, to gaze at the pinnacle. His face was paler than normal. He said, 'It's hard to think they might die. They have made us what we are. I was born in the land they made, lived there as a child.'

'The sands are not that far from them now. They may survive,' Samia said. 'And the Ravage is doomed.'

Oh, Tarran, can't you hold on a little longer?

'There's a breeze,' Garis said, suddenly alert. 'If we get another Ravage-gale tonight the last of those beasts might seek a way out into Kardiastan.'

'Yes,' Arrant said. 'Tarran warned me of that too. About

twenty Mirage Makers have been captured by Ravage beasts.'

'We can try to stop it if it comes. If we've regained some of our strength by then,' Garis said.

'How can we stop a wind?' Samia asked, dismayed.

'We'll power our own whirlwind,' Sarana said. Her anger was sharp in the cooling air; her anxiety an acrid overlay. Her gaze kept straying in the direction Temellin had taken. 'We won't let any of them escape, not if I can help it.'

Garis looked across at her. 'Still can't sense him?' he asked.

She shook her head. 'I'm going after him.'

'We have a shleth on this side of the channel,' Samia said. 'One of Firgan's. And the wreck of a wayhouse mount too. They are on the other side of the crest, near the Shiver Barrens. The Ravage beasts didn't get that far.'

'I'll get you Firgan's,' Garis said to Sarana and walked away.

'How did you get here?' Arrant asked Samia, suddenly realising that she had been on the other side of the channel.

'Papa built a warded tunnel for me and I walked through.'

He nodded, and lay there thinking of Temellin. He stirred in misery, which was a mistake because pain settled into his skin as though he were lying on a shard-impregnated blanket. He sucked in a breath with an audible groan. Samia frowned at him to be still and renewed her pain block.

Sarana must have felt his despair, because her hand tightened on his. She knew exactly what he was thinking. 'He wouldn't have turned back to get you,' she said. 'He would have had faith in you, in your ability to look after yourself. He went on to Raker's Camp because they had to be warned. They had to be told what was needed. He might even have made it.'

He was silent. They both knew there was no way to be certain until someone brought news, or one of them went to find out. 'Help me to sit up,' he said to Samia.

'Arrant,' Samia said, deliberately changing the subject as she eased him into a sitting position, 'I am aching to know. What made you think of cutting that channel?'

He opened his mouth to begin an explanation – and was knocked flat, whacked down hard as if he'd been trampled on. Fortunately he fell back against Samia. She made a sound somewhere between a squawk and a whoosh. He shrieked as agony rasped down his back when he fell.

Sorry about that, said a familiar voice. *Just passing through*.

'*Tarran?*' Arrant asked, unbelieving. His brother had always slipped into his mind so silently, so gently. By contrast, this visit – if that was what it had been – had possessed all the subtlety of a Tyranian legion on the march. What was going on?

Tarran didn't answer; his presence had vanished as abruptly as he had arrived.

Sarana drew in a sharp breath. 'It disappeared! Just – just winked out. I was looking at it.' She was staring out over the moving sands where they battled the edge of the Ravage sea. Where the two met, a thrashing, choppy wave stretched off to the right and left, apparently without end. The pinnacle that had been the Mirage Makers had vanished. 'Arrant, what just happened?'

He levered himself up, gritting his teeth, wanting to see. There was nothing remaining, not a ripple. 'It's all right,' he said. 'They left. They went somewhere else. I think – I think what is left of the Ravage must be so weak the Mirage Makers were finally able to leave it behind.'

He closed his eyes. Samia was flooding him with the opiate of her healing. He tried to fight it, but it felt too good. He dozed. He was vaguely aware when Garis returned with the shleths. He heard him arguing with Sarana. She wanted to ride after Temellin, and Garis wanted to go with her. She refused to let him, and it was she who prevailed.

He felt her take up his hand, and opened his eyes. He saw

her smile, but there was little joy in her expression. 'One way or another,' she said, 'I will find him. I have my senses. I will return as quickly as possible. Or I will send a messenger.'

He nodded.

'You did well, Arrant,' she said softly. 'You saved us all. Garis tells me that the Shiver Barrens still pour out through your channel, and that the level of sand in the Barrens has dropped noticeably.'

'I—'

She placed a finger over his lips. 'I'll tell him everything. I'll tell him his son will be Mirager one day. Ten years,' she added. 'I'll give you and Samia ten years of peace and time to yourselves. The time Tem and I never had. Then I will happily relinquish the post of Mirager-heir to you again.'

She blew him a kiss and mounted her shleth to ride away into the gloom.

'Does she really think he's alive?' Samia asked.

'She hopes,' Garis said.

'She can't bear to think of the alternative,' Arrant murmured and then added, speaking to Garis, 'And she didn't want you there when – if – she finds out he's dead.' Fatigue caught at him once more, and he began to drift away, thinking, 'You wanted me to survive, Father, and I did. And I will go on, no matter what happens. And nothing will make me love you less – or more – than I do right now.'

He woke several times that night. The first time he was dimly aware of Samia moving around the shleths, fixing nosebags; of Garis cooking over an open fire. Mirage knows where he'd scrounged the fuel from – shleth pats, perhaps?

And towards dawn he woke aware that he was surrounded by an outpouring of power. He jolted upright.

Garis and Samia were standing together, facing what had

been the Ravage sea. Garis held his glowing Magor sword pointed up, and a beam of light ran from its tip. A line of red power coming from Samia's cabochon joined it not far above their heads. Just past the point where the two met, Magor power transformed to a twisting gyre of light and wind, speeding upwards. Arrant stood, his gaze following the gyre until it vanished into the looming darkness of cloud in the sky. He could hear it: the rushing, howling whine of a ravage-gale.

'Sarana's idea,' Garis said as Arrant came to stand beside him, 'in case some of the last Ravage beasts try to escape on their wind. We're letting our wind rip that gale to pieces in the hope that the beasts will fall out.' He nodded to the east. 'Look, you can see where she is doing the same thing over there. And people from Raker's Camp have seen and are copying us, too.'

The spin of glowing wind met the blackness above; silence met howl, a Magor whirlwind met the Ravage in explosions of light and colour and rage. Something keened high up in the air. A moment later, a body crashed down onto the rock of the rake, followed by a thud further away on the now-stilled sands.

Arrant looked at what Garis and Samia had created and then down at his cabochon. Samia had sealed it once again the night before, and the colour was returning, but when he called on it, nothing responded. 'Nothing has changed,' he thought with wry amusement. 'The whole world has altered, and still Arrant has no control over his power. I remain an incompetent Magoroth to the end.' At least he could laugh about it now. It no longer mattered. 'I am what I am.'

He wrapped himself tight in his cloak and watched the battle overhead, just as when he was a child in Tyrans he had stood in the Stronghold and watched the lightning of thunderstorms over the canyons. There was no way of knowing what was happening. Garis, as a precaution against being hit by a falling Ravage beast, built a ward over their heads, anchoring it to the rake. Gradually the wind dwindled, but by then, the clouds seemed to have dissipated.

'There might be some that reach Kardiastan,' Samia said.

Her father nodded. 'Possible. But before Temellin left Madrinya, he sent messengers to warn every single vale and town.'

'There will be deaths nonetheless,' Arrant thought, but he didn't voice the fear.

'How do you feel?' Samia asked.

'Sore. Like a duck that's been plucked alive. Weak.'

'You must eat,' Garis said. He fetched a bowl of food and gave it to him. Whatever it was, it was cold and tasteless, but he ate it anyway.

Garis yawned mightily. 'Dawn is not far off. In the morning we will know more. In the meantime, I think we can all safely get some sleep. I don't think there is much left of the Ravage now.' He rolled himself in his cloak and lay down with his back to them.

Arrant fell asleep in Samia's arms, her healing power gently washing through him even as she slept, taking away the last of the pain, easing the aches and furthering the healing of all the sores and the grazes.

His last thought before he slipped into sleep was of his father.

Temellin couldn't understand why he wasn't dead. He slumped against the rock, incapable of movement, beyond anything except the next tortured breath.

They'd torn off his left leg and eaten it. He had heard the slurping, the crunching of bone – and for the first time in his life he had been glad he was blind. He'd managed to stop the bleeding by tying his cloth belt around what remained of his thigh, but he'd refused to use the faint remnants of his power to ease the agony that had begun once the initial shock had subsided. He preferred to keep that tiny pulse of power alive so he could sense his enemies.

And sense them he did, as they unexpectedly died. He didn't understand what had happened, but he felt them fade out around him, a slow slide into oblivion, until he was surrounded by dead bodies.

The irony was almost too much to bear. Their deaths came too late to save him. There were too many poisonous bites, too much blood loss, too little power left to call upon for healing. His right arm was broken and bleeding, his right leg bitten to the bone. His flesh burned with the corrosive saliva they had left behind. And now they were dead, and the only thing that kept him alive was the kernel of Magoroth magic he kept safe in his cabochon, leaking it drop by precious drop so that he could survive a little longer.

He was waiting. Waiting for the right ending. He would wait as long as it took.

'I knew you would come,' he whispered.

He was bathed in golden light. Magoroth light. The magic of what he had been, symbol of all that had made him special. Its gentle caress was a balm to all his wounds, rendering them irrelevant. He felt at ease, without pain at last. It would be the last thing he would see, that light.

'I'll heal all I can and then fetch Samia—' she began.

He laughed, and used the name he loved best for her, the one he had first known. 'Ah, Derya, when have you ever refused to face the truth? Before this night is over, I'll be gone. No healing would repair what has been done here. The only reason

I am alive now ... is because I refused to go before I said goodbye to you. Now tell me what happened.'

She rested his head on her lap and stroked his forehead. 'A happy ending,' she said. He could not see her, but the golden light glinted in the tears on her cheeks, sparks of pure light in the grey world of his vision. 'Arrant and Tarran worked out a way to kill the Ravage and smother its sores. The Ravage is gone, Tem, drowned by the Shiver Barrens.' Quickly she told him what had happened, finishing by saying, 'We aren't too sure what happened to the Mirage, but Arrant is positive they are alive still. He saved them. He and Tarran. Your two sons.'

He smiled as he felt her truth, the relief and joy almost too much. 'You wouldn't lie to a dying man, would you?'

Her laugh was more a hiccup. 'All right, I'll admit Arrant is sore and bruised, but nothing more than that. He and Samia and Garis are fine. Sandhells, Tem – can't you hang on? For me? We have a life to live.'

He raised his hand and caressed her cheek with the back of his fingers. 'We had our moment, and it was good. Better than I deserved. We loved – sands, Derya, how we loved! Was that not fine?'

'Yes. Yes, it was. The best. I don't want it to end. I don't want it ever to end.'

'All things end. And a poor ending doesn't make the good times sad. As for Arrant – we didn't do so badly after all, did we? He is a man worthy of this land and the sword he will have one day. And you are the Miragerin now.'

'I never wanted it.'

'Yet you will do well.'

He felt himself slipping away. He couldn't feel his legs any more. He was dying a little at a time. 'I return to the land to nurture those who follow,' he whispered. 'What more can one of the Magor ask?'

She bit her lip. He did not see. He saw nothing now, not even the Magor glow. The numbness reached his chest, his arms.

'Give my sword back to the Mirage Makers,' he whispered.

They were the last words he spoke.

Arrant was the first to wake in the morning.

Everything was quiet. He raised his head. Garis and Samia slept on. The hobbled shleths were nearby, standing quietly. Garis must have fetched their mounts from the other side of the channel. Gently, he dropped a kiss on Samia's lips and disengaged himself from her arms. Mindful of his newly healing skin, he stood to look out over the Mirage. Except he was looking at a plain of sand. There was no Ravage, no Mirage. Nothing but a desert of partially frosted sand as far as the eye could see. A new Shiver Barrens lying unmoving in the cool of dawn. And not a Ravage beast in sight.

No, not quite unmoving. Already the grains were lifting in answer to the warmth of the sun's first rays. Already a new dance was beginning, although compared to the previous day's frenzied rush, this promised to be as subdued as a mourning dance devised for burial griefs.

He wandered away to see the cut he had made through the rake. It was empty. Nothing more poured through; the flood of sand had ceased. The sides of the channel, buffed by thousands of grains on their wild rush through to the other side, were as smooth and shiny as polished obsidian. Curiosity stirred him. He walked the length of the cut, to the other side of the rake. His body was a mass of aches; even the soles of his feet hurt, but he ignored it all.

He didn't quite know what he'd expected to see, but it wasn't this. On the far side of the valley opposite him he could just see the peaks of the Fourth Rake. In between, to

the left and right, where once there had been the Shiver
Barrens between the Fourth and the Fifth Rake, there was
nothing. There was no sand left, not in any direction. It was
a scene of utter desolation, of *vacancy*. This section of the
Shiver Barrens had vanished, leaving behind a valley of
solid red rock. It wasn't quite flat; there were gentle gullies
and hillocks, all with edges softened by the aeons of moving
sand.

He found himself waiting, although he couldn't have said
for what. It seemed so obvious that such an emptiness had to
be filled.

The sunlight came first, moving along the valley floor as
the sun rose. Then he saw movement out of the corner of his
eye, several hundred paces away to his left. There was a patch
of something there, a large irregular shape a few hundred paces
long consisting of something – soil? – that didn't match the
surrounding rock. He walked towards it, and then broke into
a run. As he watched, a stream trickled out of it and ran down
into a dip. But it wasn't a stream of water. It was grass, and
other plant life. Sedges, bushes, flowers springing away from
the mound in a long living line, lush and colourful: gold, green,
emerald, purple. The stream sang as it flowed, a full-throated
warble of sound like a songbird at the dawn of a desert-season
day. On either side of it, other things began to appear, slowly
at first. A cottage roofed with flowers, a lizard with ten legs, a
low rain cloud – on its back, if that was possible, with the
droplets of water travelling upwards, then falling back down
again in a rainbow shower.

'Tarran?' he whispered, full of hope, full of wonder.

I'm here, his brother said, slipping into his mind. *Hey, what
do you know, Arrant – we both made it, after all.* Arrant felt
his laughter. *And you, my fumble-witted brother, brought off
something of a miracle.*

'Not alone,' he said.

Near enough alone. We know how much we owe to you, Arrant.

'Was that really you that thundered through my mind?'

Yeah, well I'm sorry about that. I wasn't alone either, you see. I had the others with me.

He was incredulous. 'You mean – you came through my mind *with all the Mirage Makers in tow?*'

Er, well, yes, as a matter of fact. A few thousand of them. At the time most of the Ravage beasts, what was left of them, were fully occupied with dying. It seemed a good bet that we could sever the connection and leave without taking them with us, if we could only work out a way to leave. And the only way to do that was for the others to hook themselves to me when I came to your mind. I made it as quick as possible. I didn't want to confuse them with your chaotic thoughts. Coming in was actually the easy bit; the tough bit was getting out again when there was no Mirage Maker out there anywhere to hook on to.

'So what did you do?'

We used a beetle instead. Found it trundling along the rocks by the edge of what used to be the Shiver Barrens. We're grateful it was there – we really didn't have the strength to go any further than that. I must say its mind is strange though, and I'm not sure what sort of a Mirage Maker it's going to make, but we're stuck with it now. Did you know that once a male beetle gets a whiff of a female, they can't think of anything else? It's rather tiresome.

He paused and then added, *Come to think of it, that's not much different to you whenever Samia is around. Even now—*

'Private, Tarran! Definitely not for fraternal consumption.'

Spoilsport. He added, more soberly, *We took a bit of a risk using you. More than you know.* He fell silent.

'There's something you're not telling me?'

Um, yes. For a start, if we'd been wrong about leaving the Ravage behind, we could have made an awful mess of you, brother. And to tell the truth, we did have some of the Ravage with us.

He was horrified. 'You *what*?'

Well, we couldn't leave those Mirage Makers behind, could we? The ones that had been captured by the Ravage beasts. So we sort of wrapped them up inside us and brought them along. If I'd been wrong about your mental strength, you would have died. We decided to take the risk because you had once been part of us before. Remember that time when you were asleep and joined us?

Arrant shuddered. It hadn't been a pleasant experience, waking up to find you'd become part of an entire land. 'Am I hearing this right? You're admitting there's something good inside this head of mine?'

Marvellous what keeping the right company will do. You're improving, lad, improving. I'll make a rational thinker out of you yet.

Arrant waved a hand at the crazy world spreading across the valley in front of him. 'You? *Rational?* Get out of here!'

I'm going, I'm going. Want to anyway – this is the best fun I've had in years. Arrant, we are without pain. It is – wondrous.

'But you brought part of the Ravage with you! Won't the same thing happen all over again?'

Not this time. The rest of me is absorbing the beasts back into themselves, a little here, a little there. They will be different – a bit more like me, perhaps, which will be interesting. It was wrong what they did, so very long ago, Arrant, and we all know it now. To be complete, you have to acknowledge the evil within and deal with it – not parcel it up and pretend it doesn't have power. He nodded Arrant's head in the direction of the new Mirage. *It won't be quite as it was before. They have changed.*

'I think we all have. You – you don't know if Temellin's all right, do you?'

There was a pause that lasted too long as Tarran considered the implications of the question. *No. I'm sorry.* One of Arrant's hands, without any volition of his own, waved at the spreading Mirage. *That's all we are at the moment. Some of us didn't make it. It will be a long time before we have the strength to be what we were, to know what happens at a distance.* He paused once more, and added soberly, *Temellin is Magor-strong, Arrant. And wise. Do not grieve yet. Perhaps he rode on to the safety of Raker's Camp.*

Arrant nodded. 'Perhaps.' Perhaps not. He had also been a blind man riding alone. A single Magor sword.

You aren't alone now are you? Tarran asked.

'No. Samia and Garis are here. I left them asleep on the rake.'

You feel hungry. And a bit . . . gritty. Why don't you go and get them? Bring them for breakfast and a bath? I'm sure we can arrange something.

'Are we welcome?' Arrant asked, remembering the terms of the Covenant.

Always. Without you, all of you, we wouldn't be here at all. We will have to draw up a new Covenant, I think.

'You will stay here, in what used to be the Shiver Barrens?'

For now, anyway.

'A bath does sound inviting.'

Good. I'll talk to you later, then.

Tarran slipped away, but Arrant stood for a while longer, watching as the Mirage Makers produced a grove of fruit trees. Too bad they seemed to be growing goldfish.

'Oh, sweet cabochon,' Samia whispered in his ear.

He jumped. As usual, his positioning powers had not given him any warning.

She put an arm around his shoulders. 'They're building a new Mirage. How wonderful. Tarran?'

'He's there. We're invited for breakfast. And he mentioned a bath.'

'Oh! That's even better. A *bath* – how did he know what I needed? I'll go and get Papa. And all our things.' She lingered, though, to ask, 'The – the Mirager?'

'No news yet.'

'You think he died, don't you?'

He hesitated. 'I think the Ravage would have found it easy to overwhelm him because he couldn't see.' There, he'd said it. Put it out in the open. 'I'll cope, no matter what. Because he would expect it of me.'

She touched his cheek in concern. 'If the worst has happened, you will not be alone, you know. Not ever again. I don't care if you are Mirager-heir, or Mirager or just plain Arrant the bridge builder of Madrinya, and I don't care if I only have a red cabochon to your gold. You and I are going to wed.'

He took her into his arms and buried his face in her neck and hair. 'I think I could bear anything if you were there. Have you any idea of how much I love you?'

'Probably about as much as I love you,' she said matter-of-factly. 'I could stand here and kiss you and have you murmur sweet nothings in my ear and all sorts of nice things like that, but I think I need breakfast and a bath more. Wait here – I'll be right back.'

He had to laugh as she strode purposefully away to fetch Garis. Prosaic, pragmatic, wonderful Samia. Still the same girl who had dug him out of the ward Lesgath had placed over him.

He shifted his gaze back to the Mirage. The grass spread out towards him, followed by a paved path that led straight to his feet from the cottage.

Tarran reappeared in his head. *Live well, brother. I'll drop in from time to time no matter where you are, if only to help you out with that cabochon of yours. There's no reason you can't be Mirager one day, not if I can be around when you need me.*

'It's true,' Arrant thought in sudden wonder. With the Ravage gone, Tarran could come whenever he felt like it. Whenever Arrant asked. 'Do that, Tarran,' he whispered, still choked with emotion. 'You do that. Oh, and one other thing.' He fumbled deep in his belt pouch and drew out the marble vial he had placed there. He tipped the contents into his palm. A few tiny gold splinters sparkled in the sun. 'Serenelle,' he said, and his voice was husky. 'Would you, I don't know, make something to remember her by? I'd like to think that some part of her goes into building a new Mirage. She deserved that much, at least.'

Serenelle? She's dead?

He nodded. 'Firgan.'

Ah. The bastard. We'll do something. A breeze came out of nowhere and whisked the flecks of gold from his fingers, into the air and out of sight. *Leave it up to us. And when you meet the Miragerin-sarana, tell her thanks from me.*

'Thanks?'

Yes. For winning that fight with my mother. I am eternally grateful I wasn't born human.

He touched Arrant's mind with love, curled his brother's lips up in a smile and then blurred back into the Mirage.

The smile lingered, and then faded as Arrant's positioning powers chose to work. He raised his eyes to the top of the crest of the rake. A rider was poised there. A Magoroth sword lay across the pommel of her saddle. Not hers. She was wearing hers.

And she was alone. From where he stood he could feel the shattered pieces of her grief tearing her apart.

The Mirager was dead.

Long live the Miragerin.

From my early childhood, my life was paved with the mosaics of illusion, each piece another tale of deceit, delusion, betrayal . . .

I watch the child play in the sunlight, running under the apricot trees, squelching the fallen fruit with her bare feet, laughing at the soft sweetness of them beneath her toes. She has Temellin's laugh and Samia's freckles and Arrant's bright courage. The cabochon my sword bestowed on her shines gold.

I have been an Exaltarch and ruled an empire. I have achieved the revenge I sought. My enemies have begged for mercy at my feet. I have ruled the nation of my birth, although they did not at first welcome me. I have loved and lost and grieved and thought I would never love or laugh again.

And then the child creeps into my arms, and love overwhelms me, laughter bubbles up when she chuckles. The mosaic of my past is fractured by a child's laugh, melted by her smile, banished by her very existence. And I who have trodden its patterning find a peace I once thought I'd never know.

EXTRAS

www.orbitbooks.net

About the Author

Glenda Larke is an Australian who now lives in Malaysia, where she works on the two great loves of her life: writing fantasy and the conservation of rainforest avifauna. She has also lived in Tunisia and Austria, and has at different times in her life worked as a housemaid, library assistant, school teacher, university tutor, medical correspondence course editor, field ornithologist and designer of nature interpretive centres. Along the way she has taught English to students as diverse as Korean kindergarten kids and Japanese teenagers living in Malaysia, Viennese adults in Australia and engineering students in Tunis. If she has any spare time (which is not often), she goes bird watching; if she has any spare cash (not nearly often enough), she visits her daughters in Scotland and Virginia and her family in Western Australia. Visit the official Glenda Larke website at www.glendalarke.com

Find out more about Glenda Larke and other Orbit authors by registering for the free monthly newsletter at www.orbitbooks.net

GLENDA LARKE

Can you tell us a bit about your background? How did you get into writing fantasy?

I grew up on a small farm in Western Australia. Playmates were few and far between, which is probably why I developed both an excessively inventive imagination and a love of all things outdoors. As a child, I read everything I could lay my hands on, including old National Geographics, and for as long as I can remember I wanted to write and to travel. I was writing fully-fledged stories by the time I was eight, and as soon as I was old enough to work in my school holidays, I was saving money to travel.

I've been writing and travelling ever since. As well as Australia, I have lived in North Africa, continental Europe and Asia – both on the mainland and the island of Borneo. My first published works were non-fiction travel articles!

You were a teacher for many years. How do you think that affects your approach to storytelling?

Well, I was telling tales long before I was a teacher. I seem to remember enthralling my classmates back in the play-ground of a country elementary school on a regular basis by reading my stories to them. Perhaps the teaching that helped me most as a writer was when I taught English as a foreign language (in Malaysia, Austria and Tunisia) and gained a depth of understanding about the structure of my own language as a result.

A bit of a logistical question, but just how do you find the time to write with another career and family to visit all around the world?

I can – and do – write anywhere. Without that ability, I would never be able to submit a book on time to meet a deadline.

I now work as an environmentalist, not a teacher, and much of my work takes me into the field. I have read first proofs in a tent in the middle of the rainforest. I have dealt with copy edits while sweltering by a roadside waiting for transport. I have plugged my computer into the wall in airports, coffee shops and waiting rooms, or I've hooked it up to generators in muddy logging huts or rainforest research camps. I've used my laptop as long as the battery would last on buses and beaches and coral atolls, in peat swamps and on fishing boats chugging through mangrove inlets. I've typed while perched on gunny sacks full of coffee beans on a wharf, or on tree stumps and fallen logs in the forest, or crammed into an airplane seat for a twelve hour international flight. I've written by candlelight, lamplight, moonlight, torchlight, firelight, streetlights, and even headlights (waiting to be rescued from a bogged car in the middle of nowhere). The most challenging of all, though, is to find time to write while looking after a three-year-old grandson . . .

How much of an influence has being a conservationist and studying the natural world been on your writing and your world building? Do you often draw inspiration from your experiences or does it make it much harder to create something new and different?

An understanding of the natural world includes seeing how everything fits together, the larger picture. A logging operation means more exposed soil upstream. Run-off means the river is brown with mud. How does a riverine kingfisher see the fish it must catch to live? It's all about connections. What happens in a neighbouring country can affect what happens to the birds in your own.

World building is like that. You don't create just a house and a street. You are creating a *world*, and it is all interconnected. You can't have your pre-industrial townsfolk eating fresh tuna if your town is miles from the ocean. Your musician needs strings for his lute (what are they made of?), your swordsman won't be an expert if he never practises. In a desert, no one burns firewood in their fireplaces. Of course, you don't put everything you know about your world into your book! But you have to know it and understand how it all fits together. Only if you do, will your reader feel that when he has opened the page, he has stepped into another real place.

Because I have lived as a local within a number of different societies, I know more than the average traveller about what goes into making a culture. That gives me an edge, I feel, in creating the people and the social rules they live by within their imaginary world.

It's interesting to see how you create your worlds; do you have a method of managing them? Do you lay out the world and story-arc before you start writing or is it more of an organic process?

The story-arc begins first and the world develops alongside it.

I start by doing a great deal of thinking. My favourite time for this is while driving or doing housework. I rarely write much of this down, because I end up knowing my world – the part I am writing about anyway – just as well as I know this one. I know without looking it up in my notes that the fishing boats of my invented land put out to sea in the morning and return to port before nightfall, just as I know, without doing a Google search, that our refrigerated boats here on Earth don't have to do that.

I like to have the larger picture in place before I begin – the politics, the commerce, the religion, the landscape, the climate. Much of the detail, however, is only conceived while I am writing the story. I try to integrate these details as the story unfolds (rather than throw them in huge chunks at the reader), much the same way we learn the details of our new surroundings when we move to another country. I'm an expert on the real thing – I've lived on four different continents!

I do start with a map, though. It may, however, be altered to suit the story as I write. If a river is in the way of characters on a journey, I will re-route the whole valley!

The story-arc remains flexible until I write the last word, but when I start on the first chapter I must have a clear idea of the beginning, the end and the highlights – the key scenes. The rest is a bit fuzzy, like looking through a fog which won't clear until I get there.

Can you tell us a bit about where the idea for *The Mirage Makers* came from?

As a young mother, I was horrified by two real life stories emerging from two countries. One was an Australian tragedy of almost incomprehensible hubris, where many Aboriginal children were forcibly removed from their parents, supposedly for the benefit of the children. They were often raised with no knowledge of their own culture or families, sometimes even taught to denigrate their heritage. The second story was the tragedy of the 'Disappeared Ones' of Argentina. During this time, pregnant women caught up in the political brutality had their babies taken away at birth, to be raised by the families of their captors, while they themselves were murdered.

These events moved me. How terrible it must have been not only to lose your child, but to know they would be raised by people with different values, possibly values you despised.

A little later we moved to Vienna, Austria. One evening, I watched a TV historical drama (in Italian, which I don't speak) sub-titled in German (which I can read, but too slowly to keep up with sub-titling). It was about an Imperial investigator being sent by Rome to Jerusalem to find out why people believed that a man had survived his crucifixion a year or two earlier. The investigator scorns the story as pure fantasy. About then, it became too complicated for me to follow, but it didn't matter. My own imagination was already hard at work.

All those things came together to form the basis of the plot for *Heart of the Mirage*. I didn't do anything about it at the time because I was writing *The Isles of Glory*, but a year or two later my husband transferred to Tunisia, and I could see the ruins of Roman Carthage from my study window and we had the base of a Roman pillar in our rose garden. When southerly winds blew, Saharan dust piled up at my front door, desert on the move . . .

That was when I had to start writing The Mirage Makers trilogy.

Ligea is such a strong and interesting female character and it was wonderful to see how she grew over the trilogy. Do you have any favourites among your characters?

Part of me loves all my characters, even the villains. I do like Ligea, not because she's a lovely person – she's definitely not that – but because I feel for her. She's a woman who would probably have been kind and loving and nurturing, if she had not been raised to kill ruthlessly in the service of her Emperor and her manipulative mentor. She's the child removed from her culture and her family, to be raised by her enemies to despise both. She does not have much of a chance, yet she manages to rise above her beginnings and develop as a human being. She can never entirely leave her past behind, but in the end, she does her best.

The character whose life history tore me up most when I was chronicling it, however, was Arrant. So many awful things happened to him, none of which he deserved, and sometimes I almost wept as I wrote about them. It was heartbreaking.

Some authors talk of their characters 'surprising' them by their actions; is this something that has happened to you?

Characters can certainly be remarkably stubborn if I ask them to do or say something out of character. They just veer off and do it their way. Sometimes I have to remind them that people can do the unexpected; mostly I give in to them. They should know best, after all.

One of the major themes of *The Mirage Makers* is the choice between upbringing and birthright. It's something you obviously feel strongly about as a writer – is it also the sort of theme you enjoy coming across in books as a reader?

Yes. I love writers who look at large or universal problems within the microcosm of a character. It makes themes and theoretical concepts more personal, more understandable, less black and white. One can read an essay on 'Nature versus Nurture' – or read about a fictional character like Ligea facing exactly that problem in her personal history. The abstract suddenly becomes much more immediate and real, even though she is fictional.

What do you think of the packaging given to your books? Do you have any strong feelings on cover art?

I love the Orbit covers! I think both the design department and the talented Larry Rostant, the artist, have done a superb job of echoing the elements of the story.

As I write this, I haven't yet seen the cover for *Song of the Shiver Barrens*, but with the *Heart of the Mirage* cover there's the strangeness of the cracked pinkish sky, the importance of the translucent sword, the mysterious, shadowy people watching, waiting . . . are they real? Or just a mirage? And on *The Shadow of Tyr* cover, don't you just love the way the spear and the Imperial symbol seem to dominate, promising war and retribution? – but then look again, and you see that the feathers on one side of the wings appear to be broken. Perhaps Tyr has a weakness, a sickness? It sends shivers down my spine. Masterful.

I must admit, I have little understanding of what cover art can do to sell – or not sell – a book, but I think both readers and authors feel short-changed when a cover portrays something that is not in the book or gives an incorrect emphasis to what the story is about. A dragon on the cover should mean there's a dragon in the story!

In the past, I think the cover of mine which mystified me the most is one for a book in translation that portrays the flight deck and crew of a space ship, when the book is about a world of sailing ships and magical mayhem in an archipelago!

Although you live in Malaysia, many people still consider you an Australian author. Do you have strong ties to the Australian writing community? Do you have a similar community in Malaysia?

I am still an Australian, that will never change. Whenever I can, I go to Australian science fiction and fantasy conventions, and of course the internet makes friendships with my fellow writers so much easier. I've met or corresponded with most of the Australian published fantasy novel writers, at least those who write for adults; some, such as Karen Miller, Trudi Canavan and Jenny Fallon – and Russell Kirkpatrick from New Zealand – I count as good friends. We have acted as first readers for one another, I have a place to stay when I visit their cities, they have a place in Malaysia, and yes, we are availing ourselves of one another's hospitality! The Australian scene is large enough to be interesting and vibrant, yet small enough to be intimate and familiar, and I value my contact with wonderful writers, as well as with my Australian editors and publishers and fans.

There is a terrific group of English language mainstream writers and poets in Kuala Lumpur, Malaysia, who meet up regularly for readings and similar. But there are few fantasy writers. I am in touch with a couple, though, and one day I hope we can start something catering specifically for science fiction and fantasy genre writers.

What's coming after *The Mirage Makers*? Where do you see yourself going next?

I am working on *The Random Rain Cycle* – four books, set in a world where control of water is both power and wealth, where battles are fought over water, where sand dunes articulate and move, where rain depends on the manipulation of *not* weather, but water magic, where painting on water can chain you to a future you do not want. It's also a powerful love story. I love this one.

And, lastly, for those writers who have yet to see their books appearing in the shops, how did it feel to see your first novel in print?

Disbelief was uppermost, I think! There were a good many years between the day I found an agent and the day my first book was sold, and I was ready to admit defeat several times.

But my wonderful agent had faith in my writing and never gave up, so neither could I. When the first copy of my first book arrived in the mail I think I was as delighted for her as much as I was for myself.

If you enjoyed
SONG OF THE SHIVER BARRENS,
look out for

EMPRESS

by

Karen Miller

Despite its two burning lard-lamps the kitchen was dark, its air choked with the stink of rancid goat butter and spoiling goat-meat. Spiders festooned the corners with sickly webs, hoarding the husks of flies and suck-you-dries. A mud-brick oven swallowed half the space between the door and the solitary window. There were three wooden shelves, one rickety wooden stool and a scarred wooden table, almost unheard of in this land whose trees had ages since turned to stone.

Crouched in the shadows beneath the table, the child with no name listened to the man and the woman fight.

'But you promised,' the woman wailed. 'You said I could keep this one.'

The man's hard fist pounded the timber above the child's head. 'That was before another poor harvest, slut, before two more village wells dried up! All the coin it costs to feed it, am I made of money? Don't you complain, when it was born I could've thrown it on the rocks, I could've left it on The Anvil!'

'But she can work, she—'

'Not like a son!' His voice cracked like lightning, rolled like thunder round the small smoky room. 'If you'd whelped me more sons—'

'I tried!'

'Not hard enough!' Another boom of fist on wood. 'The she-brat goes. Only the god knows when Traders will come this way again.'

The woman was sobbing, harsh little sounds like a dying goat. 'But she's so young.'

'Young? Its blood-time is come. It can pay back what it's cost me, like the other she-brats you spawned. This is my word, woman. Speak again and I'll smash your teeth and black your eyes.'

When the woman dared disobey him the child was so surprised she bit her fingers. She scarcely felt the small pain; her whole life was pain, vast like the barren wastes beyond the village's godpost, and had been so since her first caterwauling cry. She was almost numb to it now.

'Please,' the woman whispered. 'Let me keep her. I've spawned you six sons.'

'It should've been eleven!' Now the man sounded like one of his skin-and-bone dogs, slavering beasts who fought for scraps of offal in the stony yard behind their hovel.

The child flinched. She hated those dogs almost as much as she hated the man. It was a bright flame, her hatred, hidden deep and safe from the man's sight. He would kill her if he saw it, would take her by one skinny scabbed ankle and smash her headfirst into the nearest red and ochre rock. He'd done it to a dog once, that had dared to growl at him. The other dogs had lapped up its brains then fought over the bloody carcass all through the long unheated night. On her thread-bare blanket beneath the kitchen table she'd fallen asleep to the sound of their teeth, and dreamed the bones they gnawed were her own.

But dangerous or not she refused to abandon her hate, the only thing she owned. It comforted and nourished her, filling her ache-empty belly on the nights she didn't eat because the woman's legs were spread, or her labours were unfinished, or the man was drunk on cactus blood and beating her.

He was beating her now, open-handed blows across the face, swearing and sweating, working himself to a frenzy. The woman knew better than to cry out. Listening to the man's palm smack against the woman's sunken cheeks, to his lusty breathing and her swallowed grunts, the child imagined plunging a knife into his throat. If she closed her eyes she could see the blood spurt scarlet, hear it splash on the floor as he gasped and bubbled and died. She was sure she could do it. Hadn't she seen the men with their proud knives cut the throats of goats and even a horse, once, that had broken its leg and was no longer good for anything but meat and hide and bleached boiled bones?

There were knives in a box on the kitchen's lowest shelf. She felt her fingers curl and cramp as though grasping a carved bone hilt, felt her heart rattle her ribs. The secret flame flickered, flared . . . then died.

No good. He'd catch her before she killed him. She would not defeat the man today, or tomorrow, or even next fat godmoon. She was too small, and he was too strong. But one day, many fat godmoons from now, she'd be big and he'd be old and shrunken. Then she'd do it and throw his body to the dogs after and laugh and laugh as they gobbled his buttocks and poked their questing tongues through the empty eye sockets of his skull.

One day.

The man hit the woman again, so hard she fell to the pounded dirt floor. 'You poisoned my seed five times and whelped bitches, slut. Three sons you whelped lived less than a godmoon. I should curse you! Turn you out for the godspeaker to deal with!'

The woman was sobbing again, scarred arms crossed in front of her face. 'I'm sorry – I'm sorry—'

Listening, the child felt contempt. Where was the woman's flame? Did she even have one? Weeping. Begging. Didn't she know this was what the man wanted, to see her broken and bleating in the dirt? The woman should die first.

But she wouldn't. She was weak. All women were weak. Everywhere in the village the child saw it. Even the women who'd spawned only sons, who looked down on the ones who'd spawned she-brats as well, who helped the godspeaker stone the cursed witches whose bodies spewed forth nothing but female flesh . . . even those women were weak.

I not weak the child told herself fiercely as the man soaked the woman in venom and spite and the woman wept, believing him. *I never beg.*

Now the man pressed his heel between the woman's dugs and shoved her flat on her back. 'You should pray thanks to the god. Another man would've broke your legs and turned you out seasons ago. Another man would've ploughed two hands of living sons on a better bitch than you!'

'Yes! Yes! I am fortunate! I am blessed!' the woman gabbled, rubbing at the bruised place on her chest.

The man shucked his trousers. 'Maybe. Maybe not. Spread, bitch. You give me a living son nine fat godmoons from now or I swear by the village godpost I'll be rid of you onto The Anvil!'

Choking, obedient, the woman hiked up her torn shift and let her thin thighs fall open. The child watched, unmoved, as the man ploughed the woman's furrow, grunting and sweating with his effort. He had a puny blade, and the woman's soil was old and dusty. She wore her dog-tooth amulet round her neck but its power was long dead. The child did not think a son would come of this planting or any other. Nine fat godmoons from this day, or sooner, the woman would die.

His seed at last dribbled out, the man stood and pulled up his trousers. 'Traders'll be here by highsun tomorrow. Might be seasons till more come. I paid the godspeaker to list us as selling and put a goat's skull on the gate. Money won't come back, so the she-brat goes. Use your water ration to clean it. Use one drop of mine, I'll flay you. I'll hang you with rope twisted from your own skin. Understand?'

'Yes,' the woman whispered. She sounded tired and beaten. There was blood on the dirt between her legs.

'Where's the she-brat now?'

'Outside.'

The man spat. He was always spitting. Wasting water. 'Find it. When it's clean, chain it to the wall so it don't run like the last one.'

The woman nodded. He'd broken her nose with his goat-stick that time. The child, three seasons younger then, had heard the woman's splintering bone, watched the pouring blood. Remembering that, she remembered too what the man did to the other she-brat to make it sorry for running. Things that made the she-brat squeal but left no mark because Traders paid less for damaged goods.

That she-brat had been a fool. No matter where the Traders took her it had to be better than the village and the man. Traders were the only escape for she-brats. Traders . . . or death. And she did not want to die. When they came for her before highsun tomorrow she would go with them willingly.

'I'll chain her,' the woman promised. 'She won't run.'

'Better not,' growled the man, and then the slap of goathide on wood as he shoved the kitchen door aside and left.

The woman rolled her head until her red-rimmed eyes

found what they sought beneath the kitchen table. 'I tried. I'm sorry.'

The child crawled out of the shadows and shrugged. The woman was always sorry. But sorrow changed nothing, so what did it matter? 'Traders coming,' she said. 'Wash now.'

Wincing, breath catching raw in her throat, the woman clutched at the table leg and clawed herself to her knees then grabbed hold of the table edge, panting, whimpering, and staggered upright. There was water in her eyes. She reached out a work-knotted hand and touched rough fingertips to the child's cheek. The water trembled, but did not fall.

Then the woman turned on her heel and went out into the searing day. Not understanding, not caring, the child with no name followed.

The Traders came a finger before highsun the next day. Not the four from last time, with tatty robes, skinny donkeys, half-starved purses and hardly any slaves. No. These two Traders were grand. Seated on haughty white camels, jangling with beads and bangles, dangling with earrings and sacred amulets, their dark skin shiny with fragrant oils and jewelled knife-sheaths on their belts. Behind them stretched the longest snake-spine of merchandise: men's inferior sons, discarded, and she-brats, and women. All naked, all chained. Some born to slavery, others newly sold. The difference was in their godbraids, slaves of long standing bore one braid of deep blood red, a sign from the god that they were property. The new slaves would get their red braids, in time.

Guarding the chained slaves, five tall men with swords and spears. Their godbraids bore amulets, even their slave-braids were charmed. They must be special slaves, those guards. In the caravan there were pack camels too, common brown, roped together, laden with baskets, criss-crossed with travel-charms. A sixth unchained slave led them, little more than a boy, and his red godbraid bore amulets as well. At his signal, groaning, the camels folded their calloused knees to squat on the hard ground. The slaves squatted too, silent and sweating.

Waiting in her own chains, the crude iron links heavy and chafing round her wrists and ankles, the child watched the Traders from beneath lowered lashes as they dismounted and stood in the dust and dirt of the man's small holding. Their slender fingers smoothed shining silk robes, tucked their glossy beaded godbraids behind their ears. Their fingernails were all the same neat oval shape and painted bright colours to match their clothing: green and purple and crimson and gold. They were taller than the tallest man in the village. Taller than the godspeaker, who must stand above all. One of them was even *fat*. They were the most splendid creatures the child had ever seen, and knowing she would leave with them, leave forever the squalor and misery of the man and the village, her heart beat faster and her own unpainted fingernails, ragged and shapeless, bit deep into her dirty scarred palms.

The Traders stared at the cracked bare ground with its withered straggle of weeds, at the mud brick hovel with its roof of dried grasses badly woven, at the pen of profitless goats, at the man whose bloodshot eyes shone with hope and avarice. A look flowed between them and their plump lips pursed. They were sneering. The child wondered where they came from, to be so clean and disapproving. Somewhere not like this. She couldn't wait to see such a place herself, to sleep for just one night inside walls that did not stink of fear and goat. She'd wear a hundred chains and crawl on her hands and knees across The Anvil's burning sand if she had to, so long as she reached it.

The man was staring at the Traders too, his eyes popping with amazement. He bobbed his head at them, like a chicken pecking corn. 'Excellencies. Welcome, welcome. Thank you for your custom.'

The thin Trader wore thick gold earrings; tattooed on his right cheek, in brightest scarlet, a stinging scorpion. The child bit her tongue. He had money enough to buy a protection like that? And power enough that a godspeaker would let him? *Aieee . . .*

He stepped forward and looked down at the man, fingertips flicking at her. 'Just this?'

She was enchanted. His voice was deep and dark like the dead of night, and shaped the words differently from the man. When the man spoke it sounded like rocks grinding in the dry ravine, ugly like him. The Trader was not ugly.

The man nodded. 'Just this.'

'No sons, un-needed?'

'Apologies, Excellency,' said the man. 'The god has granted me few sons. I need them all.'

Frowning, the Trader circled the child in slow, measured steps. She held her breath. If he found her unpleasing and if the man did not kill her because of it, she'd be slaved to some village man for beating and spawning sons and hard labour without rest. She would cut her flesh with stone and let the dogs taste her, tear her, devour her, first.

The Trader reached out his hand, his flat palm soft and pink, and smoothed it down her thigh, across her buttock. His touch was warm, and heavy. He glanced at the man. 'How old?'

'Sixteen.'

The Trader stopped pacing. His companion unhooked a camel whip from his belt of linked precious stones and snapped the thong. The man's dogs, caged for safety, howled and threw themselves against the woven goathide straps of their prison. In the pen beside them the man's goats bleated and milled, dropping anxious balls of shit, yellow slot-eyes gleaming.

'How old?' the Trader asked again. His green eyes were narrow, and cold.

The man cringed, head lowered, fingers knuckled together. 'Twelve. Forgive me. Honest error.'

The Trader made a small, disbelieving sound. He'd done something to his eyebrows. Instead of being a thick tangled bar like the man's they arched above his eyes in two solid gold half-circles. The child stared at them, fascinated, as the Trader leaned down and brought his dark face close to hers. She wanted to stroke the scarlet scorpion inked into his cheek. Steal some of his protection, in case he did not buy her.

His long, slender fingers tugged on her earlobes, traced the shape of her skull, her nose, her cheeks, pushed back her lips and felt all her teeth. He tasted of salt and things she did not know. He smelled like freedom.

'Is she blooded?' he asked, glancing over his shoulder at the man.

'Since four godmoons.'

'Intact?'

The man nodded. 'Of course.'

The Trader's lip curled. 'There is no "of course" where men and she-flesh abide.'

Without warning he plunged his hand between her legs, fingers pushing, probing, higher up, deeper in. Teeth bared, her own fingers like little claws, the child flew at him, screeching. Her chains might have weighed no more than the bangles on his slender, elegant wrists. The man sprang forward shouting, fists raised, face contorted, but the Trader did not need him. He brushed her aside as though she were a corn-moth.

Seizing a handful of black and tangled hair he wrenched her to the tips of her toes till she was screaming in pain, not fury, and her hands fell limply by her sides. She felt her heart batter her brittle ribs and despair storm in her throat. Her eyes squeezed shut and for the first time she could remember felt the salty sting of tears.

She had ruined everything. There would be no escape from the village now, no new life beyond the knife-edged horizon. The Trader would toss her aside like spoiled meat, and when he and his fat friend were gone the man would kill her or she would be forced to kill herself. Panting like a goat in the slaughter-house she waited for the blow to fall.

But the Trader was laughing. Still holding her, he turned to his friend. 'What a little hell-cat! Untamed and savage, like all these dwellers in the savage north. But do you see the eyes, Yagji? The face? The length of bone and the sleekness of flank? Her sweet breasts, budding?'

Trembling, she dared to look at him. Dared to hope . . .

The fat one wasn't laughing. He shook his head, setting the ivory dangles in his ears to swinging. 'She is scrawny.'

'Today, yes,' agreed the Trader. 'But with food and bathing and three times three godmoons . . . then we shall see!'

'Your eyes see the invisible, Aba. Scrawny brats are oft diseased.'

'No, Excellency!' the man protested. 'No disease. No pus, no bloating, no worms. Good flesh. Healthy flesh.'

'What there is of it,' said the Trader. He turned. 'She is not diseased, Yagji.'

'But she is ill-tempered,' his fat friend argued. 'Undisciplined, and wild. She'll be troublesome, Aba.'

The Trader nodded. 'True.' He held out his hand and easily caught the camel whip tossed to him. Fingers tight in her hair he snapped the woven hide quirt around her naked legs so the little metal weights on its end printed bloody patterns in her flesh.

The blows stung like fire. The child sank her teeth into her lip and stared unblinking into the Trader's careful, watching eyes, daring him to strip the unfed flesh from her bones if he liked. He would see she was no weakling, that she was worthy of his coin. Hot blood dripped down her calf to tickle her ankle. Within seconds the small black desert flies came buzzing to drink her. Hearing them, the Trader withheld the next blow and instead tossed the camel whip back to its owner.

'Lesson one, little hell-cat,' he said, his fingers untangling from her hair to stroke the sharp line of her cheek. 'Raise your hand or voice to me again and you will die never knowing the pleasures that await you. Do you understand me?'

The black desert flies were greedy, their eager sucking made her skin crawl. She'd seen what they could do to living creatures if not discouraged. She tried not to dance on the spot as the feverish flies quarrelled over her bloody welts. All she understood was the Trader did not mean to reject her. 'Yes.'

'Good.' He waved the flies away, then pulled from his gold and purple pocket a tiny pottery jar. When he took off its lid she smelled the ointment inside, thick and rich and strange.

Startling her, he dropped to one knee and smeared her burning legs with the jar's fragrant paste. His fingers were cool and sure against her sun-seared skin. The pain vanished, and she was shocked. She hadn't known a man could touch a she-brat and not hurt it.

It made her wonder what else she did not know.

When he was finished he pocketed the jar and stood, staring down at her. 'Do you have a name?'

A stupid question. She-brats were owed no names, no more

than the stones on the ground or the dead goats in the slaughter-house waiting to be skinned. She opened her mouth to say so, then closed it again. The Trader was almost smiling, and there was a look in his eyes she'd never seen before. A question. Or a challenge. It meant something. She was sure it meant something. If only she could work out what . . .

She let her gaze slide sideways to the mud brick hovel and its mean kitchen window, where the woman thought she could not be seen as she dangerously watched the trading. The woman who had no name, just descriptions. *Bitch. Slut. Goatslit.* Then she looked at the man, shaking with greed, waiting for his money. If she gave *herself* a name, how angry it would make him.

But she couldn't think of one. Her mind was blank sand, like The Anvil. Who was she? She had no idea. But the Trader had named her, hadn't he? He had called her something, he had called her—

She tilted her chin so she could look into his green and gleaming eyes. 'He – kat,' she said, her tongue stumbling over the strange word, the sing-song way he spoke. 'Me. Name. Hekat.'

The Trader laughed again. 'As good a name as any, and better than most.' He held up his hand, two fingers raised; his fat friend tossed him a red leather pouch, clinking with coin.

The man stepped forward, black eyes ravenous. 'If you like the brat so much I will breed you more! Better than this one, worth twice as much coin.'

The Trader snorted. 'It is a miracle you bred even this one. Do not tempt the god with your blustering lest your seed dry up completely.' Nostrils pinched, he dropped the pouch into the man's cupped hands.

The man's fingers tore at the pouch's tied lacing, so clumsily that its contents spilled on the ground. With a cry of anguish he plunged to his knees, heedless of bruises, and began scrabbling for the silver coins. His knuckles skinned against the sharp stones but the man did not notice the blood, or the buzzing black flies that swarmed to drink him.

For a moment the Trader watched him, unspeaking. Then he trod the man's fingers into the dirt. 'Your silver has no wings. Remove the child's chains.'

The man gaped, face screwed up in pain. 'Remove . . . ?'

The Trader smiled; it made his scarlet scorpion flex its claws. 'You are deaf? Or would like to be?'

'Excellency?'

The Trader's left hand settled on the long knife at his side. 'Headless men cannot hear.'

The man wrenched his fingers free and lurched to his feet. Panting, he unlocked the binding chains, not looking at the child. The skin around his eyes twitched as though he were scorpion-stung.

'Come, little Hekat,' said the Trader. 'You belong to me now.'

She followed him to the waiting slave train, thinking he would put his own chains about her wrists and ankles and join her to the other naked slaves squatting on the ground. Instead he led her to his camel and turned to his friend. 'A robe, Yagji.'

The fat Trader Yagji sighed and fetched a pale yellow garment from one of the pack camel's baskets. Barely breathing, the child stared as the thin Trader took his knife and slashed through the cloth, reducing it to fit her small body. Smiling, he dropped the cut-down robe over her head and guided her arms into its shortened sleeves, smoothed its cool folds over her naked skin. She was astonished. She wished the man's sons were here to see this but they were away at work. Snake-dancing, and tending goats.

'There,' said the Trader. 'Now we will ride.'

Before she could speak he was lifting her up and onto the camel.

Air hissed between the fat Trader's teeth. 'Ten silver pieces! Did you have to give so much?'

'To give less would be insulting to the god.'

'Tcha! This is madness, Abajai! You will regret this, and so will I!'

'I do not think so, Yagji,' the thin Trader replied. 'We were guided here by the god. The god will see us safe.'

He climbed onto the camel and prodded it to standing. With a muffled curse, the fat Trader climbed onto his own camel and the slave train moved on, leaving the man and the woman and the goats and the dogs behind them.

Hekat sat on the Trader's haughty white camel, her head held high, and never once looked back.